# CO❄L

# MARCH

Having spent most of his life trapped in the frozen tundra of upstate New York, Daniel Cohen decided to dream himself somewhere new. It was from this quest for heat that the scorching world of COLDMAKER was born.

www.danielacohenbooks.com
🐦@saxophonehome

## HCP LTD

Also by Daniel A. Cohen

*Coldmaker*

# C❄LD
# MARCH

## DANIEL A. COHEN

Book Two of the Coldmaker Saga

HARPER
Voyager

Harper*Voyager*
An imprint of HarperCollins*Publishers* Ltd
1 London Bridge Street
London SE1 9GF

www.harpercollins.co.uk

First published by HarperCollins*Publishers* 2018
1

A catalogue record for this book is available from the British Library

ISBN: 978-0-00-820721-2

Set in Meridien by Palimpsest Book Production Limited,
Falkirk, Stirlingshire

Printed and bound in the UK by CPI Group (UK) Ltd, Croydon CR0 4YY

MIX
Paper from
responsible sources
FSC™ C007454

To my mother

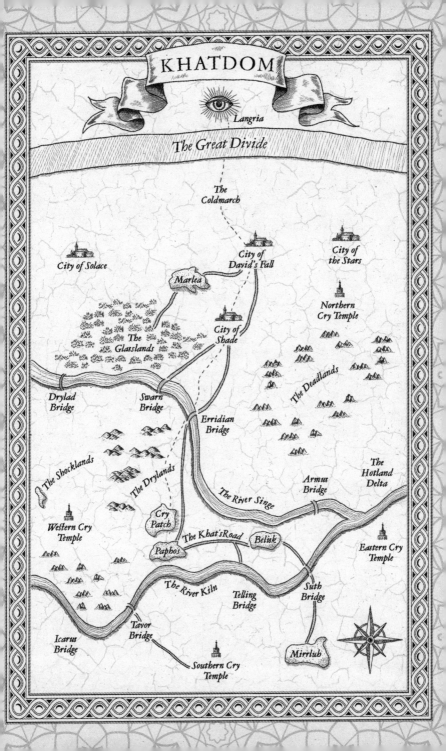

# PART ONE

PART ONE

# Chapter One

'Break in.' Shilah stabbed the shop door with a sweaty finger. 'I think after what we invented you should have no problem with a lock, Spout.'

I was still in shock and barely able to think, let alone tinker.

News of my father's death had kicked my heart halfway through my chest. And watching Leroi being consumed by the Vicaress and her army had finished the job. I had a feeling if I turned around quickly enough I'd see a red lump gathering sand and dust on the street, thumping its final beat.

My cleverness was as slow as scorched honey. Despite staring right at one, I'd forgotten how locks even work. Shilah was breathing heavily, her braided hair pasted against her right shoulder with sweat. There used to be a blade hidden in those locks when she'd lived out in the sands, but she'd given that habit up after moving to the Tavor Manor. Something at the back of my mind whispered that a traditional blade would be too big for this job anyway, but I had no access to any other memories that might spur an alternative plan.

'Spout,' she said. 'I know you can do this.'

The dark skin of her face was flushed, thick beads of sweat

dripping down her neck and staining the waterskin slung over her chest. After getting used to the comfort of Leroi's tinkershop, I think both of our bodies had forgotten how deeply the sky could bite.

Shilah, Cam, and I had somehow avoided the Vicaress, fleeing through the empty sands and making it to the centre of Paphos without getting caught. The hour was too early for the Street Jadans to be racing towards their corners, which meant only the eyes of the sky were upon us.

The enemy wasn't far behind and was quickly gaining ground. Shouts and commands flooded the nearby streets and echoed down the alleyways.

'I don't want' – *heave* – 'to rush you, Spout.' Cam's words were mostly wheeze, pitched up and squeezed. 'But I think I hear' – *heave* – 'them coming.'

If Shilah appeared overheated, then Cam was roasted and ready to serve. Unkempt yellow hair was brightly contrasted against the red of his face, making him look as if he'd been hanging upside down all night, his blood gathered in his delicate Noble cheeks. He'd somehow managed to maintain his gold-rimmed glasses, but despite his best efforts, they kept sliding down his nose, his skin as slick as Ice.

Shouting from the pursuers became more barbed as the taskmasters closed in. The Vicaress and her forces had been at our heels since our narrow escape from the Tavor gardens, where Cam's father nearly had us cornered. If not for Leroi's heroics, I imagine we would currently be strung up from the Manor gates, awaiting judgement.

Touching a Frost is punishable by death.

We didn't just touch one.

We *stole* a Frost and used it to create an invention that could shatter the entire Khatdom. We discovered a secret that could save my people.

My mind felt gummed and cloudy, the lock impenetrable.

Our only stroke of luck so far was that my years of serving as a Street Jadan meant I still knew the best passages through the city, and I had been able to lead our group down a secret route that had been somewhat abrasive. Cam's sunshirt was ripped in a hundred different places from the constant squeezing against tight bricks, and Shilah still had clay dust in her bristly hair from the roof of the Bathing Quarters Cry Temple. We were still in one piece, but time was running thin.

I cracked my knuckles, trying to figure out a way to pick myself out of the mental rubbish. My throat was parched and burning from the long run, most of which I didn't recall. One moment I'd been watching Leroi battle the Vicaress with his explosive powders, the gardens of my new home consumed by fire, and then I was stumbling through the Paphos alley-ways with the two most important people in the World Cried. It was Shilah's idea to go to Mama Jana's, as I had been in no state to form a plan. Neither had Cam. Little Langria had been burned to ash, and we couldn't go back to my old barracks, so when Shilah suggested Mama Jana's shop we didn't argue. Hiding within her unkempt piles of treasures felt like the only place in Paphos that made sense.

If we could break in.

Shilah was right; besting the lock should have been a breeze. I'd been apprenticing under a master inventor for quite some time, and this should have been as easy as breaking a Khatnut with a giant hammer. But keeping focus was impossible, as my head was ringing from explosions and visions of a stolen future.

'I don't have any tools,' I said calmly, patting my empty pockets for effect. 'I don't have anything. The supply bags. I don't know—'

'Spout, why aren't you' – *heave* – 'freaking out?' Cam asked, swallowing hard. 'I hear them on the next street over.'

I twitched my lips back and forth, barely listening to him. The lock was baiting me, the metal blinding in the heavy light of day. I used to play with them, manipulate them, learn their secrets. Broken locks were a common find in the boilweed piles of my youth. I slowly rubbed the back of my hands, trying to remember what tricks they used to hold.

Shilah grabbed the side of my face. Her palms were slick with sweat and slipped along my cheek before taking hold. 'We just made the greatest invention in the World Cried, dammit. You once talked with the Crier himself. You can break this stupid lock in your sleep, so don't go losing yourself, Micah. I'm right here.'

I blinked, everything suddenly becoming more real.

Every line in her face was defined. I could see the tightness of the muscles underneath her skin, the veins in her neck standing up and strained. I could make out each individual rivulet in her braid. Her almond eyes were boring into me, drawing me home.

The shouting and sounds of whips against stone were getting closer, the taskmasters trying to flush us out of hiding. We needed to get inside now.

I took a deep breath and tried not to picture Leroi drowning in all that black smoke. I could still feel his sad eyes on us in the tunnel, presumably knowing the battle that awaited him on the other side of the door. I could still smell the crackling fire on my shirt.

A snap of Shilah's fingers and a quick gesture reminded me that the Coldmaker was still by my side. We still had the machine.

'This is bigger than us now,' Shilah said. 'And you're not alone. I'm right here.'

Cam cleared his throat, checking over his shoulder. 'Me too.'

I nodded. The streets themselves had once given me all the tools I needed. I used to trust that the Crier would provide.

So why did he keep taking away?

'Keep watch,' I said, gritting my teeth and balling my fists. I shifted myself into the shadows of the alleyway next to the shop, headed towards the boilweed piles. Almost immediately I spotted a trove of sunclocks, broken parasols, and a large pair of Cold Bellows that I'd once fixed for Mama Jana a while back. She didn't used to have that much rubbish lying around in her alley, but I was guessing since I'd moved to the Tavor Manor, she was no longer able to salvage her broken goods.

Junked items sat piled up and dusted with morning sand, waiting to be plundered. Under any other circumstances I would have smiled at the notion that Mama Jana actually *needed* a Jadan like me, but right now I had no capacity for nostalgia. Emotions were only distractions. I did allow logic to surface, and almost instantly I spotted what I needed. Dropping to my knees, I snatched two skinny metal rods from a broken parasol, originally used to keep the shredded fabric splayed.

As I launched back towards the alley, something green and swirling on the wall made me stop. I couldn't quite make out the symbol, but I already knew what the design would be.

The Opened Eye had been painted in that exact same spot once before.

I stopped just long enough to draw my fingers across the pupil.

The Open Eye was the symbol for Langria, the only place in the whole World Cried where my invention would be safe, as North as North goes. It was the land where truth rained from the heavens, and the Jadan people had all the Cold they'd ever need to remain free. The gardens there were more lush than anything the Nobles could dream of, with forests of sugar cane miles wide, and enough lush fig trees to feed everyone in Paphos. There were troupes of animals that hadn't been seen since the Great Drought, and even such ancient things as birds. It was a haven for our lost culture, and songs and fruit were of equal abundance. I'd even heard the Langria river waters were cool enough to dive right into. Langria was hope itself, and seeing the symbol painted on the wall gave me enough to hold my tools high as I rounded the front door.

'You think those will work?' Cam asked, his nerves apparent. Wide eyes and a haunted look made him seem as good as Jadan at this point.

'Yes,' I said, shimmying the two small rods inside the hole of the lock and feeling for the pins. 'I just have to . . .'

Loud orders were barked so close that I could almost smell the burning oil on the Vicaress's blade. Either the Vicaress had a vision of our plan to go to Mama Jana's – which seemed highly unlikely, considering she was a fraud – or she had gathered more of her army, flooding the streets.

'Hurry,' Cam pleaded, sucking down a swig from the water-skin slung across his chest. 'Not that I'm rushing you.'

Shilah turned and gave him a stern look. 'Save that water, it's all you have.'

I closed my eyes and tried to recall how metal could serve as an extension of my fingertips. Leroi often told me a true Inventor's reach could be measured only in imagination.

He was dead now.

My hands were shaking with fear and adrenaline. The metal rods felt like greased needles trying to stab a single grain of sand.

'I can't,' I said, getting frustrated. The cloud had parted enough to let me remember that Mama Jana's lock was a snap-pin set-up, which meant the pins needed to be lifted at once. My flailing fingers were only making things more futile. The knowledge alone of how the lock worked was not enough to steady my grip. 'I can't feel anything.'

Shilah reached down and placed a hand on my lower back. 'What do you need from me?'

Cam was muttering to himself under his breath, his father's name appearing no less than three times within the murmurs.

'You can make it work,' Shilah said, matching my calm. It was as if we were back on our cots, taking turns telling stories as the night waned. Back then, safe in the womb of the tinkershop, I'd never thought we'd be on the run, protecting one of the most important discoveries in the history of the Jadan people.

I tried to feel for the pins in the lock again, closing my eyes this time, but the answers wouldn't reveal themselves. Over and over the proper technique slipped my touch, and I finally pounded my hand against the door out of frustration, a shock of pain ricocheting down my arm.

Shilah shot me a disappointed look, but the slamming noise had been drowned out by the blaring of a distinctive horn.

Three long blows.

Followed by two short.

And three more long.

I hadn't heard that call in years, and even then it had been faint, sounded from the outskirts of the city. It was a harbinger of death. There was a reason why the noise was rare – important Jadan runaways were quite uncommon – but every once in a while a favoured Jadan Domestic would choose baking to death in the sands over what waited back at the Manor.

That's when the beasts were sent hunting.

'Shivers and Frosts!' Cam exclaimed, eyes flitting around, almost as if he could see the echoes of the horn bouncing off the walls. 'Is that what I think it is?'

Shilah's eyes darkened, her chest rising and falling quickly. I didn't blame her. Torture under the Vicaress would be bad enough, but getting stalked down and eaten alive would be another level of agony entirely.

'The Khat's hounds,' I said, my hands shaking like loose boilweed in the wind. The needles clacked uselessly in the lock.

Cam swallowed hard. 'Sun damn.'

'You know about the hounds?' Shilah asked him with a snarl. 'You've *seen* what they can do up close?'

Cam wilted, taking his glasses off and closing his eyes. 'He doesn't let . . . I've only seen the ones he keeps in his chambers. But they're small and harmless and . . . fuzzy. Just relics from before the Great Drought.'

'Those runts are *not* his hounds,' Shilah said, her voice breaking for what felt like the first time. She absently touched her throat, her arms flexing so fast that I wondered if she might try punching the door down. At this point that might have been more effective than my trembling hands. 'The Khat keeps his real hounds in the basement of the Pyramid,' she said between clenched teeth. 'He starves them for days on end. And when he does feed them . . . guess what he uses for the meal?'

'I've heard.' Cam's face went so red he might as well have smeared Khatberries on his cheeks. 'But you have to remember. I have nothing to do with the Khat.'

'Other than your name and blood.'

'I'm only heir to the *Tavors*,' Cam said, not meeting her eyes and changing the subject fast. 'Keep trying, Spout. Please.'

'Why did the Crier take us this far?' I asked. The words came out lifeless, and I wondered who this stranger was using my voice. 'Only to let us get caught. Why would he be so cruel?'

The taskmasters' shouts were almost on top of us.

'Spout,' Shilah said, guiding my chin sideways with her finger, forcing me to meet her eyes. 'Don't worry about the Crier. I have faith in *you*.'

I followed the sweat beading off her face, which dropped quickly and flecked the stone at my feet.

Splashing up an idea.

I set the thin metal picks on the ground.

'What are you doing?' Cam gasped, hands pulling at his yellow hair. 'Maybe let's just go find a shop that's actually open, and hide there?'

'No one leaves their doors unlocked,' I said, returning to the alley, not looking at the Opened Eye as I passed. Cam softly called after me, but before he could repeat my name I'd returned with a sharp slice of glass from the pile of trash.

'Tears above, Micah. Are you going to try to fight the hounds?' Cam asked frantically. I'd never seen him so worked up.

Grabbing an Abb from the bag, I sliced off a tiny golden sliver, small enough to fit under the pins in the lock. Shoving it deep into the hole with the help of a parasol needle, I gestured for Shilah to give over her waterskin. Her lips opened in the shape of a question, but after a moment her eyes lit up with recognition.

'Do it,' she said with a smirk.

'Do what?' Cam asked.

Shilah licked her cracked lips. 'Ice. He's going to open it with Ice.'

Cam paused, looking as though the two halves of his body were trying to flee in opposite directions. 'How? What if the lock just breaks off? Or we get blocked out completely?' I could feel the buzz of fear in his words. 'This can't be the best idea.'

A harsh voice shouted from the street next to ours. 'Two of you go high and the rest of you lot go around! Check the rooftops and alleyway!'

Blood shot into Cam's cheeks, the sunburn there appearing even more raw. 'Do it.'

I nodded, holding up the waterskin to the lock and letting out a trickle of water.

Cam manoeuvred his hand to the bag on my shoulder, digging into the cloth and putting his palm directly on the bronze lid of the Coldmaker. He closed his eyes and muttered something under his breath.

The sound of Ice expanding rapidly crackled in my ears. I wanted to watch the beautiful crystals unfold, but mostly I just hoped the reaction would push all the spring-loaded pins up enough to trigger the lock. I had no idea how much force it gave or how fast it worked. Our lives depended on something I knew almost nothing about.

If the Crier really was watching, then this was his moment to do something.

Metal clicked, and the door opened a squeeze. A small peg of Ice jutted out of the lock, but hopefully it wasn't enough to be noticed by any taskmasters.

Shilah grabbed both Cam and I by the shoulders and tossed us inside, just as the next round of horn blasts split the air.

# Chapter Two

I barred the door, threw down the shades, closed the curtain of beads, and dragged the nearest cabinet in front of the entrance, sliding it flush against the door. Closed Eye necklaces jangled on the shelves, and if someone pushed their way inside, the resulting crash would at least let us know we needed to find cover.

My pulse was in a frenzy knowing the Khat's hounds were charging into the city.

The stories said that Sun blinded the hounds to teach them pain, leaving them to stalk their prey entirely by smell. And the stories said a lot more than that too. The hounds were supposed to have breath like hot fire, and fangs as long as any rattler, and could smell a specific Jadan body even lying in the dunes.

Sometimes back in my barracks, Levi would get hold of sour ale, and would tell the Jadan children about the other things that lived in the catacombs of the Khat's Pyramid. Things worse than hounds, that didn't need to smell you. They already knew you. Things that saw only through Closed Eyes, slithering in silence. Without warning. Without mercy. To drag you into the black.

I stepped away from our feeble defence of an unlocked door and single cabinet, knowing it would be all but useless against such foul beasts if they caught our scent. If only I had my old Stinger, powered by the scorpion venom I used to extract. If I'd only been able to get my hands on some of that explosive power Leroi had used to demolish the Tavor gardens, we might have stood a chance.

I tried to force a real idea that might save us, but I came up empty. Mama Jana didn't sell weapons. Nothing that we could fight an army with. I glanced around at all the Closed Eye fashion pieces displayed on the racks: reminders that Jadans deserve to be oppressed, that the Crier himself condemned us when he took away my people's Cold. As if eight hundred years of Drought wasn't bad enough, we were supposed to cower constantly to the fact that it was our fault.

I had recently stopped believing a word of those old stories, but my father and Leroi were now both dead. In my mind there was no worse punishment than that, except maybe also losing the two friends at my side. The enemy was coming: my mind had to make that a reality.

Shilah's eyes narrowed and swept the edges of the shop.

Cam stood over a basket of figs on the glass counter. Already a handful deep, he groaned with relief, digging into the food with the kind of reckless hunger that I'd only ever seen in Jadans starving in the streets.

It was odd to think that all of us, Nobles included, were just a few meals away from such desperation.

'It's not stealing,' Cam said sheepishly, noticing that I was watching. His cheeks were puffed with fruit pulp, leaving his words hard to discern. 'It's survival. I'll pay Mama Jana back when I can. She knows I'm good for it.'

'I don't think *your* people are capable of seeing it that way,' Shilah said after a pause, her eyes still scanning the floors. 'Plenty of Jadans have been killed for taking less than figs.'

'Stop saying *my* people,' Cam said, a seed bursting out and sticking to his bottom lip. He gestured around him, arms waving wildly, almost knocking over a can of Closed Eye badges. 'Am I not here with you? Did I not sacrifice everything for our cause?'

For once Shilah looked to be at a loss for words, but I could see her wheels turning even from the thick of the shadows.

I reached up and touched my forehead. There should have been sweat.

'What exactly are you looking for?' I asked her.

'It's a long shot,' she answered, still focused.

'We need to find a hiding place until Mama Jana gets here,' I said. 'The Pyramid is not that far away, and the hounds are supposed to be fast.'

'I swear,' Cam said, flustered. He wouldn't look anywhere other than the figs. 'I've only ever seen the little hounds. And they can fit on your lap.'

'That reminds me,' Shilah said, stripping down to her undergarments on the spot. She was quick and efficient in disrobing, which in no way should have been arousing, yet I could feel Cam and I both seizing up at the unexpected sight. Bare skin wasn't taboo for Jadans – our barracks were always stifling, making clothing a burden – but Shilah's body was toned and lean, and even her intense scarring was attractive in its own right.

She was a warrior. Straight out of the days before the Great Drought, when it was still possible to battle your oppressors. Once it was decided that the Jadans were unworthy of Cold, the warriors disappeared.

You can't fight the Crier's will.

Cam audibly gasped, averting his eyes – although he didn't stop chewing the figs. The room was shadowy enough that we were all mostly silhouettes anyway, but Shilah's figure was uncomfortably striking, more woman than girl, the curvy areas accentuated by the glistening sweat. I looked away as my lips recalled the passionate kiss Shilah and I had shared after discovering the secret of the Coldmaker. I didn't want to complicate an already dangerous situation with stirrings that only ever made young men like me lose focus.

'I thought you were this great lover of women, Camlish,' Shilah said with a snort, reaching for a yellow sundress on a rack and tossing it over herself, the bottom hem getting caught on her thick hair. 'Romancer for the ages. I wouldn't think you'd get shy around a little skin.'

'I— well you—' Cam turned away further. 'You deserve respect is all.'

Even though her skin was darkened to a fine mahogany by the Sun, the Noble dress seemed to fit Shilah in more ways than one. At first glance I wouldn't have been able to distinguish her from the kind of girl that dress was intended for. Her back was straight and sharp, regal in bearing.

'You two do the same,' Shilah commanded the both of us.

'I'm already in noblewear,' Cam said, finally turning back, threading a finger through one of the many gashes in his sunshirt, wiggling it against his stomach. 'Ripped and nasty noblewear, I guess.'

Shilah grabbed two handsome sets of sun-robes from a display drawer, tossing one to Cam and one to me. 'We change for the *smell*. That's how the hounds find you.'

'Aren't we going to smell like us either way?' Cam asked.

He was right. New clothes probably weren't enough to mask us from the beasts. My stomach growled watching Cam scarf down all that food, but I was also used to hunger, and my body could wait.

Shilah began to examine the perimeter of the store, and I quickly changed into the sun-robes, the silk fabric pulling against my sticky skin. Hopping around Mama Jana's main counter, I heard another horn call sounding outside, baiting the hounds. The noise was closer this time, but at least we were safe for the moment.

'Not sure if this will be enough, but . . .' I let my fingers peruse the biggest drawer. At first all I found were slips of parchment stained with writing I couldn't understand and small clay urns.

Finally, the object I was looking for rolled into my palm.

I shook the glass perfume vial and glared up at the roof.

I always associated rosemusk with Mama Jana. '*Fashion for the nose*,' she always said when applying the scent from this very bottle. She usually tipped out a dose or two whenever I was fixing things in the shop, and I knew it overpowered even the most obnoxious smells. I sometimes had to come straight to Mama Jana's after performing rather unseemly tasks for other Nobles – Street Jadans didn't get to pick the order of our errands – like cleaning up vomit from the alleys of the Imbiberies, or struggling to carry lumps of spoiled firefish out to the dunes. On times like those Mama Jana would leave the whole bottle of rosemusk out, uncorked. I think the gesture wasn't so much for her as it was for me, however, as she never wrinkled her nose at the foul odours clinging to my slave uniform, and she often left the open bottle next to whatever item I was tasked to fix.

'You think she has cool water somewhere too?' Cam asked, looking into his waterskin with complete dismay. The temperature inside the room was stifling, but I knew Mama Jana had a store of water and Wisps under her nail-colouring kit. What I didn't know was how soon the hounds might arrive to gnaw on our bones.

'We should probably do this first.' I unscrewed the rosemusk cap.

Cam nodded, tossing his ruined shirt onto the ground and snatching up the garment Shilah had passed him. It was a

formal green silk robe that was far too big, the embroidered
bottom billowing around his knees.

I raised an eyebrow.

'This is no time for fashion,' Shilah said. 'Pour.'

I sent a stream of perfume down the back of Cam's neck.
His nose scrunched with a grimace, the scent overpowering.
I dabbed my fingers on the watery puddle, and spread it down
over his arms. The hairs lining his wrists were so fine they
were nearly invisible, yellow and thin. As I was rubbing, I
noticed how sunburned the backs of his hands had become,
and I tried to remember if Mama Jana had any groan salve.
His jaw went tense as I smeared around the wounds, and I
could tell he was trying not to wince.

Shilah marched over and gave me a nod, Cam slipping back
behind the counter. My fingers trembled as I tipped a thin
stream of the rosemusk down the back of her dress, trying
not to think of all that creamy brown skin. The perfume fell
across her skin quickly because her back was so razor straight.

'More,' she said, her face as serious as stone. 'And rub my
arms too, if you don't mind.'

I swallowed hard, seeing and feeling her flesh under my
hands. As I spread the bright scent on her arms I could feel
her radiating heat, and I could make out the individual clus-
ters of freckles around her elbows. Her skin was rough with
scars, sending a jolt through my heart, my movements nervous
and jerky. The flaws in her skin made the liquid less easy to
spread, and so I had to take my time, making sure I covered
everything evenly.

'Do my back too,' she said without any hint of embarrassment, lifting her dress and revealing her muscled stomach.

Cam looked away, occupying himself by sifting through
the rest of Mama Jana's shelves, his voice more pinched than
when our lives had been in danger. 'Surely there must be a
few Wisps lying around.'

'We don't need Wisps,' Shilah said with a hint of a smile, looking at my hands and then at my face. 'We have Ice now.'

Cam gave a nod of consent, keeping his eyes on the inside of the drawers. 'You're right, but it probably wouldn't hurt to have some with us. So we don't raise suspicion all the time.'

His words trailed to a murmur as he pulled out a stack of books. A little blue tome in the middle caught my attention, looking about as old as the Khatdom itself. The writing on the spine was white and languid, and also somehow . . . familiar? I couldn't quite make out the design in the dim light. I also quickly lost interest, as Shilah had just taken my hands and moved it to her naked lower back.

'Here,' she said. 'Where the sweat gathers.'

I reapplied the perfume and began spreading it across her skin, trying not to linger at the dimples studding her backside. I allowed my fingers to move slowly, nearly forgetting about the hungry creatures clamouring for our blood. Shilah leaned into my touch and time slowed to a crawl – which was most welcome, as every breath had the possibility of being my last.

'And my hair, too,' she said.

I dabbed the rosemusk into her locks, making sure to massage her scalp. Her head rolled along with my touch. All of a sudden her eyes flicked over, boring into mine with strong passion.

'We can change things,' she whispered. 'We have to change things. Look at how far we've come.'

I nodded. 'But the hounds—'

She took my hand in hers, gripping tightly. 'Are nothing. We made the Coldmaker. We're going to get through this together.'

I saw that my fingers had dried faster than I would have liked, and so Shilah spun me around and emptied the bottle, holding me still with one hand and spreading the perfume evenly with the other. Wherever her fingers traced I felt life blossom, and I was suddenly aware that the room had filled with the potency of a hundred gardens.

Shilah's hand lingered on my forearm as she put the empty bottle down, her voice going back to normal volume. 'Now let's just hope all the perfume doesn't attract suspicion from outside, then—'

'Not you!' a voice groaned from the back of the shop. 'Curse this whole Sun-damned land, not you, Spout.'

All three of us spun around to watch the figure sweeping her way out of the dark. It couldn't have been Mama Jana, however, as the shopkeeper I knew was always meticulously maintained, not a grey hair out of place. The approaching figure was dressed as poorly as the dead-cart Jadans, with dirt smeared all over her face and more rips in her clothes than Cam. Her hair was the same shade of grey as the real Mama Jana, but it was frayed like a broomstick. Heavy shadows tugged at her eyes. She wandered through a beam of light seeping in from the space beneath the closed window, revealing the face of the kind Noblewoman I once knew. I couldn't fathom what sort of darkness must have devoured her and left this hag in its wake.

'Not you,' Mama Jana said again, dropping the knife in her hand. 'You were supposed to be safe.'

'I'm sorry,' I said, tucking my chin to my chest in shame.

Cam looked shocked. 'Mama Jana! Were you sleeping somewhere back there?'

Mama Jana walked right up to Cam and poked him in the chest, her fingernails broken and chipped. For the first time since I'd known her, the nails weren't painted any particular colour, which was even further cause for worry.

'You were supposed to take the boy back to the Manor, Camlish,' she snarled. 'You were going to keep him safe.'

'I did,' Cam said, backing away, keeping his eyes off the fig basket. He nearly stumbled over a wooden chest trying to find reprieve from her gaze. 'I tried. But you don't understand—'

The next horn blast from outside was muffled, but distinct. Closer.

'What happened, Camlish?' Mama Jana asked, tears forming in the corners of her eyes. 'Why the hounds, and why are you wearing a girl's Paphesian flutter-dress?'

Cam glanced down at his shirt with a hearty frown. 'Is that what this is? They just looked like regular robes to me . . .'

'We need your help,' Shilah said, stepping in between them, standing tall.

Mama Jana gave Shilah a fleeting look and then did a double-take. Her eyes widened, the streaks of dirt making her aged face look demonic. 'Aren't you Veronica's daugh—'

'We're in danger,' Shilah said. 'Can you hide us? Please. I heard you used to be a Marcheye. That's why I brought us here.'

I cocked my head. *A Marcheye?*

'Your mother told you about that?' Mama Jana asked, mouth gaping. 'But you're too young for the ceremonies. And besides, it was shut down ten years ago.'

Shilah stood rod straight, her eyes flitting around the room, almost as if ignoring the Noblewoman standing in front of her.

'And you said nothing to anyone?' Mama Jana asked, lump visibly forming in her fleshy throat. 'You didn't try the March, did you?'

'Nothing,' Shilah said, puffing further with pride. 'No.'

'Mama Jana,' I said, giving the shopkeeper a respectful bow. She seemed smaller and more hunched than I remembered. 'I'm sorry that we came here and burdened you. But we have good reason. We—'

And then a pang in my chest, seizing my words.

'What is it, child?' Mama Jana asked, looking me over with concern.

I shook my head, unable to speak over the rebounding emptiness.

Shilah gave me a concerned glance and then picked up where I had left off. 'We discovered something that's going to change the whole World Cried.'

'Please help us,' Cam added, bowing, which was something the High Nobles never did for the lowborn Nobles. 'It will pay you back for the figs a hundredfold.'

'Oh, I don't give a beetleskin about the figs, Camlish!' Mama Jana was nearly snarling. 'You were supposed to keep him safe!'

I was about to grab the Coldmaker out of my bag and show Mama Jana, but she waved me still and quiet.

'No more talking,' she said, navigating the dark shop as easily as a whip snapping through open air. 'No more talking until we get down to the chamber. The hounds can hear almost as well as they can smell.'

Mama Jana's shop only had the one level. I'd been there dozens of times and never noticed any stairs or hidden doors. There was no *chamber*.

Mama Jana grabbed one of her fancy canvas bags and began stuffing our soiled clothes away, staining the inside with our sweat and dirt and sand. 'It was a smart idea to change clothes and scents, Spout. I'd expect nothing less from you, but it's not enough. You need to be away from here.'

I went to open my mouth, but her glare could have cooked clay to brick.

'No talking,' she spat, her eyes flicking over to the drawer where I'd discovered the rosemusk and clay urns. 'I mean it.'

She grabbed our clothes bag that must have stunk like a taskmaster's armpit and gestured for us to follow her to the back of the shop. Keeping the Coldmaker tight against my side, I followed through the darkness, the pungent smell of flowers clinging to us.

Mama Jana stopped at her giant Khatclock with the Closed Eye for a face. Even though the huge timekeeper was a beautiful display of craftsmanship, I'd never paid it much mind. Besides the giant timepiece being a looming symbol of Jadan inferiority, it was also broken, its two hands forever stiff. The Khatclock only ever pointed in one direction, straight up. Mama Jana had never asked me to take a look inside the machine to see if I could get the gears and cogs working, and so I'd never offered.

'Wait here,' she said, eyes already planning her route back through the dark shop. She threw the bag of soiled clothes at Cam's feet. 'And say nothing.'

I gave my friends a confused look, which was returned by a helpless shrug from Cam, and a perplexing smile from Shilah.

Mama Jana careened around the room gathering things with the swiftness of a wraith. Darkness nor clutter were able to stop her. She gathered clothes, waterskins, velvet bags of Cold, assorted vials, and a compass. Last she grabbed the half-empty basket of figs, balancing it in the palm of her hand. Another series of horn blasts sounded outside and my stomach seized up.

I ran my fingers against the smooth bronze metal of the Coldmaker, my nails scraping along the engraved Opened Eye I'd carved with a hammer and chisel. The machine was small enough to fit in my arms, but still quite heavy, as it was made mostly of dense bronze. It also walled in a whole Frost, and was filled with salt water, two of the main components that made the invention work. Jadan tears were dropped onto the Frost inside, which caused a visceral reaction at the catch-point. I didn't know exactly why it worked that way, but the machine's presence bestowed me with strength and kept me from having a breakdown; so even if it weighed more than a whole caravan cart, I would have found a way to keep it by my side.

Mama Jana reappeared as fast as she had gone, shoving the basket of figs into Cam's hands and the bags of supplies into mine. 'Free of charge. My first flock in so long.'

'Mama Jana, what's—'

She put a hand to her lips, cutting me off and giving me a stern look. 'No. Talking.'

I nodded, hearing every rapid beat of my heart in my ears. Shilah looked far too calm considering the circumstances, as if none of this surprised her. Cam at least looked as lost as I did, as he was drenched in sweat, and squirming with a hand over his stomach as if he was about to spew.

Mama Jana pulled back the glass face of the Khatclock and took hold of the spindly hands. Before doing anything else, she gave me a look, as though she'd been waiting on this moment for some time.

'North.' Mama Jana nodded, and then spun the hands one full rotation. 'The March is always North.'

As the Khatclock's hands completed their circle, the entire Closed Eye face opened with a faint click, revealing a startling display of strange writing beneath the mechanical lid. The whole clock swung forwards, revealing a hidden hole that was lit faintly by a distant flickering light. The dark corridor led to descending stairs not unlike the ones in Leroi's study, and brought with it a frightful sense of dread, reminding me what had happened last time we took one of these secret passageways.

Mama Jana put a hand on my back and gently nudged me along, handing me the soiled clothes to take with us. 'Go, children. I'll seal you in and hold them off as long as I can. It's airtight, so those foul beasts shouldn't be able to smell you. Remember, the March is always North. Follow the signs, and when you get to the shack, ask for Split the Pedlar. He probably won't answer to Shepherd any more. Now, hurry!'

I went to spin around, but Mama Jana's arms were stronger than I remembered. 'Wait, what March?'

'The Coldmarch,' she said, glancing over her shoulder at the front door.

Cam gasped, sucking in a breath so fast he almost choked. 'It's real?'

Mama Jana licked her cracked lips, her eyes feverish and crazed. 'It used to be real. And I guess it is again. Now take these words with you if you can. Hold on. Okay, let me remember. *Shemma hares lah . . .*' She stopped, her tongue rolling on the roof of her mouth, struggling to find the next part. '*Shemma hares lahyim her*— no, that's not it.' She flexed her gnarled hands with frustration. 'It's been a while. Let me get the Book of the March.'

I clutched the Coldmaker more tightly against my side and offered: '*Shemma hares lahyim criyah Meshua ris yim slochim.*'

From the look of shock, I thought Mama Jana was about to faint.

'My father told them to me,' I explained.

The sharp memories of Abb made me bite down on my tongue, and I might have drawn blood.

Mama Jana composed herself with a sigh, but her words moved quickly. 'Fitting for such a name. Now go. There's still a lantern burning, and candles. Take the lantern with you, you'll need it. Move with caution as there are certain dangers down there. Eat the lizards if you must. You'll find water eventually. What am I forgetting? Hmm. I was just down there . . . don't stop, even if you hear my voice behind you . . .' The circles under her eyes deepened. 'I've not broken yet, but the Vicaress has certain ways.'

'The Coldmarch is real,' Cam said to himself, looking quite flustered. 'I can't believe it. My father always said "If the Khat can't find it, it's not real."'

Mama Jana said nothing, just made another shooing motion, brushing us towards the dark.

I rifled through my bag until I found one of the loose Abbs, handing it over.

She took the Abb gently, holding it up against the bit of light trickling in from the passageway. 'What it is, Spout?'

'Put a slice of it in water and tell as many people as you can,' I said, keeping my voice hushed so she wouldn't yell at me.

Mama Jana gave me a curious look, but the horn calls were explosive now, even through the walls of the shop. She finally brushed us through the threshold and swung the Khatclock back in place, sealing us away.

# Chapter Three

Grabbing the lantern from the bottom of the stairs, I lifted it high so we might get our bearings. Glancing back at the Khatclock, I found the space now to be one solid wall, not even a single crack where a horn or a shout might pass through. I knew there had to be a way to slip back into the shop, but I found no sign of a knob or release, and from Mama Jana's tone it didn't sound like she intended for us even to try.

Spinning around, I let the light shine down the empty corridor that stretched deep into the earth. The passageway was wide enough to accommodate us if we walked in single file, the walls so smooth they almost looked wet. The air tasted strange in my mouth, and not just because of our collective rosemusk bath. I smacked my dry lips. The air was so much cooler than back up in the shop, but I saw nothing in the way of Cold Bellows. The temperature must have been natural.

The passage took a sharp turn left after about ten paces, cutting off sight to whatever lay beyond.

Cam put his forehead against the clay wall, closing his eyes and taking a moment before speaking. 'It's real. I knew it.'

'You know what this place is?' I asked, feeling rather

childish as nightmare images jumped into my mind. I knew I should be thanking the Crier for the incredibly fortunate fact that Mama Jana had a passageway out of her shop, but ever since childhood I'd been bombarded with stories of haunted holes and cracks in the land. Places where the unforgiving spirits lived, bottled up and angry.

Beneath the ground was where the foul creatures lurked, plotting how they might make it up to the surface where they could partner with Sun and do his bidding. Sobek lizards and sand-vipers would be the least of our problems down here, and a part of me wondered if it would be better to take our chances with the hounds.

Cam kept his head pressed against the wall, but looked at me with a small tear dotting the corner of his eye beneath his glasses. His face was still blood red from exhaustion, but at least he was smiling. 'I mean, I knew it was real, and you *did* invent a miracle. And my father really is a monster, but this proves everything once and for all. I would go back to the library and burn all those paintings and—'

'Cam, stop babbling and talk to me,' I said carefully.

Lifting himself away from the wall, I thought he might start dancing. He threw his arms wide. 'Spout, you're going to change Sun-damned EVERYTHING! And I get to help you!'

'Keep it down, idiot,' Shilah snapped at him, pointing to the door.

Cam gave an embarrassed nod, his chest rising and falling with incredible speed.

'I would have thought you were a true believer when you took us in, Camlish?' Shilah said with an eyebrow raised, standing in the centre of the chamber with her arms crossed over her chest.

'Why am I the only confused one?' I asked. 'What is the Coldmarch?'

'I'm surprised you haven't heard the stories,' Cam said,

standing straight and grabbing at the end of his Opened Eye necklace. 'I would have thought it would have been pretty common lore in the barracks.'

I shook my head slowly.

'The Coldmarch,' Shilah said, stepping up to me and putting a hand on my shoulder. 'There's a reason I kept bugging you about leaving the Manor. There's already a path to Langria.' She paused, considering something. 'Or there was.'

'Hold on,' I said, needing a moment. 'Just stop. We don't know what's down there. Just . . . hold on. This tunnel goes all the way to Langria?'

Shilah pointed back up the stairs with an impatient look. 'Like she said, the Vicaress has her ways of getting information, and I don't want to be near that clock if the hounds track our scent to the shop. Now come on, I'll fill you in as we walk.'

'You told me dozens of stories before we went to sleep on those cots.' I suddenly felt a tad betrayed. 'Why wouldn't you tell me about an *existing* path to Langria?'

'Like I told Mama Jana, I'm a girl of my word.' Shilah kissed her finger and waved it at the sealed entrance in some foreign gesture of gratitude.

Did I really know anything about this girl?

She grabbed the lantern, holding it at arm's length as she traipsed down the passageway, forcing back shadows.

Cam wiped his single tear from his cheek and held it out towards the Coldmaker, his excitement dipping. 'I wish you could use it to make Ice. One day the Crier will forgive me.'

I had no idea what to say to such a thing.

'Maybe one day,' Cam said again with a hopeful shrug. 'Maybe I can be chosen, too. A Jadan, like you both.'

Even the finest Inventor in the World Cried couldn't tinker with someone's blood, but still I said: 'I'm sure.'

Shilah kept quiet, but I could see what she burned to say.

'Come on,' I said. 'We have to hurry.'

Cam took both the supply bags, the dirty clothes and the basket of figs, not seeming to mind the burden, leaving me to carry only the Coldmaker, which I clutched dearly against my hip.

Shilah led us through the tunnel and I followed last in line, my head swarming with visions and possibilities.

'The Coldmarch,' Shilah said, only loud enough for me to get a trace of her words, 'is a web of stops, stretches, and people along the path North. It's a journey, not necessarily a place. There were hidden chambers like these run by Jadans and Noble sympathizers all across the Khatdom, set up so they could usher people in secret. Obviously no one could dig out a tunnel all the way from Paphos to Langria, as that would take all the Builders in the world thousands of lifetimes.' She looked back with a wink. 'I thought you were smarter than that, Spout.'

The way she said it, playful and wry, didn't seem to connect, and I had no joke in response. I wasn't in the mood to joke anyway.

'Some brilliant Inventor could have come up with a digging machine to do all that work,' Cam said. 'I've seen some pretty impressive things in the tinkershop.' He looked back over his shoulder, beaming. 'That your next invention idea, Spout? I have to say, you'll need something rather big to follow up' – he gestured with his elbow to my bag – 'a miracle.'

'Flight,' I said without pause. I expected a pang to strike my heart like a battering ram, but nothing shook. I thought back to my time under Thoth's wool hat. I wondered what Matty might say if he could see me now, protecting something that could change the world, walking through the dark veins of myth. 'Flight is next.'

Cam smirked. 'If anyone can do it, I'd bet my Cold on you.'

'What Cold?' Shilah whispered with a scoff. 'You don't have any claim to the Abbs.'

'I brought you the Frost!' he said.

'You mean the one that your father stole from the hard-working Patch Jadans?'

'Wait.' Cam suddenly stopped short, and I nearly crashed into his back. 'This is wrong.'

I looked from side to side for talons or teeth. A drunken Levi had once assured our barracks that hounds' eyes glowed red before the beasts pounced.

Cam shook his head, pressing himself flat against the side of the cave wall. 'You go in the middle of us, Spout.'

'Why?'

'Just do it. You deserve to be in front of me.'

'No, it's okay, I can—'

'Just. Please,' Cam insisted, pressing himself harder, his face squished against the cool rock.

'Why?' I asked.

Shilah sighed from up front. 'Boys. *Hounds*.'

'And maybe worse,' I said under my breath.

Cam tried to angle his way behind me, sliding along the smooth walls, his loose shirt and bags dragging. I tried to stop him and we did an awkward dance, both of us shimmying backwards.

'What are you doing?' I asked.

'You're the most valuable of us,' Cam said, not meeting my eyes. 'You stay in the middle. Just in case.'

All of a sudden the Coldmaker felt very heavy.

I didn't say anything, letting Cam filter around in front of me. He was still balancing the basket of figs in one hand, and I snatched one, shoving it in my mouth and biting down hard, hoping some food might help me feel more normal.

'Let me at least take the bag of dirty clothes,' I said between bites.

'I need to carry them.' Cam craned his neck so he could see Shilah. 'This is also for you, you know.'

Shilah kept walking, her back straight as the edge of a knife. 'Drop the dirty clothes, Camlish. Mama Jana just needed them out of the shop.'

I was surprised how authoritative Shilah could sound. Cam gave a conceding shrug and did as commanded, tossing the bag aside and giving it a frustrated kick as he passed it.

We followed the corridor around a bend and found that the ceiling sloped lower and the walls pinched closer. I'd never had a problem with tight spaces before, but something about being underground made the musty air – cool as it may have been – feel as if it was going to suffocate us. My chest felt tight, and I dug my thumbs into my ribs, trying to loosen the knot.

Shilah didn't seem to mind, and she picked up the pace, guiding us deeper into the dark.

'Anyway,' she said, 'the Coldmarch has been kept extremely secret for obvious reasons. No mention of it in writing, and everyone involved kept about as tight-lipped as they could. The March supposedly only let a handful of Jadans North every year, most always young girls. It was shut down a while back, apparently ten years, but I don't know why.'

'But why would they shut down something like this?' I asked. 'Every Jadan should have known. No. Every Jadan should have *gone*.'

I drew my fingers along the wall. Feeling the stone, the damp texture and tiny imperfections, I understood the importance of such a place as this. That didn't mean I wasn't detached. I was walking through a secret that could have started a revolution, a place that proved us chosen, or at the very least worthy, and I should have been struck with something powerful. Awe perhaps. Disbelief maybe. Flames of righteous indignation. Something that infused life back into my soul.

But all I could feel was the stone.

My father was gone.

Shilah shrugged, urging us onwards. 'Maybe the Khat found out. Maybe something changed. I imagine the whole situation was delicate to begin with.'

'If the Khat found out about it,' Cam said, all of a sudden looking very pale. 'That means we might be walking right into their hands.'

Shilah picked up the pace. 'Yes. It's possible.'

Cam stopped. 'So . . .'

'So we have no choice, *Camlish*,' Shilah said, holding the lamp higher, her feet slightly splayed.

'Why do you keep saying my name like that?' Cam asked gently.

'Because it's not a Jadan name,' Shilah said with a huff.

'I didn't choose to be born Noble,' Cam said, his face strained. 'But I'm damn sure doing everything I can to make up for it.'

'I know,' Shilah said softly. 'But you still don't know what it's like to be Jadan. You never will.'

'I'm going to prove it to you,' Cam said over my shoulder. 'I'm going to show you that—'

All of a sudden the corridor ended in a wall with a large smear of dark red cascading from edge to edge. I didn't need to examine the colour to know that it was blood, and my stomach tightened.

The Coldmarch was over as soon as it had started.

My machine was heavy; my foolishness weighed more.

'Mama Jana sent us into a trap,' I said, still oddly removed from the situation at hand. I stopped short, wondering how long it would be until we were cornered by beasts. I didn't blame Mama Jana. Life was hard enough in Paphos, even for the lowborn Nobles, and everyone had to do what was necessary to survive. I didn't blame her. I ached. Even with all the whips and stabbings I'd suffered as a Street Jadan, I had come to find out the worst sting came from betrayal.

Cam came up next to me, his throat visibly stiffening. 'Is that blood on the wall?'

Shilah kept pushing forwards, swinging the lantern.

'She's probably keeping us down here until they arrive,' I said matter-of-factly. 'Then the hounds can rip our throats out without any fuss. I bet we're worth half the Khat's fortune, and Mama Jana will be set up for life. It's smart, really.'

I held the Coldmaker closer to my chest, wondering how I could at least save the machine. Even if I was disposable, the discovery was of the utmost importance. If I had enough time, I could have used the metal corners of the machine itself to dig a proper hole into the clay where it might hide.

Cam unshouldered all the supplies he was burdened with, shaking the basket of figs. 'But why would she give us all of this, if it's just a dead end?'

'It makes sense,' I said, sniffing my arms and enjoying the scent of life for what might be the last time. Even beneath the rosemusk I could smell ash and fire. 'Now they can do everything in secret and not worry about rebellion. Like the mistake they made with Matty.'

'For someone who helped crack the secret to Cold,' Shilah said, turning to me, 'you're being quite glum.' She stabbed a finger against the red on the wall. 'Alder. Also known as Alder of Langria.'

I paused, trying to remember how I knew that word. 'Like the plant Leroi had on his table?'

Shilah nodded.

Cam gave a blank-faced stare.

'Look closer,' Shilah said, beckoning us forwards. 'This *blood* spells out a word.'

Tentatively I stepped forwards and saw that without the cover of shadow the smears did indeed look like letters.

'It says *hope*,' Cam read, astonished. 'How'd you know that stuff wasn't blood?'

'Because all Jadans know how blood dries,' Shilah said, pushing open the whole wall with a single thrust and revealing a much larger chamber behind, dust clouding the air.

'Huh,' I said, my eyes having trouble taking in everything at once.

Cam nearly dropped the basket of figs. 'Wow.'

'Hurry,' Shilah said, letting the wall close behind us and rushing forwards, practically ignoring all the sights before us that demanded admiration. The vast room itself was still encased in long clay walls, but unlike the crawlspace leading up to it, this chamber had overwhelming signs of past travellers.

The Opened Eye of the Crier was painted everywhere, in all different styles, drawn on with the same red alder as on the entrance wall. Hundreds of Eyes looked over the chamber and gave the room a hopeful air. Small assortments of trinkets and keepsakes sat along the perimeter of the walls, like shrines. Jadans were never allowed to own much, and even though the dust and neglect made it clear that none of my kin had been down here in a decade, the sense of creativity felt alive and electric.

There were makeshift dolls posed to look as if they were tearing off their slave-uniforms. And little ceramic bowls with gold paste filled the cracks around the shrines. Ragged sleeping blankets of all colours were pinned to the walls, making one broken, yet beautiful tapestry, while whistles carved out of broken cane sat poised and ready to sing. Broken hourglasses were fitted sideways so the sands would never fall, and links of rusted and shattered chains were woven between all the Opened Eyes. I saw a few taskmaster whips – obviously stolen – buried up to the hilt in the floor, as well as statues of ancient animals that must have been painstakingly chipped out of barrack bricks.

And prayers.

So many prayers, all carved directly into the walls. Words

of thanks and fear and hope and pleas for guidance. They weren't all written in the common tongue of Paphos, either. There were letters I didn't recognize, ancient designs with tails and loops and dots studding the bottom lines. I couldn't stop looking around at the words, stunned by how many Jadans had been down here; all hopeful, preparing to make the journey to paradise.

Cam plucked a Wisp off one of the shrine tables. 'Someone left Cold behind.'

Shilah shrugged. 'You'd probably give anything you had too, if you knew it might help keep you safe. Sacrifice is a big thing with my people.'

'But Cold?' Cam asked. 'Wouldn't they want to use it? It's a long way North, and the Sun is even stronger there.'

Shilah shook her head, as if Cam was missing something obvious.

'What?' Cam asked, putting the Wisp back down. 'Is that offensive to touch?'

Shilah looked at me, her eyes resolute. 'The Vicaress can read, too. And I guarantee she knows the difference between alder and blood. We need to keep moving.'

I nodded, but a part of me wanted to read every single prayer down here, and touch every gift, thinking about the Jadans who might have left them behind. They'd challenged the Khat's Gospels to try their luck in this Coldmarch. They must have believed our people were more than dirt, that we weren't supposed to be slaves.

Even without a Coldmaker, they had taken a leap.

If only they could see the machine in my arms.

'You're right,' I said, my hand trembling as I pressed it against my machine. The metal was cool to the touch, even after all that time under Sun.

Shilah quickly led us through the decorated chamber, which at the end funnelled into another small space. Before we pushed into the mouth of the new tunnel, Shilah stopped and moved her head from side to side. If possible she drew her back even straighter, whipping her braid around so it was out of her face. The walls were closer near the exit, and two tallies of names had been etched on either side.

'Lost,' I read on top of the left wall.

'Saved,' Shilah said, pointing to the right.

The 'saved' side had considerably fewer names than the 'lost' side – which had hundreds, if not thousands, of names carved in, spanning floor to ceiling. I let my eyes scan the rows top to bottom, feeling more and more dismayed the closer to the ground I got, even spotting a few 'Micahs' along the way. Had all these Jadans really been killed in the name of freedom?

And then I reached the final name on the wall.

It looked entirely fresher than the rest, scraps of clay sprinkled on the floor underneath. It must have been why Mama Jana had so much earth trapped under her cracked fingernails.

She'd scratched his name in by hand.

*Abb.*

Cam bent over and put a hand on my shoulder. 'I'm so sorry, Spout.'

I swallowed hard, my knees shaking as I crouched.

It's not that I didn't know he was gone, but here was the first physical proof. Not just a vision, or the Vicaress's words that could have turned out to be a lie. Here was the name of my father, the best slave I'd ever known.

Emotions tried to flood in, but I had no capacity to deal with them right now, so I swallowed them back.

It wasn't even that hard.

'Drop the bucket,' I said casually under my breath, opening the lips of my bag and showing him the invention. 'All because of you.'

'Hmm?' Cam asked.

I put the Coldmaker on the ground, and, instead of grabbing one of the Abbs already tucked into the inside pocket, I flipped the machine on.

The air in the cave quivered as my invention went to work, a cool breath drawn from the entire tunnel. Wind whipped across the shrines, the temperature changing in the room. Why the machine worked was a mystery I intended to examine, but at least for now I had a general idea. The vials were opened as the gears turned. A few tears fell on the Frost first, which sat in its Cold Charge bath. This caused the initial reaction. Then a drop of my Jadan blood was let out at the catch-point as a starter material, where the gold gathered and bundled to form an Abb.

From a strictly inventive standpoint, the procedure was simple and straightforward, nothing other than a natural response.

Cause and effect. Simple. Emotionless.

As the new Abb came to life, I shut off the machine and plucked up the golden bead. A crisp scratching came from behind me, so I spun around and found Shilah with a long blade in her hand. It was folded steel, the silver handle ornate as they came. She was doing something to the bottom of the 'saved' wall. From my vantage it looked almost as if she was crossing a name out.

'What are you doing?' Cam asked.

Shilah finished and pressed her back to the place she'd marred, hiding the evidence. 'Let's keep moving.'

'Can I borrow that?' I asked, pointing to the blade. I was actually glad of Shilah's thievery. Mama Jana had a decent collection of blades behind the counter, and we would need it more than the shopkeeper did.

Although perhaps not if the hounds had found her.

Shilah tossed the blade at my feet. I gently prised a nook out of the second 'b' in Abb's name, big enough so as to make my own kind of shrine. I stuffed the fresh, golden Abb in the space, snug and secure, and then closed my eyes, offering a prayer I was sure was not the first of its kind to echo across these walls.

'Let's go,' Shilah said, this time gently. 'We don't know how long this next stretch of tunnel is going to be.'

'One more thing,' I said.

I picked an empty spot on the wall and carved in a small feather.

# Chapter Four

We were stuck underground for much longer than expected.

Whoever had built this part of the Coldmarch had used the natural cracks in the land for a foundation, presumably to decrease the amount of actual digging that needed to be done. Since the Builders had used the existing spaces already waiting underground, the way through ended up being complex and disorientating. The compass told me we were zig-zagging back and forth beneath the city, quite often straying from North. Some of the natural cracks in the earth were huge, the size of Cry Temples, with sporadic holes that plunged downwards into a forever sort of darkness. Often in the distance we heard the sounds of rushing water, leaving me to wonder how close we were to the River Singe. We made sure to follow the red alder line painted at our feet so as not to get lost or stray off the designated path. In other sections the walls became incredibly congested, scarred with hundreds of scratches. I imagined the marks were from bodies and supplies trying to squeeze through.

We had no way to tell time in the darkness, but I imagined it was a few days. We stopped to sleep twice, both times finding sanctuary off the path in case the Vicaress had found her way down here. We only intended to rest for a few hours, just to gather our strength, although it was hard to judge how long we slept, since we had to extinguish the lamp each time to conserve fuel. Shilah and I slept with our bodies pressed together, our arms linked, belts looped together. This was both for warmth, but also for safety, in case something foul tried to snatch one of us away in the dead of night. Shilah thought I was being paranoid, but she was the one who'd suggested the knotted belts. I offered to have Cam sleep on my other side, tied to us, but he kept declining, insisting on staying awake and keeping guard. I'd told him this was unnecessary, since he wouldn't be able to see, but he wouldn't listen, keeping at the edges of whatever nook in which we took refuge, constantly vigilant.

By the third leg of the trip his eyes were as red as the alder line.

He also refused to eat any more of the figs. They didn't last long anyway.

Not much was said as we made the journey. There was no reason for the silence, but I had a feeling Cam and Shilah were nervous for the same unsaid reason. None of us wanted to be the one to startle something ancient living down here in the dark. So far there had been no red eyes or grinding of unseen fangs, but anything was possible so far beneath the sands of Paphos. The world was different down here, cool and dark, and apart from the threat of Hookmen and Firegogs, it was a fitting start towards paradise. There was no Sun to bake us dry, no taskmasters waiting to scar our backs, no Nobles using our bodies for their own gain. For the Jadans who took their chances on the March, it would have been their first taste of peace.

'Do you like being called Jadans?' Cam asked, his quiet voice thunderous after so much silence. We were trudging through a thin clay corridor with crystal cones hanging above our heads and sometimes reaching the floor. The pointy wedges made it feel as if we were threading our way through a giant mouth. There had still been no sign of the Vicaress on our heels, no flaming dagger in the dark, so we'd been able to slow the pace down a bit. The overall mood had grown a bit lighter, since, despite the constant threat of danger, we had yet to be eaten. Even I was feeling the smallest twinges of hope. Unfortunately, every time my chest tried to kindle the sensations into happiness, all I could think about were the names carved into the 'lost' wall.

I examined a particularly thick crystal tooth, wondering what sort of benefit the shiny material might have offered crushed up. Leroi would have known.

'As opposed to?' I asked Cam, ducking low as I moved away, so as not to be speared by the tip.

'Well,' Cam said, lowering his voice. 'Since the Great Drought, there's a negative connotation involved with the word.'

Shilah glared back at us.

'Not that I think anything is wrong with it,' Cam said quickly. 'It's just that I've heard my brother and uncles – and obviously my father – say "Jadan" with such hate. They make it sound *worse* than saying slave. Is there something else you want to be called? Because I'll call you that if you want.'

'What brought this on?' I asked.

'I figure if we get out of here alive then—' Cam got flustered, the crystal cones gently reflecting the redness of his cheeks. 'I don't know, I thought that maybe you'd want your people to be called something else. And I could be the one to start it now. It's dumb, sorry. Forget it.'

'*When* we bring things back to how they were supposed to be,' Shilah said with a snort, 'just don't call us Nobles.'

Cam adjusted the bags of supplies on his shoulder so he could avoid a crystal pillar more easily. I imagined the bags must have grown quite cumbersome after so long, not as much as my burden, but unwieldy nonetheless.

'Just forget it,' he said.

'It's considerate of you.' I tried to sound consoling. 'But Jadan is something to be proud of. If anything, we'll just have to change the connotation.'

'Whatever you need,' Cam said, giving an agreeable bow, as low as he could manage without spilling everything. His eyes went to Shilah. 'Just let me know.'

I stared back at him, blinking a few times. The lantern light barely reached him, and his shiny yellow hair now looked black from all the dirt and dust it had attracted.

'What?' he asked.

'Nothing.' I nodded, noting his eyes had moved to the Coldmaker. 'I believe you.'

I licked my finger and touched the nearest pillar, bringing it back to my mouth. My tongue recognized the delight better than my eyes.

'Salt,' I said.

Cam immediately reached up and cracked off the tip of the nearest pillar, stuffing it in the bag. Shilah shot him a look, as if reminding him we shouldn't be drawing attention to ourselves.

Cam licked his dry lips. 'When we get to Langria we'll have to have a feast, and I can say I brought the free Jadans salt from the Coldmarch. As a gift.'

I smiled, although it didn't climb past my lips.

'And,' Cam said with a glimmer of pride, 'you need salt for the Coldmaker, right? To keep the Charge.'

'Good thinking,' I said with a nod. 'Let's get a few.'

Shilah shrugged, and we all snapped off a handful of salt each, adding it to Cam's supply bag. I pressed my hands to my nose afterwards, but there wasn't any scent.

'Salt and Abbs and revolution,' Cam said as we started

moving again, following the alder. He immediately stopped and then gestured for Shilah to lead us, giving her a respectably wide berth. 'It should be quite the feast.'

Our next stop took place beside a tiny stream, which had carved a shallow bed into smooth rock as it cascaded endlessly into the darkness. We'd heard the rushing waters from the alder path and wound our way to its shores to fill up our waterskins. Gentle currents had brushed the endless tunnel wide, making the passage seem both frightening and serene. The waters were some of the most delicious I'd ever tasted, possibly because they'd been kept away from Sun for an eternity. We only needed to add the smallest slices of Abb to get them to cool.

The journey had already begun to thin Cam out, his voice hollow and cheeks sunken. I asked him to sleep. Begged him even. It ended up taking three direct commands to get him to agree to shut his eyes for one hour. I gave him much longer. While he snored, one foot hanging limp in the waters, Shilah and I talked of fragile things. She kept dipping one finger in the water and bringing it over my hand, letting the single droplets fall on the back of my palm. She did this until the puddle at my feet trickled its way back to the source, rarely meeting my eyes as we spoke.

We talked of meeting out in the dunes behind my barracks, when I invited her to join our family, but instead she disappeared out into the sands. She told me she used the Rope Shoes that I'd traded her for the Khatmelon quite a bit, which is something I'd always wondered. We joked about the days working with Leroi back in the Tavor tinkershop, hiding under the floor grate whenever anyone unfamiliar came knocking. We discussed at length all the plants she'd cultivated for Little Langria. About where she got the soil and seeds, and vines. About the humour of the weaver beetles

that lived on her persimmons. She asked about the feather
I'd scratched into the wall, and I told her about Matty and
the board game we were creating; how close we'd come to
finishing. About how Moussa, Matty, and I lessened the harsh
tinge of the day by playing 'whatsit', where we made up
stories to go along with the shapes of our bruises. She told
me of the time she visited the Hotland Delta, having stowed
away on a merchant ship. About how the High Nobles there
had a certain ritual that they performed each night to pay
tribute to the Crier. Each Sundown they would fold little
boats out of Droughtweed and sail them along the Singe, a
single Wisp floating in each hull. Shilah's smirk was stupen-
dous as she told me how she would wait downstream with
a net to collect the boats. Over the course of a week she'd
made a small fortune.

I told her what it was like with such a large family.

She told me what it was like to live alone.

We didn't mention my father or her mother once.

Some things can live delicately in memory, but shatter
when put into words.

We didn't have much fuel left for the lantern, so I had to
wake up Cam sooner than I would have liked. He whimpered
at my touch, but when he grew conscious his face hardened
and he sprang to his feet, grabbing our supply bags and empty
basket of figs, leading us back to the path.

Finally, after more endless tunnels, the single red line led
us to our escape. The sleek and spindly cave once again
widened into a proper chamber, funnelling us towards an
actual way out. The wooden slab was slanted so much it was
nearly horizontal, and no light spilled in through the cracks
on the sides, but it looked like salvation nonetheless.

Wiping the layered crust of dirt from my forehead, I debated
thanking the Crier for getting us here alive – but I decided
that I was only ready to open one door at a time right now.

Cam pointed to the tilted door in front of us and the buckets sitting at its base, lowering his voice. 'Where do you think it lets out?'

'Honestly,' I said, matching his volume. 'I've been so turned around this entire time I have no clue.'

Shilah brought the lantern over to the door, where something was written in more alder. As she scanned the lines, her lips moved and I couldn't help but notice how full and plump they were. My focus shifted to her hair, long and tattered and matted with dirt. And her eyes, spilling over with all the sad things she'd already seen in this world.

'Imagine if we didn't have a lantern,' Cam said quietly. 'And we had to do this whole thing in the dark.'

'We almost did,' I said, pointing to the oil reserves, which were dangerously low.

'Right now we're at the edge of the Drylands, just North of Paphos,' Shilah read. 'Two days' walk until the next stop on the Coldmarch. The shack is in the bottom of the three-humped valley, and will be marked by a green streak over the threshold.' She turned to us with pinched lips, pointing to the empty buckets. 'It says please take all the water and Cold we need. And may the Crier watch over our family.'

'Two days.' Cam did the sums in his head, looking into the bag of supplies. 'No food, but plenty of water. Should we wait until night-time to leave?'

Shilah peered back into the dark chamber, the shadows flickering and ominous. 'Not sure we'll have until night.'

Pressing my fingers against the door, I found that it didn't have much give. There was no latch to undo, and the hinges told me that it was set up to swing outwards.

'We need to push together,' I said.

Gathering ourselves, we gave the door a hard, collective shove. The pressure should have made the wood budge at least, but it was immovable.

'Is it locked?' Cam asked. 'Want to try the trick with Ice in the lock again, Spout?'

I ran my fingernail around the cracks at the edges of the door, noting the gritty sand. 'I don't think there's a lock. Just ten years of sand pressing down on the other side.'

'You think we're under a dune?' Shilah asked, crossing her arms.

'I took a girl to see the Drylands once,' Cam said, looking down and scratching the back of his neck. 'And from what I remember they're pretty barren, but it's possible the dunes have shifted.'

Shilah put a hand on the door, as if to ask it through touch. 'I don't think it would let out so close to the dunes. Maybe the Khat barred it from the other side when he found out?'

Cam put both arms on the door and shoved again, the vein in his neck showing heavily through his light skin. He started pounding on the door with his shoulder to try to get more leverage, but I quickly put a hand on his arm to stop him.

'We have to be quiet and strong,' I said. 'We don't know what's out there.'

We all tried to push at the same time again, but the door wouldn't budge more than a hair upwards. It was then I noticed the middle of the wood distending inwards, gently caving under all the weight.

'Wait,' I said, remembering myself. 'Let me see that knife.'

Shilah reached under her dress and unstrapped the knife from her thigh. She handed over the blade and I tried not to think about the heat lingering in the metal.

Cam stared at the blade, his eyes softening.

'In case of the Vicaress?' she asked. 'You still think this is a trap?'

'No,' I said, going to work on the door's hinges. 'I'm just trying to think like an Inventor.'

Leroi had taught me that when it came to tinkering, sometimes the best answer was also the simplest. The door may have been intended to open upwards, but Inventors worked with their own intentions. After a flurry of careful twisting and prising, the hinges groaned, letting me know things were about to give.

'Get back,' I warned, heart pounding as I gave the blade back to Shilah and reluctantly handed the Coldmaker over to Cam.

I made the final twists by hand, and the metal cracked, the horizontal door giving way under an explosion of sand. An entire dune practically spilled into the cavern and pushed me backwards. Smacking my head against the wall, everything went a hazy beige as I tumbled to the ground, instantly buried up to my waist.

Things settled, and my head throbbed as I spat the sand out of my cheeks.

Arms threaded beneath mine, helping me up and out of the slice of dune, and hoisting me through the threshold. Shilah said something by way of appreciation, but my head was still ringing too heavily to make it out.

My friends kept a steady hold of both my sides, carrying me back into the glaring Sunlight, where I shook the sand out of my ears. Indeed, we had emerged North of the city, the brown land compact and walkable. There were plenty of boulders for cover, although the air up here tasted more dead and dusty than I was used to. Once I had found my footing, I took a look back at distant Paphos, just barely able to make out the web of streets and monuments and barracks and shops and temples and walled gardens and High Noble Manors and the First Khat's Pyramid, all built on the backs and blood of my people.

'Come on, Inventor,' Shilah said, gripping my elbow. 'We should get moving. We won't be safe until we get to that shack.'

I nodded to the city, promising I'd be back to set it free.

And then we marched North.

# Chapter Five

'Sunlash and blisters,' Cam said, hunching over as we reached the rocky face of the next hill. 'How many is that now, Spout?'

I paused, trying to come up with something poetic. 'As many as the freedom songs they sing in Langria.'

Cam tried to smile, but ended up wincing, his lips crimson and blistered. He had one of Mama Jana's sunscarves wrapped around his head, keeping his delicate yellow hair tucked away. There were other shirts in the bag, but Cam insisted on wearing a green blouse pulled over his robe, as he claimed it let in more air.

'I like that one,' Cam panted, covering his lips with his fingers. Sweat dripped down both his cheeks, which had begun to freckle.

I nodded, continuing to hum under my breath with each step. I finally realized that I'd been humming the Jadan's Anthem along with each step. It was the song Moussa, Matty, and I had created in my barracks, back when my childhood was torturous, yet somehow strangely whole.

The melody was sharp and painful. I didn't stop.

Cam took off his glasses and wiped the sweat from the lenses. His red face and struggling frame made me realize how well my people had adjusted to this harsh world. How we had been *forced* to adjust. My skin was dark and leathered, hardened by the strong glare of the Sun, and I was still wiry from the years of scavenging the city for tinkering supplies. Even though Cam's people were deemed '*Worthy*', it was the Jadans that could withstand treks under a merciless sky.

'How long do I have to wait before the next one?' Cam asked, wincing against the Sun.

'Not long,' I said.

To pass the endless monotony, we'd invented the Game of Paces. Since there were really no landmarks to judge how far we'd gone, we decided to keep track of the steps taken. There was a distinct possibility that there was nothing out here, that the shack had been swallowed by the dunes or burned down by the Khat, and that we would need an escape plan. So for fun we matched our steps to certain things in the World Cried, starting with small numbers like *figs in a garden* and *stones in the Pyramid*. By the end of the first day we had reached things like *beetles in Paphos* and *Jadan whippings*. Now, on the second day of hard walking, our numbers were so incredibly high that we had to get creative.

Water rations were tight, and since we found nothing living in the sands, our stomachs had already begun to harmonize their grumbles. The hunger hadn't been so bad last night, as we'd all passed out at the sight of good shelter – three huge boulders that came together to make a little nook – but it was hitting hard today. Cam had taken to chewing on strips of boilweed, and Shilah had begun to spend more and more time with her hand resting on her stomach. I'd been trying to keep track of how much water we went through each stop, and judging by the diminishing weight of the skins, I knew that soon we were going to buckle against the point of no return. The Sun was laughing at us, only getting stronger the further North we walked, its rays cracking down like fiery whips. The irony was that we had as much Cold as we needed, glorious, miracle Ice, but right now I doubted we'd have enough water to make it back the way we'd come.

I think both Cam and Shilah were aware of this, but they helped keep up the pretence, smiling through the dread.

'That's quite a few freedom songs,' Shilah said with a raise of her eyebrow. 'To sing that many they must not have stopped since the Great Drought.'

I adjusted the Coldmaker again, the machine heavy and the metal edge continuing to dig into my hip. I had a feeling I'd be walking with a permanent crook if we ever made it through the March.

'I imagine that's true,' I said softly.

I rubbed the sore spot on the back of my head, looking out over so much dead land and consulting the compass Mama Jana had been savvy enough to put in our supplies. We were still headed due North, but the barren sands and rocks weren't showing any signs of letting up. As far as I could tell, this was a fool's journey. We would surely perish, and the Coldmaker was going to be lost out in the middle of nowhere, along with any hope for the Jadan people.

'This is brutal,' Cam said, wiggling his toes underneath his sandals. 'It's like I stepped on a pile of needles, and the Sun is trying to lick my bones.'

'Welcome to life as a Jadan runaway,' Shilah said, unfazed and standing tall on the flattened stretch of earth. 'Enough of this suffering and maybe you will start understanding us.'

I had to admit it was a smart idea to have the Coldmarch positioned here, since no taskmasters would ever be caught out in this nightmarish terrain for no reason. The ground near Paphos had started as compact and easy, but the March had taken us across thick dunes, unstable rock faces, and the vertical climbs of the Drylands, all in the name of secrecy. I had yet to see any bleached bones sticking up from the sands, but I doubted all of the brave Jadans who'd attempted this journey had made it through.

The only benefit of this treacherous terrain was that the land here was not even, meaning frequent patches of cool shadow in which to rest. But all the shade in the World Cried wouldn't matter if we ran out of water.

'I bet they'll have groan salve at this next stop,' I told Cam. 'Mama Jana said this Split is a Pedlar, and Pedlars have everything. You'll barely feel the burns tomorrow.'

Cam nodded, taking a breath before standing up again. 'I'll call it penance.'

'Maybe you Nobles just aren't *worthy* of the March,' Shilah said.

'Shilah,' I said, shooting her a stern look. 'Stop. Cam is family, and he saved us both. Don't forget that.'

She looked poised to argue, but bit her bottom lip, and eventually nodded.

'And correct me if I'm wrong,' I continued, the timing perfect. 'But doesn't that look like the tip of a three-humped valley in the distance?'

Cam gave me a thankful look, his glasses still in his hand. 'You'll have to describe it to me. Things are a bit fuzzy at the moment.'

'Three humps in the rocks and sand,' I said, smiling for what felt like the first time since we'd started walking. 'Just like the alder writing said.'

'Shall we celebrate with Cold water all round?' Cam asked, his whole demeanour changing in an instant, looking practically giddy. 'We earned it.'

Before Shilah or I could answer, Cam gave a frantic nod, answering himself.

'Why, yes, Camlish, what a delightful offer. Thank you!' He rubbed his hands together eagerly. 'You're most welcome,

Camlish. You've always had the finest taste in celebrations.'

'Fine, but not all of it,' Shilah warned gently, rolling her eyes. 'It's been ten years since the Coldmarch shut down. We don't even know if there's anyone down in that valley.'

I reached into the Coldmaker bag, fishing for the side pocket where I kept the Abbs. 'Maybe not, but if this Split is still around, then it's another person we can share—'

My wrist exploded with pain.

I snatched my hand out of the bag. The sting was too overwhelming for me to even form a shout. My throat immediately closed up. Even though my tongue was silent, I could feel my arm howling.

'Spout,' Cam said, frowning. 'You okay? You cut yourself?'

I was unable to answer. The shock was still registering, pain increasing with every rapid pump of my heart. My wrist looked normal at first, but after an instant, two puncture marks began to make themselves known, my dark skin rising and bubbling from the venom.

I dropped the Coldmaker far harder than I should have, the machine giving an angry clank. The canvas lips of the bag fell open, and a baby Sobek lizard skittered from the bag. It looked up at me unafraid, its tiny red eyes glistening in the Sun. The scales around its neck puffed up, as if readying itself for another bite, although I already knew a second one couldn't do me further harm.

I was as good as dead.

'Oh,' Cam spurted. 'Oh no. That's really small.'

I snatched my wrist up to my lips and began sucking out the venom, my heart thundering and my head clouding with fear. Run-ins with Sobeks were common, and I'd been bitten before, but always by an adult lizard. The grown ones knew only to release a bit of venom in a single bite – meaning a night of vomiting and cramps for the victim – which was bad enough.

This was far worse.

Young lizards always emptied their entire poison sacs at once, not yet knowing how to control their portions.

Sobek lizards are a nuisance.

Their babies are assassins.

My tongue began to fizz with pain at the edges.

Shilah was quick, pinning down the creature with her sandal and cutting off the back half of its tail. Normally she was reverent of all living things, so I knew hurting a Sobek would not have been an easy thing for her to do.

Cam's face scrunched in frightened confusion as the lizard skittered away, unharmed by the loss of its tail.

'For the medicine,' Shilah said, her face severe. 'They say it's always best if you mix in some of the creature itself.'

I tried to say that it was true, that Abb had imparted that same bit of wisdom, but words were no longer possible.

Cam's face went mad, tearing at his headscarf. 'What do we do? How do we make medicine?'

Shilah didn't answer, pocketing the tail and rushing to my side.

'Alternate with me,' she said, bringing my wrist to her lips and somehow keeping calm. 'Five spits each. I'm right here. This isn't going to stop us.'

I nodded, feeling the Sun's rays pulsing with menace. The baby lizard must have crawled into the bag while we were passing through the caves, as they usually didn't stray far from water supplies.

But why hadn't I noticed it until now?

Perhaps this was *my* penance: punishment for trying to change things.

Shilah wrapped her lips around the punctures. She sucked hard, and the pressure was excruciating, like a shard of glass being driven out of my wrist. She pulled deep five times, spitting after each, rubbing her tongue on her sleeve.

I took a deep breath and went to take my turn, but the pain was too much, the wound burning like hot iron, and I flinched away.

'Let me do it,' Cam said, coming over and taking my wrist. He took one deep pull of the poison and then started coughing violently. 'It's like burning coals!'

'Move,' Shilah said, pushing him aside. She looked me right in the eyes as she grabbed my wrist. 'You're going to be okay, World Partner.'

Her words were slurred, and I knew her tongue had gone numb as well.

I nodded, but my forehead wasn't feeling as confident. I was heating up to a dangerous degree, beads of sweat falling into my eyes and sprouting all down my infected arm.

This was the end.

Cam breathed heavily, his face lost to fear.

'Micah,' Shilah said, gripping harder. Her words were slurred from the poison, but her eyes were focused and sharp. 'You're going to be okay.'

I pointed down to the valley with a shaking hand.

Shilah nodded with understanding and went back to work extracting the poison. She reached her limit after three more pulls, her lips flooding with colour and swelling. Scooping a hand against the ground, she sprinkled a layer of sand over her tongue and then angled my arm up.

'Kpp it elvted.' She spat. 'Make th bld wrk to rech the wnnd.'

'What can I do?' Cam asked, checking the Coldmaker bag for more lizards before tossing it over his shoulder. 'How can I help? Tell me what to do!'

'Kpp up,' she said, wrenching my arm and dragging me forwards.

We sprinted all the way to the middle of the three humps of the valley, my legs shaking. The pain in my arm was so furious that it almost felt like pleasure, which I knew wasn't a good sign. My vision was starting to swim and everything had taken on a beige hue – something that had never happened with any other Sobek bite. Hope was quickly draining with each step.

Down at the bottom of the steep valley was a stout shack huddling in shadow. Attached to the side was a small wooden stable, a beige snout poking out, dipping into a water trough.

*Is that a hound?* I thought, trying to pick out any red eyes through the haze. *Did the Vicaress beat us here?*

'You see that?' Shilah asked, nodding down, clarity in her voice returning. 'I think it's a camel.'

'It's alive,' Cam said. 'Which means someone must be home.'

Shilah grabbed my wrist and drew out three more pulls of poison and blood, but I couldn't feel her lips this time.

'Yrr gong to be okay,' she said, wiping her mouth.

My legs began to buckle. I turned to Cam, pointing to the Coldmaker, thinking maybe Ice could help. I was taken aback by the sight of my arm, which was riddled with sweat. Like the boiling bubbles that ran along the top of the Singe.

Shilah pinched the skin on the back of my neck, jolting me out of the fog. 'Stop being dramatic. You're going to be okay. I'm not going to Langria without you. And I'm *going* to Langria.'

She was stronger than I thought, or maybe *I* was stronger, because we made it to the bottom of the valley without me falling over and passing out, the land growing more solid the deeper we traversed. I knew I needed to stay awake, to keep from death's alleyway, or I'd be gone forever.

'No green mark over the door,' Cam said as we stepped in front of the shack. 'You think this is the right shack?'

'Are you kidding me?' Shilah asked, pounding the door with the palm of her hand. 'You see any other shacks around?'

I wasn't able to peel my eyes away from the stable. The

snout poked out further, revealing a beast with kind eyes, accentuated with long, thick eyelashes and knotted tufts of fur awning its forehead. The creature reminded me of a camel, but it was much smaller, the tufts at its neck lumpier. It's head only reached my chin, and it stuck out a pink tongue playfully, wiggling it in my direction.

I stuck mine out as well, but I couldn't get it to wiggle.

Shilah pounded the door again.

'You ever see one of those before?' I asked my friends, smiling at the beast. I much preferred this creature to the hounds that were probably still on our trail. 'I think it wants to be friends.'

No one answered me.

The words were only in my head.

'The secret is tears,' I whispered silently to the camel. 'Isn't that funny?'

'That's not the only secret,' the camel responded, ruffling its furry neck. 'I know your name.'

I laughed, wondering why only I could hear the little camel.

'He doesn't look so good,' Cam said, snapping his fingers in my face. 'Micah, you still with us?'

Cam's face was a beige smear.

Shilah kicked at the door now. 'Hello! Please, we need your help!'

The door opened just a crack, enough for us to find a very sharp arrow pointing at Shilah's forehead.

'No,' a gruff voice inside the shack said.

'Yes,' the camel whispered.

Down at our feet a heavy smoke curled out of the opening of the door. The black cloud was like an old scar. A shameful part of me wanted to drop to my stomach and start huffing, as it would certainly make the journey to my death more pleasant.

*What's the opposite of penance?* I wondered to myself.

'We're here for the Coldmarch,' Shilah said, unafraid and standing tall.

The arrow lowered to point at her mouth.

A pause from inside, the smoke continuing to escape. 'No.'

'No what?' Shilah asked.

'That's not a real thing. I never heard of no blasted Coldmarch.'

'Mama Jana sent us,' Shilah said. 'And my friend here has been bitten by a Sobek. We need your help.'

The arrow shook. 'He'll live. Tell him to suck it up. Least it's not a sand-viper.'

Shilah grabbed the severed lizard tail out of her pocket and held it up. 'It was a baby.'

'Well, you shouldn't have been out in the sands if you didn't want to get bit. Go back to your barracks and get medicine there, damned Jadans.'

Even through my fog of panic I found it interesting that he used the word 'Jadans' instead of slaves.

Cam nudged Shilah out of the way, stepping in front of the arrow and puffing up in the haughty way at which High Nobles tended to excel. I wanted to laugh, as the billowy green flutter-robes wasn't helping to toughen his image.

'Sir, I'm Camlish Tavor, first in line for my House, and I'm escorting these Jadans on the Coldmarch.'

'No such thing as a Coldmarch,' the voice growled. 'Now take your spoiled, High Noble ass back to your daddy, *Tavor*.'

The miniature camel began grunting loudly in its stable, the overhanging tuft of fur on its forehead spilling into its eyes.

'Hush, Picka!' the man grunted. 'Thisn't none of your business.'

*Picka*, I thought with a grin as I wandered over to it, looking into its long face. What a fine name for a talking camel. *Hello, Picka.*

'Hello. Thank you,' the camel said with a smirk in its eyes. *'Micah.'*

'My friends call me Spout,' I said with a bow, wondering if the camel was pronouncing my name funnily on purpose, or if it just couldn't make the sounds with its large, lolling tongue. 'You can call me Spout. It reminds me of my father.'

Shilah caught me under the arms as I fell, keeping me upright. I glanced down and saw that my feet were now two large sweat bubbles.

'Look, sir,' Cam said, giving an arrogant bow. 'I appreciate your discretionary behaviour, obviously a necessity for such a position as yours, but we know very well that you're Split the—'

The arrow released, impaling the bag on Cam's shoulder. I imagined most of our supplies had just been compromised in one single blow.

'Drat,' the man said with a menacing tone. 'Missed.'

'Please, won't you help us, sir?' Cam asked with a gulp.

'No such thing as a Coldmarch,' the voice inside warned, grunting a few times before another arrow appeared. 'And I'm pretty sure I don't miss twice.'

I wanted to reach out and touch the arrow to see if it was actually dripping with honey, or if that was just my imagination.

'You dare threaten someone of House Tavor?' Cam asked, aghast.

A silver token hopped out of the crack in the door, landing on the ground with the crest face up. I hadn't seen a coin like that since the days of endless errands as a Street Jadan, and all of a sudden I was back on my corner, the Vicaress parading around a group of my chained, young, and scared kin.

*'You* dare bother someone from House Suth?' the voice inside said in an imitation of Cam's arrogant tone. 'You hold no sway here, boy.'

The camel gave a throaty grumble, broken in frantic brays.

The arrow pointed down at Shilah's throat. 'I'm closing the door now.'

Cam's face was all fire. 'Sir, I demand you lower your weapon and talk to us about the Coldmarch.'

The smoke at our ankles had stopped drifting out. 'Scarabs on your shitty demands, Tavor.'

'Please,' Cam said, breaking into panic. 'We went through the tunnels beneath her shop, we saw the red alder—'

'Say it, *Micah*,' Picka whispered to me. 'Remember? You should say it now.'

I heard my father's voice beneath the words of the camel, which was disconcerting, but didn't stop me from taking the advice.

My throat opened just long enough to allow the prayer. '*Shemma hares lahyim*—'

The arrow swung to me, pointed right between my eyes.

'You don't finish that sentence, slave!'

At least the words were real this time, and not just in my mind.

More importantly I'd struck a chord, his words cracked with emotion down the middle. I had to use my tongue before it hopped out of my mouth and grew wings.

'*Shemma hares lahyim criyah*—'

'I mean it!' The man was at full alarm. 'Not another word, or I shoot!'

Shilah reached over and put a hand on my lower back to get me to stop, but I knew what I had to do, even if my vision was slowly narrowing to a pinpoint, and my arm felt as if it had been buried at the bottom of the dunes.

'*Shemma hares lahyim criyah Meshua ris yim slochim.*'

'DAMN EVERYTHING TO BLEACHED BONES AND SHRIVELLED TONGUES, FINE!'

The arrow disappeared and the door was flung open by

way of a swift boot kick. The man stormed out, revealing a paunchy stomach, thin and wispy hair, and a nose that was craggier than our way back to Paphos. After closer inspection, I realized this man was also another beige smear. Everything was beige now, actually.

'Fine. The Coldmarch is real,' the smudge said. 'I'm Split the Pedlar. Is that what you want to hear, you little brats? Years of peace you just upended. Now get your friend inside and—'

Beige went black.

# Chapter Six

'In your opinion,' I said, putting the vial marked 'Gales breath' back in its potion slot, 'what are the most important ones to know?'

Leroi crossed his arms, something the Head Tinkerer did quite often. 'All of them.'

'No, I know that,' I said, turning away from the cabinet full of solutions and giving him a smile. 'But I mean the most important specifically for inventing.'

Leroi gave me an incredulous look, raising an eyebrow.

I selected the next vial, marked 'Crushed Marjoram', and tapped at the bright green powder, a colour I'd only ever seen in Noble eyes. 'I know it's important to recognize them all, but we can't really use *everything* for inventing. So what I meant is, what are the things in this cabinet to focus on for our line of work?'

Leroi sat back on his chair and crossed one leg over the other, giving a ponderous scratching of his goatee, looking around the Tavor tinkershop. 'What is it that you think we do, Spout?'

'Make things,' I said with a shrug. 'With metal, and gears, and Cold Charges.'

'And that's it?'

I shrugged. 'Obviously not, but you know what I mean.'

'Course I do. But just because you're Jadan don't think I'm going to take it easy on you.'

I laughed. 'I don't think that's ever been the case.'

Leroi spread his rough facial hair down at the corners of his moustache. I expected him at least to smile at my joke, but his eyes had become distant and heavy. 'I imagine that's true.'

I nodded, taking out the next vial, with was filled with preserved newtworms from the Hotland Delta. I shook the glass, wondering how much better Jadankind would be if, like these slimy creatures, we didn't need Cold to survive. I wondered how much Leroi had already experimented with these life forms, trying to discover their secrets.

'What you have to remember,' Leroi said, 'is that you will never be finished learning. You will never have only certain things to focus on.'

I put the newtworm vial back. 'What do you mean?'

Leroi sighed, taking his hand away from his face and wiggling his fingers. 'Art. Inventing is art. The hands of Creation itself. Sometimes you work for the hand of the Crier, sometimes for—' He stopped himself, shaking his head. 'Sorry, you don't need to hear that nonsense. What I mean is, your life isn't going to be like the Builders or the Patch Jadans or even the Domestics, with certain quotas to fill or tasks to be completed. Inventing is not like other lines of work. There's no cap, no finishing. Inventors don't get to specialize in paint, or words, or music, or clay, we work with *all* of reality itself. Creation to destruction. You need to know *everything*, and you can never know everything. You need to know that Golemstone reacts violently with Milk of the Dunai. You need to know at what pressure Glassland Black will shatter, and at what temperature it will melt. You need to know how many ounces of Halia's elixir will dissolve diamonds, or how many drops will make a grown man scream. You need to know your metals and poisons and your powders and your mathematics and your poems, dammit, you need to know what the world needs, Micah, what Jadans need, and Nobles, too, and what this desecrated, Sun-damned, piece of—'

Cool water splashed my face, snapping me awake. My mouth instinctively gaped, collecting all the water it could. I sputtered and choked as it washed down my throat, but it felt wonderful against my burning tongue. Everything was still out of focus, and I blinked wildly, trying to figure out where I was.

'There. He's alive,' a voice announced. 'Now we get this over with.'

'Give him some time, man.'

A throaty grumble.

'Spout.'

A snap of fingers in my ears, then pressure on my chest, rubbing back and forth.

'We can have him ride Picka. She's small, but strong enough for your little friend. If the Khat's hounds are on the scent, we need to move.' Another grumble. 'Can't believe you got me into this.'

I finally heard Shilah's voice: 'Spout.'

'Do you know if the baby Sobek bites can have lasting effects?' Cam asked.

'How should I know?' the gruff voice asked. 'If you're smart, you avoid the damned things.'

I blinked again, wiping the water off my face, and three bodies came into focus above. Shilah and Cam were pressed against each other, vying for the spot closest to my side. Cam smiled, giving me a rather sheepish wave. He still hadn't changed out of the loose fluttering robe and blouse and looked like a green cloud. Shilah was straight-faced and standing tall, but her hand was resting gently on my ankle.

My arm was now covered in a waxy cotton, soaked red all the way through. I imagined Split the Pedlar wasn't nearly as proficient with needle and gut as my father, whose stitches almost never leaked.

I felt a wave of nausea, and my body spasmed under the weight of falling memories. I whimpered once, but disguised the next sound by sitting up and coughing, keeping my eyes averted. I pressed down hard over the cloth on my wrist and doubled the pain shooting up my arm. This flushed my mind of anything other than pure physical agony.

'Don't do that, kid!' Split demanded. 'You'll ruin the stitches! You think this house is made of needle and gut?'

I didn't listen, pressing even harder, digging my fingernails through the cloth. It was working. After a few more fake coughs my composure returned.

The first thing that I noticed was that the shack was rather dull for a Pedlar. The bare walls were decorated with splinters and flecked paint, and the empty shelves were stocked only with dust. The bed was a simple boilweed mattress, with no sleeping sheet. This was unlike the lavish silk accommodations I imagined all High Nobles slept on. A healing box sat open on the counter – recently rifled through – but I couldn't see any food in the kitchen.

The one oddity that struck me was the wooden Khatclock in the corner, smaller than Mama Jana's, but equipped with the same time-locked hands hanging over the Closed Eye face.

Hands that pointed North.

I gave the broken clock a nod, as it told me we were at least in the right place. 'Are you still a Pedlar?'

Split grunted. 'Hmm? What's that?'

'It's pretty empty in here.' I worked my jaw and lifted my

face enough finally to get a good look at the man. 'Did you sell everything you own?'

He crossed his hairy arms, tapping his thumbs against his soft chest. The stout man had the look of someone who could have once picked up his camel, but was now more likely to pick up a plate of cheese. Fair and flabby skin hung loose around his neck, and his belly protruded over his waist. A receding hairline tugged back the top of his head, which was bald and burned red from exposure. Beady eyes were sunken in beside his crooked nose, and his waxen face was chiselled with a deep frown. He wore a hollow sort of sadness I'd seen only once before.

'I peddle big piles of "you're alive thanks to me",' Split grumbled. 'So stop asking dumb questions that don't matter, and get off your ass and let's get going.'

I had a feeling my friends had yet to show him the Coldmaker.

Cam scowled. 'Spout is alive because Shilah got so much of the venom out. You even said so yourself.'

Shilah's cheeks flushed just a little bit darker.

Split waved a dismissive hand. 'I said she helped. Your sweaty friend here would be a blathering pile of useless meat if not for me. Now let's cut the chat and get my section of the March over with, before the hounds eat all of our faces off.'

'Lovely,' Cam said. 'Now hold still, Spout, let me check that burn.'

He leaned in and wrapped a hand around the back of my neck. Forehead to forehead, he whispered so low that only I could hear. 'Don't use your real name.'

I pondered for an instant and then nodded, deciding it was probably wise. 'It's fine,' I said at normal volume. 'It doesn't hurt any more.'

Cam stood up and gave Shilah a secretive wink.

'I thought you said there was no such thing as the Coldmarch,' I said to Split, testing the waters.

Split went red. 'Listen, kid. I don't know what you think you know, but you basically just left the womb. Maybe you were a really good errand boy in the city, finding colourful parasols on sale in the Market Quarters for ungrateful Nobles' – he did a fancy twiddle with his fingers and then pointed to Cam – 'or rushing towels to his bare-butt relatives in their baths, but you've never been outside Paphos. This is the Drylands, boy, this is where stupid young Jadans step on baby Sobek lizards, and then they die.'

Cam looked as if he was about to melt under the heat of his own fury, but I found myself drawn to Split, especially after seeing the Droughtweed pit cut into the middle of his floor. The ashes within the charred grey leaves were still smouldering. A small part of me wished just a bit of the smoke would waft my way and help ease both the burning in my throat and the stabbing in my wrist.

Split followed my eyes, his face getting even darker. 'You going to judge the High Noble who just saved your life? You know what, I don't care if you knew the sacred words, or that you were picked by Mama Jana, I don't have to—'

I waved him off with a bleak smile. 'I'm not judging. You and I are kin. Broken kin.'

Split huffed, but his face softened a bit. Tiny red lines cut the whites of his eyes, and his fingers absently scratched at his thigh. I never got so dependent that I scratched, but I knew plenty who did.

'How's your arm, Spout?' Shilah asked, cutting in and gently holding the back of my hand.

'I'm okay,' I lied, the whole left side of my body throbbing. 'Is the Coldmake—'

Shilah shook her head, cutting me off. 'Yes. The *World Crier* has been watching over us.'

'World Crier,' Split said with a huff, and then clapped his hands. 'Yeah, there's a chuckle. Now let's get this over with. And I hope you know I'm only in charge of taking you to the next stop on the March. Did Mama Jana tell you that? The flock always get passed to another Shepherd at Gilly's, so I'm not responsible for you once we get there.' Then he grumbled under his breath. 'Just letting you know now, there ain't going to be any other Shepherds left. But that's your problem, not mine.'

'*You're* still a Shepherd,' Cam pointed out.

Split kept scratching, the other thigh this time. 'You forced my hand.'

I brought my wounded wrist against my chest and pointed to the Coldmaker bag in the corner, looking at Cam. 'I assume you waited to show him our *supplies*?'

'You sure he needs to know about our *supplies*?' Shilah asked pointedly.

Cam nodded. 'Up to Spout. It's his miracle.'

Shilah tensed up at the declaration, her face turning sour.

Split looked about as confused as you could get, his thick face going red. 'What miracle you blathering about? Miracle that you're alive? That's not a miracle. That's a decrease in my healing supplies. Which Mama Jana is going to pay for, by the way.'

'He should know about it,' I said to my friends, deciding to take the gamble. Our secret was too powerful to hide anyway. I wanted the world to know. I wanted every Jadan and every Noble to know the truth that would set us all free.

Cam hesitated before reaching into the bag, and then he tossed me one of the Abbs.

'S'that gold?' Split said, finally a hint of interest in his face. 'You know it's customary to give something of value to your Shepherd.'

The Ice was going to make one of two things happen.

Either the Pedlar would slit our throats and take the machine for himself, or he'd sober up with hope. Once this man had dedicated his life to saving Jadans. Maybe I could return the favour.

Shilah's brow furrowed, her hand running along the end of her braid. 'That so? Mama Jana didn't mention that.'

'Well, I imagine you never been on the Coldmarch before,' Split said, looking away, his fingers scratching harder at his leg. 'And also you're not allowed to look at me, girl. Not for the whole trip. That's got to be part of the deal.'

Shilah raised an eyebrow.

'May I have a cup of water, please?' I asked Split with a blank face, even though my heart was pounding.

'*More* water?' Split asked, glancing at the Khatclock. 'You think I'm made of Wisps?'

'You *did* destroy our supplies with an arrow,' Cam said. 'And you're a High Noble. Which, as we both know, comes with a weekly stipend from the Pyramid. So technically yes, you are made of Wisps.'

'Just water, please, Split,' I said, shooting Cam a disapproving look. 'No Cold.'

Split went still and then grumbled something about a well behind the shack. Grabbing a bucket coiled with rope, he barrelled through the front door and kicked it closed behind him.

I went to open my mouth, but Shilah cut me off. 'You sure you want to show him what our machine can do?' She pointed to the nook in the centre of the floor, a haze of smoke still rising. 'You can't trust Droughtweed.'

'You still have that knife?' I asked.

Shilah tapped her thigh.

'I trust *you* to keep us safe,' I said. I tried to stand up, but I was still a little woozy. 'Keep it close.'

Cam came over and helped me to my feet. 'What do you think of the name Mordechiah?'

Maybe it was the lingering Sobek poison, but I couldn't follow. 'Mordechiah?'

'For your fake name,' Cam said, peeking through the healing box on the table. 'It still starts with an "M" so it'll be easy to remember.'

The old me would have laughed, but all of a sudden the pain in my wrist was extraordinary.

'No!' I spat, my stomach stewing with something thick and sour. 'No.'

Cam's head dropped. 'Sorry, I just—'

'No,' I said, holding up my wrist. 'It's just really painful. And I think I'll stick with Spout.'

'Spout's a nickname, though,' Cam said, lifting his eyes just a bit. 'What if he asks your real name?'

'Clearly Split is a nickname too,' Shilah said. 'But I think that kind of stuff must have been common on the Coldmarch. Fake names and disguises.'

Cam shrugged, a bit of colour returning to his cheeks. 'So you think Split's going to faint when he sees the Ice?'

'Maybe,' I said, looking around again at the bareness of the shack, nursing my wrist against my chest. 'What do you think he used to peddle?'

Shilah was over by the Khatclock now, tapping at the glass. 'Probably Droughtweed. Lots of profit in addiction.'

Cam gestured around at the bare walls and decrepit ceiling. 'This shack doesn't exactly scream Cold.'

Shilah continued to tap on the face of the Khatclock, the glass nearly silent against the calloused pads of her fingers. 'You think this leads to some secret tunnel as well?'

'Just think,' Cam said with a smirk, pocketing a vial of groan salve. 'When Spout figures out how to fly, we won't need tunnels. We can just fly Jadans to Langria. We'll call it the Coldfly.'

I gave him a warm smile. 'The Coldfly.'

Shilah gave a light snort, reaching for the latch on the glass face.

Just then Split burst in, boiling water sloshing over the rim of his bucket. 'Hands off that clock, girl!'

Shilah didn't startle, but she slowly took her hand away and folded her arms across her chest. 'My name's Shilah. Not girl.'

Split's face went blank as he turned away. 'Fine. Whatever. I don't want you to leave your scent on the glass.' He looked uncomfortable. 'Because of the hounds.'

Shilah bared her teeth, giving a low growl.

I knew she was joking, but Split looked poised to pick up the crossbow.

'Split,' I said. 'I'll just take the whole bucket of water if you don't mind.'

Split looked to Cam, who was still lingering by the healing box, the Pedlar's eyes narrowing. 'You going to pay me back for all this Cold I'm wasting on your Jadans?'

'You can't waste Cold on Jadans,' Cam said with a scowl, crossing his arms over his blouse. 'And by the way, you should prepare yourself for quite the opposite.'

Split shook his head with disdain, even the stubble on his cheeks looked a bit darker. 'You get bit by a Sobek too, boy? Crawled in your ear and nibbled on your brain?'

I gestured for the bucket.

The Pedlar grumbled, thrusting it over. The steaming water sloshed onto my foot, but since the underground water always ran cooler than in the boiling rivers, it didn't raise blisters.

'Close your eyes,' Split demanded. 'All of you.'

'Sorry?' Cam asked. 'I thought that was just Shilah who wasn't allowed to look at you during the March.'

Split was redder than any alder paint now. 'I don't want you to know where my Cold is hidden, boy! In case the Vicaress catches you and tortures you. Damn the damned

Khat, he doesn't need my Cold. A man should always die with a few secrets.'

'Like I said, I don't need Cold,' I said, letting the anticipation build. 'I have what I need.'

Split sighed, rubbing his temples. 'A mad flock. And I thought two boys was going to be obstacle enough.'

'What's that supposed to mean?' Cam asked.

Split huffed, wiping away a little leftover grey ash from under his nose. 'You obviously don't know much about the Coldmarch, *Tavor*.'

'Never mind that.' I asked the Pedlar as seriously as I could, 'What do you *believe*?'

Split's beady eyes narrowed even further. 'In regards to?'

'Everything,' I said simply.

'A mad flock,' Split muttered again, rubbing the sides of his head.

'We're the best flock you've ever had,' Cam said, still indignant.

Shilah tapped at the Khatclock glass once more.

'Don't *do* that!' Split chided.

Shilah turned around with a glare. There was a plan in her eyes.

I waved my friends off, needing them to be still. This was going to be the first time a stranger witnessed what my machine could do.

'What do you believe?' I asked Split softly again, holding my palm over the bucket, the Abb ready to fall in the water. I didn't relish the idea of wasting a full golden bead, but the Pedlar's trust and obedience was equally as important.

'About the World Cried?' I continued. 'About the Khatdom? About the Jadans? You don't call us slaves, not like most High Nobles. What do you *believe*?'

Split paused, gathering a huge breath in his ruddy face. Everything inside the shack went quiet enough that I could hear Picka braying gently outside in the stable, knocking her hooves against the trough.

'You really want to know?' Split asked quietly.

I nodded.

The pause was so heavy that I thought the floor might crack. When he finally looked at me, it was with something emptier than anger. His eyes stirred in the realms of loss, which was all too familiar.

I wanted to dig my fingers back into my wrist, but I had to keep the Abb steady.

'I believe that we're alone,' Split said quietly, his cheeks trembling. 'That no one is watching. I believe that everyone consumes this World Crier crap all the time, and they drop down on their knees to get their doses, and they say "give me more, please, let me have the truth". But you know why everything around us, the whole damned world, is all still sand and shit? You know why when people say *Great Drought* I say my *great pale ass*? There was no 'chosen', no 'unworthy'. It's all Sun-damned coincidence. There's no such thing as the World Crier, or if there was, then he died long ago and left us on our own. You know what I believe?' He paused, looking into the steaming waters in the bucket. 'I believe we're alone as can be.'

I let the gold bead fall.

The bucket creaked and screamed at the rapid change from water to Ice, the seams splitting loose and cracking in half. The scorching water completely changed in the blink of an eye, pushing hard enough to break the metal entirely apart. This wasn't just a few Drafts in the bottom of a barrel, or a Shiver in the wind. This was a complete and utter shift in reality. This was snuffing out the Sun. This was taking the Vicaress's fiery blade and turning it around so *she* could be Cleansed.

This was sanctuary.

The solid block of Ice was both shield and weapon. I had a feeling I could stick it in the heart of Paphos and it would never yield, even after being gnawed on by the Sun, hacked at by taskmasters, stabbed by the Vicaress, and prayed away by the Priests.

Split's face went slack, his eyes processing the impossible. His fingers had stopped scratching at his leg, and were now sweeping through the air in front of his face, as if he were trying to swat away the devastation of a mirage.

I picked up a piece of the metal scrap that had exploded from the bucket, which still lingered with the touch of Ice, and pressed the flat of it against my injured wrist. The pain and throbbing ceased immediately against the impossible Cold.

'*Meshua*,' Split whispered, and then stumbled backwards, smacking into his counter, his body jerking stiff. 'Meshua.'

I gave up the scrap, the residual Cold quickly becoming too much. A gorgeous mist drifted from the top of the Ice, white and lovely. The Inventor in me wanted to grab an empty bottle from the healing box and see if I could bottle the stuff, thinking it might be useful in its own right.

Split's face had gone so pale I could almost see the bones underneath. His eyes were flashing with something that looked unsettlingly like worry. 'Damn it to dust and rot. After all these Sun-damned years.' His expression grew murderous and sorrowful at the same time, his hands clenching into fists so tight I thought his knuckles might dissolve to powder. 'It can't be Meshua.' He clenched his teeth and his face trembled, as if he were about to hiss. His breathing quickly grew stunted, his breath shallow and infrequent. His hand went over his chest, pain registering in his face.

I hoped the lingering Droughtweed wasn't reacting with the shock in some unforeseen way. Abb had taught me some rudimentary healing techniques, but nothing extensive, and I wouldn't know how to deal with a failing heart.

'It's not possible,' the Pedlar said between his teeth. 'Can't be real. Not now. Not after all this time.'

'Split,' I said, staying behind the Ice. 'It's okay. It's safe.'

'Man or woman?' he said, pallid face somehow seething red.

'Sorry?' I asked carefully.

'Is Meshua a man or a woman, you little brat?' he barked, far removed from any semblance of patience. His eyes kept flicking to the Droughtweed pit in the floor. 'You must know, since they gave you the Ice.'

Mist from the Ice rode up the front of my shirt and it took everything in me not to swoon from the spectacular sensation. 'I don't know what you mean.'

Split sucked in a breath, his clenched hand rubbing the spot over his heart, as if he were attempting to loosen his lungs up for air. His movements were frantic, and the muscles in his shoulders strained.

Shilah walked over to Split and reached out to put a hand on his shoulder. 'It's okay. We all felt the same way the first time—'

He swatted her away, not meeting her eyes. 'Don't *touch* me. Back up, girl!'

'Whoa,' Cam said, holding up his hands. 'Take it easy, Pedlar. She's only trying to help.'

'Dammit! *Meshua!* Man' – Split's breath had constricted to a wheezing now – 'or woman?'

'What is Me-*sh*-ua?' I asked, enunciating each syllable. I recognized it from the sacred words Abb had sung to me, but he had never revealed what the prayer actually meant.

Split pointed at the Ice, his finger shaking. 'The Crier's child. Meshua. The one who made that.'

I paused, not following. '*I* made that.'

'Yeah, Spout made that,' Cam affirmed, snapping his fingers at Split. 'Weren't you watching?'

Shilah crossed her arms over her chest and gave Cam a dark look.

Split kept rubbing his heart, his knuckles frantic now.

'Yes, I know that, Tavor moron,' Split chided. 'But the Jadan who shed that golden tear. The Crier's child. *Meshua*. Simple question. Man. Or woman? The Book of the March isn't clear.'

Cam stepped closer, holding his palms up innocently. 'I think you're mistaken, my friend.'

Split grabbed his crossbow from the ground, and all three of us stiffened. Before Shilah could extract her knife, an arrow was once again threatening my face. Split's hands were shaking so badly I had no idea if the arrow would end up in my eye or chin, but he kept looking at the Droughtweed pit, so I knew his aim would not be true.

'Are you with the Vicaress?' Split seethed. 'Or did you steal the golden tear?'

Cam went to step in front of me, but I kept him at an arm's distance. As long as the arrow wasn't pointed at my friends, I felt perfectly calm.

'I didn't steal anything,' I said. 'I found the secret that's going to set us all free. *All* of us. Jadans and Nobles alike.'

'You *found* it?' Split asked, aghast.

I nodded, looking at Shilah. 'With help, of course.'

'Did they—' Split nearly choked on the words. 'Was it— Did they put it in the ground?'

I wasn't shocked to hear the suggestion about 'putting it in the ground', but I was most certainly intrigued. There had always been Old Man Gum's endless prattles about 'they put it in the ground' when I was young and living in the barracks. And then the Crier had said something similar in my vision when I'd been put under the Thoth's wool hat. Leroi had only agreed to let me stay in the tinkershop after hearing the phrase. It must mean something. I pointed to the Coldmaker bag, to the chiselled bronze Eye peeking out from the canvas. 'No. It was put in my mind. And my heart. And my hands.'

Split's face broke, and he turned the crossbow around, holding the tip of the arrow against his own throat. The metal pressed into the soft flesh and scratched against grey stubble. The Pedlar's hands were no longer shaking, which somehow seemed worse.

No one moved.

'I was loyal,' Split sobbed, a tear racing down his cheek. 'I risked everything, and this is how I get repaid! I believed for so long! And the Crier takes everything from me. Then ten years later sends salvation like it's nothing! Like it's Sun-damned NOTHING! Meshua was all supposed to be a lie, I could handle a lie, because if it's real . . .' His thumb crept closer to the arrow release. 'If Meshua is actually here. If you are here with the golden tears, standing in the same place where . . .'

My jaw had gone slack, completely at a loss for what to do. Mist from the block of Ice swirled upwards, curling around Split's fingers, which I prayed wouldn't flinch. If the Pedlar pulled the trigger, the Coldmarch was over.

Shilah raced to the Pedlar without fear, inching her hand in between the arrow and his throat. It wouldn't stop the weapon if Split chose to squeeze, but her confidence was as good as a steel barrier.

'You're part of this,' Shilah said softly, curling her palm around the tip of the arrow, almost enough to make a fist. 'We need you, Split.'

Split gulped as his eyes slipped sideways and fell again on the Droughtweed pit.

'Tell Meshua to go burn forever,' Split exhaled, his thumb shaking so badly it was now tapping the release. 'Didn't save anyone.'

Shilah slowly removed Split's hand from the trigger. 'You

can save *us*. Help bring the machine to Langria. Be a part of this.'

The Pedlar's face cycled through a dozen emotions, and finally he let out a long sigh and dropped to his knees, the crossbow skittering across the floor. Shilah was quick to pick the weapon up and take the arrow off the shaft, giving me a calm nod, almost as if she did this sort of thing every day. The knife never even left her thigh.

Saving my admiration for later, I reached over the Ice and put a hand on the Pedlar's shoulder, my whole arm tingling.

'She's right,' I said. 'We need you, Split.'

'Show mercy, and tell me it's a trick,' Split said, his eyes closed tightly, refusing to look at the Ice. 'Is it expected that I forgive everything? Just like that?'

'It's real,' I said. 'And I'll tell you everything you want to know.'

'You have the miracle,' Split said, face still scrunched tightly. 'The golden tears of the World Crier's child. And you don't know Meshua.'

'I don't know. But we need to keep the Coldmaker safe. Now can you get us to Langria before the hounds track us down?'

Split opened his eyes and pressed his palms on the ground as flat as he could, the mist that had settled against the floor slipping through his fingers. Then he looked up at me, boring into my eyes. Anger had slipped away, and of all the things plaguing his face, regret now ringed his eyes the most.

'Don't you understand?' he asked, pointing a finger at the block of Ice. 'This is the miracle; *this* is Langria. And it's not just hounds that they're going to send.'

# Chapter Seven

Split's hands moved like heat lightning as he scooped out mounds of ash, burned leaves, and slag from the small pit in the floor. Tossing the residue aside, he wiped his hands on his already ruined shirt, leaving long black smudges. The air in the shack quickly became dusty and thick from the flurry of upended Droughtweed remains, making me hold my breath so I didn't cough or inhale too much. Once the plant touched fire, the smell turned from earthy to sickly sweet. The tang caught in the back of my throat and reminded me of things of which I didn't want to be reminded.

I looked at the Ice, over which Split had reverently draped his thin sleeping blanket, making sure that it wasn't sullied by his senseless digging.

Cam leaned in and whispered in my ear. 'I don't think this is the time for him to huff Droughtweed and go on some vision quest, Spout.'

'I'm not sure that's what's happening,' I said. 'You add leaves to make the slag more potent, you don't wipe it clean.'

'You do know your stuff. Can you say something to him?' Cam asked. 'I don't think he likes me very much.'

I nodded, making my tone as gentle as possible. Split's

reactions were interesting to behold, making me wonder if I should have kept the Coldmaker secret.

'Split,' I said gently. 'Perhaps it's not the best time for that. We should be moving, and it's best we take our wits along.'

Split had already removed most of the old deposit, and he grabbed a new strip of boilweed, wiping the pit clean. The cleaning didn't make much sense, knowing from my weeks beholden to the Roof Warden that compounding the grey residue only made the visions and high stronger. He was ruining his supply.

'Meshua and Ice,' Split said to himself, his coughs coming out grey. 'Wits don't exist any more. So I have to get Baba Levante. I have to get Baba Levante. I made a promise that I would.'

'Split,' I said again, hoping the sound of his name might snap him back to reality. 'We have to get moving.'

'Absolutely,' Split said, practically shining the pit now. 'But first we have to go under.'

Shilah had returned to her place near the Khatclock, scrutinizing the edges for signs of a secret passageway the device might be hiding.

'Okay,' Split said, stopping and sitting back on his thin ankles, looking over the pile of ash and slag next to the pit. 'It's ready.'

I swallowed, taking a step back. 'I don't do that any more.'

I thought back to Old Man Gum from my childhood, curious about what event had sent him over the edge of sanity. We had to respect him, since he was the oldest and most weathered in the barracks, but no one ever took his babbling seriously. Now I had to know, who put *what* in the ground? Had the crazy loon from my past, with his toothless mouth and wild eyes, known about this Meshua as well?

'Girl,' Split said gently, still staring into the pit. 'Shaylah. You can do it now. Open the clock and give it a turn.'

'Shilah,' she corrected firmly.

'Fine,' Split said, waving a hand. 'Just don't look at me.'

Shilah lifted the glass off the face of the machine. She didn't seem nearly as lost as Cam and I in all of this. She spun the hands one full rotation in the same way Mama Jana had, and the large Eye clicked open, revealing gears behind. But instead of causing the whole creation to swing forwards, the Khatclock stayed where it was.

The floor opened up.

With an angry creak, the bottom of the Droughtweed pit fell to the side, revealing a tight passageway wide enough only for one person. Thin stairs dropped down into the darkness at an alarming angle, steep and slick.

Split coughed at the wave of dust stirred up by the floor's disappearance, and gave a satisfied nod, his body visibly loosening. 'Okay, let's be quick. They're going to be coming for us.'

Cam covered his mouth and spoke between fingers. 'Shivers and Frosts, Spout. What is he—'

Split turned to Cam, his eyes still red and raw. 'You don't get to touch anything down here.'

Cam turned up his palms, taken aback. 'Why are you singling me out?'

Split scoffed, turning back around and threading himself through the hole. '*Tavors.*'

Once the Pedlar had disappeared into the secret chamber, a tiny light blossomed within, casting flickering shadows back up the stairs. Shilah came over and gave the back of my neck a squeeze, her fingers lingering on my tattooed numbers. 'He's right. About what we made.'

'Hmm?' I asked.

She pointed to the Ice, and then, without another word, followed the Pedlar into the hidden space. Her upright posture was perfect for slipping down the steep stairs, and the grey dust swirled and eddied in the wake of her swift descent.

A sudden gasp returned back up, but it sounded more of awe than danger.

I clapped Cam on the shoulder, finally wanting to smile at the adventure in it all. I should have been dead a dozen times over – we all should have – but my father would have been proud to watch me attempt this Coldmarch. There was no time for me to grieve, so I knew the second best thing was to do his memory proud. Abb had had a great sense of humour, but an even greater sense of story.

'Better keep those hands to yourself, *Tavor*,' I whispered with a smirk, hovering over the open pit listening to the sounds of muffled conversation.

Cam's face fell. 'I wasn't going to touch anything.'

'I was joking,' I said as quickly as I could.

'Oh.' Cam gave me a sullen look. 'You seemed serious.'

'I didn't mean it like that,' I said. 'I was just kidding.'

Cam waved it away. 'No, I know that. It was funny.'

I put a hand on his shoulder. 'You're family. I don't lump you with the rest of— I just—'

Cam's smile grew wider, but I could see his true expression behind his eyes, as if I'd punched him in the gut, or taken a taskmaster's whip and added to the scars on his back.

'It's okay,' Cam said.

'No, we—' I tried, my stomach sinking. 'You're not—'

'It's okay, Mic— Spout,' Cam said with a nod, finding his eyes on the hole instead of my face. 'Let's go see what this crazy Pedlar is hiding.'

I pressed my teeth together, promising myself I'd make it up to Cam later. Before going into the chamber I slung the Coldmaker bag over my shoulder, wincing as a metal edge of the machine caught my injured wrist.

'You can leave it up here,' Cam said in a gentle manner. 'I don't think anyone is going to take it.'

'I know,' I said, but couldn't bear the thought of leaving the machine behind. 'But just in case.'

Then I proceeded down the stairs, holding the bag close

and trying not to slip. Since I only had one good grabbing hand to begin with, I had to keep most of my body pressed sideways for balance, the lips of the stairs scraping into my ribs, worsened by the weight of the machine.

But once I settled at the bottom, I was unable to withhold my own gasp.

The place was a museum.

Or a tomb.

Or a vision.

Or the finest shop, selling equal parts treasure and equal parts dust.

I couldn't tell.

'What is this place?' I asked, clutching my machine close.

This was completely unlike the other secret chamber we'd discovered since starting the March. Even though we'd found spaces with little shrines and gifts from past flocks, mostly those rooms had consisted of crude drawings on clay walls.

This third chamber made the first seem practically empty.

Split's chamber was the size of a small Cry Temple, the ceiling high enough that even Slab Hagan – the tallest Jadan from my barracks – wouldn't have been able to touch the top without a stool. Two dark corridors snaked away near the back of the room, dimly lit by a fresh candle flickering on a centre table. Overstocked shelves rose up from every available part of the stone floor, bursting at the seams with artefacts and maps and tapestries and treasures that screamed at us from every corner of the room, dizzying in their array and sense of age. Statues. Beaded clothing. Pottery. Jewellery. Scrolls. Everything down here had a tinge of neglect, but even under the shawls of dust, the items glowed with personality and life.

The paintings shouted the loudest.

Hundreds of decorated canvases fitted together like flush gears all along the walls, so that very little blank space existed between them. The paintings were splashed with every colour imaginable, but looked faded, possibly older than the Khatdom itself. After one sweeping glance I knew that these images were important, more important than any of the famous pieces in the basement of the Paphos library. I couldn't put my finger on why, but something resonated.

There were long landscapes and vibrant hills, decorated with beasts the likes of which I'd never seen; muscled, horned, and dragging contraptions through impossibly green grass bursting with life. There were animals that walked on all fours, velvet black, with thick fur all over their bodies. They rested in trees that had too many limbs, alongside tiny insects with colourful wings. Birds streaked the sky, many of them with dull beige plumage the colour of Wisps.

I couldn't stare at the birds for too long.

And next to the cluster of animal paintings were images of ships, built with more wood than I'd seen in a lifetime. They practically sailed off their canvases, floating on gigantic rivers that weren't boiling from heat. They caught wind with giant silk sheets embossed with symbols I didn't understand, and I had to wonder if such massive bodies of water ever existed.

Detailed paintings of the night sky sat clumped together, swirled and streaked with infinite Cold falling to the ground. The Crying wasn't happening just in a few Patches, however, but everywhere across the land.

Other sparse canvases gave life to wizened men with dark skin, but not so dark as to be quite Jadan. They smiled and wore long beards and woollen hats that looked torturous, as the thick fabric would have drained even the most resilient of us today. The ceiling was covered with paintings as well, showing mountainous dunes that looked taller than the Khat's Pyramid, the same kind of white mist rising off their peaks that came from the block of Ice.

There were costumed bodies dancing in festive halls,

laughing and spinning within circles of Frosts. The piles of forbidden Cold were so large that they must have been exaggerations, as that many Frosts couldn't possibly have fallen since the beginning of the Drought.

My dry mouth began to water over the pictures of exotic fruit, most of which I didn't recognize, gluttonous amounts of green berries just waiting to be devoured. Next to the food, some of the other frames simply held numbers painted on tablets, set with indiscernible markings. There were even a few that looked to be the work of children, streaky and with no particular purpose.

I moved from paintings to statues.

Clay bodies stood sentry around the place dressed in the strangest clothing I'd ever seen. Their shirts were made of heavy cloth, as thick as my thumb – so thick and stifling in fact it would be enough to kill the wearer after five minutes under the Sun. At first I thought the shirts might be primitive torture uniforms used by the Vicaress, but the cloth was colourful and decorative. There were also beadwork vests with a lot of empty spaces interwoven between the fabric, as if there were once round objects there that had since been plucked. None of it made any sense.

There were shelves of diamond-encrusted swords with blunted edges, dusty vials of petrified medicine, silver tokens bearing unfamiliar crests, candelabras with eight arms, and stone carvings of rulers who looked nothing like the Khat.

A slight turn of my face revealed a whole cabinet of musical instruments, stringed and buttoned and keyed, their bodies carved from giant gourds that couldn't possibly have grown in this dying world. A twist of my neck revealed black parasols and black tents – which would be useless, as they'd just gather all the heat – and rusty tools with odd shapes. There were even a few once-shiny inventions with enough tattered knobs and copper spooling to make my empty hands itch.

And then I spotted the group of paintings suspended on the far wall that stole my breath away. These were clustered by theme as well, and the subject of each one revolved around the same powerful figure. His long hair was braided to one side, his chin prominent, and his cheekbones high. He held a Frost in one hand and a razor-sharp fan in the other. I knew from all the myths that this fan was a gift from Sister Gale, imparted with the hope of stacking the odds against their older brother Sun.

The World Crier.

Instinctively, I tossed a hand over my eyes and buckled, half falling to my knees.

'It's okay,' Shilah said softly from my side.

Remembering who and where I was, I took my hand away from my face and stood up, feeling rather foolish.

'Habit,' I said, still not looking directly at the paintings.

Shilah gave a wry smirk. 'I almost kneeled too. But don't you dare tell anyone.'

'Me too,' Cam said quickly from my other side. 'I almost kneeled, too.'

I swallowed hard, squinting my eyes and walking across the room, threading around the stacks of objects glazed with dust and age. Split was in the corner pushing a pile of thick sheets off a marble trunk. I ignored the Pedlar and rounded in front of the group of spectacular paintings. My eyelids trembled with effort, wanting so badly to close against the images.

It was him.

Our divine Creator.

But as I got closer, I realized I was wrong.

'This isn't the World Crier,' I said, my throat going dry.

'I think it is,' Cam said in certain tones, tapping the place on his chest that normally held a pocketed book. His fingers slipped across the smooth silk. 'Or rather, it was.'

'Finally a shred of intelligence from the Tavor,' Split said from his knees, the lid of the trunk now open. His voice was still full of pain, but at least I could no longer see the matching expression on his face. '*Meshua*. Of course Meshua just happens to be real. Ice right in the place that she used— where is this blasted thing?'

'I don't understand,' I said to Shilah, reaching out without actually touching the paintings. They all had the same telltale signs that they were representations of the Crier, but these paintings were different from those in Paphos. Here, his face was softer, and his braided hair was not yellow, as the Crier was always portrayed. These weren't right, since everyone knew that the Nobles were created in the image of the Crier.

I brought my fingers to my eyes and then traced my nose and chin and hair. I gave Shilah's face a scrutinizing look as well, going over her angles and colour and smile.

'His hair,' she said, her face just about glowing with pride. 'It's dark as coal. And just as rough.'

'He sort of looks like . . .' I almost couldn't get the word out, my throat gritty from shock. 'Us.'

Split got up from his knees. 'That's why those images are the most illegal things in the Khatdom.' He moved on to another trunk, this one beautifully striated with red lines, and I could see a mad smile forming at the corner of his lips. '*Were* the most illegal. Ten years later. Baba Levante, *where are you hiding, you old crone*?'

The last part was said in singsong, making me wonder what parts of the Pedlar's mind had broken under the stress of seeing Ice. Or maybe it was inhaling that residual Droughtweed slag that had sent him over the edge.

Split dragged something carefully out of the bottom of the next trunk, cradling it like a small child. He made clucking sounds as he pulled it free, rocking it back and forth. The object almost looked like an infant, but the shape was wrong, the head too big and the limbs too thin. The figure also had string and wooden dowels rolled up against its back. It was a puppet, an ancient Jadan woman puppet to be exact, carved from wood and meticulously painted with deep wrinkles. The puppet was wearing shiny tin shoes and a miniature silk sundress, the kind Nobles wore, but from the skin tone and hair, the doll looked distinctly Jadan.

'Baba Levante, you old rascal,' Split said. 'It's been too long.'

'And from the rotundness of your belly,' the puppet's imaginary answer came from the corner of Split's mouth, in a raspy and out-of-breath voice, 'it's also been too fat.'

Split beamed, but his eyes were all shadow and loss. He unrolled the strings and paddles, letting the puppet dangle, the tin shoes dancing above the dusty floor. 'Got me again, Baba.'

Then I spotted perhaps the most interesting item in the room.

On the shelf next to me was a stack of books. They were all so old that I thought the bottom one might disintegrate under the weight of the others, the pages maybe holding more rot than words. They all looked important, as if they held the secrets of the Coldmarch. Of Langria. Of why the World Cried was so miserable; but it was the book on top that nearly made me gasp.

A thin blue tome with white writing on the spine, just like the one at Mama Jana's. It was nearly obscured by a layer of dust, but this time I could make out what was written on the spine.

A name.

I clutched the Coldmaker close.

'I'm not a loony,' Split said, turning around and giving me a look that might have proven otherwise. 'It was . . . it was our routine. The jokes always made my girl smile, so just— just let me have this, okay?'

I gave a simple nod, keeping my voice even. I tried to keep calm, knowing that what was on the book had to be a coincidence. Micah was quite a common name in Paphos. I was just searching for meaning where there was none. 'You're our Shepherd, Split,' I said. 'You take whatever you want so long as you lead us on the Coldmarch.'

'Did you call this tubbo a Shepherd?' Split baulked as the puppet, his voice rising in both gravel and pitch. The tiny dancing feet wiggled as the puppet jostled. 'You starting that up again, Fellezehall?'

'Yes, Baba. I think so,' Split said. 'And you know only my mother called me Fellezehall.'

'Hmmph,' the puppet said, Split's voice changing back to his own. He tilted his grip on the paddles, and if I didn't know better, I'd have said he somehow made the puppet's wooden wrinkles appear to deepen. 'Didn't know that. I only ever heard her call you a mistake.'

Split chuckled, the sound of loss dripping into his voice. 'Got me again, Baba. And yes, we're going to go back on the Coldmarch.'

'Good,' the puppet said. 'Because if I had to spend another minute stuck in that damned trunk with your old underwear I might have cut my own strings.'

Split paused with a sniff, wiping away a single tear that had fallen to his cheek. A thin line of blood dribbled down from his nose. 'You're too kind, Baba.'

'Um, sir,' Cam said, clearly perturbed. 'Have you lost your mind?'

Split wrapped up the puppet's strings with care, threading them around the paddles. He pulled out a small carrying case from the trunk and lowered Baba in, closing the lid and patting it down.

'I was in charge of these artefacts,' Split said, standing up and gesturing around. 'Jadan culture. Things the Coldmarch leaders didn't want burned, just in case Langria ever became truly stable.'

'What do you mean stable?' I asked, perking up at the mention of Langria, eyes coming off the book. 'Isn't Langria where we're going?'

Split nodded, but his head didn't move completely up and down, as it was too busy trembling. 'Yes. But, well, I'll explain everything on the way. I guess we have to do supplies first.' He started grumbling something unintelligible and gestured to one of the side corridors, his eyes still decidedly as far from Shilah as possible. 'I have stuff here, shelves full of waterskins and groan salve and beige clothing. And decoy goods so I can pass as a Pedlar. It's not like us Shepherds *planned* on shutting the Coldmarch down, you know. The order came all the way from Langria. Although I would have demanded it be shut down myself if I knew you were going to be—' Split took a deep breath, bringing his volume back down, his hand scratching his thigh once again. 'Never mind. Just. Never mind.'

I was struck with an idea, rubbing my fingers against the tattoo on the back of my neck. Individual birth and barracks number. The markings had been there since I was assigned to barracks forty-five, all Jadans in Paphos inked to keep order and in case we tried running away. The numbers weren't there so we would be sent back to the right barracks, however, since runaways were taken to the Khat's Pyramid. Rather, they existed so the taskmasters knew which barracks family to whip bloody as punishment for allowing one of us to escape.

'Split,' I said. 'Do you have ink and needles down here?'

His face creased as he looked around, but then he spotted a desk, and his eagerness returned. 'We didn't write much to each other, just in case the notes were found, but yes, I think I have— wait!'

I gave a start, snatching my hand back from the bookshelf and turning his way.

The Pedlar suddenly blinked over and over, his eyes red

and raw and distant. He looked at his fingers, touching them to his tongue one at a time. 'My skin is Cold. Why is it Cold?'

I nodded. 'Ice.'

Split squinted as he surveyed the room, genuine confusion clouding his eyes. 'What are we doing down here?'

Cam shot me a look as he quickly brushed a finger under his nose and sniffed.

I waved him off. 'We're preparing for the Coldmarch, Split. And we're hurrying.'

'We are, aren't we?' Split asked, a second line of blood from under his nose joining the first. His smile was easy, almost wistful.

'And you're finding me ink and needles,' I said.

I turned to Shilah. From the look on her face I would have bet she already knew my plan.

'But of course!' Split said, shuffling off. 'Ink and needles. I've peddled those!'

Shilah pulled her sleeve back, giving me a wink. The Opened Eye tattoo on her arm looked darker than ever, reminding me what a spectacular feat Little Langria had been, and how lucky I was to have her by my side.

'I'll do you first,' Shilah said to me under her breath as Split went searching. 'You have a lucky number?'

I shook my head, an idea striking. 'Maybe not lucky. But important.'

'Do what now?' Cam asked, fixing his glasses as he glanced around. His eyes focused mainly on the stacks of faded books and sealed scrolls.

'How often have you heard other Nobles say, *all Jadans look the same to me*?' I asked.

Cam looked down at his feet, mumbling something.

'Bastards,' Split said, practically spitting as he rifled through some drawers, the mysterious contents glinting within. 'We're all bastards.'

'If the Khatdom is going to be looking for us,' I said, tapping the back of my neck, trying to peel my eyes off the painting of the World Crier so I might concentrate, 'then taskmasters will check our numbers first, since it's the quickest way to identify us. I say we change the numbers.'

'A crime punishable by death!' Split said almost happily, his voice slightly slurred now.

I looked the Pedlar over, remembering how potent the Droughtweed could be. I was glad I only spent a few weeks under its influence before Abb had pulled me out of my hole.

Split pulled a bottle of ink and a needle from the drawer and stared at me for an uncomfortable amount of time, his soot-stained bottom lip starting to tremble. Finally, he shook his head of whatever thought was bothering him and returned his attention to the puppet. 'I need a few minutes. I'm going to go back upstairs.'

'What are you going to do?' I asked carefully, hoping he wasn't planning on heading for a secret Droughtweed stash. If we were going to trust this Pedlar to get us through this next part of the Coldmarch, I'd prefer he be able to recognize the difference between his feet and the rocks beneath them.

'This may be ten years too late,' he said quietly, setting down the needle and ink on a table and picking up the puppet, his hand trembling. His face was now so close to breaking I knew a single word might shatter him, 'but I guess I'm finally going to pray.'

I nodded and wrenched my eyes away.

'Take your time,' I said, holding the Coldmaker close.

# Chapter Eight

As I watched Picka attack the miracle from her pen, I wondered if there was anything in the World Cried that sounded more excited than a dwarf camel licking Ice. After years of living between the thin walls of my barracks, I thought I'd understood the extremes of pleasure, but nothing even came close to this.

Picka brayed and snorted and happily grumbled, her long tongue running over the glistening block. She explored every inch of the Ice as her eyes bulged, showing off their long, sand-proof lashes. The soft tufts around her neck jiggled to match her hysteria, the fur thin enough to reveal patches of irritated pink. I wondered whether the wounds were from Sun or neglect, but otherwise the camel looked healthy enough to travel.

Shilah stood by with her hands covering her mouth, face lit up with tenderness; she looked as if she might squeal along with the camel. She didn't seem to be bothered by the new numbers on her neck, which once again proved how much tougher she was than me. I couldn't stop pressing a palm against the sting of the ink settling into my skin.

Split tried to snatch the block of Ice away from Picka, his

eyes set with worry. 'This is a holy substance! She's just a beast, and doesn't deserve it.'

I'd never seen such a caring look in Shilah's eyes. 'I'm sure the same thing was and will be said about the Jadans. Now tell us about Langria.'

Split looked stunned for a moment, mumbling something under his breath as he backed away. His eyebrows furrowed – his face was so dirty from Droughtweed soot that it looked like one long eyebrow – and turned his gaze back towards the top of the valley from whence we had come.

'Not yet,' he said. 'Coldmarch rules.'

'I don't believe you,' Shilah said bluntly.

Split turned his back on Shilah and started to go back inside, leaving the Ice where it was. I'd brought the block out to share with Picka before our journey and I'm glad I had, because the little camel was reacting the way I hoped everyone would after seeing what my machine could do.

I ran my hands over her shaggy mane as she howled with excitement. I finally smiled, feeling her delight through her shaking fur. I wondered if her ancestors had ever tasted Ice before the Great Drought.

I gave Picka a last pat on the head, but I doubted my touch even registered over her happy indulgence. Going to follow Split inside, I adjusted the Coldmaker bag on my shoulder, but before I'd taken so much as two steps, the Pedlar turned and put up a halting hand.

'You'll not be helping, Spout,' he said, deadly serious.

I gave him a curious look.

'Your wrist,' he said with a narrowing of his eyes.

I looked down at my bandaged left hand, having nearly forgotten the pain of the Sobek bite. 'I'm fine.'

Split gave me a sad smile, his crooked nose drooping a little lower. 'You and me both, kid.'

Without further explanation, the Pedlar guided me behind

the shack where the shade was the thickest, giving me a pat on the shoulder. His eyes did not stray from the Coldmaker bag. Shock and the nasty heat of the Sun seemed to have cleared the Droughtweed from his system, but there was still something off in his expression, as if he was constantly about to wince. 'You have to keep it safe.'

'I—'

But before I could argue, he was gone.

I leaned against the stone rim of the well, the place where his water must have come from, as there was no other source within a day's walk of the shack. I pressed my palm against the sting on the back of my neck, and continued to listen to the sounds of excited licking coming from the stable. The stillness gave me time to think about the nature of my invention, and I was left agonizing over how I might get my hands on another Frost to make a second machine. The other components would be easy enough to obtain, but each Coldmaker would need its own Frost to work. There might be one buried deep in the sands from before the Great Drought, but I would have bet everything that they had Frosts in Langria. The free Jadans would have their own Cry Patch, otherwise the place would be as dead as everywhere else in the world.

But if they had Frosts, they would have shared them with the rest of Jadankind. Possession of the holy Cold would have proven us worthy and begun the long climb towards freedom. Our biggest shackles weren't the kind made of metal.

I strained to keep my mind away from darker thoughts while I watched my friends make a few quick trips from shack to stable, carrying up decoy goods under the Pedlar's direction. My hand once again went to the back of my neck, and I suddenly realized it wasn't so much the pain that was bothering me.

I snatched my hand away, not letting my mind wander

too far in that direction. A true Inventor had to have as much control over his thoughts as his materials.

Instead, I stuck my hand in the Coldmaker bag, reaching for the side pocket where I'd stowed my new acquisition. I felt a bit bad about stealing the book from Split's chamber, but I couldn't leave it down there. Not when it had my name etched into the cover. The letters were a bit ornate, and the 'i' and 'c' had tails that they usually didn't, but it almost certainly spelled 'Micah'. I could read as well as any other Street Jadan, and had seen the word written out before, but there was something about the way it was written on this book, about how the letters melted into one another, that called to me.

I would eventually get around to telling Split that I had stolen one of his artefacts, but not right now.

I peeked around the corner of the shack to make sure everyone else was preoccupied, and once all three had gone inside, I took out the little volume and blew off the remaining dust. Carefully opening it, I found time-weathered pages ready to crumble, filled with rows and rows of Ancient Jadan I couldn't read. I frowned, my heart sinking; I had hoped that it was going to be written in the common tongue. There were a few drawings of the Opened Eye, however, and what looked to be a map, but I didn't get a chance to look closer because Split shot out of the shack.

Still hidden in shadow, I stowed the book as the Pedlar tossed a few rolled-up beige parasols on the ground. Cam and Shilah came out behind Split, each with armfuls of ornate silk. Everything was colourful, and much more modern than most of the stuff I'd seen in his chamber, which was comprised mainly of linens and small trinkets and jewellery. The heaviest thing in the pile looked to be the puppet's carrying case, although there were a few wind-up trinkets and Khatclocks that I knew might come in handy.

The last thing they brought up from the chamber was a cart with wheels and a harness for Picka, setting it down with care.

The dwarf camel was still going at the block of Ice with fervour, launching attacks from every conceivable direction. It was curious that even under the heat of the beast's tongue and the bite of the Sun, the block of Ice looked just as solid as when I'd set it down.

I swept out from behind the shack as Split piled all the decoy goods on the cart in a hurried manner, without any sense of order. As he bent over to grab the parasols and Coldboxes and Closed Eye necklaces, I saw the tops of a few glass vials peek out of his pockets. He was moving quickly, but the flash of grey gave them away.

'They'll be coming,' the Pedlar said, not meeting any of our eyes. 'They know how to find anything.'

'The hounds?' Cam asked, plastering down his hair. He'd changed from the billowy green blouse into a form-fitting shirt that Split had offered, although already it was soaked through with his sweat. 'But we doused ourselves in rosemusk and are days away from Paphos.'

Split scoffed, stuffing the rest of our personal supplies on top of the cart. The final pieces to go in the cart were all the fake documents he'd shown us before leaving the chamber. He assured us the scrolls proved him to be a shipper of slaves, and although a bit dusty and out of date, that this would swiftly be overlooked with the help of a bribe.

The Pedlar turned to me, scratching his thigh with frantic fingers. 'Rosemusk and distance ain't enough.' With a grimace, he bowed. 'Anything else you need before we go, Spout?'

Cam smirked, cutting in, 'Any chance you have any Marlea cheeses and roasted—'

Split snapped a warning look at Cam. 'I wasn't asking you, Tavor!'

'Take it easy,' Cam said, retreating into himself. 'I was just joking.'

'We don't need jokes,' Split said, spitting on the ground. 'Jokes ain't going to cut the ropes when they string us off the Pyramid. Jokes ain't going to remove the hooked blades from our—' He took a deep breath through his nose, whirring with the sounds of snot. 'Nothing, dammit. Let's just go.'

My eyes went back to the block of Ice, which still refused to yield. Picka continued to make exultant sounds, but her eyelids were droopy and her tongue moved slowly, as if she were finally losing herself in a pleasant dream.

'We need to move,' Split said, pointing to the thin road that led from the shack up the other side of the valley. 'You can put the chest of golden tears on the cart so we can walk—'

'No,' I said, instinctively clutching the Coldmaker more tightly.

Split looked at me with a blank stare, his wheels clearly turning. Then he snapped out of it and gave a single nod, taking Picka out of her stable and hooking the camel up to the cart. Now out in the light, I noticed the poor creature was frailer than I realized, her legs bony and thin, and her fur missing patches near her rear.

Shilah held up her hands, looking ready to protest.

'She's stronger than she looks,' Split said, not looking over at Shilah as he gently guided the ropes around Picka's chest and legs. 'I'm sure you can relate.'

Shilah crossed her arms over her chest, but for the moment looked satisfied.

I finally touched the back of my neck, the skin still throbbing from needle and ink. Perhaps it wasn't the smartest decision to have Shilah change my tattoo in such a way, but I couldn't help myself. I should have just had her ink the markings into completely random numbers that couldn't point back to my old life, but the opportunity was too great to ignore. Abb and I had belonged to the same barracks, and the numbers were already somewhat close. Shilah had to take some liberties in order to get them to match, but if I was going to wear any branding other than my own, it was going to be that of my father.

'North,' I said. 'The March is always North.'

Two days later I sat against a cool wall of rock, massaging my tired feet, the sky dark and the stars blazing. We couldn't see the Crying at this distance from Paphos, but I looked back in the direction of my home city, over the countless dunes and endless stretches of barren land, imagining all that Cold falling from the sky. I wondered if the Crier was staring back, looking at my machine. If so, a part of me wanted to hold up the invention and scream until my throat burned. And if the Crier wasn't listening, then maybe someone else up there was.

This leg of the Coldmarch was far more intense than the first, and I looked over at Cam. He was in worse shape than me, but not by much. My body had become weak since working in the tinkershop. My skin used to be like tough leather, impervious to hot stone and sand, but life in the Manor had softened me, and even under the protection of heavy sandals, I was left with embarrassing cuts and blisters all the way up my ankles.

I knew I should have just added the Coldmaker to the cart, but fear kept the bag slung on my shoulder. Although it added a considerable weight, the machine was one of the only things that kept me from sinking.

We had stopped to rest in a small, hidden canyon. The walls of the natural nook were close and high, filtering starlight down into a clearing. The protection was better than most of the places we'd stopped, so I had a feeling that this time the Pedlar would actually let us relax. There had still been no sign of the Vicaress, but that hadn't kept him from insisting that we didn't talk unless necessary, and that we always kept hunched to lower our profiles. Shilah had ignored both rules most of the time, keeping her back straight, and constantly asking about Langria. Cam doubled her questions whenever Split skirted around them. Our Shepherd didn't give us any more information than necessary; and he also didn't ask much in return. I would have thought he'd want to know every little detail about the Coldmaker and how it had come to be, but he refused even to look inside the bag.

Now that we had slowed for the time being, Split unhooked Picka from the harness and kissed the top of her snout. The camel slumped down and curled against herself in a heap of exhaustion, bleating softly. Shilah looked poised to toss Split up and over the canyon walls for letting the tiny camel suffer, but her fury seemed trapped beneath a blanket of exhaustion.

Ambling up to the stone, the Pedlar brushed his fingers against a long streak of older red painted onto the rock. 'I'll be boiled dry. Still the same as it was.'

Cam was huffing and panting as he snatched a waterskin off the cart. He looked to me with a thin-lipped smile, and I took out an Abb and removed a slice with Shilah's blade. Cam gave me a thankful nod, tossing the golden sliver into his container and giving it a heavy swirl.

'Here,' he said, handing the cooled waterskin over to Shilah. 'You first.'

'I can get my own,' she said, nose twitching, her posture remaining upright. 'Spout can cut me a piece.'

'Please.' Cam shook the container again. His yellow hair had stiffened like straw from all the heat.

Shilah paused and gently took the water, but kept it at her side.

'It's not because I think you're the weakest or anything,' Cam blurted out. 'That's not why I gave it to you.'

Shilah raised an eyebrow, lowering the water further from her mouth.

Cam gave a firm nod, as if he had come to a serious conclusion. 'It's because you deserve respect.'

'Damn right I do,' Shilah said, taking a swig.

Cam distributed water all around, my High Noble friend waiting until everyone else had had their fill – including Picka – before taking furious swigs from his own waterskin, relief visibly washing over him. Split took swigs as well, but he was shaking in a different way, his eyes more than once glaring over at the Coldmaker bag. The scratching at his thigh had only become worse the longer we'd travelled, and I'd seen him run his thumbs over the corks on his pocketed glass vials more than once.

The Pedlar wiped his mouth, staring at his hand. 'It's the Coldest thing I've ever felt.'

'You said that last time we stopped to drink,' Cam said, rolling his eyes. 'And the time before. And before.'

Split glared at his fingers. 'I keep hoping it won't be true.'

Picka twitched her way upright and strutted over to me, slumping against the ground with a happy harrumph as she nuzzled her head into my lap. I stroked her mane as the beating of my heart slowed, the camel's beige fur rough from hours under the Sun. The little beast grunted happily, rolling to her side so she could put a hoof up on my leg, her fuzzy lips drooping down so her yellowed teeth showed.

'Damn it to the black and back,' Split said through clenched teeth.

'What?' I asked, snatching my fingers from behind Picka's ear. She immediately gave an irritable grunt, a cool breath escaping her snout.

'It's just . . . she doesn't do that any more. She only ever used to—' Split's face became unreadable, his hand drifting to his pocket. 'This area is notorious for runaways. Or it used to be, ones trying to meet up with the March. And that means we might have prying eyes. I'm going to check the perimeter.'

He grabbed a handful of headscarves from the cart and left our little sanctuary, silence settling in his wake.

Eventually Cam leaned towards me, his eyes glinting with dark humour. He cupped his hand around his mouth and kept his voice low. 'So what are the odds he murders us in our sleep and steals the Coldmaker?'

Shilah was struggling to twist her hair around the new blade, the weapon proving to be far too thick for concealment. 'He could only murder those of us dumb enough to sleep.'

I reached out my fingers to scratch behind Picka's ears, the echoes of the Sobek bite arguing with my movements. I leaned in and whispered to the camel: 'Who did you two lose?'

Picka answered with a low grumble, nuzzling her head deeper into my stomach.

'You think that's what it is?' Cam asked.

The connection I felt was too apparent to overlook. My body felt a hundred times heavier, and not because there was a pack animal in my lap. 'He doesn't remind you of anyone?'

Shilah's jaw sharpened a bit at the edges. She stared at the Coldmaker bag, a strange gulping sound rising to her lips. Then she glared at Cam, as if daring him to say something. 'It's hiccups.'

Cam gave her a soft look and then dropped his gaze. He started cracking his knuckles, the normally creamy skin on his fingers now red and burned.

'It was hiccups, dammit,' Shilah said again, and turned her face away, the braid whipping around.

Everything went quiet once again, my stomach tensing up. As tired as I was, I thought we should keep moving, pushing towards Langria.

'They can't have killed him,' Cam said, barely a whisper. 'I know they won't. Maybe they'll lock him in the Pyramid, but Leroi is too brilliant a mind for the Khat to waste. And he's High Noble.'

My stomach had tightened so much I doubted I could even fit water around the knot, so I left the last few sips in my waterskin. 'Can we talk about something else?'

Shilah reached into her pocket and unfolded the old parchment map given to her by her mother. Her long fingers traced the sheet up and down, lips parting gently as if she might start humming, which is something I only ever heard her do in her sleep.

'I wonder if she ever made it this far,' Shilah said, gesturing to the small canyon around us.

'Who?' Cam asked.

'My mother,' Shilah said, her fingers lingering on the parchment. 'She told me she tried to get on the Coldmarch every year, but they always turned her away. She tried to figure it out on her own once, but it's impossible to do it without help.'

Cam and I both exchanged a stunned look.

Shilah went quiet, staring at the Coldmaker bag. 'I guess paradise isn't for everyone.'

Cam made an indistinguishable noise, looking at his feet.

After a moment, a rare smile perched on Shilah's lips as she looked over at the supplies cart. 'You know, I kind of like the puppet. Is that weird?'

Cam snorted, eyes returning with a smile. 'Spout should put an Abb inside its head and see if it comes to life.'

I offered a small grunt.

'Spout,' Cam said, snapping his fingers.

'Hmm?'

'That was funny, right?'

'Yes,' I said, forcing a smile.

Cam swept aside his overcooked hair, the ends frayed like a broom. 'I say a talking puppet might be a good way to distract any hounds. Like those Decoy Boxes you used to make. It can sing songs and—' Cam stopped himself with a sigh, picking up a handful of pebbles and tossing them back to the ground one at a time. 'What do you think he meant about other things hunting us down too?'

Picka bristled at the question, which made me lift an eyebrow.

'She can't understand what we're saying,' Shilah said, reading my face. 'She's reacting to *you* reacting.'

'How do you know?' I asked.

'Because Picka's a woman of the world, so she's bound to be good at picking up cues.' Shilah gave me a quick wink and then walked two fingers through the air. 'Besides being slow, you're very readable.'

'Then I'm glad to have you both on the team to round me out,' I said, taking a few pebbles of my own and adding to Cam's rubble pile.

Cam got up, bending back and forth, stretching out his back. He looked skinnier than I was comfortable with. 'Let's celebrate.'

Picka eyed Cam with suspicion, but I kept scratching her neck.

'And what are we celebrating exactly?' I asked.

Cam peeled open the Coldmaker bag, but didn't seem to spot the book-shaped bulge in the inside pocket. The bronze along the machine's top shone in the starlight, stout and strong. Even though it was turned off, I could sense a glow from the Coldmaker's centre, as if the machine was just waiting to be put to use. A wonderful chill flooded back into my chest as I looked at the invention.

Cam clapped his hands and opened his arms. 'We celebrate the fact that Shilah—'

Split stumbled back into the clearing, a thin rivulet of blood dripping out of one nostril. His eyes were puffy and raw, but his smile was so wide it could have been used to measure the Great Divide.

'We're celebrating the fact that it's all true!' the Pedlar said, stumbling towards us, keeping his hands on the stone wall for support. 'The Crier is watching once again! Meshua! What's ten years in the grand scheme? We celebrate the fact that it's here. Meshua!' Each repetition of the word '*Meshua*' was garnished with a little flip of his wrist. 'We celebrate the fact that tomorrow we'll reach Gilly's Tavern and announce that the Coldmarch is open for business once again!' He started laughing in a manic way, slumping to the ground, cross-legged. Pursing his lips, he blew a kiss at the machine and then slapped his hands on his knees. 'Shepherds unite, there's a miracle in the sands.'

Shilah went rigid, her hand hovering over her blade, but I had a feeling the Pedlar wasn't planning on being violent. I remembered what Droughtweed could do to someone, what it could dredge up, and the man didn't have any bloodlust in his expression. It was more the look of someone walking barefoot over the shards of memory.

Abb once told me: 'Some losses aren't there to get over, but rather to make you change direction.'

I raised my waterskin, still partially full, and sloshed it in the Pedlar's direction. 'Then to the Crier.'

Cam mimicked the gesture, and Shilah raised her drink as well, her lips pinched in silence.

'To *Meshua*!' Split said, another flippant toss of his wrist, the blood droplets from his nose finally reaching his top lip.

'Split,' I said, gesturing for him to clean himself. 'You've got some . . .'

The Pedlar cocked his head to the side and wiped his sleeve across his mouth before smiling again. 'Just happens when you get older. Age leaks, I calls it. Don't mind the stuff.' He sniffed, and a little bit of grey dust fell from his right nostril.

'Now what do you want to know, kiddos?' He drummed his fingers on his knees happily, his movements frantic. 'You're talking to a genuine Shepherd here. A *Pedlar* Shepherd, even better! Forty-five successful trips on my stretch from shack to Gilly's. And all those Jadan artefacts in my basement. All those ceramics, all those books, smuggled out of the wrong hands, folks that couldn't even read them. I doubt anyone knows more about Jadans than me!'

'What about the Jadans themselves?' Shilah asked in a defiant manner.

Split blinked a few times, his face blank. Then he broke out laughing again; big thunderous chuckles. He addressed me when he spoke again. 'Don't you know that's what this is all about? We were *all* Jadans before the Great Drought. Problem is, some people ain't satisfied sitting on the ground with the rest. Some people don't like being common. And now here comes the end of it all.' Split hawked up some spit and wet the ground.

I paused. 'What exactly is Meshua, Split?'

The Pedlar's lips pinched into a tight smirk. Then he burst out laughing again, wiping the bloody spot under his nose. 'You could ask me about Ancient Jadan culture, and Ancient Jadan food – which was limitless back then, mind you – or art, tinkering, alchemy, horticulture, anything at all. But you start with Meshua. Hah! A sandstorm always swirls back on itself.' Then he shook his head, deadly serious, his whole demeanour shifting in a heartbeat. 'Meshua is nothing, just a story that got made up when the world started dying.'

I went to say something, but Split flailed his arms, cutting me off. His words were getting slower now, the blood from his nose moving faster than his tongue. 'Meshua is a shift in the rivers. And a sky made entirely of shade. Meshua is twenty feet tall with arms like wrought iron and fists that can smash pyramids to pebbles.' He paused, words trickling out now, the tap slowly being shut. 'The child of the Crier, who walks the earth, with tears that can turn anything to Ice.'

My breath caught in my throat.

Split cackled, blood from his nose spraying over his upper lip. 'But I guess in reality, Meshua was put in the ground, found by a skinny little slave with a lizard bite!'

Shilah reached over and took my hand in hers. She'd done this a dozen times before, usually a platonic gesture, but this one felt different, her fingers pressing more tenderly than usual. I went to squeeze back, but at the first sign of pressure she snatched her hand away.

Split's eyelids were closed now, the dribbling blood under his nose having ceased. Cam swirled a finger next to his head, eyes wide with implications.

'Split?' I whispered.

The Pedlar snorted himself awake, blinking furiously. 'Huh? Where's Picka?'

'Right here, Split,' I said. 'Why did you become a Shepherd? You're High Noble, why do you care so much about Jadans? Why do you love our people?'

Split gave me the saddest look I'd ever seen, a rather impressive feat. 'You know what love is then, do you?'

I nodded, straining to keeping my face forwards. 'I think I do.'

The Pedlar's eyes were shut again, his fingernails scratching the burned bald spot on top of his head. 'Love is licking honey off a sharp blade and only worrying about the taste.'

'Davliss Erridian said that, right?' Cam asked. 'From Khat Vivus the Fourth's Dynasty?'

'Split the Pedlar said that, son,' he chided, sniffing with only one side of his nose. 'Brainless and blond, you must know less about the world than they do.'

Cam's shoulders slumped, his expression going dark.

'Cam is the only reason I'm alive,' I said. 'I'd say he knows plenty.'

Split didn't reply, his eyelids tightly shut now. In only a moment his breathing was deep and nasal, snores trickling into the air.

I slowly removed myself from under the camel and walked over to the Pedlar, reaching into his pocket. Four vials of Glassland Dream came out, just as I'd suspected. The powder was grey, expensive, deadly, and the closest substitute to pure bliss. A lot of High Nobles liked to use it between their bouts of Droughtweed highs. Huffing slag was unpredictable and could lead the mind to dark places, but Glassland Dream could always lift it back. The catch was that the powder had terrible side effects, bleeding from the nose being the least of the bunch. Even Leroi on his worst days would never touch Glassland Dream. The Tinkerer's cabinet contained a small vial of the grey powder for research purposes only, and he had me memorize which doses were lethal and which would send a person to sleep.

'Is that what I think it is?' Cam asked.

I nodded, stowing one glass container in my pocket in case Split showed any withdrawal signs. Then I tossed the other vials one by one over the nearest rock ledge, the silent night punctuated by the faint shattering of glass.

'Why did you do that?' Cam asked, swallowing hard. 'If the Vicaress finds us, it would have been nice to numb ourselves up.'

'We need our Shepherd functional,' I said, 'or the Vicaress might actually find us.'

'Besides,' Shilah said, 'the Vicaress would wait to kill us until the stuff had worn off anyway. It would only be delaying the inevitable.' She bit her bottom lip with delight, stretching the thirsty scabs. '*Brainless and Blond*. I'm remembering that.'

Cam ignored her slight, turning to me instead. 'Good thinking.'

Split snorted, drool sliming his chin.

I went over to the cart, having already mentally prepared the necessary components for my next idea. The little blue book with my name on it wasn't the only thing I'd pocketed from Split's chamber. It wasn't stealing, after all, since Split said everything in the chamber was a Jadan artefact to begin with.

'And if it's not only the Vicaress out there looking, then we need to be prepared for anything.' I pulled out some springs and wires I'd taken from one of the trinket shelves. 'And what good is an Inventor who's out of practice?'

# Chapter Nine

Split didn't mention the missing vials of Glassland Dream. I think he was rather consumed with the effort of not passing out or vomiting up his morning rations of dried figs and Khatnuts.

Cam, Shilah, and I had spent the night taking turns as lookout, and not only had we all grabbed a few hours of deep sleep, but we'd managed to make it to morning without being eviscerated. Eventually we woke our Shepherd – who flailed and sputtered back to reality – and made sure to leave the canyon before Sunrise, always heading North.

Split was talking a little louder than normal and digging a pinky into his ear from time to time, but he managed to keep pace and his hands weren't trembling. The fact that he wasn't burying his head in the sand or staring at us as if we were demons in Jadan form told me it probably wasn't the first time the Pedlar had come down from Glassland Dream. He was shamefaced towards me, downright mean to Cam, and he ignored Shilah altogether.

Since Split didn't ask about the vials, I didn't offer an explanation. Instead he insisted we keep quiet on the journey, but soon we were talking of small things that wouldn't worsen his headache, like the kinds of rocks and gemstones that could be found out in these dead sands. He made sure to point out fossils of ancient creatures that he'd discovered on previous Marches, leftover impressions in certain boulders. I mulled over these physical memories from times that pre-dated the Great Drought, and the glimpses into the past that they gave me. There were small, shelled fossils that looked like flat beetles, willowy plant-shaped rods, and a few single bones. When we reached a low pass that dipped into the land, Split pointed out the indentation of a large skull that sort of reminded me of Picka, if her snout had been longer and she had fangs. Split assured us those kinds of creatures were long extinct, but still I imagined they were the type of thing that lived deep underground, having long ago taken refuge from the Sun. These were the creatures the older Jadans whispered about on warm nights in the barracks, when the young ones couldn't sleep. I'd heard enough tales of wraiths, the Saberdim, Hookmen, and sheedimah to have shivers of fear run up my spine at the sight of the skull. There were more terrible things than taskmasters lurking in the dark places of the World Cried.

We snaked North through rocky valleys, and talked of the different kinds of merchants that used the Khat's roads – the ones we were actively avoiding – to transport goods and Cold to the Northern cities like the Glasslands and the City of David's Fall. Split knew a lot of the trading lines, left over from his peddling days. He had intimate knowledge of the stretches the caravans used, which came in handy while trying to remain unseen. Eventually we ventured into more important conversational territory, as Split asked about recent events in Paphos, and I told him of the Cleansing and the Opened Eyes everywhere. He quickly changed the subject to his favourite kinds of Jadan pottery. I asked about the puppet once, at which Split's lips clamped shut faster than a scorpion trap, his whole body clenching and giving off a distinct sourness.

We used beige parasols as camouflage, and so the Sun wouldn't burn our skin, and we stopped to drink Cold water and have rations every hour or so. On the second day we stopped less frequently, our supply pouches withering down. The Abbs kept our bellies filled with as much Cold water as we could take, but the machine couldn't make food, so we had to keep moving. We made good time across empty stretches of stone and sand, Shilah leading almost as much as Split. Cam demanded that he be the one to use the thinnest of the parasols, and he did his best to block the sky, but his poor Noble skin was crisp and red all over, and his little vial of groan salve didn't last long.

We accidentally encountered a few other travellers filtering towards our destination, almost exclusively caravan merchants. Apparently, Gilly's Tavern was one of the most popular drinking establishments on this side of the Singe, which seemed an odd place to host a stop on the Coldmarch, but Split's confidence didn't ebb even as we got into more populated areas and had to travel on more open paths. He always assured us that he had his methods to remain inconspicuous, and we ended up seeing these rather bold manoeuvres implemented whenever anyone came too close to our group or turned devious eyes towards the cart.

'Friends!' Split would yell, waving his arms and whistling. 'Let me sell you my cart! I've got fantastic goods, all cheap! So cheap! Let me sell you my slaves, too! So cheap! The Khat's personal stock. These are the ones that rub honey on his feet. Just a few Shivers for the lot! Fine, a few Drafts. Please, just come closer and look! I'll sell you my camel if you just come closer!'

Without hesitation the caravan merchants would always snort and turn away, silently going about their business. Split would drop to his knees and howl, pleading with the passersby just to take a look, saying things like: 'These goods are too cheap to be passed up on, you damn fools! You're all making a *grave* mistake!'

'Why don't they stop?' I'd asked him after his method worked the second time, my heart beating wildly. 'You're High Noble. This doesn't make much sense.'

'There are different rules out here,' Split had said, winking at me. His left eyelid sagged a bit, having trouble coming back up. 'A desperate Pedlar? It's supposed to be the other way around, so it looks very suspicious. A Pedlar would never sell his only camel, and the Khat never lets go of his personal Jadans, so when I say these things it makes me reek of lies. We could be planning an ambush.' Split kicked up some of the thin sand that gathered on the Khat's road, staring at the Coldmaker. 'Just like the world itself.'

'Why wouldn't they just try to take advantage of a desperate man?' Cam had asked. 'They are Nobles after all.'

Split gave him a look as if Cam was about as dumb as they get. 'Because, if the caravans leave us to die, then they can just come back later and scavenge the cart and all the stuff for free. No hassle.'

'Charming,' Shilah said.

Split grunted, digging a pinky in his ear, not meeting her eyes.

Eventually I showed him the machine.

I hadn't been at all sure how he was going to react. He kept referring to the Coldmaker as a chest of 'golden tears' and not asking any further questions. I had begun to realize that he assumed I'd found the thing somewhere in the ground, already stocked with the Abbs. My instincts told me that I shouldn't leave him ignorant as to how it worked, especially since the more people who knew the truth meant the greater chance for its survival, and eventually I decided to take the gamble.

On the third night of wandering I opened the bag and explained.

'So the Frost sits in the Cold Charged water,' I told him, pointing at all the parts. I'd made the bronze lid so it was removable, as long as the person knew how to manipulate the Belisk puzzle box which I'd built in as an obstacle.

Split's face was alder red. 'The Cold Charged . . .'

'We put scoops of salt into the water first,' Shilah said, 'and when the Cold dissolves, the salt and Cold battle each other, life and death at odds, making a charge that can be harnessed.'

The Pedlar nodded.

'But since Frosts don't dissolve,' I said, 'the water constantly keeps the charge.'

'And that's Jadan blood,' Shilah said, pointing to the vial that drops the bead into the catch-point. 'Spout's for now, mine next when it goes dry.'

'Why in the Crier's name would you put your blood in there?' Split asked.

I shrugged. 'That's just how it works.'

Cam shrank into himself, becoming uncharacteristically quiet.

'Okay,' Split said, his lips cracked and dry. He pointed to the vial next to the Frost. 'And that one?'

'Tears,' I said.

The Pedlar paused, blinking far more than was necessary. 'Tears?'

'Yes,' I said, too excited to linger. 'So when I turn the machine on, these gears here let out tears onto the Frost, which causes this crazy reaction where it pulls Cold in from every side—'

'But we lined the bronze with lead,' Shilah said, leaning in and tapping the inside walls. 'Which keeps the pull restricted only to the one spot. Oh, and also, it has to be *Jadan* tears.'

Cam mumbled something, going over to Picka and scratching her behind the ears. 'She looks tired. Long day.'

The dwarf camel brayed happily at his touch, and Shilah gave Cam a curious look.

'And that's how it works,' I said simply. 'That's how you make Cold.'

I closed the lid back up and flipped the machine on. All of a sudden the air around us changed, swirling and pulsing, and a golden bead formed at the catch-point.

'Impressive for a skinny little slave with a lizard bite, huh?' Cam asked with a smirk.

Split wobbled a little on his feet, blinked, and then passed out, falling slowly to the ground.

Shilah dashed over and checked the Pedlar's pulse, giving me a shrug over her shoulder. 'Don't worry, he's still breathing.'

'Sorry,' Cam said, turning to me. 'You know I meant *Jadan*, not slave. I was just using his own expression from before, so—'

'I know,' I said, putting a hand on his shoulder. 'And it was funny. Let's get some sleep.'

The following morning, we revived our Shepherd and immediately he launched into dark giggles, looking anywhere but at the machine. He kept us moving across canyon and deadlands as fast as the cart would allow, not talking or looking back over his shoulder. The pace was blistering. A few times blood started leaking from his nose, but I never saw him snort any hidden stash of Dream, and his eyes were clear.

Night fell once more, and at last our destination eventually came into view. The timing couldn't have been better, as we were down to our last scraps of food. Split's house had been bare to begin with, as he only went to the nearest House Suth trading post once a month to get his Cold and food

stores replenished. We'd shown up a few days before he was
due to resupply. This meant we were running dangerously
low on rations, and I'd begun debating whether or not to
hunt the deeper dunes for sand-vipers that we might cook
and eat. This would have been dangerous in more than one
way, since not only could the snakes kill with a single bite,
but they preferred living around patches of cloud sand, which
looked normal until the dune's surface billowed apart and
plunged unlucky wanderers into an inescapable chasm.

Thankfully the building of our salvation rose against a
backdrop of craggy hills, tilting from the earth like a loose
tooth. Gilly's Tavern had simple mudbrick walls, big enough
for perhaps a dozen rooms for lodging, but right away I could
see that the refuge from the Sun itself wasn't the main attrac-
tion.

A thin stream jutted out from the stony hills behind the
building, making a slight twist and heading back underground.
The small body of water looked near steaming, but the top
of it wasn't crusted with heat bubbles like the rivers Singe or
Kiln, which meant rations scooped out of this stream would
take less Cold to make it drinkable. A stream like that, already
hidden from the Sun for quite some time, meant that travellers could make a Wisp act like a Draft. I opened the lips
of my bag and wondered what a single Abb could accomplish
with such a water source.

Shilah put a hand on my lower back, leaning in close so
only I could hear. 'Let's get in and out, I don't have a good
feeling about this place.'

I whispered out of the side of my mouth: 'It's part of the
March. We're obviously not the first Jadans to come here.'

She shook her head. 'Maybe it *was* part of the March. I'm
not so sure what our guide here is thinking. Just stay close
to me.'

Split snapped his fingers, and Picka came to a halt. I gave

a quick glance at the bottom of the cart near the wheels, making sure my newest little invention hadn't come untied. The rolled-up scroll – with special alterations – was still in place. I'd tied it to the cart with what Leroi had dubbed an 'Assasiknot'. I needed the invention to be easily accessible, but not have it jar loose at the first bump. Once again, Leroi's teachings were paying off, even though I was no longer by his side. There could be no finer sign of a good teacher.

'I just want you to know,' Split said, scratching the rough scruff on his neck, his eyes still red. 'I been thinking about it. And, well, I guess I'll be your damn Shepherd.'

I paused, giving him a confused look. 'You already are.'

He turned away and crouched to his knees, picking up a flat stone and balancing it on top of another. He stewed in his silence, picking up more stones and heightening the stack. 'No, I mean, the rest of the way. I want to take you there. To Langria.'

Shilah crossed her arms, but I could tell a smile waited behind her lips. 'I thought you said you were only in charge of *this* stretch of the Coldmarch.'

'Things change. And I know the way.' He cleared his throat and looked at Shilah. He didn't glance at her, or peek, but finally met her eyes straight on. 'Please. And besides, rumour had it that Boahz moved to the City of the Stars.'

'Who's Boahz?' Shilah asked.

Split looked away, to the hills about the tavern. 'He was in charge of the next stretch of the March. He always took the Jadans from here.'

'And you're just telling us that now?' Shilah asked, her hand inching towards her hip.

'I told you that earlier,' Split said, his words speeding up. 'That I was only going to take you this far. I told you that. I'm sorry, but I did tell you.'

Shilah crossed her arms. 'Yeah, but—'

'It doesn't matter,' I said. 'If he wants to take us the whole way now, he can take us the whole way.'

'You're not going to murder us in our sleep and take the machine, are you, Split?' Cam asked with a straight face and a deadpan tone.

I nudged Cam's ribs with an elbow, giving him a look.

'What?' Cam asked with a shrug. 'It's important information. Especially since . . .' His words trailed off as he gave an over-exaggerated scratch of his thigh.

Split stood up, the stone tower toppling. 'What can I do to prove myself?'

'Swear it on the puppet,' Shilah said, jabbing a finger at the cart. 'On your Baba Levante.'

Split's face lit up with both shock and dread. 'You know about Baba Le— the puppet? How do you know about that?'

'You showed it to us in the chamber,' Shilah said, not missing a beat. 'The puppet is on the bottom of the cart as we speak.'

Cam raised an eyebrow, wiping the sweat off his brow. 'How can you not remember? You did the crazy voice and everything? You called yourself *rotund*.'

Shilah waved Cam off as if he were an annoying beetle, her eyes narrowing. 'Split. Swear to Baba Levante that you are on our side, that you won't sell us over to the Khat, and that you'll take us where you say. To Langria.'

Split swallowed hard, looking at the cart. 'I really brought the puppet along? Out into the open?'

Shilah didn't let him waver. Even under the shade of the parasol, her eyes glistened like jewels. 'Swear it.'

Split nodded without hesitation. 'I swear it on the strings and buttons and woollen hair and wooden heart. Okay?'

'And on whoever she belonged to,' Shilah said, her words slicing the air faster than her blade ever could.

Split met Shilah's eyes again, his face going pale. 'Yes,' he said quietly, his thick hand flexing in front of his thigh but not scratching. 'Salt in my tears I swear on whoever she belonged to.'

Shilah turned to me, completely relaxed. 'Good enough for me, he can be our Shepherd.'

I returned an innocent shrug. 'I never had a problem with him in the first place.'

Shilah smirked, staring at the beast. 'Mostly he can stay so we can keep Picka.'

The little camel grunted, stamping her feet and buzzing her fuzzy lips; again I was left questioning whether the beast understood more than we thought.

Split nodded, his eyes moistening at the corners as he looked me square in the face. 'The world's been waiting a long time for you, Meshua. Doesn't mean they're going to be ready. They're going to try to kill you. And truth be told they're probably going to Sun damn succeed.'

Cam clapped a hand on my shoulder. He still smelled overwhelmingly of rosemusk. 'That's what I'm here for. To jump in the way.'

Shilah crossed her arms, but she didn't argue.

Split gave a derisive snort. 'A High Noble brat jumping in the—'

'Listen, *Pedlar*,' Cam said in cutting tones, letting the parasol fall, his face wincing against the sudden splash of heat. 'I know you're important to the Coldmarch and all, but don't forget that you're High Noble too. If you're going to be our Shepherd, I'd like for you to show me a little respect. It *was* me who offered Spout a safe place to hide when the Vicaress was after him. It was in *my* tinkershop that he built the machine. And I may never have taken a Jadan to Langria, but I think it proves that you're not the only one of us who cares.'

Shilah put a hand on Picka, stroking the fur along her hump. 'It belonged to your uncle.'

Cam frowned, his face glaring red from passion and burns. 'Hmm?'

She didn't look at him when she spoke. 'It was your cousin's tinkershop.'

Cam took a deep breath, trying not to lose his patience. 'Yes, I know. But it was also the *Tavor* tinkershop. And since I'm the heir to the Tavor— *was* the heir—'

'It doesn't matter,' I said quickly, feeling so irritated I thought I might scream. 'I wouldn't háve found the secret and built the machine without either of you. And Leroi, too.'

Shilah looked somewhat placated, and Cam's face had gone even redder, which I would have thought impossible.

'Sorry,' Cam said. 'I just—'

'And Cam is right,' I spat. 'Split, I would ask that you be nicer to him if you're going to be our guide.' I turned to Shilah. 'You too. What happened with Leroi wasn't Cam's fault. And I can promise that Cam misses him more than you do.'

Silence fell, the echo of my harsh words turning to dust.

Split went back to scratching his thigh. 'We just can't forget who the enemy is here. The Tavors have an especially cruel history when it comes to your people.'

I gently spun Cam and pulled up his sunshirt so I could show Split the whipping scars running all the way up and down my friend's back. The taskmaster who had brought down the multi-tailed whip had shown no mercy in her swing. The blow was intended for me, but Cam had thrown himself on my back like a shield, and had paid the price in blood.

'He's not the enemy,' I said, letting his shirt fall back. 'This here is family. Maybe not by birth, but by deed. So, if you want to shepherd us, then you shepherd all of us. Walking North alone wouldn't be that difficult considering it's one simple direction, and we have a compass.'

The muscles in Shilah's jaw tightened, but then she gave a solemn nod. 'You're right, Spout.' Then she turned to Cam, her chest rising as she breathed deeply. 'It wasn't your fault. And I know you care about our people. I'm sorry.'

Cam turned slowly, putting the parasol back above his head, but not quickly enough to hide his embarrassed expression.

Split bowed low. 'I apologize, Meshua.'

'And don't call me that,' I snapped, feeling as though sand was caught in my chest, grating all of the delicate places. 'That's not me.'

Shilah gave me a satisfied nod and a wink, her hand teasing the end of her braid.

Split held his crossbow and snapped his fingers. Picka stopped nuzzling Shilah's hand and started dragging the cart into motion. Shilah caught my eye, and I nodded back, touching my fingers to my lips as she had behind the first Coldmarch door. I was immediately confused as to why I'd made such an odd gesture in that moment.

Shilah didn't return the finger-kiss, but she did wander next to me as we crossed the final stretch of road, every once in a while touching my elbow to remind me that she was there.

'You trash-slinging, knuckle-licking, faht-in-a-jar, sorry excuse for a swindlah,' the barkeeper said in a heavy Marlian accent as soon as the door sealed behind us. His voice was heavy on the vowels and crackling with cold tones. 'You think after ten yeahs you cans just waddle back to me place without wiping yer feet? On second thought, don't wipe, the grime on yer shoes is probably cleanah than you is. Those *slaves* are probably cleanah than you is.'

Every patron in the room had gone silent. The metal tables were populated mostly with middle-aged Nobles, and the glares were unanimously so foul that my stomach dropped. As far as welcomes went, it felt as if we'd just stumbled into a nest of starved taskmasters, and I was ready to grab the back of Split's shirt and tug him back out to the sands. We could always refill our waterskins from the underground river, and what was a few more days without food rations? According to Shilah's map, the City of the Shade wasn't too far east.

Split turned and gave me the kind of nod that said 'go along with it', cleared his throat, puffed out his chest, and announced: 'And what's it to you, you Wisp-pinching, mud-baking, piss-serving barmaid?'

'You think yer still welcome heah, you clotted wound of a High Noble? With yer craggy nose.' The innkeeper squirted extra venom into his tone as he cleaned a glass with a dirty rag. His grey hair was slicked back with the kind of expensive grease that would need to be reapplied every few hours to maintain its hold. 'I'm surprised yer welcome anywhere with the worthless shite you pass off as merchandise.'

Split paused and scratched his thigh. I spotted a large Cold Bellows waiting in the corner, and even though the tavern was somewhat chilled, I could feel sweat on my forehead. I scanned the tables for suspicious faces that might recognize me. Lord Tavor and the Vicaress both would have put out a serious ransom on my head, and if word of a reward had reached this tavern before us, then any of these people had the potential to be carrying a very lucrative dagger. Whatever supplies Split had wanted to pick up at the inn didn't seem worth our heads on pikes.

Shilah leaned closer to me, her fingers brushing the back of my hand. 'I told you. Let's get out of here.'

'Just stick close to me,' Cam said, standing a little taller and fixing his glasses so they were straight. 'These are Nobles. I know how to deal with Nobles.'

Shilah looked unimpressed, but she didn't step away.

The Pedlar squirmed as he worked up a response to the barkeeper. 'Guess I'll go try my luck at your mother's house. I'm always welcome there. And I have it on good authority that she quite enjoys my . . . *merchandise*.'

A few men at a corner table chuckled, but were swiftly quietened by a wave of the innkeeper's rag. The mood of the room became tense again, enhanced by the flickering candles around the tables. I looked to Cam for some guidance, but he seemed at a loss for a plan too.

The barkeeper slowly set down the glass he was polishing. Although his words were ripe with disdain, there was something at odds sitting in his eyes. His glance flicked back and forth from Shilah and me, to Split's face, almost as if trying to convey some important secret. 'Ah, you must be the one who sold me mother that "disappointing needle" she carried on about in her last lettah. I thought maybe she'd been trying her hand as a seamstress. Makes more sense she was speaking of *yer* little needle.'

'Oh, yeah?' Split swallowed hard. 'Well, from what I hear. You— your ale— I heard you . . .' Gritting his teeth, he threw his hands up in defeat. 'Leaky puss in my sunburns, you got me.'

The crowd erupted, thrusting their mugs into the air. Patrons slapped hands, clapped one another on the back, and a few Wisps even changed hands, rolling from one side of the table to another. A group of High Noble girls in fine silk dresses sat at a table in the corner, uninspired by the exchange of insults; rather they seemed eager to finish their round of violently coloured drinks for a different reason. A fancy red-headed Noble girl sat in the centre, a perfectly white sundress hugging her curves, and she was already eyeing Cam, giving him a flirtatious little wiggle of her fingers from the stem of her crystal goblet.

124        DANIEL A. COHEN

Cam was quick to flatten his golden hair, keeping a straight face.

The barkeeper broke into a huge smile, gesturing to himself proudly. 'You had ten years to plan yer attack and still I bested you!'

'I was distracted, Gilly!' Split tried calling over the noise. He pointed at the rest of our group, as if the presence of two Jadans and a Tavor explained it all. 'I'm distracted, got a shipment I'm transporting. *Yer* win doesn't count.'

Gilly raised a glass in triumph, not a single grey hair on his head shifting out of place. 'Course it counts, you boot-licking husk of a limp lizard.'

The crowd burst into sounds of celebration again, draining mugs. A toothless man at the bar smirked wildly, his black tongue dancing across the gaps in his gums. The dirty patron looked as if he might embody the exact opposite smell of rosemusk, yet there was a House Erridian sigil prominently displayed on his chest. If the ragged Erridian wanted, he could have bathed in pretty much the same kind of perfume as the Khat.

Split sighed audibly. His disappointment sounded real, but his eyes were speaking in a language of their own, hurling something important back across the bar to the innkeeper. He gave a double-tug of his earlobe. 'Fine, Gilly. You earned it.'

'Hey, Pedlar!' a wrinkly patron in the back of the crowd slurred over an empty mug. 'Didn't I know you once? You the one who sold me a rusty compass that barely ever worked?'

Split scratched at the scruff on his chin. 'Ain't you the one who shorted me two Drafts on that deal when you tossed a velvet bag at my feet and ran away cackling?'

The patron's face paled, and he slunk back into the shadows, a round of laughter circling his table. Blinking away my confusion, I continued to look around the room. A moment ago I thought we were destined to be hurled through the door, but the murderous glares had become placid and disinterested. Split was right; I didn't know much about life outside Paphos.

The Pedlar bent over and spoke to us so low that only we could hear. 'Remember, be smarter than you were in those damned caverns, and keep quiet. If anyone asks, you're slaves that I'm transporting to the City of the Shade. And, Tavor,' he cleared his throat, 'you're a distant nephew, and you're interested in renting Shilah for the evening.'

Shilah's upper lip curled back into a snarl at this proclamation, and her almond eyes bulged wide, as though she wished to murder everyone in the room – starting with the Pedlar.

Split held up his hands. 'Okay, okay, sorry.' He lowered his voice, an evil smirk forming at the corner of his lips. 'Tavor, you want to purchase *Spout* for the evening.'

Cam had been eyeing the redhead at the table, who was now seductively running her fingers around the rim of her goblet, so it took a moment for Split's comment to register. When it did, Cam's smoulder flopped into horrified mortification. 'No— what— how come—'

Split chuckled. 'We need *authenticity*, Tavor. And from what I understand that is an authentic desire with the overly spoiled Nobleboys who get bored with young women. I call it the "too many figs" syndrome. Seems to me like a small lie to pay to keep your friend safe.'

Shilah shrugged, giving Cam an innocent look. 'Happens plenty in the Drifthouses.'

Split's eyes once again wandered to the Coldmaker bag around my chest, an unreadable expression crossing his face. I could see his fingers tense up slightly.

'Seems fair,' I said, reflexively clutching the bag tighter. 'Just go with it.'

Cam went to protest, his face redder than his burns, but Split was already shuffling through the tables, working his way across the room. Gilly wiggled out from behind the bar, and when they reached each other, they embraced heavily, but only for a second. The innkeeper took a step back, cocked his fist, and sent a blow soaring into Split's stomach.

Split's loud *oomph* gave the room another small cause for celebration, but from where I was standing, I noticed that as he was hunched over, Gilly quickly whispered something in the Pedlar's ear. A few mugs were raised at a corner booth, but at this point most of the Noblemen had already turned their attention back to each other. Card games were resumed – I recognized a few matches of Conquer – goods were examined, and dice were tossed alongside harmless insults. The young girls at the table hadn't reacted to the punch, as they were too busy gathering in a tight giggling dome, decidedly not looking our way.

I fell into slave stance, nudging Shilah to do the same, the way we used to have to stand on our street corners. Bend at the knees, shoulders in, slouching. She reluctantly put a crook in her perfect posture, and did not appear happy about it.

Split was clutching his stomach, laughing and enunciating so the whole room could hear. 'Your punch about as strong as your ale, Gilly.'

The innkeeper slicked back his shiny hair, focused on Shilah and me. 'So yer gonna be making bad decisions later, then, Peddlah?'

Split nodded to the small door beside the bar, his eyes urgent. 'I only come here for the bad decisions.'

The quip sounded like something practised. Split hadn't told us if Gilly was also a Shepherd or simply a sympathizer, only that the man would refill our supplies without need for payment or delay. To me it didn't matter what Gilly was, because that sort of support from Noblekind deserved to be repaid in full; and when I had my army of Coldmakers I'd come back and make the innkeeper rich. So much so that he could reapply the silvery grease to his hair every hour for the rest of his life and never run out.

Gilly gave a serious nod, adding a Wisp to his Cold Bellows and cranking the place a shade cooler.

'I poisoned one o' the barrels,' he then announced to the tavern. 'Any of yoose lot try stealing my ale and I'll be able to tell by the blood welling out of yer eyes.'

'I like poison,' the toothless man at the bar muttered, his gums flapping wildly.

'I'm aware of that, Roland,' Gilly said, opening the side door Split had been so focused on and closing it tightly once he and the Pedlar were both inside.

I glanced around the room using only my peripheral vision, a skill I'd honed during the years when it was necessary. Mostly the crowd looked to be weary travellers, grateful for the time out of the Sun and a stomach full of something stronger than water. There were, however, a few dubious Nobles who'd gravitated towards the shadowy sections of the tavern. Not far from where we were standing one older man with a pair of coloured glasses had a cage full of spiny skink-manders. They were set on the table before an eager cohort, the buyer examining the scuttling creatures from a safe distance.

The lighting was dim, so it took me a moment to realize, but behind the table, standing hunched just like Shilah and me, was a battered Jadan about my age. He was skin and bones, and even though his complexion was a shade darker than mine, I was still able to notice all the scars around his wrists. A Closed Eye was embossed over his uniform, and the lines on his face spoke of a permanent frown. And if the oppressive symbol on his chest weren't humiliation enough, the side of his neck had been branded with the 'unusable' symbol: a triangle with a line through the middle. This symbol on the neck let other Nobles know that he'd been purchased outright by a merchant.

The man in the coloured glasses sneered and snapped his fingers, my shackled kin sweeping around the table and bowing low. It was difficult to pick up their conversation out of the din. I could sense Shilah trying to hone in as well.

'Yessir,' the Jadan said, completely devoid of personality and life.

'Take one skinkmander out for our guest here, Sunpillow. So he can see that the fangs haven't been milked.'

Hearing the derogatory term 'Sunpillow' made my blood boil. It wasn't the first time I'd come across the word, but 'Coldleech' was the more popular slur in Paphos. I understood that each city had their own special insults for Jadans, but now that I knew the truth of things – at least the partial truth – the name made me tense up. Especially because of the way the merchant tossed it about so casually.

'Right away, sir,' the Jadan said. 'If you want me to get the tongs from the wagon—'

The man smiled from behind his coloured glasses, head slowly turning. He drummed his fingers against the table, making the skinkmanders more frantic. The little lizards buzzed about the cage, whipping their spiny tails at one another's hard carapaces. 'Did I say get the *tongs*, Sunpillow?'

'Nossir.'

'What did I say?'

The crook in the Jadan's back deepened. 'You said take one out for our guest.'

'So why would you suggest tongs? Do you want to ride to the City of the Shade in the crate again?'

'Nossir. Pleassir.'

Only the merchant and the buyer were at the table, and the buyer sent his hands up defensively. I didn't see any visible rashes anywhere on his skin, making me think that he must have been interested in purchasing the skinkmander venom for someone other than himself. Even Leroi hadn't understood why it was that only Nobles were affected by diseases like firepox when Jadans weren't, or why the cure for such a disease was found only in such a ferocious little lizard.

The buyer gave a nervous chuckle. 'It's okay, I don't want to—'

'Nonsense.' The man in the glasses sat back, giving a go-ahead motion. Fingers were snapped multiple times, emphasizing his impatience. 'You should feel confident in your purchase, good sir!'

The Jadan reached out a trembling hand, slowly flipping open the lock on the lizard cage. The skinkmanders started hissing at his approach, the spines on their tails raised and sharp and ready to draw blood. And before I knew it, the seller had removed a cudgel from somewhere beneath the table, raising it above the Jadan's hand.

'It's them or me gonna sting you, boy,' the seller said, entirely composed, brushing the cudgel gently against the Jadan's cheek.

The buyer sat back in his seat, face flushed. 'I don't think that's . . . Gilly doesn't allow—'

The man in the glasses gestured to the ceiling with his blunt weapon. 'It's Gilly's bar, but the Crier's world. And our Lord and Creator wants the lessers disciplined. Decree of Unworthiness, good sir! Now hurry up, Sunpillow, or I'll stick your whole head in that cage.'

Shilah tensed up, but there was nothing we could do without drawing incredible amounts of attention to ourselves.

Cam was already halfway to the table.

'Hold on,' my friend nearly shouted. 'Don't put your hand in that cage, slave!'

Dice games were halted, heads were turned, and conversations died immediately. A whole troop of curious eyes turned towards Cam. The toothless man called Roland even stopped reaching over the bar, his dirty hand holding a mug beneath one of the taps.

Cam realized his misstep, but instead of backing down he puffed up and wagged his finger at the room, snapping at everyone at once. 'About your business, fools! This doesn't concern you!'

Cam spoke with such force and authority that even I slumped a little lower. The redhead in the tight outfit practically swooned, whispering something to her group of friends.

I moved forwards in Cam's wake, head down. Shilah did the same, only less demure.

'Cam,' I hissed out of the corner of my mouth. 'Cam, stop.'

But he seemed determined. Cam gave a curt bow when reaching the table, quickly brushing the Jadan's hand aside and closing the cage. One of the skinkmanders leaped up and whipped a tail at Cam's fingers, but the bars were tight and thick, the attack rebuffed with a metallic clang.

'And who might you be?' Glasses said, pushing his eyewear tighter for further anonymity.

Cam tried to whip his golden hair in a majestic way, which didn't quite work since it was matted down with sweat and dirt. 'Salvatore of House Erridian.'

The seller gently put his cudgel on the table, trying to decide whether or not to buy the claim, as the Erridians were the most powerful house outside of the Khat's immediate family. Scrub away a few layers of grime, and Cam could obviously be the real deal, considering he had the blond hair, fair complexion, and correct haughtiness. It wasn't a terrible lie.

'And you have a token to prove as such?' the bespectacled man asked.

Cam scoffed. 'I hardly think that's necessary for someone of my status. And I hardly think you're in any position to ask, House Icarus.'

'Salvatore Erridian is notorious for wickedly grotesque eyebrows,' the seller said carefully. 'Like two chunks of serrated boilweed from what I understand.'

'Yes,' Cam said with an irritated roll of his eyes. 'And anyone well *informed* of the true happenstances in the Khatdom knows there's more than one Salvatore in the Erridian family. Uncle Sal doesn't groom his eyebrows, but I obviously do. And along those lines, if you're going to represent House Icarus, as low as they have fallen after their bungled incense deal with the Paphos Cry Temple Priests, then you might want to scrape away some of that grime from your fingernails, sir.'

The glasses man sat back, placated for the moment. He put his hands under the table. 'So what interest is the safety of my slave to you, Salvatore of House Erridian?'

Cam looked back at me, his bravado still present, but a nervous look creeping into his eyes. 'I— I just.'

My eyes widened, hoping he might miraculously come up with something feasible.

'You're not a sympathizer, are you?' the seller asked, the wickedness in his eyes apparent even behind the glasses. 'I heard there are some sympathizers that stop here from time to time. Gilly's a softy on the decrees.'

The shackled Jadan backed away nervously, hunched low and looking fearful at Cam's interference. Even though the din of the place was back to normal, everyone in the tavern was keeping half an ear open for Cam's answer. The reward for turning over a sympathizer could keep a Noble drunk on stout ale for a year. The circle of girls had opened into a crescent, each one wide-eyed with the hope of fresh gossip. The redhead's adoration was put on hold, her head cocked in a curious manner.

'Sympathizer!' Cam scoffed. 'How dare you make such implications!'

The seller gave a flippant opening of arms, as if to say 'prove it'.

Cam hesitated and picked up the cudgel, giving the shackled Jadan what could only be described as a light tap on the shoulder. I wanted to slap my forehead, my stomach clenching as my friend continued to dig himself deeper into trouble. I sneaked a glance at the side door behind which Split had retreated, praying the Pedlar would come out soon so we might scatter.

The branded Jadan gave a polite bow, nursing a hand over the spot Cam had struck, and said a meek: 'Ow, sir.'

The seller looked at the Jadan, and then at Cam, an eyebrow rising far above the glasses as he slowly cracked his knuckles.

'Fine,' Cam said, throwing his hands up, his face going bright red. 'I'm bored with what I got. Too many figs syndrome. I want to rent your Jadan boy for the night and I want—' He took a deep breath, the next words straining with effort. 'I want his hands to be . . . untainted.'

The seller clucked his tongue, a deep grin forming. 'So you think Sunpillow here is a handsome slave, do you, Salvatore Erridian? Fancy his luscious dark skin?' The man leaned in, giving an over-exaggerated sniff of the air in front of Cam. 'That why you got yourself smelling like pretty rosemusk?'

Cam swallowed hard, looking at his feet as he nodded, his freshly opened sinkhole only growing wider. 'So what if it is? I'll pay big Cold.'

The red-headed girl turned her back to Cam faster than an arrow. Fortunately for us, this sort of scandal didn't seem as exciting or lucrative to the crowd as their gambling, so attention started to wane. The clacks of dice soon filled the space, eyes returning to their own dealings.

I started to breathe again, but not all that easily.

We still weren't in the clear.

Glasses man dipped to the side, looking past the cage of hissing skinkmanders and over at Shilah and me. 'Looks like you already have some young company.'

Heat shot into my cheeks. And even though I couldn't see Shilah, I imagined she was fuming.

Cam gave a flippant wave. 'They've been with me for days now. I've tasted those figs plenty. And us Erridian boys have needs. Us Erridian boys want . . .' He coughed, trying to force the words out. '. . . something new.'

Just then the side door beside the bar swung open, Split and Gilly spilling out. Split was holding a giant bag of supplies over his shoulder, his pockets bulging at the seams. Gilly looked pale as white limestone, his eyes bulging as they focused on the bag on my shoulder. He cleared his throat, running his hand over and over through his grey hair, which speckled greasy goop on the bar. 'Round of ale on the house! Finest brew, Coldest mugs!'

The place erupted, and any rogue attention that was clinging to us was quickly scraped away. Split sifted through the celebrations, accidentally bumping people with the supplies sack, reigniting a few glares.

'What's going on here, Nephew?' Split asked, his voice imperious.

'Nothing, Uncle,' Cam said. 'We were just having a conversation.'

The seller gave Split a scrutinizing look, suspicious eyes going right to his eyebrows, which were dirty and thick, but not enough to be considered notorious.

Split waved his hand impatiently. 'No time for conversations. You know we have that deal to make by nightfall.'

'Hold on,' the seller said, holding up his palm and smirking. 'Young Salvatore here promised me big Cold for a night with—'

Cam dropped the cudgel. 'Misunderstanding. Come, Uncle. Let's leave and go do that deal.'

The glasses man began to stand up, hunched over with his hands on the table looking as if he might join the skinkmanders in their chorus of hissing. 'I'm an honourable man. I expect others to be as well. I was already promised Cold for my slave, and if Sunpillow here is not sleeping with your nephew then he's sleeping in my crate—'

'I'll take the whole litter right now,' the original buyer across the table said, his cheeks pinched with worry. He pointed frantically at the skinkmanders, forcing a smile. 'Double the price.'

The glasses man swung his attention back. 'You said *double*?'

'Double.'

'You have that much on you?'

While they were distracted, I reached into the Coldmaker bag and grabbed an Abb, cupping it in my palm. Shuffling a few steps, I got close enough to the shackled Jadan to reach out and drop the gold bead into one of his ripped pockets, hoping it didn't fall out. I gave the bead a quick pat and winked as the poor soul met my eyes.

'Put it in water,' I whispered.

I don't know why I risked the gift, especially since I couldn't explain the importance of the Abb to him now, but I knew my Jadan brother was going to be punished later for this interaction between High Nobles. I wanted him to have a bit of wonder to keep him occupied through the lashings.

'I have no time for this,' Split said, his face jiggling with anger, but his eyes calmly gesturing for the door. 'Your *tongue* has got you in trouble once again, Nephew.'

Cam flared with embarrassment, his fist clenching at his side.

Split snapped his fingers. 'Slaves! Out!'

Shilah and I turned heel, Cam and the Pedlar trailing

behind. We all made it to the door without being followed, or questioned, although I did hear the most incredible scoff escape the redhead's lips as we passed her table.

Once outside, the door sealed tightly behind us, we started running towards the mudbrick stables. Shilah had begun shaking, her arms wrapped around her body.

'You okay?' I asked.

She stopped beside the dwarf camel, her quaking erupting into a fit of delighted giggling, head tossed back and face lighting up brighter than the sky. Cam was as flustered as they come, not able to meet our faces, but after a moment of wordless babble, he too was doubled over with laughter. Picka sensed the hilarity and started braying happily, and of course I had no choice but to finally let go.

'What?' Split demanded, tossing the large sack of supplies onto the cart. 'What did I miss?'

Tears were too busy leaking from my eyes for me to stop. It felt like such a release to laugh again. Shilah was wiping away her own tears, giggling like I'd never heard before.

'If you have a good story, you have to tell your Pedlar!' Split said, crossing his arms. 'Rules of the Coldmarch!'

# Chapter Ten

We made our way North for half a day, the Sun blazing overhead, our packs full, and our hearts lighter than they had been in a long time. Split's mood had improved considerably, and he even ended up sharing a few stories about other Jadans who he'd shepherded to Gilly's Tavern. He smiled particularly about a girl called Lop, who was apparently so quick on her feet that she insisted on scouting ahead of the group. Her spryness ended up saving them from a run-in with the Vicaress of Belisk, who had been slinking around Gilly's looking for a runaway. There was also a boy – 'a rare case' – who everyone jokingly referred to as 'Shaman Eli'. Eli had a pet scorpion that he'd de-barbed and insisted that he'd figured out the secret to making crops grow faster. He also spat at people's feet when they got too close or pried too much. Split had shepherded great healers and storytellers, and plenty of young women who'd just come of age, and I could feel the gap closing between myself and the answers I so desperately craved. Soon he'd be telling us about Langria, and why the Coldmarch so abruptly ended ten years ago.

The land up here was firmer than I was used to, the dirt almost springy, which allowed the cart to roll smoothly and our pace to quicken. Even though Split hadn't directly taken anyone on this next stretch of the March, he'd still walked the route once alone, to understand what lay ahead for his flock. So now he was leading us towards one of the Great Bridges where we'd cross the Singe with speed and confidence. The Sun was blazing, but at least we had parasols and supplies, Gilly having even thrown in a few vials of groan salve for our future rashes and burns. There had been no sightings of the Vicaress on the Khat's roads, and the hounds were a distant memory. Even Shilah's hesitation towards Cam had waned, and, though they didn't fall into friendship, she at least began to chuckle at his jokes.

Everything was going surprisingly well until two ominous silhouettes popped up on the horizon, headed right for us.

Jabbing a fingernail in between his teeth, Split picked out grains of sand and said, 'These here, my little flock, are the moments that separate the Peddlars from the merchants.'

'What's the difference again?' Cam asked, moving his body in front of mine so I'd be out of view from the approaching lawmen.

'Don't do that,' I whispered. 'That only makes it more obvious.'

Cam weighed what I was saying with a bobble of his head, eventually stepping aside. The figures heading towards us had their chests proudly thrust out, displaying the symbol of the Khat's law. At the sight of the design – black flames being crushed beneath a Pyramid stone – I pulled the Coldmaker close to my side. Split was unperturbed, spitting out the loose grains of sand with a wry smile.

'Merchants sell goods,' Split said. '*Only* goods. And any brainless oaf can slap a price on a box of gem candy and stick it on a table.' Split wiggled his eyebrows, a bit less sullen. 'But Peddlars sell *themselves*.'

Cam nudged me in the side. 'So, selling tips on how to eat more and bathe less?'

'Blisters and boils, you're insufferable, Tavor,' Split said, waving his arms about dramatically, which I hoped was not conceived as aggressive. 'We sell our words, our attitudes. Our stories. And you attach the right story to an item – I don't care what that item is – and the price becomes irrelevant. People don't want to buy things; they want to buy the story behind things.' Split gave a dramatic wave of his hands and feigned an overzealous voice. 'This necklace, sir, why it was worn by the great designer Halia of House Plindus, back when the Belisk Towers were being erected. Oh, and this piece over here? Glad you asked, ma'am. This long wooden rod with the snakehead on top is the dowsing rod that belonged to Darlish the Unrelenting. Does the staff work any more? Another great question, ma'am. It's never worked for me, hence why I'm selling it, but it could always be saving its magic for the right hands.' Split let out a small belch, his eyes widening with surprise. 'Wow. Gilly's cheese is denser than I remember. Good stuff.'

'You seem rather sure of your skills,' Shilah said.

'You don't become the most successful Shepherd ever to work the Coldmarch without being sure of yourself,' Split said, his smile toothy and confident. Now that the Pedlar had sobered up, he almost had a charm about him, and I could see why the Pedlar title suited him. 'Doubt and lies have a remarkably similar smell.' He paused, giving a little huff through his crooked nose. 'Not that I would know.'

Picka matched the huff, stamping her toes.

'What's that mean, when she does that?' I asked, pointing to the camel's foot.

Split shook his head, rubbing his hand on Picka's neck. 'Nothing. Now stand short, my Jadan friends. And Camlish, let me do all of the talking. Please.'

Shilah and I deepened our slave stances as the lawmen

approached. I tried not to get too nervous, as these men were travelling North to South, and there was a good chance they had not heard news of precious runaways.

'Ho, lawmen!' Split practically cried out, waving a friendly hand. 'Praise be the Khat!'

The lawmen didn't answer, keeping their faces stern and their hands on the hilts of their swords.

'Please, do examine my scrollwork for these slaves!' Split said, coming right out with it, making me tense. 'Examine my luxurious goods for yourselves. And just so you know, the law's Cold spends twice as well with Peddlars!'

'I thought desperation was suspicious,' Cam whispered out of the corner of his mouth, waving jovially at the lawmen before raising his voice. 'Praise be the Khat, sirs!'

Still no answer from across the vast stretch of stone, and if anything, the lawmen's lips stiffened further, turning to each other with a wordless glance. The brutal Sun lit them from the back, casting their shadows long and sharp across the dead land.

'You've done this before, I assume?' Cam whispered again, keeping his smile wide. 'Dealt with lawmen, while you had a flock?'

'My number one customers,' Split said quietly. 'Trust me, if we have to choose between what's in front of us versus what's behind, I'll take the law every time. Don't forget it's just regular Nobles hiding behind those fancy sigils.'

'The Vicaress is a regular Noble, too,' Shilah said, head bowed.

'The Vicaress,' Split scoffed. 'All the Vicaresses in every city have their heads too far up their arses to be able to sniff us out. It's the Hoo— hounds that we have to worry about. The hounds.'

'You think the hounds still have our scent all the way out here?' I asked.

'PRAISE BE THE KHAT!' Split waved even more furiously at the approaching danger. 'Now hush, all of you.'

At last the lawmen got close enough for me to make out individual faces, both their hands resting on their swords as if they were expecting to use them. The one in front looked as self-important as they come, a neat yellow goatee rimming thin pink lips, his mouth just begging for an excuse to curl into a smirk. The man behind him was tall and curiously round in the centre, shaped like a sand-viper that was only halfway through digesting a hearty meal. His face was decidedly less expressive, and I imagined he did far less talking over the course of their partnership.

'Gentlenobles,' Split said with the friendliest grin I'd ever seen, his yellowed teeth and blackened gums stark against the Sunlight. Gesturing to the cart, the Pedlar rubbed his hands together. 'Everything is for sale except for the puppet in the case. And that's not for sentimental reasons, I just know if you purchase it you'll return the damn thing, as her ugly old face has been known to scare the—'

'*Khatfists*,' Yellow Goatee interrupted with the exact smirk I'd been expecting, pointing to his chest. 'Not *Gentlenobles*. We earned the Khatfist title, we expect you to use it, Pedlar.'

'Of course,' Split said with a bow. 'I meant no disrespect. First and foremost, let me offer you honourable Khatfists some fancy headscarves for any women you might have in your life, free of charge. The dyes employed were mixed by the experienced hands of the Tefflin sisters in the Hotland Delta, guaranteed to get your women in a state of complete and utter—'

'Papers.' A wet tongue circled beneath the lip above the goatee as his eyes simultaneously circled Shilah. It made me want to ball my fists and shove her dagger into each of his eyes. 'For the slaves. If you wouldn't mind, Pedlar.'

'Of course, of course,' Split said, sighing as if overwhelmingly bored. 'Let's get the boring stuff out of the way. Then the gifts for your women. I'm transporting these two slaves from the chains of—'

'He said papers,' the Khatfist with the bulbous stomach barked from the back. 'Unless you're a swindler.'

The Goatee turned, his voice gentle. 'Francis, my dear. Give respect, get respect. We've discussed this.'

Split bowed low, his bald spot revealing itself to be pretty severely burned. 'Thank you kindly . . .'

The Goatee didn't offer a name yet. His meticulously groomed eyebrows raised, glancing to the top of the cart where the scrolls sat.

Where *most* of the scrolls sat.

Cam reached out one hand and smoothed his long yellow hair with the other, almost as if to draw attention to the fact that it was a similar colour. 'Salvatore Erridian, pleased to make your acquaintance.'

The Goatee kept his hand on his sword, fingers tapping the hilt. 'From what I understand, Salvatore Erridian has eyebrows about as smooth as a bucket of nails.'

Cam would need to pick a better name to hide behind in the future.

'Yes, my uncle does have quite the peeper-hair,' Cam said with a gulp.

The Goatee's smirk somehow grew larger, so large it would have broken any normal face in half.

'Do you have any tokens to prove your lineage, Salvatore Erridian?' he asked.

Cam made an innocent turn of his palms, his face going red. 'Well, you see, I was with this young Noblewoman last night, and she was incredibly attractive, mind you, so obviously I didn't have all my wits about me, and in the morning she'd taken—'

'Tokens,' Francis barked out from behind. 'Unless you're liars.'

The Goatee made a *tsk-tsk* sound, which either completely negated or completely matched the amused look on his face. 'Francis, we've discussed this.'

No apology was offered from the Khatfist behind, only a folding of skinny arms over the protruding belly.

Cam's face soured, huffing in that way only High Nobles could. My friend was probably ten stations above these Khatfists, and it really was a shame he hadn't grabbed a fistful of Tavor tokens before leaving the Manor.

'So let's see. I've got two Khatfists to report for unprofessional conduct,' Cam said, eyes narrowing. 'What are your names and ranks in the law?'

The Goatee slowly withdrew his sword from its sheath, the sound long and shrill. The tip of the blade swung back and forth playfully in front of Cam. 'What's unprofessional is a Pedlar refusing to give over his papers to two respectable Khatfists, and a supposedly High Noble, of House Erridian no less, having no way of identifying himself.'

'Very unprofessional, Harrold,' Francis said with a sneer from behind. 'Unless they're thieves.'

Split held up his hands defensively, shooting Cam a dangerous glare while grabbing the scrolls from the cart. 'No one's refusing anything. Here, take a look.'

Harrold kept the tip of his sword swinging, making all of us tense. He kept eyeing Shilah, his glance resting in places that made me cringe. I was secretly hoping they didn't believe Split's scrolls, so I was forced to use my own.

Without removing his lingering glare, Harrold nodded back to the much larger Francis, who stepped forwards and snatched the scrolls out of Split's hand. The parchment crunched under fat fingers as he wrenched the scrolls open without care, his eyes narrowing.

'Stamps are out-of-date,' Francis said.

'And I'll gladly pay the fine,' Split said without missing a beat. 'Anything for the Khat's grace.' The Pedlar sighed dramatically, but gave the lawmen a conspiratorial wink. 'That's what I get for losing sense of time in the Glassland Pleasurehouses. Lots of pleasure to be had. Yes, *lots* of pleasure. Now how many Drafts is that again for out-of-date stamps? Three, I believe? Let's make it a clean Shiver? The Khat's law deserves the utmost respect and it's my honour to—'

'*Ten years* out-of-date. And it says here two girl slaves for transport.' Francis pointed at me, tearing the parchment in half and tossing it on the ground. '*That* is a boy slave.'

'Might have to check down below,' Harrold sneered.

'Ten years!' Split exclaimed, aghast. The tone was believable, but his forehead was betraying him, sweating profusely. 'Outrageous! I must have grabbed the wrong papers. Or maybe the last checkpoint accidentally switched them on me. Please, first let me give you some scarves for your women, and then we can—'

The point of the sword aimed at the Pedlar's throat. 'Are you attempting to bribe members of the League of Khatfists, Pedlar? Francis, what's the punishment for such a transgression?'

Francis cracked his knobbly knuckles. 'Out here? Anything we want.'

Split gave a nervous laugh. 'I've never heard such a thing.'

Harrold beamed, the tip of the sword moving away from Split's throat and instead caressing the folds of Shilah's shirt. 'We are joking, of course. Bribes are the preferred communication between respectable Nobles like us. The question is, what's the quality of the bribe? Is the bribe diseased? Can the bribe handle what's coming to her without bleeding out? Because she'd better be able to handle all these things, or she is no bribe at all.'

And that was enough of that.

I gave Cam the double-cough we'd practised.

Harrold's attention swung to me. 'Why are you carrying that against your body instead of in the cart, slave? What's your master got you lugging?'

Cam sighed loudly. 'Fine. You caught us, okay?'

'Hmmph,' Francis grumbled from behind. 'Can always spot lies.'

Harrold drew the tip of the sword across Shilah's chest, examining her curves with the metal. His hand wasn't entirely steady, and he clumsily drew a line of blood. Maybe it was on purpose. Shilah remained unflinching, refusing him the satisfaction of so much as a squeak.

'Caught you, you say?' Harrold's smirk outlined by the yellow goatee was a work of sinister art that could rival anything in the Paphos library. 'Caught you doing what exactly?'

'I'm going to grab our _real_ scroll from the bottom of the cart,' Cam said, keeping his hands up as he scuttled sideways. 'Just don't stab me.'

'Stab Salvatore Erridian's nephew?' Harrold said, making a sarcastic flap of his hand over his mouth, the tip of his sword still dangerously close to Shilah's heart. 'Who would dare do such a thing?'

Cam bent low, pulling loose the thread that held the invention in place.

'But if you come back up with a blade, boy,' Harrold growled, 'it goes down your gullet. High Noble or not.'

'No sword,' Cam said innocently. 'Just secret information. More valuable than blades in the right hands.'

Harrold's sword was now plucking away the lower cloth covering the swell of Shilah's chest, the small new cut on her breast dripping red onto the metal. The lawman was only half paying attention to Cam, the dark hunger obvious in his face. Shilah didn't give him so much as a flinch, her cheeks tight and eyes narrow. Her hand was poised dangerously close to her thigh, and I hoped she would let the invention get us out of this before trying something drastic.

'Haven't had a good bribe in a long time,' Harrold mumbled to himself. 'And this bribe looks like she needs a breaking. Do you concur, Francis?'

The large man grunted, scratching under his sword belt. 'Concur.'

Split's face was stuck in helpless shock, clearly oblivious to what was going on. I probably should have informed him about our scroll plan, but I had my reasons for keeping him out of the loop.

'Here,' Cam said, looking at the rolled-up parchment wistfully before holding it out. 'Just . . . this information is extremely secretive to the Erridian family, and I would ask that once you read it, please—'

Francis grabbed the scroll with a grunt, beginning to unroll the end.

'Manners,' Harrold said with a scoff, dropping the sword and taking a step closer to his companion. 'Now let's see what's so secretive that—'

The reaction was explosive.

And as the cloud of grey powder erupted against their faces, the name 'Snapscroll' shot into my mind. Francis had ripped the paper low enough to trigger the side-spring I'd coiled inside, smashing the plunger through the glass trap, making the back-up Glassland Dream spray out like a sandstorm. The paper itself kept the cloud from travelling backwards, so the powder was left with only one direction to escape.

Right into those bastards' faces.

But I never expected it to burst so hard.

Francis got the brunt of the cloud in his mouth, immediately making him cough and splutter, staining his entire face grey. Harrold unfortunately was still a few feet away the moment

146 DANIEL A. COHEN

the trap was sprung, turning his face away from the puff of Dream, and only receiving a weak dusting on the yellow goatee. It didn't much matter though, because in the commotion Shilah had swung around behind the man, holding Mama Jana's blade firm on his windpipe.

Just like we'd discussed, should a situation like this arise.

And, unlike her captor, Shilah's hand didn't shake.

Francis, his face now the colour of a dead man, made some garbled sound, dropping the Snapscroll. With the amount of Glassland Dream now in his lungs he had no chance of staying upright. The normal dose of the powder for relaxation purposes – from what I understood – was supposed to fit on a fingernail. A full vial could last an addict weeks, and the lawman had just had the entire supply in one flurried dose.

As expected, Francis's eyes rolled back and his oddly shaped body collapsed, his arm making a sickening crack as it slammed against a large rock on the ground.

'Drop to your knees, *Khatfist*,' Shilah commanded of Harrold, her voice steelier than her weapon.

Harrold's face was pure vengeance, but he couldn't quite hold the menacing expression beneath a fit of coughing. As he jostled, the knife cut into his skin, but Shilah didn't back off.

'Knees!' Shilah shouted.

This time the Khatfist decided to listen.

'Hands behind your back,' I said, trying to match Shilah's ferocity and failing. 'Now.'

Instead of listening to me, the Khatfist hesitated, his eyes judging how quickly he could pick up his sword. Shilah let the knife dig further into his neck, and soon enough both of Harrold's arms were behind his back. I had coils of thin rope ready in my pocket, and I quickly bound him at the wrists and ankles, using a technique Leroi had taught me that was far more binding than an Assasiknot.

Cam went over to Francis's limp body, checking for a pulse.

'He's alive for now,' Cam said, keeping his head as far away as he could from the fallen lawman, transferring the grey powder from his fingers to his sunshirt. 'And I think his arm is broken.'

'It is. And his breathing is slowing,' I said, moving back to our other captive. 'Now listen closely, I will leave you here, also alive, and put a sharp piece of metal and a waterskin a thousand paces North of this spot. After we leave, you can crawl to the metal and cut your bindings—'

'You listen to me, slave,' Harrold spat, trying to blow the powder out of his once-perfectly-yellow goatee. The whites of his eyes had gone red from Dream and disgust. 'I swear on the Khat's law that I will find you and end you and make you obey like no slave has ever done before.'

'How are you going to make him do things no slave has ever done *after* you end him?' Cam joked, a nervous lump in his throat. 'You've got to get your timeline right.'

Shilah let her blade taste more of the Khatfist's flesh. 'You sure you want to make that threat?'

'Shilah,' I said with a bit of warning. 'It's fine. Now, as I was saying, your release will be one thousand paces North, and I'll put a Wisp in the waterskin. Now, I know that's asking a lot of crawling, but we have to be sure—'

A gob of spit carrying flecks of powder splattered into my face. I saw it coming enough to be holding my breath as I spoke, but I made sure to wipe it away quickly with my sleeve. Picka gave an excited grunt from behind, Split trying to calm her with ear scratches. The Pedlar had had his back turned to us ever since the grey cloud burst, muttering something to himself and presumably doing his best not to look at all that powder.

'Respect, Khatfist,' Cam said in a taunting voice. 'Do we need to discuss this?'

Harrold's breathing had grown ragged, from a combination of the powder and emotion. 'And you, girl,' he laughed, so high-pitched it was almost a giggle, 'oh, just wait to see what I have planned for you. Your body is just the beginning. Shilah, was it?'

'Watch it,' Cam said, at last serious.

Shilah was smiling, stroking a hand against her captive's cheek. 'You *sure* you want to make that threat?'

Harrold's breathing was now so fast I wondered how much longer he'd be able to stay awake. 'You don't understand. You'd better slice my throat with that blade, *Shilah*, otherwise I'm going to track you down and you will be my rug, and my dirty bathwater, and my soft boilweed that I rub in the cracks between—'

'Watch it!' Cam warned again.

Harrold's eyes were wide and frenzied, and I worried that he might try to bite Shilah's fingers. 'Do you know how much practice I've had with your kind, girl? Do you know how many Jadan slaves I've consumed whole?'

Shilah looked poised to cut his throat, the muscles in her arms tense.

I quickly reached in and put a hand on her wrist. 'It's fine. Remember. There's a reason the Crier chose us.'

'Chose you!' Harrold giggled, high-pitched and fast. 'Amazing. How droll. I hope she makes jokes like that while I have her tied to a post, giving her my cudgel. I'm swelling just thinking about it. Oh, the fun we're going to have. Let me tell you, the last time I took a bribe in the form of a Jadan girl—'

'Just stop,' Split said quietly, finally turning around, all the composure he'd gathered since Gilly's gone.

'It's okay, Split,' I said. 'Let's get on our way. He won't be able to follow us in those bindings.'

'Absolutely. On our way.' The Pedlar sucked in a breath,

puffing out his cheeks as he picked up the large rock the other lawman had broken his arm over and moved next to Shilah. Split gently brushed her aside with one arm, so he could loom behind the bound-up Khatfist, raising the stone high.

'Excuse me, dear,' Split said, his eyes on fire.

Then he brought the stone down with all his wrath, splitting open the Khatfist's skull with a single blow.

The reaction was explosive. Split lifted his weapon and stepped sideways.

The second blow was just as violent.

We buried the bodies.

Two pools of blood marked the sand.

Split insisted on keeping the rock.

# Chapter Eleven

'Well I'll squeeze puss from an old wound and sit on a pile of bleached bones,' Split cursed under his breath, grabbing the parchment with Shilah's likeness off the wall and squeezing with such fury that I thought he might set it aflame. The Wanted Scroll was just one of many that featured Shilah's picture, all within view of our hiding place behind the hovel. They were tacked up all over the port, littering the walls and signs and even a few Pedlar carts near the entrance to the Great Bridge, so everyone would know our faces. A quick glance across the main corridor allowed me to see a few Cam scrolls and at least a dozen Micah scrolls as well.

'They beat us here,' Split continued. 'These blasted things are everywhere!'

A part of me was flattered that the Khat's scribes would waste so much paper and ink on our images, although I still couldn't figure out how it had been done. I had to blink away my light-headedness at seeing my drawn face staring back at me. The scrolls peppering the walls of the buildings were all uniform, perfect copies of each other, all drawn up with our likenesses, and really the only difference from reality was that their creators had somehow skewed our faces to look menacing and evil.

The Pyramid obviously held inventions to which the rest of the Khatdom was not privy – the Khats always snatched up the best minds for themselves – and I could only imagine the beautiful slab of machinery that had produced these papers with such swift and perfect abundance. The images were rather accurate, and if I ever had ample time in a tinkershop again, I'd try and figure out the process. Such a thing would come in handy when trying to spread truth.

We had made our way to the port city surrounding the Great Erridian Bridge. I understood these shabby half-communities popped up around all of the Great Noble Bridges not only out of convenience, but out of sheer necessity. Fruit merchants, Imbiberies, brothels, Coldbaths, fishmongers, and temples were just some of the attractions for weary Noble travellers who intended to cross the Singe.

Even though, as far as I knew, Cold was only Cried in Paphos, the Khatdom's major cities were still numerous and spread out. Crossing the Singe was necessary for merchants who wanted to expand their businesses and work their way towards higher house status. The Priests had taught us that the Great Bridges had all been erected long ago, stout, strong, and glorious to behold. Monuments to the power of the Khat. They were wide enough to fit three caravan carts side by side, the raised stone easily spanning the boiling waters.

There seemed to be a problem at the port, however.

The massive doors to the bridge were barred shut, the jostling crowd of travellers bottlenecking before a line of armoured guards standing in front. Our group kept to the back, hidden behind a clay hovel, watching the irate travellers waving Noble tokens and yelling vulgar things at the guards, including insults regarding the integrity of their mothers' bedroom affairs. A few of the merchants had regular-sized camels to help carry their wares, but most of the travellers had their own Jadans instead, burdened, chained, and with signs of recent beatings.

I wished I had enough spare Abbs to sneak one into each Jadan pocket.

I vowed that one day I would.

Split's blasphemous rant about the Wanted Scrolls went unnoticed in the mess of noise, but we were still conspicuous just being so close to our likenesses. The headscarves and thin disguises that Gilly had bestowed would only do so much if any of the merchants decided to take a closer look. We needed to scatter to a more deserted section of the Singe as fast as possible, perhaps to the next closest Great Bridge – which belonged to House Swarn, according to Shilah's map.

Cam reached around the side of the hovel, peeled another Wanted Scroll off the wall, whispering as he held it up to my face. 'You're much uglier in person, Mic—'

Shilah coughed and snatched the parchment out of Cam's hands. She folded it in half, tossing it on the ground. 'Idiot. Don't draw attention.'

'Relax, no one's going to pick us out over all these people,' Cam said beneath his floppy hat, yellow hair tucked up underneath.

Shilah's eyes widened with a conspiratorial look, gesturing to the scroll on the ground with a quick nod of her head. She mouthed: 'Name.'

Cam's face scrunched with confusion, and then lit up with understanding. 'Ah, you're right. We shouldn't draw attention. No looking at the names on the scrolls.'

Shilah slapped her forehead with her palm.

Split grumbled under his breath, his fingers scratching his thigh. Ever since burying the dead Khatfist bodies, Split had been itching his leg almost nonstop, his little finger wiggling into his ear during any reprieves.

Shilah put a hand on my shoulder. 'We need to move. They're obviously watching for us.'

'And go where?' Split nearly growled, his eyes verging on madness. 'Crossing the Singe is the only way to continue the Coldmarch. And if they are watching *this* bridge, then I guarantee they're watching all the bridges, and they're going to find you two, and—'

'We find another way North,' Shilah said.

The bridge doors suddenly opened enough for a man dressed in white silk to sneak through, his high hat decorated with a silver Erridian crest.

A bulbous merchant with a loose neck shouted at the brightly dressed arrival, his thick chins flapping as if to underscore his sentiment. 'You can't shut down the bridge, you fools! We have to get to the other side of the Singe! Are you going to pay transport boats for all of our carts?'

A High Noblewoman with more skin-gloss than face chimed in. 'If I miss the annual Chosenball in Marlea, I'll have all your heads on next year's appetizer platters!'

'We supposed to swim?' a crotchety Nobleman barked, waving his gemstone-encrusted cane and smacking the shins of his personal Jadans hunched at his side. 'We supposed to ride across on slave backs? Because I'm not using *my* slaves for that! Give me Erridian slaves to drown.'

The armoured guards just stood at the entrance to the Great Bridge, unfazed. Their pikes gleamed in the harsh Sunlight as the man in white squeezed to the front, his face pinched, eyes hidden behind ostentatious golden glasses. The eyewear was similar to Cam's, but embellished with jewels. I could hear the Singe roaring from behind the walls, steaming and angry.

I'd always wanted to see a Great Bridge, as each one was supposed to be an incredible feat of tinkering and determination. The High Noble families who controlled the bridges took credit for the marvels, toting their might and influence for besting the river, but it was obvious that the bridges would have been built by Jadan hands. Nobles wouldn't risk their lives constructing such a thing, constantly under threat of being scorched or drowned or lost in the dangerous waters as the slabs of stone and metal were set in place. No, the bridges would have been built under threat of whippings and death, it would have been the Jadan people who'd bested the river. The Jadan people who'd suffered to find a way across. And considering the marvellous invention pressing against my side, one that could actually make Cold, it was going to be the Jadan people who were going to best the Drought.

'My apologies to all who have chosen to use this, the most venerable Erridian Bridge!' the man dressed in white said, loose sleeves flapping over his arms. His words came out just as pinched as his face, compact and nasal. 'We are working as fast as we can to minimize the threat to the Khatdom, so please be patient!'

'Who cares about some slave runaways!' some Noble in the crowd shouted. 'Not all of us suck all our Cold from the Pyramid's teat! We have jobs to do!'

The man in white bristled at this, making sure his tall hat wasn't tilted in the slightest. 'Now now. A decree is a decree. Please stay calm as duties are fulfilled. Seeing as the Khat has his best five on the job, I imagine the threats will be captured in no time.' The man offered a patter of a laugh. 'We will be providing Cold Oolong tea and figs for everyone delayed at the port, free of charge, while—'

'Let us through!' someone shouted. 'We don't want your damned slave food and piss tea!'

All eyes were on the bridge's defender, which meant it was time to make our move. If the Wanted Scrolls with our likenesses had made it here, the hounds, and the Vicaress, and whoever the 'best five' were, must be close by.

'Come on,' I said, rubbing a hand across Picka's fuzzy back. She nuzzled against me, offering a low humming sound that reminded me of the crank-fans I used to make. 'We'll try the House Swarn Bridge.'

Cam nodded. 'Or maybe we can wave down a boat or something.'

'If you were a ship's captain,' Shilah said with a cluck of her tongue, 'would you risk anchoring your boat over the rocks to pick up a few Jadans and a camel? I don't think so.'

'I would anchor for two stranded *High* Nobles,' Cam countered. '*And* the greatest Jadan Inventor ever to walk the sands. *And* a stunning Jadan girl with dark skin like fine mahogany.'

Even amidst the complimentary words, Shilah looked ready to take Cam's floppy hat and pull it down over his ears until it ripped in half.

'We'll see what happens,' I said, holding the Coldmaker close. 'Most importantly we need to get out of here, now. We'll stay along the banks and make a new plan.'

I nodded deeper into the shadows of the building and began backing away. Cam and Shilah followed suit, but Split remained still, his hands clenched into fists, eyes lost amongst the boiling crowd.

'Split,' I said. 'It's okay. We've got water and food, and there's no guarantee they've got guards or scrolls at the next bridge, too.'

A tear dripped along the Pedlar's cheek as he scratched his thigh so hard I heard the fabric rip. 'Hookmen. That glib bastard is talking about the Hookmen.'

I turned my eyes to Shilah, trying my best not to faint.

She looked as though all the blood had just drained from her face, her hand absently going to her braid.

'No,' I said. 'They're not real.'

Hookmen were just legends made up to scare Jadan kids. From the way Levi used to put it in the barracks, Hookmen were half-snake, half-person, trained by Sun himself to taste the scent of a Jadan anywhere in the Khatdom. They'd slither under you without any warning and drag you under the sands. The Hookman had a special poison that made it so you didn't need air. You'd be trapped under the weight of the dunes, and they would nibble away at you, piece by piece, forever.

'Oh, they're Sun-damned real,' Split snarled, his fingers flexing wildly. He looked more dismayed than he had after he'd killed the Khatfists. 'I promise you that they're real. And they're coming for Meshua.'

Cam slunk further into the darkness, his body disappearing in shadow.

'Cam,' Shilah said, sneaking around him and cutting off his retreat. 'What do you know?'

'Come on,' Cam said, not meeting her gaze and pointing to the crowd of frustrated merchants fleeing the closed bridge, headed for the next. 'Now or never. We can blend in with the group, and no one will be the wiser.'

Split rubbed a hand under his nose, staring at the crust of dried blood. 'He's right, let's move.'

'Camlish,' Shilah said, for once not standing tall. 'Are they real?'

'Yes,' Cam said. Once again he had shouldered more than his fair share of supplies; already his back was settling into a crook that was all too familiar. 'My father has boasted of using them before. I've never seen one, but apparently they never fail.'

Split grabbed Picka's reins and led her out into the glaring Sunlight, the rest of us filtering behind as the bulk of the crowd swept by. Shilah kept pressed up against my side, and I knew it must have been my imagination, but I thought I could feel her tremble. We met up with a few other Pedlars and some silk merchants, their grumbles and threats towards the Erridians creating a light smattering of noise in which to hide. A few Noblewomen holding bright white parasols held out their Closed Eye necklaces towards Shilah and me, but it seemed more out of habit than anything else. It was because we were Jadans, not because we were fugitives.

'Cam,' I whispered, glancing at a paper picture of myself. This Micah was scowling from a signpost, looking ready to rip out Noble throats with his teeth. 'If they're real are they monsters?'

Cam swallowed hard, pulling the floppy hat further over his face.

# Chapter Twelve

Picka knocked her toes against the wet stone, braying loud enough to mute the sizzling waves crashing against the shore. We'd been travelling along the banks of the Singe with exactly the hope that the turbulent waters might mask our scent and sounds, but the disproportionately loud camel was ruining our plan. If something unnatural were hunting us, the task was being made easier with each explosive whinny Picka blurted out.

'Quit it, girl!' Split shouted with a scowl, readjusting his grip on the handles of the goods cart, hoisting the wheels over the next gap in the rocks. 'You're not even dragging this blasted thing any more! I'm doing all the work!'

Picka answered with a resounding razzle of her tongue.

'She's got such a big coat,' Cam said, wiping his forehead free of sweat and the hot spray gathered from the Singe. 'Let's stop for a bit. Shilah's got that knife, maybe we can give Picka a haircut?'

Split spun around – almost losing control of the cart – aiming an accusatory point at Cam's face. 'You touch my camel I cut off all *your* hair.'

'Just a suggestion.' Cam held up his hands and ran one

through his locks. 'Besides, I don't think I'd mind that too much. I've been told I have a very shapely head. And the fashion for young High Nobles now is keeping the head shaved because it draws focus right to the eyes, and when they're sparkling blue like mine—'

Split waved him quiet and turned back to the slippery rocks. An annoyed grunt followed, and I wasn't sure if the sound had come from the Pedlar or Picka.

Shilah gave Cam a gentle nod. 'It was a good suggestion.'

Cam blushed, hiding his face under the parasol.

'Split,' I said, tired and parched. 'Maybe we should finally stop for a while. I think we could all use a break and some Cold.' I knocked my knuckles against the Coldmaker.

Split pointed up, bringing attention to the fading Sunlight. But then he jerked his hand back to the handle of the cart after it nearly slipped again. 'I don't think that's wise, Meshua.'

'Don't call me—'

'Spout.' Split actually sounded sincere. 'I just mean, even if the next bridge is closed, we should try to at least find shelter somewhere before nightfall. Maybe even try proper lodging if we have to.'

'You really think the safest place to hide is near lots of people?' Shilah asked. She was once again next to Picka, giving the camel long scratches under her chin.

'There is no ruddy safest place to hide.' Split picked up the pace, wrenching a back wheel out of a crack in the rock, a small black tongue rising from the rocks with a hiss. 'Not with what's coming after us. I just don't know what else to do.'

'How can they know where we are?' I asked. 'We're so far from Paphos.'

Split sighed, keeping his pace. 'We're going to need another of your miracles, Spout. So please see if you can get the Crier to give us a sign.'

'I don't actually talk to the Crier,' I said, not wanting to mention the visions I'd had while under the wool hat. 'I'm not Meshua.'

Split threw down the handles of the cart, turning back at me. Steaming spray from the river continued to fleck his cheeks, almost as if it was attracted to the Pedlar's budding fury. 'You don't want to be Meshua, then you don't get to make damned Ice!'

Cam stepped next to me, holding up his palms. 'Easy—'

Split's pinky wiggled into his ear, his face distorting with rage. 'You don't think I want that? You don't think I want you *not* to be Meshua?' His eyes bored down once again on the Coldmaker. 'After everything I loved was taken away I was perfectly fine with the prophecies in the book being lies! If the world was screwed to begin with, then at least it all made sense. The Crier wasn't real, so he couldn't help us. End of story. But now, if the secret all along has been Jadan tears—' Split gathered a glob of spit and sent it flying into the Singe, waving two knuckles at the Sun.

I had no idea what to do. I only lowered my head.

Split made a heart-wrenching *arrrrghh* sound before gathering the handles of the cart again and wrenching the wheels across the cracks in the rocks. 'Just. I'm sorry. I just don't want to watch the same thing— Let's go.'

Picka came up to me and licked the palm of my injured wrist, but I pulled away.

I couldn't bring myself to meet Shilah's eyes as we made our way down the shoreline. Cam came up to me and clapped me on the back, whispering: 'Ignore him, he's just coming down from that stuff.' And I nodded, but what the Pedlar had said had a ring of truth to it. If the Crier was real, why wait so long to let someone discover the secret of making Cold? Did that mean every Jadan before the invention of the machine was truly destined to be enslaved?

What was the purpose of such misery?

'Sorry,' Split said at last, keeping his eyes on the slippery rocks. 'I didn't mean to go off like that.'

'I don't want an apology,' I said quietly. 'I want to know what happened to you. I want to know why the Coldmarch shut down. About Langria.'

Split shook his head, the corners of his eyes wet. 'I can't.'

'Rules of the Coldmarch, Split,' Cam said, cutting in. 'If the Shepherd has important information, they have to share it with the flock.'

Split scoffed, yanking the cart back on its way. 'Like you know anything about the Coldmarch, *Tavor*. Now let's move.'

We travelled in silence for some time, Cam fuming at my back, and I thought I could hear stabs of sound in the distance, dark and low. I decided they were just my imagination, my mind playing tricks with fear. Picka continued to skip along, her knobbly legs taking her all over the rocks. She was putting herself in danger of slipping into the waters, but Shilah held her reins tightly, making sure the beast was safe.

'Why are we called a flock?' I asked Split after a while, thinking I could start with something simple and work my way up.

'It's what a group of sheep were called, before the Great Drought,' he said in even tones. 'And a Shepherd led them around.'

'Did you say a *group* of sheep?' Cam asked.

'Back then there were dozens of sheep to each Shepherd,' Split said. 'Hundreds. Countless. Now there's probably only a few dozen sheep left in the whole Khatdom. And most of them are in the Khat's menageries at the Southern Cry Temple. As I understand it, the amount of Cold required to keep those animals alive is staggering.' Split waited for another loud bray from Picka to settle. 'But the Khat has got to keep a fresh supply of wool to dye black and kill you Jadans with. The irony is just too sweet to pass up.'

I thought back to my time beneath the wool hat, the absolute torture of the fabric as it squeezed every drop of water and Cold out of me. Anger surged in my stomach thinking about all my brothers and sisters who were probably getting the hat today back in Paphos, and my jaw clenched. 'The Khat's going to wish the wool *had* killed me.'

'I'm liking the fire, Spout,' Shilah said, touching the knife at her thigh. 'Going to need it if you're serious about that revolution.'

My cheeks grew warm, and I tapped the Coldmaker hanging from my shoulder, giving her a warm smile. 'I'll just stick to inventing. I've got you for all the fighting and revolution stuff.'

'Also for inventing,' Shilah said, the edges of her face more prominent for a moment.

'Huh?'

'Inventing,' she repeated, straightening her back, this time attitude seeping into her voice. 'I mean, you weren't alone when—'

'FLAME-LICKING DUNG-GUZZLING MAGGOTS!' Split's knuckles went white on the handles. 'You've got to be kidding me!'

The Pedlar's outburst made Picka's outrageous grunts seems like quiet whispers in the dark, and I nearly tumbled back in surprise. Cam lost his balance, falling to a knee on the stone, but Shilah stayed straight and tall.

I hopped across the stones, rounding the cart so I could see what Split was reacting over. 'What's the— Oh.' My stomach plummeted. 'Sun damn.'

Split kicked a heavy stone through the brush of boilweed and into the Singe's tributary, which happened to be directly in our way. The rock splashed up some of the white-capped waters, which we'd never be able to jump across. This block-ading arm of the River was a few paces wide, but it cut off our path completely, perpendicular to the main body of the Singe. There would be no way to cross the sizzling waters, and my neck craned West, following the stream across the deadlands to see if there were any sort of boulders in the waters that could be used as stepping stones. Or if the trib-utary dipped underground. As far as I could see, there was nothing.

We were stuck.

Echoes of barking and horns reached our ears, coming from behind us, from the direction of the Erridian Bridge.

So the sounds had been real.

We were dead.

Sights of the Great Erridian Bridge were no longer possible after all the distance we'd travelled, which meant the distant noises of savage beasts were too close to be coming from the port marketplace.

The Vicaress and her hounds must have tracked us into the sands.

She must have been led.

Hookmen.

Split paused and then burst out laughing. The fire in the sky was draining, but I knew darkness wouldn't hide us. We were truly and utterly doomed. I had no more inventions prepared, no materials with which to tinker, and the only obstacles that stood in our enemy's way were Shilah's knife and some slick rocks that might make the hounds slip.

Split's chuckles were dark, bubbling up from somewhere far deeper than his doughy belly. 'Here to complete the set, I guess.'

Cam's face had gone wan. Shilah's wheels were turning fast, her blade already unstrapped and gleaming.

I sat down on the rocks and tried to tune out Picka's furious whinnies. She must have been able to hear the snarling of the hounds before we could.

'Dump the goods from the cart,' Shilah ordered. 'We can make a raft.'

'It's too damned thin to float, and will never carry us all,' Split said, still laughing. He reached into an inner pocket of his tunic and pulled out a vial I hadn't known about, shaking the grey powder. Uncapping it, he poured out a bit of the Dream onto his finger and snorted it all in one deep sniff before I could protest. Sighing with relief, he jiggled the vial in each of our directions. 'No Droughtweed to make it pleasant, but anyone else want to at least be numb for death?'

I shook my head, although I was very tempted. 'What else?'

'Spout,' Cam said, his voice nearly breaking. 'What if we just put the *machine* on the raft and float it downriver so at least—'

'Hold on,' I said, raising a hand, an idea flashing in the back of my mind.

I slipped the bag off the Coldmaker and let the Sun take one last look at the machine that deserved to be its undoing.

Shilah came to my side and touched my elbow. 'What are you thinking?'

I motioned to the Coldmaker, and then brought our hands to the switch together. 'Do it with me.'

We turned the machine on, stirring up its magic.

Not magic, I reminded myself. Tinkering.

No. It *was* magic.

Perhaps nothing as holy as a miracle, but here was a machine that proved why our people were in fact just as chosen as everyone else. Here was an invention that proved the Opened Eye, and could break every kind of suppression in the Khatdom. Here at my feet was our salvation; a salvation that was not only earned, but necessary. There had to be a reason why the machine was allowed to exist, why we were able to get it this far. It couldn't all be some accident.

In the distance, the barks were now deeper and more menacing.

Shilah pressed closer against me as the air grew strange and turbulent around us, the machine making a new Abb. She grabbed a fistful of Cam's shirt and pulled him close as well, the three of us huddling around the Coldmaker as it hummed.

The gold gathered at the catch-point, and the wind picked up, all the air around us dropping in temperature. I glanced at the offshoot of the Singe blocking our path, which seemed to have grown angrier, the white bubbles popping at an alarming rate.

The new golden Abb grew from the size of a pinhead to a Sobek egg in a matter of moments, the shine enough to allow me to relax a little, the knot in my stomach unravelling. While the Abb continued to pile on itself, the machine humming like all was well in the World Cried, I grabbed two Abbs from the bag's pouch – there were six left in total – and took Shilah over to the rushing waters blocking our path.

I closed my eyes and tried to say the words from my heart instead of just my throat, which was difficult because that particular path through my chest felt jammed with fear. 'Shemma hares lahyim criyah Meshua ris yim slochim.'

Drop the bucket.

I gave one Abb to Shilah.

'Together,' I said.

She nodded and we let them go as one.

The surface of the water buckled as the gold broke through, the beads shocking an entire section of the offshoot. The intense crackling sound echoed across the rocks and water, loud and violent, and in the distance the hounds' barks answered with a rousing curiosity. Crystal arms of Ice reached out from the impact points of the gold beads, snaking in a hundred directions at once, broadening into something strong and solid. The Singe didn't seem to know how to react, its waters only adding to the phenomenon, the hot white bubbles smoothing out and becoming slick and clear. The cloud of white mist rising off the waters hissed upwards, obscuring the sky with ethereal waves, until the fading Sun could no longer see us.

My heart surged with hope as the platform of Ice flexed outwards from the shore of the offshoot before the current could pull it away. In a matter of moments, the white blockage spanned to both shores, its crystalline claws digging into the rocks and sand and boilweed roots on each side and gripping tightly. The rushing waters bowed to the Ice, dipping underneath the slick mass.

And just like that, we had a way across.

'Come on!' I shouted over the hissing waters, which pushed at the edges of our small Ice bridge. I should have been shocked, frozen over with awe, but the Singe's reaction to the Abbs didn't surprise me. It felt like something I always knew would be true.

It was *my* people who'd bested the River before.

'We need to move fast!' I shouted.

Picka gave a happy grumble, looking at me as if she wasn't that stunned either, her toes clopping her way across the glossy rocks.

'Shivers.' Cam gulped hard, swaying on his feet. 'And Frosts.'

Shilah slowly tied the knife back beneath her shorts, the lower half of her face dropping in awe, her eyes remaining hard.

Split just blinked slowly, staring at the Ice mound. His beady eyes had become so wide that I could finally see that they were a delightful green.

'Come on!' I yelled again, grabbing the Coldmaker, leaving

it humming. I closed up the lips of the bag and threw the strap around my neck, positioning the machine at my stomach instead of my side; this way I could pull the cart behind me. Split seemed to be in no state to bear a burden. Even through the canvas bag I could feel the intense Cold caught in the bronze walls of the machine, sending a shock through my body.

I took hold of the cart's handles and began heaving it towards the Ice.

I thought I heard Split gasp about 'Meshua' over the crackling, but I didn't have time to argue.

Shilah moved around to the back of the cart and began pushing until we scraped through the rocks and reached the crystal platform. I turned to offer her a nod of thanks, and when our stares connected something strange passed my way.

It almost felt like a challenge.

Confused, I turned back to the Ice and put a foot out to see if the bridge was even crossable. Stepping down with half of my weight, the mist rushing up over my leg, I found the opaque material to be solid, although it did have a bit of give. The block probably didn't stretch all the way to the bottom of the waters, and I had a feeling it was holding steady mostly by the shore.

We had to act fast. The Ice would get eaten from the bottom up.

'Careful, Spout!' Cam called. 'Are you sure—'

My first step out nearly sent me toppling sideways, my foot slipping out from underneath me. Right away I realized that I couldn't treat the Ice like rock or sand or metal. This material was slick and ancient, and demanded more respect than that.

I gave the Ice a nod of apology and then stepped on with care, dragging the cart behind me. I prayed the whole thing didn't give and send me sputtering to the bottom of the waters, my bones being boiled on the way down, although I would have bet a swift death would be better than what the Hookmen and hounds had planned.

Shilah continued to push the cart from behind so the burden wasn't entirely on me. The crackling of the Ice was heavy in my ears, and I held my breath with each gentle step I took. Slow and careful.

Three.

Five.

Seven.

Before I knew it I was across, back on solid rock.

Still far from safe.

I turned and found Shilah suspended in the middle of the Ice now, her back straighter than ever, gripping on to the rear of the cart for support. Her face was steely and determined, and I rolled the cart the rest of the way, bringing her over to me. She slid off the Ice and grabbed the back of my neck, placing our foreheads together.

She smelled of sand and Ice and sweat, and too soon we'd broken contact.

Cam and Split exchanged a look from the other side of the tributary. If I hadn't known better, I would have thought Cam was disappointed. The hounds were getting louder, and the rest of our group had no choice but to cross.

Some of the frosty mist was lingering in Shilah's hair, and, without thinking, my fingers touched her glistening braid, enjoying the cool sensation of her rough locks. She raised a coy eyebrow, and I blinked with embarrassment, backing away and setting the Coldmaker down beside the cart.

'Get them over here,' I told her, and then began frantically digging through the cart for the large rock. I still didn't understand why Split had wanted to keep such a horrendous reminder, but now I was grateful. The North side of the offshoot had only boilweed and pebbles along the banks, and I needed something heavy that wouldn't shatter on impact.

Shilah turned and began coaxing our remaining flock across the bridge, assuring them that it was safe. Even over the hiss and crackle of the River nibbling the edges of the Ice, I could hear the barks getting more real and ravenous. I could see the flicker of a fiery blade cresting a distant dune, and from the multiple roving shadows, it looked as if it wasn't just the Vicaress marching towards us.

I tossed out linens and parasols and jewellery boxes, finally finding the hefty stone resting in the bottom corner of the cart. I drew it out, my fingers trembling as they brushed the red stains over its surface.

I had killed today.

Even though Split was the one who put stone to flesh, I hadn't stopped him.

I was a murderer too.

And I regretted nothing.

I lifted the stone over my head, testing the weight as Cam hunched over on all fours like a beetle as he crossed the Ice, scurrying in a frantic manner. His eyes appeared almost entirely closed as he scuttled, but he made it to our shore. He rolled onto his back on the muddy shoreline, his chest rapidly rising and falling.

'Sorry,' he wheezed out, looking at me with profound relief. 'It's not that I'm scared of drowning. I'm just really scared of drowning.'

'We all are,' I said. Then I looked across the offshoot at Split, who was scratching his thigh and holding Picka's reins loosely in one hand. In no way did he look prepared to cross.

'You go on without us!' Split called out, scratching his thigh. 'We can stall them. I can talk my way out of this!'

'They'll kill you!' Shilah screamed. 'And we need you! Get moving right now!'

Split shook his head, pulling Picka's snout against his stomach. The dwarf camel brayed and stamped her feet, looking just as impatient with the Pedlar as the rest of us. 'I can't do it,' Split said. 'Take care of Baba Levante! Don't let her get wet, and don't worry, I can talk my way out of—'

Shilah marched back across the Ice, her step firm on the slick surface. The crystal platform had more give this time, and I knew it wouldn't be long before the whole thing got washed away by the current.

Shilah crossed the Ice and shoved a hand in Split's shirt, taking out the Dream vial. She turned and hurled the powder as far as she could into the Singe.

Split groaned. His expression glazed over, and he mumbled something under his breath.

Shilah undid her knife, the tip hovering right over Split's throat. 'I swear to the Crier above I'll slash you a hundred different ways unless you get to the other side. You're a part of our group, and you're not abandoning us.'

Split went to say something, but Shilah jabbed the tip of the blade into his shoulder. She pierced skin and left the blade there for a moment, before wrenching it back. Blood came out with the metal.

Split screamed, a hand going to his shoulder, but his eyes came back into focus. Nodding at Shilah, he took Picka's reins and began scraping his way across the Ice, leading the camel at his side. Shilah was right behind him. The hissing at the edges of the tiny bridge grew louder, as the camel and Pedlar weighed a considerable amount more than the rest of us combined, but the Ice managed to hold, and after a tense moment everyone was on the right side.

The hounds finally crested the dunes, their barks needles in my ears.

The beasts were far more horrible than I could have imagined.

Their sleek bodies were inky black, and had no fur. They moved at a terrifying speed, muscles rippling beneath their skin. Eyes black as a starless night bored into us, and their mouths frothed over with drool and hunger.

Picking up the pace, they whipped across the rocks and sand, their legs impossibly fast.

They were headed right for us.

Shilah grabbed a handful of my shirt. 'Do it, Spout!'

I brought the rock up and smashed it over and over against the edge of the Ice.

It wouldn't break.

Heart and bile in my throat, I kept smashing. It felt like trying to cut a diamond with breath. I put every ounce of strength I had into each blow, chipping away small shards, but it wasn't enough. The hounds were closing in, snarling. My injured wrist exploded with pain, but the bridge began to groan under the stress of my attack.

Shilah dropped to her knees at my side and flipped her knife upside down, slamming the Ice with the ornate handle. Time was running out. The hounds were thrashing their way across the land, close enough that I could see their gleaming fangs, stained red. They didn't care about the Ice or the offshoot. They wanted blood. They weren't going to stop.

A fiery slash moved across the dunes, in the hounds' wake.

The Vicaress.

Cam grabbed a small bust from Split's cart, bringing it down with shocking brutality. Chunks of Ice were demolished. His face was caught in a vicious sneer and he kept smashing the bust down at the shore. The cracks were astounding. Shilah and I joined him with all our might. Boiling water erupted from beneath, spraying our arms and hands and faces, burning, seething.

The Ice screamed in protest.

The hounds were seconds away. Their shoulders bulged.

Their mouths snarled. I could see death dripping from their snouts.

Cam yelled as he swung. Shilah howled like a wraith. I was swinging so hard my whole left arm went numb. Picka was all panic now, her bleating deafening. Split finally dropped beside us, smashing down with his fists and crying out.

The Ice clung with its last hope.

Cam raised the bust over his head, and with a warrior cry he slammed the marble head down once more.

The Ice broke free.

The Singe wrenched the last of the bridge loose, the resulting crack sounding like an entire caravan cart being ripped in two.

The explosive noise was enough to halt most of the hounds, but one had already leaped, snarling and gnashing its teeth as it arced through the air. Its sharp claws pierced the Ice just as the whole bridge spun sideways and washed down the offshoot.

The terrifying creature fell flat against the Ice and made a surprisingly tender whimper as it was swept away.

We were saved.

Shilah collapsed sideways onto me as she gasped for air, but she managed to hold the knife out just in case.

Cam fell to the shore, clutching the bust close.

Split stared at his bleeding palms.

The other hounds barked and howled at the far shoreline, gnashing their teeth and clawing scars into the rock face, but noise was their only way to attack.

Cam was breathing so hard I thought his lungs might fall out and float down the tributary as well. But he was alive and unharmed except for a few water burns on his hands.

I kissed my fingers and held them to the sky.

Split raised two knuckles towards the fading Sun. 'That's right! Keep your beasts over there, you overgrown firecracker! Meshua, you bastard!'

We slowly backed away from the shore, keeping our eyes across the span of water at our approaching enemies. The Vicaress and her army didn't seem to be in a hurry, staying in formation as they moved.

A group of sleek-armoured guards trailed in her wake, their pikes high and their swords polished. The poles didn't have blades at the end, but rather rounded tips made of what looked like cloth. I couldn't fathom the use of such things, but at least the men were regular guards and not Hookmen.

The Vicaress was up front, her black dress clinging around her curves, ambling with a grace that shouldn't have been possible on such terrain. Even Shilah looked clumsy by comparison.

As the Vicaress approached, sauntering too slowly for the occasion, the hounds quickly dropped their hind legs, going silent without so much as a command. The Vicaress slithered between them, patting one beast on the head. Then she poised herself at the edge of the shoreline.

We looked at each other across the boiling waters, close enough that I could see the startling blue in her eyes, shining even in the fading light. Her dark hair was coiffed with golden pins, each one tipped with the Closed Eye, and her lip grease was precise. Everything about her added to her regal and stunning nature, but I knew all that beauty was just a clever disguise, allowing the true form underneath to roam the World Cried unchecked.

The hounds were grotesque, but the Vicaress was the real demon.

'You lost the Khat a favourite pet,' she said quietly, eyes following the floating hound down the tributary. 'Not good, Camlish Tavor.'

'Well, you lost me an uncle, you damned bitch!' Cam shouted back, the veins popping out on his forehead.

The Vicaress ignored Cam, her face sidling back towards

me. Standing just across the tributary was the woman who'd slaughtered one of my closest friends. Here was the monster who'd killed my father, just to make a point. I should have been consumed by such a righteous fury that I could have walked across the water and added another bloody tally to Split's stone.

Yet there I lingered, trembling. I was a scared little boy once more.

Perhaps she'd killed more of me than she'd left alive.

A smile curled onto the Vicaress's face as the army of guards filed in at her back.

'Hey, Little Builder,' she said to me, waving her flaming dagger in front of her face. 'Been looking for you.'

I buckled.

Little Builder is what Abb used to call me. I don't know if my old Barracksmaster Gramble would have told her that, or if it had come from my friend Moussa when she'd tortured him, or if she'd cut it out of the source himself before she took Abb's life.

Either way, it cast my soul into darkness.

Spout was gone.

There was a stranger left standing in my body.

'Nice trick, but you wasted the Frost,' the Vicaress said. 'You have nothing left.'

'You don't know shit!' Split called in a happy voice, his eyes glazed over once again. 'We have the Coldmaker!'

The Vicaress glared him down. 'Is that what you think, Split of House Suth? Where's your family?'

Split took a breath so quickly that it contained a slight squeak.

The Vicaress licked one of her gloved fingers and pressed it against the fiery blade, igniting a small sizzle. 'I know who you are, *Pedlar*. You think the Crier would hold anything back from me? First you breed with one slave, and now you try to protect two more. The Hookmen should have hung you from the Pyramid next to your abomination of a daughter.'

And there it was.

Things clicked into place, and I felt a well of sorrow carve into my stomach. No wonder the Pedlar had been in such a state when we'd found him. No wonder he hadn't believed in the Crier or the Coldmarch any more. How could he be anything other than wretched?

Split couldn't meet the Vicaress's gaze. Instead he buried his hand in the cart, tears forming at the corners of his eyes.

'You don't have anything to do with the Crier,' Shilah snarled across the gap.

The Vicaress gave a lazy shrug. 'The words of Jadan whores don't bother me. I know what that symbol on your arm is covering up.'

'Don't you dare call her that!' Cam tried to shout, still struggling to find breath.

'What should bother you is the fact that you're stuck,' Shilah called across the water, pulling her sleeve down and hiding the rest of the Opened Eye tattoo. 'You have nothing. And we'll be long gone by the time you figure out how to get over here.'

One of the hounds rumbled a low growl. The Vicaress stabbed the beast under the chin. She pulled her blade back so fast I'd have thought it my imagination if not for the pained whimper. Then the Vicaress stabbed the mewling beast behind its left ear. This time the hound made no sound at all, but cowered down against the rocks. Now that the mist had cleared, I was able to make out the scarring on its black skin. All the hounds were scarred. The Vicaress must have tortured them as well.

'I wouldn't say I have nothing,' the Vicaress said, looking over her blazing blade as if to check that the fire was unharmed. 'I have the Crier. And the Crier has whatever he wants.'

The Vicaress turned and sauntered back to her line of guards. They stood at the ready as she brushed past each of them, touching her blade to their metal poles. A piece of her fire began to climb, quickly circling the shaft of each pike. I had to squint, but it looked as if there was some sort of wick wrapped around each pole.

The Vicaress stood back and admired the rising buds of her flame. The guards' faces were stiff, the muscles in their forearms flexing underneath their armour. I yanked Cam and Shilah around behind the goods cart in case the pikes were some sort of weapon that could fire at us, but the guards kept them pointed at the sky.

The flame on the first pike reached the top, and the orb exploded with a sharp crack. A gigantic trail of red shot up into the sky, blasting upwards at a speed I didn't know was possible, straining through the air and rising to a point at least as high as the Khat's Pyramid. Cam almost toppled over, and Split clapped his hands over Picka's ears.

The other fires climbed to the top of the remaining pikes. Consecutive blasts sent a dozen more trails into the sky, the spectacle so bright and shocking I imagined it could be seen all the way back in Paphos.

The red streaks of light lingered in the sky, the bars of a giant, fiery cage. Eventually the trails reached their peaks, arching back down towards the sands. I thought maybe the light was going to make its way down to us, attacking us from above, but after returning a quarter of the way to the land, they fizzled and popped out of existence.

I blinked, the flashes of light leaving a scorching echo behind my eyelids. Leroi had taught me about flamepowders, how to mix them and pack them so they made colourful puffs, but at the time I had thought the technique no more than a banquet trick. The Inventor in me wanted to know the proportions the Vicaress had used.

The son in me wanted her dead.

Shilah's fingernails were piercing the skin of my arm. 'What do you—'

All of a sudden, there was another eruption from the North, this one coming from our side of the tributary.

I spun around, a plume rising in the distance. This was unsettling to say the least. The line shot straight up just like the others, but this one was a sickening yellow, electric at the edges. Right after, three more plumes raced into the sky. They were all the same abrasive colour, shooting up from behind the dunes.

I got to my feet and tried to gauge how soon we'd die.

At best, these new lights originated less than a few thousand paces away, which meant we didn't have long before the enemy closed in from the North.

'Four,' Shilah counted, her brows furrowing.

'Hookmen,' the Vicaress called in casual tones across the gap. 'You think this stream is going to save you, Little Builder? If *Meshua* was real, he'd know that the Crier doesn't leave things to chance.' She dipped a gloved finger into the waters, and let a few drops fall on the snout of the nearest hound. The monster whimpered, but didn't flinch away. 'I'll just stand here and watch. This should be a most satisfying end.'

The red plumes from the Vicaress began to drop back to the sands, sizzling as they plummeted. I presumed these streaks were calling the Hookmen from the bowels of the sands, showing them exactly where to slither to find their prey.

The Vicaress to the South.

The Singe to the East and West.

Monsters to the North.

Fear slammed into my chest.

# Chapter Thirteen

But so did a new idea.

My eyes flashed to the main body of the Singe, the boiling waters rough and wide and angry. I handed the bloody stone over to Cam as I stared the current down. 'Hold this.'

Cam's mouth was agape, but I gave him a reassuring look.

'Trust me,' I said, trying to sound confident. My new idea had a rather high chance of death, but if we stayed on the North shoreline, death was guaranteed. As far as I was concerned the odds were stacked in our favour.

I bent over the goods cart and tossed open the lips of the Coldmaker bag, revealing the machine. The Opened Eye I'd etched into the bronze stared back. The Coldmaker had stopped humming, so I assumed the vial of tears inside had finally gone dry.

On previous creations of Abbs, I hadn't wanted to strain the Frost, in case it had a breaking point. I always stopped the machine after a few moments, only letting a few tears cry out of the vial. But now they'd been falling on the Frost nonstop, exhausting its magic. It should have seemed like a slip-up, but now it appeared more like a secret plan the back of my mind had conjured without me.

I yanked the bag wider and saw the massive slab of gold at the catch-point. The bronze was painfully Cold against my knuckles as I wiggled the giant Abb free.

Shilah came up to my side, a dark grin on her face. 'What do you need from me?'

My hands trembled around the massive piece of Cold. 'Strength. Lots of strength.'

She leaned in and pressed her lips against my cheek. There was almost no pressure behind them, but they were warm, and she let them linger.

When she pulled away I handed her the Abb. 'And you hold this.'

I reached into the cart and found the rest of the rope I'd used to bind the Khatfist. Split brushed passed and dug his hands through the cart as well. He pulled out the case with the puppet inside, and ambled over to the banks of the Singe. Undoing the latches, he whispered something inside.

I had to ignore the crumbling Pedlar. I began uncoiling the rope. I just hoped there was enough.

'Are you planning on tying up the Hookmen?' Cam asked, hugging the bloody rock close to his chest. 'They're demons.'

'Demons?' the Pedlar interrupted, turning his head away from the case. 'They're worse than—'

'I don't think we can fight them with rope is all,' Cam said a bit louder, cutting Split off and shooting me a fearful look.

'Trust me,' I said.

I counted twenty paces of rope. Then I began making a 'cradleknot' at the end of the rope, the way Leroi had taught me. I looped the nest around the Abb, which was roughly the size of a small orangefruit. I doubled the cradle, tying it as tightly as I could.

Then I placed the Coldmaker, food bags, and waterskins – the essentials – out of the way. A strong heave, and I overturned the whole cart, sending the rest of the goods spilling onto the rocks.

I gave Cam a go-ahead look. 'Smash it, please.'

'Come again?' Cam asked.

'I saw what you've been hiding in you,' I said quietly, gesturing to the cart. 'We're going to need oars. So if you wouldn't mind, please smash the cart to pieces.'

Cam blinked. 'Did you say oars? Like oars that they have on boats?'

My fear had been overtaken by giddiness. Or perhaps madness. If we were going to die, we'd die with glory.

'Like they have on boats,' I said, testing the strength of the rope. 'And I would say at least four oars would be preferred.'

Shilah's eyebrow went up. 'So you're really going to . . .?'

'Absolutely,' I said under my breath.

Shilah nodded. 'My kind of partner.'

The hounds were still sitting patiently on their hind legs, their fangs hanging menacingly over their black lips.

The Vicaress's face grew suspicious. 'You can't fight the Hookmen, slaves! They know you! They *are* you!'

Cam picked up the bloodied stone and went to work destroying the cart. The cracks of wood elicited a flurry of snarls and barks from the hounds. The Vicaress hushed them quiet with a wave of her dagger.

Cam's forearms were starting to blister from where the boiling waters had splashed up, but he wasn't holding back.

The Vicaress began laughing, a smooth, serene howl. 'You have no idea what sort of creatures are descending upon you.'

'Not planning on fighting,' I said under my breath. 'Not yet.'

Split closed the puppet's case, held it over the waters, and set it adrift on the current. The case was buoyant, and the Singe's angry current snatched it away, taking it out into the centre waters before carrying it downstream.

Cam kept splintering the cart's wood into planks, his face

red with effort. I nodded to Shilah, who sifted through the wreckage and selected the longest pieces.

I began swinging the Abb end of the rope in a circle to check the momentum. If the giant Abb landed too close to the shore the Ice would fuse to the rocks. If that happened, we'd never get offshore before the Hookmen arrived.

'Okay, you two,' I said, pointing North along the shoreline. 'Come with me.'

'*Towards* the Hookmen?' Cam gulped.

'This might get heavy,' I said, making sure to walk at least twenty paces upstream from the tributary, dragging the rope behind me. 'I'm going to need you both. As always.'

Split was still slumped near the wreckage of the cart, his knees pulled up to his chest as he watched the puppet's case floating away.

Once reasonably far enough along, I handed Cam and Shilah one end of the rope and kept the end nesting the Abb for myself. 'Brace yourselves.'

Shilah put a hand on my shoulder and squeezed. 'I bet he's looking down. I bet they both are.'

I knew she wasn't talking about the Crier.

I took the Abb end and wound it in a large circle over my head, getting it up to speed. I hoped I could at least count on Great Gale to nudge my throw steady with a kiss of her wind. I had to make sure to get it far enough into the raging waters.

At last, heart in my throat, I let the rope fly.

The Abb soared out perfectly.

The reaction was immediate.

The whole section of the River tinged gold, expanses of waves concussing with light and colour. The severe popping of Ice coming to life made the sounds of the little bridge feel like muted footfalls. Golden hue soaked into shorelines, disappearing as fast as it had shot out.

The spot where the Abb landed beneath the waves coalesced

into a solid block. A huge slab breached the surface like a creature starved for air. The massive block grabbed out at the nearest waters, the crystalline sides exploding outwards.

And gave birth to a raft.

Made entirely of Ice.

It was the size of a caravan cart, thick as a slab of Pyramid stone. Stout and mighty, it floated near the shore tethered by the rope, looking ready to carry us down the Singe as far as we needed.

Then it began to pull.

The yank nearly launched me off my feet. The current swung the Ice downstream, the rope going taut as a bowstring. Fortunately, Cam and Shilah were ready, digging their heels into the stone. The current was desperate, but we dragged the raft towards the shore, retreating one step at a time. The rope held, acting like a fulcrum and swinging the Ice around, eventually getting it to rest against the shoreline, right in front of the spot where Split was brooding.

'Shivers and F—' Cam's throat clammed shut, unable to finish the thought. 'Miracle.'

The Vicaress glared at us from the other shore, her face distorted with rage.

'Hurry, Split!' I yelled. 'Take Picka and get on the Ice!'

Split staggered to his feet, looking longingly downstream. One hand grabbed the rope that was anchored in the centre of the Ice, and the other took hold of the camel's reins. Picka readily hopped onto the raft, as though she was leading the Shepherd. The thick raft barely dipped under their combined weight, but the edges were already starting to hiss, and I knew we didn't have time to waste. Picka went flat on her belly, braying happily as she scratched her toes back and forth.

I threaded my forearm through the rope and nodded to Cam and Shilah. 'Go.'

'Absolutely not,' Cam said. 'You're getting on first.'

'Trust me,' I said. 'Go. Don't forget the oars. And you take the Coldmaker.'

Cam went to say something, but I shot him a finalizing look. The Vicaress was stunned into silence, her flaming blade hovering low by her side. The fire licked the ear of the closest hound, which stretched and tried to shy away without actually lifting its paws.

'Fine,' Cam said, releasing his grip with a grumble, the tug of the Ice increasing. He tossed the food bags, waterskins and oars onto the raft, and then wrapped the Coldmaker bag across his chest. Using the rope to guide himself, he crawled onto the Ice and inched his way safely to the middle, tossing his arms around the slumped camel for stability. Picka folded her neck back and began licking the spots on Cam's arms where he'd been burned.

The Vicaress started screaming something at her army of guards, but they seemed at a loss as to what to do. She kicked a hound, sending it sprawling into one of its monstrous brothers.

I looked back over my shoulder to Shilah, the rope digging into the bandages on my wrist. 'Can you believe we made this?'

She gave a start, and almost dropped the rope. 'What did you say?'

'Shilah.' I could hear my heartbeat in my ears now. 'We just made a boat of *Ice*. Straight out of the Singe. Did you ever think that something—'

She leaned in and kissed me again, catching mostly cheek, but a small bit of the kiss landed on the corner of my lips. She pressed hard this time, like she actually meant it, and I almost let the rope slip.

'What was that for?' I asked.

'*We* did do it, world partner. And we're going to go together. Like this.' She crossed behind me, her chest pressing against my back as she grabbed the section of rope ahead of my hand.

The contact of her body brushing against me made me stumble, but I managed not to drop the rope. She jostled in front, both of us maintaining our hold as the other slid in front. Cam was waving us on, shouting for us to hurry. The Vicaress had finally lost her control over the hounds, and they were barking with a fervour that made my guts shake. Her blade slashed back and forth, piercing the hounds, their cacophony of barks morphing into shrill yelps.

One step at a time Shilah and I scrambled around each other. Holding the rope tight, we made our way to the raft. We reached the shoreline just as the Ice started to buck, the hissing mist it was now producing like a miniature white sandstorm, rising up and blocking our line of sight to the waters.

'On three,' Shilah said, her face tense with strain. 'We jump together.'

I nodded, gathering the slack on my shoulder.

'One. Two. Three!'

We leaped, still holding onto the rope. Our knees slammed against the Ice. Pain shot through my legs, but the Ice didn't crack. A little sting was better than slipping into the Singe and being cooked alive.

Then the raft took off.

I gathered the rope up behind me, since we were hovering near the shoreline.

'Cam,' I shouted. 'Oar! Now!'

Cam slid one my way, and with the last of my strength I thrust the jagged wood against the rocks. The Ice felt terribly heavy, especially with us on top, but Shilah steadied her hands over mine. Together we shoved out deeper into the waters. The current worked with us, angling the whole slab away from the boilweed and rocks and enemies.

Our raft swept by the Vicaress and the barking hounds, and I kept the oar ready in case one of the beasts tried to jump. The Vicaress seethed, her fiery blade in hand, but the cover of mist was thick, and the gap between Ice and land had widened enough to leave her helpless.

After a moment we'd already floated past.

The enemy was helpless.

The Hookmen were behind us.

Now all we had to deal with was the mercy of an angry river dragging us East.

Split waved two knuckles at the Vicaress. 'Death to your Hookmen! Death to the Khat! Meshua *is* real!'

Picka had flattened herself against the Ice, her tongue slapping back and forth against the surface. She seemed unfazed by the fact that we were suspended above death, and was happy to lap at the Cold, making small grumbling sounds.

Shilah and I pulled ourselves along the rope to the centre of the raft, laughing hysterically. As soon as I was in arms' reach, Cam tossed his body across mine. The scent of rosemusk was still powerful beneath his shirt. He unstrapped the Coldmaker from his chest and pushed it my way, his teeth already starting to chatter.

'Figured you'd want-t-t to hold it,' Cam said, his face full of mist and life.

I tied the bag near the centre of the rope to make sure it held steady. The Ice felt strong beneath our feet; slippery, but confident. It was unbothered by the boiling current lapping at its underparts. I knew, however, that the Singe had eight hundred years of Sun dissolved inside, and we had to get to the far shore quickly. 'It's not over yet.'

Cam nodded frantically, wrapping his hand over my shoulders and shaking. 'This is crazy! Spout, look where we are! Look what we're doing!'

I nodded, looking back at the Northern horizon, which was quickly wrapping itself in night. The streaks from the flame-powder still hung in the air, and I let myself feel the smallest bit of pride at having eluded the Hookmen, hoping the legendary demons couldn't survive swimming in boiling waters.

I looked back at the Northern dunes, and could just make out swift streaks of beige bursting into the open.

Their forms were not what I was expecting.

Four massive bodies stormed across the land, running as if weightless, their huge curved blades at the ready. They moved with impossible speed, but didn't have claws or tails or massive gills like the stories implied. I couldn't see them particularly well through the Icy mist, but they looked more or less like men. Swiftly they raced across the rock and stopped as one unit, lining up silently on the shore. They were dressed in uniform beige, and their heads were shaved and branded with what had to be the Closed Eye. One of the men in the middle – the largest of them all – lifted both his arms, the curve of two blades pointing in our direction.

'We have to get across the river,' I said, forgetting my confidence, a lump swelling in my throat. 'Everyone take an oar.'

Our Ice raft careered along, the water sloshing against the sides, but it wasn't strong enough to splash on board. Split tried to stand up straight, immediately slipping and landing violently on Picka's back. The camel grunted, huffed, and then went back to wiping her tongue across the boat.

'Stay low,' I said, trying to sound as if I knew what I was talking about. 'Keep on your stomachs and spread out.'

'Spout,' Cam said seriously.

'Hmm?'

'You're smiling,' he said, slapping a hand against the Ice with a laugh. 'It's good to see you smile.'

I hadn't noticed, and I touched my lips to see if he was right.

'If we make it across,' I said. 'I'll smile until my lips fall off.'

'We don't want that,' Shilah said. 'We need your lips.'

My chest clenched, and suddenly I found a bit more

strength in my fingers, my oar not so heavy. Everyone wiggled towards the tips of the Ice, each of us taking a different side. The insane Cold numbed the whole front of my body.

'Okay. We have to work together so we don't spin!' I shouted over the sizzle of our raft's edges. I wished Abb was here to be our leader, as he was confident enough to deal with such mayhem. But if my father *was* looking down on us, I knew he'd find it amusing to see that my first time on a boat was on one that I'd created.

Little Builder, indeed.

'Ready?' I shouted, dipping my oar through the waters. 'Pull!'

The raft resisted, but eventually it began to lurch.

'Ready!' I dipped the oar back in, trying not to cough on the mist. 'Row!'

Another jolt.

Over and over I shouted the commands, and bit by bit we inched our way towards the far shore. The Singe was at least two hundred paces wide at its narrowest, and already the edges of the Ice raft were retreating. It wasn't major, but it was noticeable, and I now had to slide back towards the centre.

We rowed with precision and fury, everyone following my commands. Split blundered his strokes a few times, stopping to dig a pinky into his ear, but mostly we held course.

Before I knew it we were in the middle of the Singe.

'Great work!' I shouted, trying to keep up spirits. My shoulders felt like they were about to pop with each pull, and I hoped the others were holding up better. I expected the water colliding with the side of the raft to be scalding, but the Ice took away most of its sting, and by the time it splashed up on my arms it was powerless.

I wanted to laugh again.

We were actually pulling this off.

'Row!' I shouted, feeling more alive than I had since leaving the Manor.

Picka whinnied at my back, echoing my sentiments.

Everyone kept rowing at my command, but our pace was beginning to slow. The impossibly Cold Ice was making my tongue and arms sluggish. I looked over and saw both Cam and Shilah shivering, but we had gained some momentum, and soon enough we were nearing the other shore. The river kept eating at the Ice, at least a quarter gone now. We had to scoot a little tighter towards the centre, but the shoreline was almost in reach.

'Just a litt-ttle more,' I shouted, my teeth chattering. 'We're almost-t there! Pull!'

I thought I saw something moving over on the far shore-line where we were heading, swift and low in the dunes. After blinking a few times, I realized it was just a trick of the mist. The amount of effort I had to exude for each stroke was beginning to get to me. Picka had started to make uncomfortable brays, struggling against her bindings. She must have reached her limit as well. The Cold was everything.

We yanked and thrashed our oars through the water, our techniques sloppy and frantic, but we were picking up speed.

Shilah's teeth were bared.

Cam put his cheek against the Ice to cool himself down.

Split grunted with every pull, sounding all too like his camel.

And my left wrist felt as if it was going to fall off with every stroke.

But a few dozen uncoordinated strokes more and we were cruising along the shoreline, just about to touch rock. My heart was thumping wildly. We had bested the Singe.

Then I realized our new problem.

We were going too fast downstream.

The rowing had taken us next to the shore where we needed to anchor, but the current had been dragging us at a blistering pace. We were speeding faster than we could run, and I knew if we tried to jump off the raft we'd likely end up missing the shore. We'd fall right back into the deadly waters.

The Ice bumped against the rocks, scraping off bits at a time.

'What do we do?' Cam shouted back, retreating his oar so it didn't snap off against the shoreline.

'I—' I gaped at the passing rocks and boilweed, all a blur. 'I don't know.'

'Meshua!' Split called. 'Another miracle, please!'

'I don't know,' I said, shutting my eyes so I could think.

Just then we crashed into a section of rock jutting out from the shore. The whole raft spun. Picka's reins tightened and she whinnied so loudly that I nearly lost my grip. Everyone managed to hold onto the rope, but only just.

My heart sank.

The raft was moving faster.

Shilah crawled towards me, her skin as pale as I'd ever seen it. The normal lovely brown was now like wet sand. Her whole body was shaking.

'You still have some Abbs?' she asked.

I nodded, my hand going to my pocket. 'I d-do.'

'Let me have one.'

I reached out, and the raft bucked against the rocks again, nearly knocking the golden bead from my hand. Shilah took the Abb, biting her bottom lip as she appraised the shoreline. 'Split! Make sure Picka's reins are secure!'

Split scowled at her and then immediately withdrew his gaze. His pinky went back in his ear. 'I think we should let Meshua make the decisions, girl.'

Another crash.

'Just check before I push you overboard!' Shilah yelled. 'And everyone else tie yourselves on like Picka!'

Cam reached out and dragged his oar across the shoreline,

presumably to slow us down, but it didn't do much.

I looped the rope twice around my leg and then placed my free hand on Shilah's shoulder, feeling what was left of her warmth. 'Are you going to—'

'Absolutely.' She winked, her eyelid struggling to come back up. Then she nodded to my lingering hand. 'There will be time for that later. You're going to want to use the other hand to grab our machine. Cam!' Shilah yelled. 'Tie yourself!'

Cam jerked his oar away from the shore, looping his belt around the rope and cinching tight. I pulled the Coldmaker against my chest. Everyone tied themselves as tightly as they could, and we all grabbed on.

Once Shilah's side of the raft lined up with the shoreline, she rolled the Abb into the bubbling waters.

The golden Cold exploded with another flurry of Ice. The crystals grabbed hold of both the raft and the rocks at the same time. Everything seared together, and our boat immediately scraped to a halt. The lurch was astounding. Picka's limbs flew out from underneath her, Cam's gold-rimmed glasses went skittering to the edge of the Ice, and my leg nearly ripped out of place.

But no one went into the Singe. The rope didn't break.

I paused, looking around with disbelief.

Shilah had expanded the Ice and brought us to shore.

We now had a perfectly good platform from which to disembark. We were also well out of range of the Vicaress and her Hookmen.

I burst out laughing again.

We undid our bindings, gathered our things, and crawled our way to the shore, Cam squinting as he reached across the Ice. The land felt blessedly solid beneath my feet, and I grabbed Shilah's hand, looking her in the eyes. She was standing as straight as ever, even though her body was still shaking from the incredible amounts of Cold.

'You saved us,' I said quietly, giving a slight bow. 'Meshua.'

She beamed, her face flushing with relief. 'I say if it's true, then it is both of us, or neither of us.'

I nodded, placing her hand on the Coldmaker. 'I couldn't agree more.'

Split ruffled Picka's mane, which had hardened into clumpy locks from the Ice. He kissed her over and over on the snout, the camel reluctantly grumbling in return, as she was staring longingly past the Pedlar and back at the Ice.

'We made it, girl,' Split said in between kisses. 'Can you believe it?'

Cam smoothed down his hair, which looked clumpier than Picka's, and surveyed all that we'd crossed. His teeth were still chattering, his eyes nearly squinting closed, and his face had gone as pale as the Wanted Scroll-version of himself. 'If only t-t-the whole World Cried could have s-seen that. We wouldn't-t even need Langria.'

Shilah took her hand off the Coldmaker and brushed my injured wrist, a question on her face.

'I'll live,' I said with a smile, giddiness abounding.

She cocked her head to one side, her face completely blank. 'Now don't go smiling those lips off. I thought we'd discussed that.'

'I—'

She winked, then her eyebrows flicked quickly upwards. Heat swelled back into my chest.

Cam smirked heavily, pointing back and forth to both sides of his mouth. 'What about me? I'm very happy about not being eaten or drowned or having my head chopped off.'

Full colour returned to Shilah's cheeks, the Cold beginning to wear off. 'Smile away, Cam.'

'Ready to continue this Coldmarch, Split?' I asked, fixing the Coldmaker bag on my shoulder and finally feeling the fatigue wash over me. Night was falling fast, the stars peeking out, but I knew we had to put some distance between us and the Vicaress. She'd find her way across soon enough.

Split gave Picka one last kiss on the snout and then looked up and nodded. 'If I remember correctly, the next stop is—'

Cam wheezed, his tongue nearly popping out as he stumbled backwards, pointing frantically. 'Death.'

I spun around and nearly vomited.

'Five,' Shilah whispered, her whole body stiff with fright.

Looming behind us was a man who could have been carved out of stone. He was nearly two heads taller than us, and as broad as a Pyramid stone. Darkness hovered around his frame, adding to the menace. Like the rest of the Hookmen, he was wearing beige and wielding a giant curved sword that could cut us lengthwise in one swipe. His head was completely shaven, the Closed Eye branded into where his hair would have been, and his nose was wide and flat, as if pressed against invisible glass. His entire being oozed muscle and strength.

Shilah had her blade out and ready, but it was laughable in comparison.

There was no way we could fight this behemoth.

The Hookman raised his blade, going for the kill. As I prepared for the black, I noticed two strange things about the man's skin. First was the fact that his whole body was littered with scars. The faded lines were grouped in neat rows, tallies spreading across his entire body from the neck down.

And the second oddity was the colour of his skin.

He was dark, like me. Like Shilah.

The Hookman was a Jadan.

# Chapter Fourteen

The curved blade thundered downwards, travelling so fast that I didn't even have time for a final prayer. All I could do was appreciate the fading light dancing along the length of metal.

At least the Sun wouldn't get a clear view of our demise.

I closed my eyes and gripped the Coldmaker tightly.

*I tried, Dad.*

A heavy crunch of rock and sand.

My lids jerked open and I saw the weapon dug into the ground at our feet, buried up to the hilt. The rough land proved no match for the monstrous power behind the swing, and the Hookman swiftly fell to one knee next to his blade.

I stiffened, wondering how many times in the history of the Khatdom a Hookman had missed. First we bested the Singe and the Vicaress on a boat of Ice, and then right away we met an assassin who failed to assassinate.

I was almost ready to believe the Crier was real. And that he was helping.

Shilah wasted no time, hurling her tiny blade at the Hookman's face. It twisted through the air, whipping like a viper tongue, but her aim was off, and the throw was wide.

Faster than I ever believed possible, the Hookman snapped up a hand and caught the blade right out of the air. In one smooth motion he brought the tip of Shilah's blade around to his own cheek – his face being one of the few patches of unmarred skin – and looked me head on. His eyes were pools of sorrow, so deep that I imagined no amount of Cold or Abbs might reach the bottom.

One look at the Jadan man and I could tell he held just as much pain as Split. As much as Leroi. Perhaps more so, because the Hookman's eyes weren't cloudy from slag or ale.

His gaze was as sharp as his curved blade. And there was resolve there, too.

The Hookman hadn't missed his strike at all.

He sliced Shilah's tiny blade down his cheek without flinching, drawing a deep line of red. Closing his eyes, he almost seemed to savour the pain.

'For Hamman,' the man intoned, his voice as dark and gentle as a shadow. I could feel the mountainous wave of relief in his words. 'Hamman is gone. The Hookman is finally free.'

I looked over to Shilah, my head swimming with confusion. She looked just as perplexed as I felt.

The Hookman's eyes shot open, and he brought the blade down to the spot above his heart, his chest corded with thick muscle.

'Is this your command?' the Hookman asked beseechingly, his eyes not leaving my face.

'Is what my command?' I asked, barely able to get the words out.

I couldn't believe I was still breathing.

The Hookman held steady. 'Have I failed the Father for plotting to kill the Child?'

'Wait? You know—' I cleared my throat, nearly fainting at the turn of events. 'You knew Abb?'

The Hookman's eyes shifted into uncertainty, the knife trembling. 'Have we had his name wrong all this time?'

Now that the Hookman was still, I could see that not only was he Jadan, but older than I'd previously thought. The hair in his eyebrows was speckled grey, and the lobes of his ears drooped. Looking past the disfigured skin, I estimated the Hookman to be around the same age as my father. How could Abb have associated with such a creature?

Ice still lingered in the front of my body, my heart hammering. 'You're Jadan.'

'Sun in your ears run, dammit!' Split screamed, grabbing Picka's reins and yanking her towards the dunes. 'Don't talk to the blasted thing! Run away! They have no pain or mercy!'

I raised my palm, standing my ground. We were obviously in less danger than the Pedlar thought, considering the Hookman was kneeling before us. And now heavy questions were anchoring me down, and I doubted I could have budged anyway.

'How did you know Abb?' I asked, clutching the Coldmaker bag tightly to my side. 'How did you know my father?'

'Abb.' The Hookman rolled the word around in his mouth, as if tasting it for the first time, nodding solemnly. 'Abb. A beautiful name. I shall carry it with me always, into eternal service or the black.'

Cam sidled up next to me. His teeth were chattering as he whispered in my ear. 'Maybe while he's distract-t-t-ed we can do the *thing* with the rock again? There's a fat-t one over th-there behind him, and me and Shilah can—'

I waved Cam off with a gesture of annoyance, feeling woozy. Of all the things that I'd come across since fleeing the Manor – the impossible Ice raft included – the kneeling Hookman was the strangest. I couldn't see Abb associating with someone whose entire purpose was to hunt down Jadans and lead them to the slaughter. My father would never befriend such evil.

'How did you know him?' I asked again, my voice trembling.

Split clapped his hands furiously to get my attention, pointing across the Singe. 'We *need* to go, Spout! If this thing found a way across, the other bastards will too!'

'I'm not with the Hookmen,' the Hookman said in serious tones. 'I abandoned them when I heard. Hamman is gone.'

Shilah came up to my other side, pressing against me. 'What do you want to do?'

The Hookman held the blade steady at his chest, the tip finally drawing blood through the beige cloth. 'I've been a loyal servant and I have done everything asked of me without question. I was his sickle for the chaff.' Tears formed in the corners of the Hookman's eyes, emotions welling up thick and wet. He pointed with his thumb across the Singe. 'In my duties I have learned many secrets of the Jadan people. And then I heard your name and what you possessed. No one else believed, but I believed. I told my kin I would wait on this side of the Singe to kill you in case you found a way to cross, by bridge or boat, but that was not really the case. I believed you would cross by your own hand. Hamman wanted to kill you, but Hamman is gone, and I know the truth. "The Child shall part the rivers and make the shores cry with life." I wish to watch you rebuild the world, Meshua, to protect you from all harm, but if it is my time to die, I shall gladly—'

'Did you say *Meshua*?' Split shouted. I could practically hear the blood boiling beneath his words. 'Did you just Sun damn use that word, you piece of shit? You murderer of children. You call my little girl chaff and just—'

'QUIET!' I shouted, trying to get everyone to shut up for a moment so I could think. 'You.' I pointed at the Hookman. 'Take the blade from your heart right no—'

Before I could even finish my sentence, the blade was thrust into the sands next to the other weapon. The Hookman nodded, looking at me as if begging for another command. 'By your word.'

'You.' I pointed to Split. 'Listen. If Hamman here wanted to kill us—'

'I am not Hamman. Hamman is gone,' the Hookman said, and then put his head down. 'My apologies for interrupting. I am Unworthy.'

'Okay, well, if whoever *he* is wanted to kill us, he would have done so,' I said. 'Just calm down for a moment so I can figure this out.'

I could hear the echoes of the Vicaress's screams from across the Singe and upstream, her wild shouting for Hamman to kill us immediately.

The Hookman continued to kneel.

'Calm down?' Split seethed, his fists clenched tightly and his face completely red. The rage was making him shake so much I wondered whether his nose was going to get another crook. 'You don't know these creatures, Spout. You don't know what they're capable of. They are liars and killers and—'

'I understand,' I said, pressing my palm against the Icy bronze in the bag, trying to draw strength from the machine. 'But this man is Jadan, which means he is family.'

'He's a *Hookman*,' Split said from beneath clenched teeth. 'He's not your family! And if he says he'll do what you command, then command him to slit his throat twice and let's be done with it.'

I took a tentative step towards the Hookman, which I knew was dangerous, but it also put me in grabbing range of the blades. In case this was all some sort of ploy I would soon need a weapon. Glancing at the incision his curved blade made in the land gave me pause, however, as I doubted even Slab Hagan was strong enough to wrench this weapon free.

I took a deep breath. I was not in any way prepared to deal with a situation like this. Abb was always the one with

the wisdom. I had no experience leading. I had only ever
wanted to tinker with things, not people.

'Tell me who you are,' I said. 'And why I could possibly
trust what you say.'

The Hookman nodded. 'I was called Hamman. I was a
Hookman in the service of your father, the World Crier.' He
pointed to the scars on his arms and chest and legs. 'The best
Hookman in the Khatdom. I gave myself one scar for every
Jadan I had to send away.' He pointed to his cheek. 'The final
scar is for Hamman. Now I shall only ever do your bidding,
Meshua, and my name shall henceforth be whatever you
desire. I am yours to—'

'Stop saying *Meshua*,' Split said, furiously scratching at his
thigh. 'You don't get to use that word. Hookmen don't get
to Sun-damn believe in a saviour!'

Hamman nodded, keeping his eyes on me. 'I will make it
so the Vicaress cannot hunt you. I know how the Hookmen
track. I know how the hounds smell. I will protect you with
my life. You and *all* of your companions.'

Shilah stepped forwards. 'What makes you think Spout is
this "Meshua"?'

Hamman looked confused. 'Meshua shall part the rivers
and make the shores cry with life. I saw it with my own
eyes.'

'It wasn't just him.' Shilah gathered herself as straight as
possible. 'More than one of us made the Ice.'

I gave Shilah a stern look. 'I agree, but now's not the time.'
Then I turned back to the Hookman. 'Okay, well, I'm just
going to call you Hamman for now—'

'Hamman. Is. *Gone*.' Tears followed the Hookman's words,
his face all sorrow. 'Apology for interrupting. I am Unworthy.'

Picka grumbled, shaking the fur around her neck and
looking longingly back at the Ice raft, which still clung to the
shore by a few crystal threads.

The Vicaress kept shouting from across the waters. The other Hookmen had disappeared from the shoreline, leaving tracks back into the sands. They'd find a way to cross the Singe and descend upon us soon, and I had to make a decision.

'Fine.' I looked the Hookman over and did a quick assessment. 'If you don't like *Hamman*, what do I call you?'

Hamman gave a dramatic nod. 'Whatever you wish. May I be reborn by your word.'

'Okay, fine.' I shrugged, so far out of my depth that I decided just to lean into the madness. 'What was your father's name?'

Hamman's whole body stiffened and I could tell it was a sore subject.

'Never mind,' I said quickly, trying to drown out the Vicaress's frantic orders echoing from across the waters. 'How about . . .'

'Dammit we don't have time for this!' Split shouted, trying to yank a reluctant Picka away from the shoreline. 'Don't speak to a Hookman like it's a person, Spout!'

I turned on Split with a snarl. 'Never call a Jadan "it".'

The Pedlar's jaw tensed, but he eventually nodded in agreement.

I kneeled down and tried to meet the Hookman's sorrowful eyes. 'Are you really going to protect us from the others?'

The Hookman gave a single nod. 'I'd stand in front of Sun himself to keep you alive.'

I put a hand on his shoulder, recognizing pain when I saw it. 'Considering everyone calls me Spout because I sweat, you can be . . . Dunes.'

His face tilted up. 'They don't call you by your real name?'

'Why Dunes?' Shilah asked.

I felt my cheeks grow a bit warm, embarrassed. 'I don't know, because that's where he left Hamman behind.'

The Hookman's face broke with fervour and awe, which looked all the more eerie because of the blood raining down his cheek. 'Dunes. Yes. Thank you.'

Split's fists were clenched. 'The dunes can also suck you in and suffocate you. Spout, you can't trust this—'

I glared the Pedlar silent.

'This man is Jadan,' I said. 'Whatever his past, he's still family.' I turned to our kneeling guard. 'You said you know how we're being tracked?'

Dunes went to stand, but I made a halting gesture and he remained on his knee.

'I do,' the Hookman said, showing us his empty hands and then slowly reaching under his shirt. 'And this can—'

'Watch it!' Cam said, his body jerking as if it was trying to decide whether or not to flee.

'It's okay,' I said. 'Show us.'

The Hookman took out a few vials filled with a viscous substance that I recognized. 'Gales breath. To make you invisible to the hounds' noses.'

I nodded, hope springing into my chest. 'And you can find us somewhere safe to hide?'

'I can and will.' The Hookman pointed to the side of his head. 'The Hookmen get her close and the hounds track you from there. I can give you their secrets, if only you wish, Mesh—' His eyes darted to Split, who was already tensed up waiting to go off on the utterance of the name. 'Micah.'

'You know my real name?' I asked carefully.

'Of course.' The Hookman nodded, the tears and blood continuing to spill over his cheeks, one side of his face entirely wet and red. 'That and so much more. The Hookmen are told everything about—'

'Hold on, Spout!' Split nearly doubled over, his body jolting, looking at me through a steady stream of blinking. 'Your real name is *Micah*?'

I paused. 'It is. Sorry, at first we thought it best if—'

'Micah!' he shouted, throwing his arms wide.

Picka whinnied, shaking her head and clopping her feet.

Shilah shrugged. 'It doesn't really matter now.'

Split was staring back at the Ice raft, laughter bubbling into his words. 'His name is Micah!'

'Your companion didn't know your name?' the Hookman asked quietly.

'We were keeping as much as we could secret,' I said. 'But now we know he's trustworthy. He's been leading us on the Coldmarch.'

Cam groaned, pulling at a tuft of his disarrayed hair.

'Oh.' I felt my stomach tighten. 'Well, it was obvious that's what we were doing anyway.'

The Hookman nodded. 'Langria. Yes. And the Hookmen figured that too. But, I will help you get there without them seeing. I will protect you.'

Split dropped to his knees at the shoreline, his laughter spilling into sobs. 'Micah. His name is Micah.'

Forehead furrowing with confusion, I reached into the Coldmaker bag and pulled out the little blue book that I'd found in Split's chamber. I kneeled down next to the Pedlar at the shoreline, holding out the old volume in shaking hands.

'Why *did* you have a book with my name on it?' I asked.

Split's gaze went from the Ice to the ancient tome. The next mix of chuckle and sob came with a large bubble of spit.

'Of course you took that,' Split said, wiping the moisture away and then giving his temple a severe rubbing. 'It's too real. I need more— It's all too real.'

'What is that?' Shilah said, appearing at my side.

'The Book of the March,' Split answered with an uncomfortable air of giddiness. 'All the secrets. All the prophecies.'

'I saw it in your chamber,' I said with a shrug, careful not to turn my back completely to Dunes. 'And since it was called *Micah*, and I was curious, I borrowed it.'

'It doesn't say Micah,' Split said, laugh-sobbing again.

I raised an eyebrow, touching the white letters painted on the spine.

The Pedlar shook his head, a sad smile on his face as the last few chuckles fizzled from his stomach. 'It's Ancient Jadan. All of us Shepherds are required to know it. You see the tail on the I? That softens the vowel to "eh". And the curly little extension on the C? It softens it to "shu". It doesn't say *my-cuh*, It says—'

'M-eh-shu-ah,' Cam said, sounding it out.

'Meshua,' Shilah said, her eyes wide with astonishment.

'Meshua,' Dunes said in a definitive manner from behind us, somehow bowing further from the one knee.

'Oh,' I said, feeling woozy.

All sorts of memories and emotions and feelings flooded my mind at once.

My whole life was upturned in a single moment.

My name.

Had such a secret really been hiding in front of me all along? Had my father known the significance? He must have, considering everything he'd done and said. The lessons he'd tried to teach me. And had Leroi known the truth? Is that why he took me in to be his assistant when all he wanted was to be left alone?

I dropped the book.

Above me the Sun had finally receded behind the horizon, the first of the night stars winking into the sky.

'Meh-shu-ah,' I said, wiping the sweat from my forehead.

Cam looked at me with new-found awe. 'Shivers and Frosts! You really *are* him, Spout.'

Shilah went over to her knife and strapped it back to her leg.

'Split,' I said, trying not to look at Shilah. I was becoming so overwhelmed I worried I might black out. 'Can we— how do— we need to go North.'

Split had gone back to scratching at his thigh, the cloth having ripped in the places his fingernails continued to scrape. The poor Shepherd looked beaten, burned, and arguably more tired than the rest of us.

'There's a few stops along the way to the City of David's Fall. I don't know if there are Shepherds left, but if so . . .' Split sniffed, not meeting my eyes. 'I'm not sure how they're going to feel about your timing. Eight hundred years is a bit later than desired.'

'Apologies for the interruption,' Dunes said. 'But there's a caravan of captured Jadans headed for the City of David's Fall as we speak. And it's not far from here. I can get you and your companions on.'

'How do you know that?' I asked, my vision fuzzy.

Dunes's eyes went glassy, and he let his head drop further. 'Oh,' I said. 'I see.'

'You caught some of them yourself,' Shilah said, acid in her voice. 'Those slaves, with the same blood as you.'

Dunes pulled aside his shirt and revealed some fresh cuts along his shoulder, three angry red lines, swelling and tallied up. '*I* didn't catch any. That was Hamman.'

Shilah went to open her mouth, but I cut her off.

'Easy,' I told Shilah. 'We've all been made to betray our kind. He's as much a slave as the rest of us.'

Shilah's eyes went to the blue tome, her fists clenching as she nodded.

'Split, are you okay with this plan?' I asked, turning away from the Hookman's mutilated skin. 'You're the Shepherd.'

Split tensed up, still staring at the Ice. 'Not if *Hamman* is coming with us.'

'Hamman is gone,' Dunes said, the corners of his eyes

having once again grown wet. 'The Crier has finally released me.'

'Split,' Cam said gently, stepping over to him. 'The real Hookmen are coming for us. And as the only other Noble here, I know that—'

Split whisked around, hitting Cam with a look that made the Singe seem gentle and loving in comparison. The little hair the Pedlar had on his head was askew in every direction, and his beady eyes looked hard, and heavy enough to sink to the centre of the world. 'What do you know, *boy*?'

Cam backed off, holding up his hands defensively.

Dunes rose to his feet, ripping the hooked blade out of the ground in one quick swoop. I almost stumbled backwards from the power of it all, the ease with which he defeated the grip of sand and stone.

'Do not fear,' Dunes said, a bloody droplet falling from his cheek. 'I will lead you to the caravan, but I will not be coming with you.'

'Why not?' I asked, worried for a moment that this had all been a lie.

The Hookman pointed his blade across the river to where the other Hookmen had been standing just moments before. The muscles in his shoulder tensed and bulged. 'First, I will be dealing with them.'

PART TWO

# Chapter Fifteen

'You always knew, didn't you?' I asked, gesturing for the Cold. 'The word was *in* the prayer you gave me for my birthday.'

Abb gently cupped the Shiver with his hands, halting the flow of our game. Somehow I knew it was the Shiver I had found in the rubbish pile so long ago. The same one that Shilah saw me put back because I was too afraid of the possibilities it represented. I was much younger back then.

Abb slid the Cold on the slick surface in front of his crossed legs, admiring how smoothly the sphere moved. We were sitting a few paces apart on our Ice raft, the whole thing floating through the night sky, but neither of us seemed afraid of falling. Everything was calm and right and surprisingly warm.

'Send it back already!' I said with a laugh, gesturing again for the Shiver. 'Greedy greedy.'

Abb smirked, looking up. 'You scold for rolled Cold? How bold.'

I groaned, rolling my eyes. 'Terrible. How long were you thinking up that one, Dad?'

He finally pushed the Shiver back my way, gently closing

the gap. The perfect ball reflected the light around us, casting bright veins into the Ice.

'Forever,' he said with a shrug. 'Never. Time is mostly for the living anyway.'

I looked at the night sky around us, threads of darkness stretching for an eternal distance. But there was no despair to be found – if anything, there was only abounding joy. Because in between the patches of black were infinite pieces of Cold, countless beads of hope, all lit up and shining and banishing the dark with movements like music. They swirled and tumbled, laughing into the notches of night, moving in patterns that I could appreciate but never hope to understand. Together they made stars. I could almost feel a bigger hand at play, rolling them about. Wisps, Drafts, Shivers, Chills, Frosts. It didn't matter the size or potency. They all had their own song. They all sang together. They made the heavens dance and cry.

'Of course I knew,' Abb whispered. 'I'm very smart.'

I caught the Shiver, feeling tingles against my fingers. 'So why didn't you tell me?'

'I told you almost every story I know,' he said, clucking his tongue. 'Greedy greedy.'

I laughed, rolling the Shiver back towards him. 'You can't take anything seriously, can you?'

Abb snapped his fingers, and the Shiver disappeared from the Ice between us.

I shot him a stern look.

He chuckled as he snapped again. A Shiver bounded out of the sky and kissed the Ice in front of my feet. It was the same one that had just gone away.

'What if you knew every single thing about your inventions before you created them?' Abb asked. 'Every spring, gear, material, proportion, potion, and secret. If you knew—'

'I think life would be a whole lot easier that way,' I said, again rolling the Shiver his way.

He caught the Cold, lifting it up and staring into its centre. 'But a lot emptier.'

'But I could—'

'Micah,' Abb said, cutting me off.

'You mean Meshua?' I asked playfully.

Abb shrugged. 'That's up to you. Now what I was going to say is this. If you knew everything that went into your inventions beforehand, they wouldn't work properly. You'd still be missing the most important piece.'

'And what piece is that?' I asked.

He kissed the Shiver and tossed it back into the sky. 'Wonder.'

A whisper from above.

'Spout.'

I woke, sitting up with chains rattling over my stomach. Harsh morning light spilled between the slats in the cart's roof, searing my eyes and making me wince. I gave a muted cry, but didn't wake the other Jadan prisoners, their bodies sagging from the intense heat. The savage cart we were being transported in trapped more Sun between its walls than even my barracks, and I moved my face as far away from the light as possible.

'What's happening?' My hands grasped beside me in desperation, quick to make sure the Coldmaker was still there. The machine was tucked safely in its bag, and the profound relief made my lips broaden, not stopping until a small blister broke on my upper lip. 'Are the Hookme—'

'It's morning,' Shilah said softly, moving the chains off my stomach to my thighs. 'Relax.'

'It is,' I said, closing my eyes, angling out of a spear of Sun that was burning into my neck. The air inside the caravan cart was almost too stifling and thick, and every breath I took had the sour aftertaste of fear. 'How long was I out?'

'A while. And you've been wasting lots of fluid.' She smiled, pointing to the wet spot on her shoulder where my drool had pooled. I was surprised I'd had any moisture inside me at all after all this suffocating heat. Shilah spoke in a joking tone, but her expression didn't seem as frivolous. '*Meshua*.'

'Stop it,' I whispered, giving her a nudge. 'Like we said, if it's true, it's both of us, not just me.'

She picked at the chain rope draped across her stomach. 'Let's hope.'

We weren't locked in like the rest of the Jadans in the cart, with the links of chain threaded through the manacles around their wrists, because Split had only pretended to shackle us down when setting us in the back of the cart. I'd never ridden in a slave transport before, and the accommodations were just as bad as I always imagined. The boilweed mounds we were lying against were decrepit, stale, and full of dead scarab carapaces. The critters preferred heat but hated light, so I assumed this cart was crawling with them. The walls angled inwards at the top, intensifying the enclosed feeling, and the wooden floor was lined with old yellow stains. A small, fresh puddle of wetness sloshed back and forth with the movement of the cart, the origin not clear, but easily excused. There was only one bucket in the corner for us to pass amongst ourselves, and it was nearly full.

The place was a rolling nightmare, and even after a few moments of being awake I was itching to be outside its walls. The box stank of sweat and heat, and it only made my stomach sink deeper. At the moment I didn't care about the Sun or the Hookmen outside, I just wanted to be free.

Dunes had led us to the caravan's stopping point last night, before disappearing into the shadows. He took with him only his blade and a few slices from each of our clothing. Cam and the Pedlar had gone up to the caravan tents and offered the guides the promise of big Cold for supplies and safe passage to the City of David's Fall. Split had lied and said the wheel of his cart had broken and that's why we were all stuck, and the guides, not in any position to turn down such a lucrative opportunity, agreed to take our group on. So long as the slaves rode in the slave cart with the runaways.

Cam had protested until his face had turned as blue as his eyes, but I told him it was okay, and had passed out pretty much as soon as my backside touched the mound of old boilweed. I hadn't even had the energy to take in the state of our Jadan companions. I'd been pushed far past my normal limits. The story behind my name had been too much for my waking mind to process.

I wasn't feeling particularly refreshed, but I at least had some distance from all the blows to my sanity.

A real-life Coldmaker.

Abb.

Leroi.

An Ice bridge.

*M-i-cah*.

*Me-shu-a*.

I sniffed at my arms, winging away from the pungent smell of Gales breath that Dunes had poured over us. He'd told us that the potion originated from a plant grown at the Southern Cry Temple, and it apparently confused the hounds' sense of smell. It left them placid and disorientated. The Vicaress always kept a few vials on her. Dunes said it was rarely used, just in case her pets got rowdy while she was 'disciplining' them.

I blinked away the sleep.

Four young girls were in the caravan cart with us, all of them stunning.

Even under the gloss of sweat and filth their beauty was like a beacon. Curvier than most of the Jadan girls I knew, they had smooth, unmarred skin the colour of milky choco-late, which must have been tended by Cold baths and expensive lotions. Their eyes were the shape of full almonds, even more perfect than Shilah's. There were even traces of beauty powders on their lashes and lips, the kind that was rarely used on Jadans.

Two of them could have been sisters, their faces remarkably similar, although one of them had freckles. All four were Domestics for sure, each wearing tattered beige sunsilk. Each was likely some High Noble's *favourite* Domestic.

I didn't need the girls to wake up and look me in the eyes to understand why they'd become runaways.

Shilah kept her voice to a whisper and gave me an amused look, putting a hand on my ankle. She quickly found the raised skin where the rope had constricted the moment her Abb had sealed the Ice raft to shore. 'Sorry my brilliance can be so painful at times.'

I smiled, my hand still not straying from the inside of the Coldmaker bag. I had the inexplicable need to touch the machine, to keep myself anchored. 'You really did save us. I can't believe that actually worked.'

'Well, it was you who had the idea for an Ice boat in the first place.' She shrugged, tenderly rubbing the bruised spot above the ankle bone.

'"Ice boat", huh?' I asked, remembering all the times she teased me for being so literal with my tinkering. 'Couldn't think of a better name?'

Shilah kept gently rubbing my ankle. 'I was just using a term I thought you'd understand. You look quite out of it, and I didn't want to confuse you further.'

Her hand on my skin felt amazing, and I didn't want her to stop. 'So what's it really called then?'

She twitched her lips back and forth, giving me a serious look. 'Abb-boat.'

I had to work very hard to hold in my chuckle. 'Sounds like something Cam would come up with.'

'I know.' She winked. 'All part of why we make a good team.'

'So you're okay with Cam being part of the team?' I asked carefully. 'I thought you were mad at him.'

Shilah gave a cool shrug. 'He saved us too, from the hounds. And he really does seem to care.'

The cart jolted, but the Domestics didn't wake. I looked through the cracks in the front wall and could just barely make out the massive Jadan bodies pulling our mobile prison. It left me wondering how long we'd been travelling and how far we'd gone since I'd passed out.

'So what do you make of Dunes as part of our team?' I asked.

One of the lookalike sisters twitched at the mention of the Hookman's name, but she kept her eyes shut. The harsh Sunlight beamed through the roof, tangling in her long lashes and highlighting the dark freckles along her face. Jadankind didn't usually have such features, but I knew some High Nobles forced their personal Domestics to get the spots tattooed on their cheeks.

'He's Jadan,' Shilah said without conviction, not meeting my eyes.

'He'll be good to have on our side,' I said, tracing the bronze Opened Eye.

She looked across my shoulder, following my hand into the canvas bag. 'Aren't you worried about lizards?'

I slid my palm out of the bag with a sheepish smile. 'I doubt a Sobek would choose to live here.'

Shilah surveyed the corners of the cart. The angles of her face were always more defined when she was poised in thought, and I wished I had the patience to watch her ponder for hours on end. As it was, everything inside me was too frantic to remain motionless, and the chains on my thighs rustled audibly as I readjusted my legs.

'We need to find you some food soon,' I said. 'You're looking thin.'

'So are you. I'll grow us a whole feast when we make it to paradise.' She leaned closer to my ear, the heat of her breath causing a shiver to run up my back. Lowering her voice, she asked: 'Where do you think these girls were running?'

'Anywhere,' the closest runaway said, opening one eye and then the other. She sat up as straight as her chains allowed. 'Paphos. Belisk. Marlea. Anywhere with a Drifthouse that might take in strays.'

I had to hold onto my breath. Perhaps it was the angle the Sun was striking her face, or the fact that I was so far out of my element, but she was perhaps the most beautiful girl I'd ever seen. Her large eyes were a smoky brown and her thin eyebrows were angled to give her a permanently inquisitive look. Her hair was puffy, like yarn, black as a ravenbeetle, and held together in manageable bundles by copper twine. But the most striking feature of her face was her pouting lips, the bottom one so plump she might have been smuggling Wisps underneath it.

One of the sisters sat up next, and from the shrewdness of her freckled face I could tell she'd clearly been awake for some time. 'Yah brainless slab ah brick, Leah! Why'd juh tell them that. They could be spying fur Ka'in.'

The yarn-haired beauty called Leah shrugged. Her fingers twitched and curled as she spoke, almost as if she were having small spasms in her hands. 'We're on our way back anyway. It's not going to change anything.'

The sister rattled the chains on her arms. 'May-bee you. Can't hold the two of us forevah. We gunn get out.'

I cocked my head, having never heard such an accent. The cadence was fast, and from time to time a random letter got an extra barb. It reminded me of the Singe, swift and stinging.

'Where are you from, if you don't mind my asking?' I said.

Now the other sister finally sat straight up, reaching over and holding up a palm. 'Juss cause you lucked in here with us dun't mean we got to tell yah nothing.'

Shilah folded her arms across her chest. 'No reason to be rude. We're all family.'

The two sisters gave a collective gasp, both of their faces drawn to Shilah's wrists and then the loose chains upon her lap. Their twin bodies dipped forwards until the metal on their wrists went taut. The freckled sister's tattered shirt fell off her shoulder to reveal more than I was prepared to take in.

I quickly looked away to give the girl her privacy, but not before noticing that she'd been disfigured from navel to neck, the entirety of her breast covered in small burns. I stared instead at the Coldmaker, trying not to wince and feel her pain. 'Your shir—'

'You got out of thum chains!' Freckled Sister said. 'Show us! You pocket a key from yah master or somethun?'

'We were never chained in,' Shilah said, her eyes softening as she took in the girl's burns.

'How'd yah get out!' the fully clothed sister chimed. 'Don't lie. Don't hold out on us or me and Ellcia gunn break every one of thum fingers when *we* get free.'

Shilah paused for a second and then smiled. 'You know what, I changed my mind. I like the rude. We can definitely be friends.'

'Friends shah keys, little priss,' Ellcia hissed, tossing the cloth half-heartedly back over her chest. She attempted to spit, but her mouth seemed too dry to produce any moisture. 'Whichya single braid and straight back likes yah some priss wann-bee.'

Shilah's smile only grew broader. 'I told you, we don't have a key. But we do have something better.'

The sister without the freckles chimed in. 'You got food

and watah in yah boyfriend's bag? We dunn get to have nuthin in this cart. That's suspicious. You working for Ka'in?'

The fourth and final Domestic in the cart had yet to wake. She the looked thinnest of the group, her hair cut short and uneven, almost hacked apart. Her sunken chest was still moving up and down, but her tongue was peeking slightly from her lips. I couldn't tell if she was listening in or actually asleep, and I hoped the caravan merchants would stop and bring rations soon.

'Calm down,' Leah said, gesturing once again with twitchy hands. 'These new friends are probably just as scared as you two.'

Both sisters turned on Leah with a simultaneous hiss. 'Not scared!'

Leah tittered, her face lighting up and her hands and chain dropping back into her lap. Her laugh was something special as well, musical in a way, pitch perfect and lovely. Suddenly I wished I knew how to be as carefree and funny as Cam. Considering how I felt at the moment, trapped and desperate, I doubted I'd be making her laugh anytime in the near future.

Leah rattled her wrists in the manacles, her eyebrows angling to make her face even more expressive. 'I'm Leah, obviously. Originally from Belisk. And these lovely girls are Ellia and Ellcia, all the way from the Shocklands.'

I'd never actually met anyone from the Shocklands, which explained why the sisters' accents sounded strange. The place was practically off the map, as East as East goes. Leroi had taught me that the city's population was small since it was far from the capitol. The Nobles living in the Shocklands stayed for mainly one reason. Heat lightning was a nightly occurrence in the surrounding plains, powerful bolts whipping down from the sky to sear the dunes. The results were hardened designs of glass, trapped in magnificent sculptures. They ranged anywhere from the size of a fist to the size of a whole street. The Nobles that studied them called themselves 'statuaries' and claimed that the shock sculptures were the Crier's art. They spent days on excavation and interpretation, sending any transportable pieces to the Khat's Pyramid. I'd actually seen a few pieces being carried through the Capitol Quarter on massive wagons, looking wonderfully shiny and mysterious. Abb always told me the messages the statuaries saw within the pieces were nonsense, and were just another way to make themselves feel important.

'We all lived together in the Sanctuary,' Leah explained further, her fingers returning to their strange twitching, wrists joining in this time with quick rotations. 'Until we escaped.'

'What's the Sanctuary?' Shilah asked.

'Brainless priss,' Ellcia said with a scoff, sitting back against her lumpy boilweed mound. Ellia was quick to copy the movement and give a light echo of her sister's words. 'Priss.'

Leah rolled her eyes. 'Don't mind them, most outsiders don't know much about what goes on in the City of David's Fall these days. Not since Ka'in took over.'

'You all worked in a Drifthouse?' Shilah asked, moving her legs up because the yellow puddle was seeping closer to her feet.

Leah gave a sad shake of her head, her hair bouncier in the twine than I'd expected it to be. 'But that would have been much preferred.'

'The Drifthouses aren't exactly pleasant,' Shilah said carefully. 'What exactly were you running from?'

'A pampered plaything with no edges wouldn't understand,' Ellcia said. 'Now gimme that key you hiding, bitch.'

'Watch it,' I said, still careful not to look directly at Ellcia's shirt, which was a twitch away from falling open again. 'She's not what you think. She's special.'

Shilah's back wrenched as straight as possible, not meeting

my eyes. 'Pampered plaything? Does this look like I'm a
pampered plaything to you?' She pulled back her sleeve,
revealing the Opened Eye tattoo. 'Does it?'

I was expecting a more drastic reaction from the twins,
but Ellcia only shrugged. Ellia watched for her sister's reaction
before shrugging too.

'So what,' Ellcia said, tapping at her freckles. 'Lots of us
got ink, priss.'

'It's the Eye of Langria!' Shilah exclaimed, far too loud.

I shot her a disapproving look, but thankfully the cart kept
rolling. The cracks in the walls were small and jagged, and I
wondered if the Jadans pulling the cart along the Khat's road
could hear what we were saying.

'It's the Eye of Langria,' Shilah said again, much quieter
this time, pulling her sleeve up further.

'Yeah, well, Langria ain't real,' Ellcia said. 'Why you think
we was running South?'

'Langria *is* real,' I said, my voice giving an embarrassing
crack.

Ellcia gave a flirty grin, her teeth far too nice for a Jadan.
She reached across the cart with her foot, sliding it up and
down my calf seductively. 'All of a sudden yuh boyfriend's
got a mouth. Speak yuhself up boyfriend.'

'He's my partner,' Shilah said, pushing Ellcia's leg away
from mine and giving me a nod. '*Micah.*'

'Langria is real,' I said, trying to keep my voice from
breaking. 'We were told by someone I trust. She said the
march is always North.'

'Oh!' Ellcia giggled with delight. 'The Coldmarch. How
cute.'

Ellia looked at her sister and then let out a titter herself.
'Can you believe it?'

'You think the Coldmarch is going to get you into Langria?'
Ellcia asked, running her tongue over her top teeth.

'So you're *admitting* it's there,' Shilah said in a victorious manner.

'She never said it wun't there,' Ellia butted in, looking over at her sister with caution. 'She said it wun't real.'

'What's that supposed to mean?' Shilah asked.

'Where'd you get that tattoo?' Leah said, reaching out a hand towards Shilah's arm before she got caught by the manacles, as if forgetting she was still chained.

Shilah let her sleeve fall, gesturing to the Coldmaker bag with her head. 'I made it. And it's not the only thing either.'

'Is she okay?' I asked, pointing to the last Domestic, who still hadn't woken up. I couldn't tell if her chest was moving.

Leah frowned, the poutiness of her bottom lip making me shudder. It wasn't just the looks of these Domestics that was spinning my gears; there was something so dreamy about the way they moved.

'We don't know,' Leah said, rattling her wrists, her fingers dancing through the air. 'She's been like that since they locked her in. And I want to check, but . . .'

I reached into the bag and pulled out one of the four remaining Abbs, rolling it in my palm. I bit my bottom lip, wishing I had anything other than piss to cool.

'Wassat?' Ellia said. 'Your master has you carrying gold beads? Pretty stuff, but not worth much.'

'Shilah and I don't have any master,' I said.

'Oh, boyfriend!' Ellia said, licking her lips. 'Don't think yuh got a master? Just wait an' see where we're headed!'

'We're free Jadans, wherever we are, from now on,' I said, standing up and wandering across the cart, stepping over the yellow puddle. I reached out and put my fingers on the sleeping girl's slender neck, pressing gently. Abb had only taught me rudimentary techniques when it came to healing, but I at least knew how to check a heartbeat.

And hers was fading.

The cart was too hot.

I slammed my palm on the wall, trying to catch the attention of the muscled Jadans outside who were pulling us along, the chains slung over their knotted shoulders. 'Hey! Stop! She's dying!'

My words were rebuffed loudly in my ears, and the Jadans either couldn't hear me or didn't seem to care. The Sun was searing now, the box so hot that I needed to take a deep breath in order just to gather another shout. In a moment Shilah was by my side, slamming palms against the wooden walls, but the Sun-bitten Jadans outside kept pulling the cart. I pressed my eye against one of the bigger cracks, trying to see if I could spot Split or Cam nearby, but the caravan was long and spread out along the Khat's road.

I put my lips up to the crack instead. 'Get Camlish Tavor, please! Get our Nobles! Hurry!'

'Thought yuh didn't have no masters,' Ellcia said from behind me.

Shilah waved her quiet, her expression deadly.

'They won't stop,' Leah said from her sitting position, biting her bottom lip. Her fingers careered through the air as if she was testing the resilience. 'We've tried . . . to lure them before.'

'Dammit, she's on fire,' I said, stepping back and returning my fingers to the girl's neck. The sleeping Domestic was completely motionless now, the edge of her tongue hanging out, dry and crusted over.

I had no idea what to do. How to help.

All of a sudden I heard Split's dark laughter in my head. *Meh-shu-ah.*

Regardless of a tattered blue book with my name on it, I wasn't some prophesied saviour. I wasn't sent from the Crier to battle Noblekind. But that didn't mean that I couldn't do right by my people.

I forced myself into action and searched the cart for something suitably dense. The bloodied stone would have been another big help here, but we'd left that back at the shore. I couldn't use the Coldmaker itself as a battering ram, for fear that I break the only Frost I might ever get. The only things in the cart were girls, chains, and mounds of boilweed. The Inventor in me knew I needed more options, but the Jadan in me knew I had no choice.

Then I spotted the bucket.

I looked up at the roof and smiled. 'Always with your jokes, huh?'

'What you going on about?' Ellcia asked, pursing her lips. 'You try-na talk to the Crier, you daft man-priss?'

I turned to Shilah, hope rattling my heart. 'You still have your knife?'

The blade was out before I could swallow another breath of stifling air.

'That's how thum got out of thum chains!' Ellcia said, nudging her sister with an elbow. 'I knew she was hiding out! I'm gonn break all them pretty plaything fingers.'

Shilah gave a cool shrug, wiggling her untethered fingers towards Ellcia's face.

'Quit it,' I said, quickly slicing the Abb in half. Then in half again. If a full Abb could conjure an Ice bridge out of boiling water, then it was far too potent to use in such tight quarters.

'Remember my Cold Wrap,' I said to Shilah, cutting up strips of the lumpy boilweed that I'd been sleeping on. A scarab crawled down my arm, but I quickly brushed it away. 'How the chamber crushed the Wisps.'

'Of course,' Shilah said, watching me carefully.

'And your Shiver that started all of this? The one you threw at the Vicaress.'

Shilah shot me an unreadable look. 'You mean *our* Shiver.'

I wrapped the boilweed strips around my hands just in case. Then I went over to the bucket, dumping out its contents behind one of the boilweed mounds, not letting my nose stray too close. Sludgy wetness splashed against my toes, but I'd dealt with much worse things than that in my youth when pillaging for treasure in the boilweed mounds.

The sisters' fury crashed down on me in an instant.

'Foul!'

'Idiot!'

'Break your fingers!'

'Make you lick it up!'

'Foul!'

'Man-priss!'

Leah only laughed, angling away from the oozing puddle. The tittering sound from her sumptuous lips made me wish I had another bucket to dump out, if only that would keep her laughing.

'Where'd they pick you two up!' Leah asked with a halting smile.

'You won't believe me if I told you.' I crouched beside the dying girl and placed the quarter piece of Abb on the floor, making sure not to set it off in one of the wet spots. 'Well actually, maybe you will. Shilah, you're in charge of naming whatever is about to happen.'

'Micah,' she said.

I hesitated with the bucket, looking over. 'Yeah?'

She backed into the wall, and I could feel the affection in her nod. 'Yes.'

I raised the bucket in my hands. 'You might want to close your eyes, everyone. I don't know what this is going to do.'

'Foul boy!' Ellcia's face was flush with confusion. 'What yuh thinking you doing with—'

I slammed the bucket down, crushing the piece of Abb.

Everything happened so fast.

I was tossed on my back by a divine gust of Cold, the bucket hurled out of my hands. A crash sounded against the roof. The whole cart shook as the Cold air had nowhere to escape, golden waves pressing against the walls like a thousand heavy fists. Storm winds bounded around inside, jostling everyone against their chains. The pressure from the burst forced the Cold down my lungs and settled Cold behind my eyes and even thrust Cold in the cracks under my fingernails. It was all-consuming. I wasn't equipped to experience such a thing. Pain registered all across my skin, especially in my left hand. The snaps of wood were deafening as the floor splintered with Ice crystals beneath where the Abb had been, spidering out and climbing the walls. Waves of Cold wind expanded to every corner of the cart, the walls creaking and buckling outwards. My eyes were hazed with Cold.

I nursed my hand against my chest as the frozen winds made everything flail about. The bucket came crashing back down on my head, but it glanced off without doing any real damage. There was shouting, but I couldn't make it out. I was lost in the Cold sensation, gone in the cloud, paralysed by the divine temperature sweeping me inside and out. For the first time since its creation, I was afraid of the Coldmaker.

The unconscious girl sat up with an inhuman gasp, her hands grasping at her throat. She looked around in a state of complete and utter shock. Cold wind brushed through her short hair, causing the locks to stand up at bizarre angles.

She croaked something unintelligible, sucking in another gasp.

The floor gave a final clamour and fell open where the Abb had been. A spot the size of my head completely dissolved away, the ragged edges rimmed in Ice. I could see the road beneath us, but we were no longer moving.

Pain continued to bite my left hand. I tried to unravel the boilweed strip, but the old grey plant had Iced over as well, locking me in from wrist to knuckles. Slices of wall had cracked under the strain and began to snap outwards. Waves of Sunlight now spilled into the cart, filtering through the frosty gold mist, making it hard to see all the damage.

I could just make out Shilah getting to her feet, pressing a hand against her face. Her cheek was leaking red.

'Holiness,' Leah said through the crystalline fog, coughing. 'Eyes.'

The sisters were silently holding each other closely, both of them shaking.

I went over to the short-haired girl, trying to ignore the throbbing in my head. 'Are you okay?'

She sucked in another breath, her face going pale. Then she passed out.

'Crap!' I said, the pain in my hand all I could think about, needing to get the boilweed off right now. I started hitting my fist against the wall, the pain monstrous, but the frozen plant wouldn't budge.

A hand grabbed my shoulder.

'Micah!'

I flinched at the touch and accidentally elbowed Shilah in the chest, my bone sinking into her flesh. She stumbled back, falling on the mound of boilweed which had absorbed all the piss and shit from the bucket. The pile made a crunchy sound as she landed.

'Sorry! I didn't mean—' the pain in my hand was searing now, and I let out a groan of agony. 'Ah!'

Just then the door to the cart was flung open, revealing the face of a bewildered Noble. Cold air spilled outside and rushed past his light red hair, causing him to make a sort of *eeek* sound.

'Weapons!' the man shrieked loudly enough to be heard all the way back in Paphos. 'Bring weapons! Kill them! Kill them! The slaves have—'

And then his head slammed sideways, struck by something blunt and fast. His body collapsed.

Rows of scars on a giant arm loomed where he had stood.

'Meshua!' Dunes yelled, putting his hooked blade on the bed of the cart and ripping the door clean off its hinges. 'Are you hurt? Are you in trouble, Crierson?'

'Micah,' I said. 'My name is Micah.'

I was still in complete shock. The pain in my hand had suddenly disappeared, and now I couldn't feel my wrist or fingers at all. I could see the caravan guards amassing through the gaping holes in the walls, dozens of swords and whips and cudgels coming into view. Horns were sounded. Nobles hopped off their camels and dropped their goods carts and parasols, all of them grabbing daggers and shouting to one another. There were perhaps fifty enemies tensing up. I still couldn't make out Cam or Split, only the petrified and angry faces of those coming our way.

Shilah grabbed the Coldmaker bag and flung it over her shoulder. 'Come on!'

'What demons yuh bring on us?' one of the sisters shouted through the haze. 'What sort of trick is this? Ka'in did this!'

'Take me with you, Micah!' Leah said, squirming in her chains, holding out her wrists. Her fingers were twitching wildly. 'I'll do whatever you need! I can play music and sing to you! I'll do *anything* to you! Take me with you!'

'There's no time,' Shilah shouted, grabbing a handful of my shirt and pulling me out of the cart. 'They're coming!'

The horns were blaring now; the whole caravan was closing in.

Dunes pointed out into the sands beside the road, the horizon full of barren hills and crags, and even mountains of rock. 'Behind me, Crierson!'

'What about Cam?' I asked, my voice breaking. 'And Split!'

'No time!' Dunes said, his body tense and deadly. He picked up his blade, slashing it through the air in the direction of the mob, looking as menacing as a pit of vipers. 'I can track them later.'

I glanced back inside the cart at the Domestics still chained down, their faces full of fear and awe. Leah was begging me with her eyes.

'But—'

'We can't let them get the Coldmaker,' Shilah said, grabbing me by the shirt and wrenching me off the road. 'It's all that matters!'

# Chapter Sixteen

Unless I cracked the secret of flight on the spot, then there was no way to get past these fortifications.

The walls were a hundred hands high, and I could barely make out the top, my neck straining as it bent backwards. Far above, encircling the looming rim, was an unending series of Closed Eye statues. They were all different styles and textures, some small and thin, some stout and menacing, but they were all infuriating. It was curious that the walls of the City of David's Fall had a higher number of the Closed Eyes than I'd ever seen in one place.

Wind whipped around the stone walls. The fortifications were smooth and long, without any visible break. There were no obvious ways into the city other than by the few heavily guarded gates and doors, of which we'd kept out of sight. The entrances were manned by stern-looking clerics, all of whom were checking and re-checking every traveller's face against a pile of the Wanted Scrolls. I had to squint to see, but there was no denying: Shilah, Cam, and I were the prominent faces in the stack.

Dunes might have been able to get us through the gates on his reputation as a Hookman, but his betrayal meant he might have a Wanted Scroll of his own.

I held out my good hand, brushing my knuckles across the impenetrable stone. Tightly stacked bricks were gently interspersed around the entirety of the City of David's Fall, meeting up with natural rock formations that careered even higher. Some bricks were old and a bit crumbled, but mostly the whole place was sealed.

The city's layout was perplexing to say the least, raised in a series of long plateaus, dozens of staircases carved directly into the land, with not many buildings or streets visible from our vantage point outside the walls. I could just make out the shine of a gleaming dome and the scorched limestone roofs of what was surely a massive Cry Temple.

One of the defining features of the City of David's Fall was an extended plateau on the southern side, higher and more thrust out than the other precipices, its abrupt cliff ending in a completely vertical drop. I tried to follow the rock face down, but the land at the bottom was hidden by yet another wall.

All of a sudden I understood Leah's words about outsiders not knowing much about what went on here. It would be impossible to witness everyday life unless from inside.

We were currently hiding by the eastern walls of the city where it seemed the least populated, trying to figure out a plan. I continued to brush my knuckles along the grey brick. A trickle of dust and pebbles fell out at my touch, the walls more decrepit here. 'It's old.'

Dunes nodded, taking his hooked blade and picking out some of the ancient mortar. 'It looks very old. I have no idea how old it might be, Meshua.'

Shilah grunted. 'Of course it's old. This was the first Jadan stronghold after the Great Drought,' Shilah said, adjusting the strap of the Coldmaker bag on her shoulder. 'The final stand for our people. Besides Langria, of course.'

'I think I knew that,' I said, trying to recall the particulars

of the stories Mother Bev used to tell us in my barracks'
common area. 'Maybe.'

'I don't know anything about the history of the City of
David's Fall,' Dunes said, continuing to pick at the mortar.
There was something odd about his tone, distant and forlorn.
'It's probably a horrific history. Hamman knew all sorts of
those horrific things. I'm glad he's gone.'

Shilah touched my left hand, which was now wrapped in
new boilweed, freshly picked from the bubbling stream we'd
stumbled across while fleeing the caravan guards. I had
plucked a whole handful of weeds from the shoreline, as
many as would fit in my bag. The pain was excruciating, and
I was probably going to need to change the wrap often.

Shilah moved her fingers up to the spot where I'd knotted
the boilweed closed. 'Let me see it.'

'It's fine,' I lied.

She kept her face even. 'Spout.'

'I'm fine.' I pulled my hand away, too mortified by the fact
my own creation had betrayed me. It seared me to the core
with shame, and I was glad Shilah was now carrying the
machine.

I hadn't checked the damage to my hand since wrapping
everything, but if the increasing pain was any indicator, then
the wound was getting worse.

Dunes nodded, letting his head fall. 'May I see it, Crierson?
I don't know much about healing, but perhaps I can—'

'It's fine,' I repeated, perhaps a little loudly. 'Dunes, what's
with the Closed Eyes up on top of the walls? Why do they
all look so different from one another?'

Dunes kept picking at the mortar. 'I have no idea. I don't
know anything about this place.'

'You're a Hookman,' Shilah said in accusatory tones.

'No, I'm not,' Dunes said, putting a hand over the Closed
Eye scar that had been carved into his forehead. 'I'm not.'

'Fine, you *were* a Hookman,' Shilah said. 'And I thought they would know everything about the Khatdom. Otherwise how would they find all those *menacing* runaways.'

'I wasn't a Hookman,' Dunes said. 'Hamman was a Hookman. And Hamman is gone.'

Shilah gave a heated sigh, looking as though she might burst from frustration. Her hand slipped into the Coldmaker bag, resting on the bronze. 'Okay, fine, but—'

'Shilah,' I said, giving her a stern look.

She shrugged. 'Well, if he doesn't know anything about anything, why are we even keeping him around?'

Dunes slumped into himself, which almost wasn't possible considering the stacks of dense muscle.

'Because he's the only one of us who knows how to really fight,' I countered. 'And track. And he knows about the other Hookmen who are currently hunting us down and trying to kill us. *And* he's family.'

'Let me see your hand,' Shilah said quickly.

'No. It's *fine*.'

She smirked. 'I'm going to catch you off guard.'

'Also, how are we going to find Cam and Split without Dunes?' I asked.

'Well, if this place was part of the Coldmarch, I assume Split knows a secret way inside,' Shilah said. 'So if we *also* find a way inside, I bet we'll find them too. I don't think it's going to be nearly as difficult a task as crossing the Singe in an Ice boat. Which we did just fine, thank you very much.'

'This is serious,' I said.

I wanted to smirk and remind her she'd dubbed the Ice boat an 'Abb-boat', but the pain in my hand made any sort of light-heartedness impossible. I was petrified to peel off the boilweed and see my skin. Proper inventing took two hands – at least a lot of it did – and if I'd screwed up my abilities I'd never forgive myself.

Or the Crier.

'Fine,' Shilah said, turning on our brute of a companion, who was still scratching at the city bricks with his giant blade. '*Dunes*. How do we get inside the city?'

The Hookman shook his head. The wound on his cheek was seeping blood, and I wished I had some salve for him. And I also wished I had some for me, although the excruciating pain in my hand seemed far past the abilities of groan salve.

'I don't know anything about the city,' Dunes said. 'Hamman knew a lot. But I am not Hamman.'

Shilah threw up her hands in frustration. 'Wonderful news. What a lucky break in having you switch sides.'

Dunes's expression darkened and he scraped his thumb up his hooked blade, drawing blood. It looked incredibly painful, but he didn't flinch.

'Stop that,' I said. 'We need you whole.'

Immediately he snatched his thumb away and bowed. 'By your command, Meshua.'

Shilah rolled her eyes. 'Sure. Well, if we can't count on any secret Hookman knowledge to get us into the city, then we have to think logically. We need to find the alder. That's been one consistent thing this whole Coldmarch, and maybe we skipped a few shacks on the way, but I bet if we can find the alder we can get inside.'

I nodded, glancing up at the high walls. 'I can't think of anything better.'

'*Dunes*,' Shilah said, without hiding her contempt. 'Do you know of any red alder anywhere on these walls? Maybe there's a cave or something with the colour painted on the entrance? Or a picture of the flowers themselves?'

Dunes shook his head. 'I don't know anything about this city. I am reborn. I am free from the shackles of the past.'

Shilah sighed and took out her mother's map of the

Khatdom. She traced her fingers around the City of David's Fall section, her lips pinching sideways in frustration. 'I don't see anything that—'

'I can guess,' Dunes said quickly under his breath, not meeting our eyes. 'I can guess at things, Meshua. Ask me to guess and I might be able to.'

'Guess then,' Shilah said, raising an eyebrow.

'*Meshua*,' Dunes said, clearing his throat. 'Would you like me to guess?'

I gave Shilah a look that said 'please just go with it' and put a hand on the Hookman's shoulder. The muscle there was corded and hard, and I wondered if he might be able to scale the wall just on the strength of his forearms alone. 'Please, Dunes. Guess where there might be some red alder.'

Dunes paused, his face pinched with concentration. I could tell he was making the act of recalling the information look much harder than it really was. Considering my past behaviour, I wasn't one to judge how he dealt with grief.

'I guess,' Dunes said, 'you might mean the Closed Eye with the red lid. Hamman always found it strange.'

'Red lid?' I asked.

'Do you know about the Coldmarch?' Shilah asked carefully. 'Is that why it was shut down? Because the Khat found out?'

'No. But I'd *guess*,' Dunes said, hiding his face, 'that if you looked hard enough to the top of the wall, and knew the right general spot, you might be able to see the red on the small eye.'

Shilah tugged at her braid and gave me a begrudging nod, the kind that told me to press on.

'Dunes,' I said, 'which direction?'

He gave a violent shake of his head, sucking in a breath through his wide nose.

'This is going to get very old, very fast,' Shilah said.

'Guess, please, Dunes,' I said gently.

'I'd guess . . . four hundred or so paces to the right,' Dunes said, his face scrunched again. 'Around the lumpy pieces of quartz that look like hands and next to a limestone face with the three-colour striations. Probably.'

I nodded.

Four hundred or so paces later, around two pieces of quartz – that very much looked like hands – next to the limestone face with the triple striations, I stopped and looked up.

The thinnest shade of red was painted on the Closed Eye statue above the wall, the eye indeed slightly smaller than the rest.

'You can guess about things all you want, Dunes,' I said, trying not to think about the searing pain in my hand.

Dunes didn't answer me, instead dropping into a slave stance. His body looked oddly used to the slight hunch and bowed limbs.

That's when I had a revelation.

The Hookmen were supposed to be demons.

They were the nightmare of Jadan children, one of the things that kept us from moving even an inch off our sleeping blankets after curfew. Here was a creature of darkness, with hundreds of scars all over his body to signify all the Jadans he'd damned. But he was just as tortured and broken as those he was tasked to capture. Perhaps more so. I wondered, had Dunes lived his life with more or less freedom than I had? Even though he'd been able to move about the Khatdom without a taskmaster, or chains, he was still very much under the crushing weight of the Noble thumb.

I'd never been forced to capture and destroy my own kin.

My heart broke for him.

'And would you look at that,' Shilah said, pointing at my feet.

I would have missed it had she not pointed it out, but there was an orangefruit peel tucked under a rock.

'That looks fresh,' she said. 'You think someone's been here?'

'Cam,' I said without hesitation.

'How do you know?' Shilah asked.

I clucked my tongue, picking up the rind. Orangefruit had a special place in my friendship with Cam. To my astonishment, Cam had bought me one not long after we'd met, and he also left a pile of them at my side to wake up to in Leroi's study, back when I was first running from the Vicaress. If Cam wanted to leave a discreet sign for me that wouldn't draw attention from any passersby, this would be the perfect way.

'I can guess too,' I said.

She bit her bottom lip, a playful look in her eyes. 'Your sudden wisdom doesn't have anything to do with those faded dwarf camel prints over there, does it?'

A faint trail of hoof marks indented the ground nearby, just barely discernible, the wind having scraped away most of the evidence.

'Doesn't hurt to have two signs,' I said.

'Let me see your hand,' Shilah said quickly.

'No.'

She sighed, going up to the wall and running her hands over the brick until they came upon a small empty space. A line of red rimmed the top edge. She went to put an eye up to the hole, but—

'Wait!' Dunes shouted, everything about him flexing at once. This looked quite daunting.

Shilah pulled away from the wall with a start. 'What?'

'It's cooler in the holes. The Sun can't reach in those places,' Dunes said, gently brushing her aside. 'That means it's perfect for . . .'

He fitted the tip of his curved blade into the dark nook and rattled the metal around, thoroughly scraping. Two white scorpions scuttled out, dropping to the sands and burying themselves beneath the ground in quick succession. Dunes sucked in a huge breath, and gave a mighty blow into the hole. A plump scorpion waddled out next, tumbling to the sands and landing on its back, legs flailing. Dunes pressed the tip of the blade in one more time, jiggling it back and forth. Eventually he gave a satisfied nod, dropping back into slave stance.

'I promised to keep you and your companion safe, Meshua,' he said. 'I would take the pain first.'

Shilah looked as if she was about to say something barbed, but then took a deep breath. 'Thank you, Dunes. That was a very fine thing, saving me from stings.'

Dunes nodded. 'It is obvious that you are important to Meshua. I will keep you safe.'

Shilah's cheeks gave a light flush as she quickly pressed her eye to the shadowy hole.

'The alder in here spells hope again,' she said. 'With an arrow. And there's also . . .'

She gave a scoff and then reached in with two fingers, pulling out another orangefruit rind. She wiggled it in my face, annoyance and amusement splitting equal territory across her cheeks. 'Now we know why there were so many scorpions in there. Your friend needs to think twice about his ideas.'

'*Our* friend,' I said. 'And it wasn't Cam's fault. He just wanted me to know he was here.'

Shilah gently placed the rind on top of the wiggling scorpion stranded on its back. 'Eat up, girl. Looks like you're eating for many.'

'What's the message say?' I asked.

Shilah's face creased up as she felt around in the hole. All of a sudden a small section of the wall pulled back, as if on hinges, revealing a hidden Khatclock face. It was just like the ones in Mama Jana's shop and at Split's shack.

'All this time,' Dunes whispered, although there was something off in his tone.

The hands of the ancient Khatclock were both pointed downwards, poised over a Closed Eye. Shilah spun the hands North without a moment's hesitation. Gears turned, locks clicked, and once again a hidden passageway revealed itself.

The tunnel smelled damp and musty, which meant there was likely a water source somewhere inside. This was terribly lucky, as we only had Dunes's waterskin to share amongst the three of us, and it was nearly empty.

Shilah went to step in the tunnel, but Dunes cleared his throat.

'Yes?' Shilah asked carefully.

'I would like to go first. Just in case.'

'In case of what?' Shilah asked.

Dunes held his blade out and stepped into the tunnel without answering her, folding himself at the shoulders to fit. Shilah watched him shuffle into the dark, and stuck a hand on my chest.

'You have a bad feeling again?' I asked. 'We kind of have no choice at this point.'

She shook her head, continuing to watch Dunes's back as he disappeared into the dark tunnel. Then, without warning, she spun and planted a kiss right on my lips. This one was soft and dry, barely touching. My vision went hazy and I nearly joined the white scorpion on the ground, pinned on my back and flailing.

She pulled back too soon.

'I—'

She licked her top lip and then wrapped a hand around the back of my neck, pulling our faces together. This kiss was much harder, raw and full of passion. She was heat lightning to my Shocklands. I was helpless in her grip, once again a young and inexperienced boy. Her lips parted mine. I went to tilt my head to the side in case I was doing something wrong, but she kept it in place, her fingernails scratching up into my hair. She kept her tongue exploring, the wet touch letting me know it was all right. I almost melted, losing focus of everything around me, mesmerized by how tender lips could still be so commanding. The swell of her chest pressed into me, and I wanted to angle away out of courtesy and respect – and to hide my own excitement – but she kept me in place, making my whole body aware of her warm presence.

Before I knew it, she'd undone the knot of boilweed from my hand, the wrap having fallen clean off.

A lump formed in my throat. 'Hey, I—'

She *shushed* me and took my wrist gently in her hand. My elation plummeted into despair. My wound was far worse than I'd thought, and I grimaced heavily at the sight, my stomach clenching and forcing up a dry gag. The skin was blackened, darker than pure ash, consuming my pinky and ring finger. Both nails had cracked off, and the black stain stretched around into my palm. I was jagged and ugly, the Abb having proven itself to be far more than I could handle.

The Sun, seizing the prime opportunity, bit into my wound with fervour, causing the pain to flare up and my whole body to shudder with shame and fear.

'Oh, Spout,' Shilah said, her face all concern.

And then something in me snapped.

It wasn't the act of undressing my wound that set me off, or even the fact that the back of my hand looked like it had just spent a week on top of a blacksmith's anvil, but rather it was Shilah's tone that caused the break. I didn't need pity. Pity was only fitting if I'd indeed been betrayed by the machine. Pity was only fitting if I was truly out of my depth.

I'd tried to save one of my people, to harness the goodness and compassion of the Crier, and I'd been crippled for my efforts. Punished for even trying. Pity meant Shilah's kiss had been nothing but a ploy. It rubbed in the fact that only one of us had been burned.

So much for world partner.

The echo of her words grated on my soul, and because I couldn't bear to look at my hand, I snatched it behind my back and practically hissed at her.

'Give me my bag,' I said.

Shilah's face had become unnaturally soft, which made the twisted feeling even worse. 'I'm sorry—'

'Now,' I said, not meeting her eyes.

'Spout,' she said, under her breath. 'I just wanted to—'

Heat shot into my face, the corners of my eyes moistening. My hand felt as though it had been dipped in a kiln and left to dry. 'I have more boilweed in the bag. Give it to me.'

She nodded, taking the Coldmaker off her shoulder. I snatched out a new strip of the grey plant, making sure there were no scarabs hiding in the fibres, and quickly covered my hand up, trying not to snarl under the pressure.

'Spout,' Shilah said, pushing out her bottom lip. She reached out a hand towards the back of my neck. 'I just wanted to make sure—'

I hurled past and left the machine lying on the ground, following Dunes into the darkness of the tunnel.

Despite my squirming, Cam didn't let me out of his grip. His yellow hair was wild and matted, and there were shadows haunting his eyes. His ripped shirt was still tinged with Gales breath, which wasn't exactly pleasant, but I was glad to inhale the bitterness. The smell reminded me that we were all together, still on the Coldmarch, and our path hadn't become as broken as my hand.

'Do I know my Spout, or do I know my Spout?' Cam asked, finally releasing me and clapping my shoulders. He shot a careful look behind me as if expecting Dunes to lunge. When it became clear the Hookman wasn't going to do anything of the sort, Cam flattened his hair and gave Split a smarmy look.

'Told you the orangefruit would do it,' Cam said.

'Very good, Camlish,' Split said, quite sullen as he sat around the mysterious pool in the centre of the cave, his elbows resting on his knees. His face was only half lit by the few candles set by the water's edge. There was another source of light around the back of the cave, but it was dim and gritty, and I couldn't quite make out how it was being made. It looked a bit as though someone had grabbed a star from the sky and smeared it across the stones, making sure the resulting layer of dust was as thin as possible.

'Yeah, your genius plan almost got me a face full of scorpion stings,' Shilah said.

Cam cocked his head to the side. 'Oh. Sorry.'

'Don't sorry anything,' I said. 'It was a good idea, and it got us here.'

Cam clucked his tongue, turning to Split. 'In that case, pay up, Pedlar.'

'I'm not going to do it now,' Split growled.

'I thought you were the pinnacle of merchants,' Cam said. 'Someone who deals in deals.'

From the intense glower Split offered, I thought the Pedlar might grab Cam and toss him face first into the swirling water. The pool was hypnotic, its gentle rings swelling inwards. The current was drawn towards the centre, where it funnelled downwards, as if there were a hole in the bottom.

Cam lowered his voice, poking me in the stomach. 'I bet the old man that you'd find us here no problem.'

'Bet for what?' I asked.

'He has to show us the traditional Crying Dance,' Cam said, pointing to the raised platform next to the water. On the polished stone was a raised cone of earth, over which a very strange garment was draped. I couldn't make out the clothing clearly, but the object looked lumpy and stringy at the same time. It wouldn't make for a very effective armour, if indeed that's what it was.

Cam leaned in and lowered his voice, glancing over my shoulder at Dunes again, fear in his eyes. 'I thought some exercise might do his mood good.'

Split was still refusing to look our way, the light from the candles not meeting his face. He should have been at least a little happy to see his flock intact.

'Is that Adaam Grass?' Shilah shouted, pointing to the back of the cave. She'd been preoccupied rubbing Picka's snout, the little camel having rolled on its side, licking Shilah's fingers.

Split nodded, waving a flippant hand at the smeared brilliance. 'It's old and bitter, though. Not many cool places left in the world, and no one to pull the weeds.'

'I thought Adaam Grass became extinct during the Drought?' Shilah said, her hands over her mouth. 'It's beautiful.'

Picka grumbled from below, nudging Shilah with her snout.

'I told you both before,' Split grumbled, still not looking away from the waters. 'This ain't Paphos. There's a lot you two don't understand. A *lot*.'

'So tell us,' I said, trying to keep composed. My wrist hurt so much that I could feel the throbbing in my jaw.

Shilah was already on her way towards the back of the cave to look at the Adaam Grass. I'd never seen her skip before, and it was quite disorientating.

'Like what,' Split huffed.

'Like is what the Vicaress said true? You fell in love with a Jadan?'

Split hunched over further, grumbling something into his knees. 'Don't say that in front of a Hookman. He might slice your tongue out just for the notion.'

Dunes collapsed further into his slave stance. 'I am not a Hookman.'

'He's family,' I said without pause. 'And you had a daughter with this Jadan?'

Split rubbed a hand under his nose. He looked disappointed to find it clean. 'Yeah, so what?'

'So,' I said. 'So that means you're family too. And you must want the World Cried to change as much as we do.'

Split fell silent, his hands squeezed into fists.

'What happened back in that cart?' Cam asked after a spell, gesturing to the hand I was keeping hidden behind my back. 'We were just about to come and check on you, and all of a sudden there was shouting and mayhem, and everyone was grabbing weapons, and there were horns blasting everywhere. I thought those bastard Hookmen had found us for sure.' Cam swallowed hard, giving an apologetic wave to Dunes. 'The real Hookmen I mean.'

'It was an accident,' I said, making sure to keep my hand out of sight. Jolts of fire raced up my arm with each word I spoke.

'Accident?' Cam asked, trying to sneak a look behind my back. 'Must have been a pretty powerful accident. What happened, you sneeze out a big explosion of Cold?'

'Don't joke!' Shilah exclaimed from the back of the cave, hunched over the Adaam Grass. 'He's actually hurt.'

'It's. Fine.' I said between my teeth.

'Is Camlish Tavor being true, Meshua?' Dunes asked in such a serious voice that it made my stomach clench even further. 'Is that a power that the Crier above has bestowed upon you? Sneezing Cold?'

'No,' I chided. 'He's not being true.'

'I was joking,' Cam said. 'Obviously.'

'Nothing is obvious any more,' Dunes said, taking a step closer to my back. His presence was so large it felt as if he was blocking my entire retreat. 'The world will be reborn, just as I have been. A new day is dawning for Jadankind, under the Opened Eye of the Crier above.'

'Okay, that's fine,' Cam said, stepping away and making sure he didn't slip into the water. 'Anyway. That cart had traces of Ice everywhere, and those runaway girls looked like they were in shock.'

I finally took a moment to survey the walls of the vast cavern, the tunnel behind the Khatclock having funnelled us down into a wide dome beneath the land, bigger than all the other chambers combined. There were alder prayers and Opened Eyes scrawled on the walls wherever I looked, and more shrines to the Crier piled with ancient gifts. But the most interesting thing about the place continued to be the perfectly round pool, the current ushering the waters to the centre.

'Are they alive?' I asked, having trouble getting the words out. 'The Domestics in the cart?'

'Yes. I think so,' Cam said, his face betraying his uncertainty. 'We didn't stay long once we realized you both had run. And Spout, you should have seen it! All the Nobles were so scared and confused by everything and they just babbled on and tried to rationalize things. The Coldmaker really is going to change everything! They didn't know what to do!'

'They knew what to do, all right,' Split said, gently scratching his thigh.

'Split, are we safe in here?' I asked.

The Pedlar let out a dark laugh, his scratching growing more pronounced. 'Safe?'

'This is all part of the Coldmarch, right?' I asked. 'So it's still a secret? The Khat doesn't know about it in the city? Dunes said that—'

'It *was* a secret.' Split cracked his knuckles, waves of pain wafting off his face. 'It *was* safe.'

'Why only *was*?' I asked, trying to spot any ledges where bodies might hide. The cave had dozens of nooks, which did not make me feel confident that we were alone.

Split finally turned towards me, his expression pure rage. 'Because there's a Sun-damned Hookman standing right behind you, fool!'

Against the candlelight cast onto the walls, I watched Dunes's shadow grow taller.

'I am not a Hook—'

Split wrenched himself to his feet, looking wobbly and confused. I wondered if the Pedlar had somehow managed to snag himself another vial of Dream from someone in the caravan. He dug around in his pocket, fingers fumbling, and pulled out a small blade, the perfect size for coring a young Khatmelon. Split let out a frustrated cry and stumbled towards us, pushing me aside and plunging right for Dunes's chest, heartbreakingly slow for such an impassioned attack.

'My daughter!' Split cried, followed by a hiccup. 'Her little fist didn't even fit all the way in my palm, you monster!'

Dunes didn't have to react very quickly to avoid getting stabbed, wrapping a hand around the Pedlar's soft wrist to halt the blade. Dunes left the weapon's point against his chest, however. The veins in the Pedlar's neck bulged as Split pressed and squirmed, but to no avail.

'You might as well have killed her!' Split shouted, flecks of spit jumping off his lips. 'You Sun-pissed, shit-brained beast! You're all the same!'

Dunes turned to me, sadness all over his face, but otherwise completely in control. 'What do you wish me to do, Meshua?'

'YOU DON'T GET TO CALL HIM THAT!' Split tried using two hands to push the blade in, his legs slipping on the smooth stone. Dunes easily held him at bay. 'YOU BETRAY HIS KIND!'

Dunes kept his eyes locked on mine, the question still on his lips. The Pedlar started to use his feet as weapons instead, aiming violent kicks at Dunes's shins, thrusting a knee at his groin. Even with considerable blows, Dunes didn't seem to register any of the damage, remaining completely still.

'Split!' I shouted, reaching out, but then seeing the boilweed on my wrist and stopping short. 'Calm down!'

The Pedlar only grew more furious, pushing harder against the behemoth, his eyes bloodshot and distant. 'My wife was more beautiful than the night sky.'

'Do something!' I shouted to Dunes. 'Don't let him stab you.'

'The knife is so small,' Dunes said, as if commenting on the weight of a pebble. 'There is no concern for you, Crierson.'

'Get rid of it!' I shouted.

Dunes gave a single nod and performed a twisting manoeuvre with his hand. Split's blade went clattering sideways, slipping into the swirling water.

'What else may I do to serve you?' Dunes asked calmly. 'I am yours to command.'

Split's arms went down, hanging straight by his sides, hands still in fists. He stared up into Dunes's face, ready to spit. 'This pool is peace, you imbecile! You can't throw weapons in.'

Dunes shrugged. 'Apologies. I did not know. This is all new to my eyes.'

I stepped in between Split and Dunes, trying to keep my voice as gentle as I could, as fear was flooding my heart. 'Split. He didn't kill them. He had nothing to do with it.'

Dunes stepped closer to me, watching from right over my shoulder.

'Can you back up, please?' I asked him.

'Apologies,' Dunes said. 'What were their names, Pedlar?'

'I'll gouge out your eyes!' Split shouted, hurling an accusatory finger.

I heard a violent rip and turned to see Dunes ripping his shirt in two, revealing the rows of scars, not an ounce of his skin left unmarred. It made all my whipping marks seem pathetic in comparison.

Dunes took a deep breath. 'These belonged to Hamman. His name is not mine.'

'Anyah Ben-Fellezehall,' Split said, his hand going over his heart. 'My perfect daughter's name was Anyah. And her mother, Lizah. And they were stolen and butchered by one of you.'

Dunes shook his head. 'This was not by my hand.'

Split erupted, the bald patch on his head reddening. 'It doesn't matter. One of you stormed into my camp and—'

'How long ago?' Dunes asked quietly.

Split's eyes were daggers. 'Fifteen. Fifteen empty, hopeless, lifeless years.'

'Hookmen are put to death after ten years of service,' Dunes said without hesitation. 'The Vicaress calls it a reward. If it's any consolation, I can assure you that whoever took your wife and daughter is most certainly gone.'

A heavy silence descended.

'Hamman was a Hookman for eight years,' Dunes said, a tear crossing the fresh wound on his cheek. 'And made to do terrible things. I am very sorry for what has been done to you, Split the Pedlar. I am the only one here who knows what that truly means, and I will do everything I can to keep you safe on this, most holy, Coldmarch. You have my word on all the Cold that falls from the sky and on Meshua's golden miracle. I am not your enemy.'

The only sound in the cave came from the swirling water of the pool. I could hear my heart beating in my ears, trying to decide if I should intervene.

'I will never trust you,' Split said, venom oozing from his words. 'I will *never* trust you. You have the scars to prove why I won't.'

Dunes nodded. 'I am here to protect you either way, Split the Pedlar, Shepherd of the great Meshua.'

Another long pause struck. I had a feeling the *Meshua* thing wouldn't be going away anytime soon, regardless of my requests.

'You must have killed dozens of wives and children,' Split said.

'I only captured them.' Then Dunes's face jolted in shock. '*He* only ever captured them. The Vicaress kills. Hamman is gone.'

'That's the same damned thing, and you know it,' Split said. 'Innocent Jadan lives were stolen because of you.'

Shilah came back, her palm closed tightly into a fist. A bit of light escaped the cracks between her fingers. 'Split, I'm with you,' she said. 'But can't you see Dunes has been a slave his whole life, just like us? Just like your wife and daughter. He didn't have a choice. He's a victim in all of this, which is exactly the kind of reason why we have to finish the Coldmarch and get our machine to Langria so—'

'There's always a choice,' Split snarled, pointing a thumb at his chest. 'I was born a High Noble and I chose right. You don't think I wouldn't have been *captured* too if the Khat found out I chose to abandon my blood and become a Shepherd?'

Dunes nodded. 'Yes. And I finally know the path.'

'Eight years too late, *Hamman*,' Split said, hocking some phlegm and going to spit, but then keeping it in his mouth and swallowing. He thrust a finger at the ground near the pool. 'Peace.'

Then the Pedlar stormed off, disappearing into one of the dark nooks.

Cam cleared his throat. 'So . . . I guess no Crying Dance then.'

Shilah scoffed, readjusting the Coldmaker bag on her

shoulder so she could push Cam in the chest. 'Show some respect.'

Cam sighed, lowering his head. 'I'm sorry, I'm not good with these situations. I just—'

Split returned all of a sudden, his hand outstretched. In his fingers was a vial of Glassland Dream. He came up to me and placed the grey powder against my chest. 'I got it for you, Spout. In case you wanted to make another scroll. And don't ask, because I don't know why it's not full. Anyway, good luck fixing a dead world.'

Then the Pedlar turned and stumbled towards Picka. He grabbed her reins and tried to pull. The beast wouldn't give, braying with her lips pulled back from her teeth.

'Get up, you daft girl!' Split said, poking her haunches with his foot. 'We're going home.'

'Split,' I said. 'I need your help. I need to know what you know.'

'Here's something I know,' he said. 'The Khat didn't shut down the Coldmarch. Langria shut down the Coldmarch. And I never found out why.'

It felt as if I'd been punched in the throat. 'What do you mean?'

Split grunted, Picka refusing to yield. 'I know you're the supposed saviour for your people and everything, but even saviours should know that sometimes you just can't save everyone.'

I unravelled the boilweed, dropping the soiled wrapping on the stone and angling my hand so the dim light might catch my shame. 'This is what happens when I don't have my Shepherd. Please, Split. I can't do this without you.'

Split gave another yank of the camel's reins and then dropped them with a frustrated huff, turning to me instead. At the sight of my nasty wound, his face became more pinched than normal.

'You dip it in fire?' he asked.

I shook my head, my whole arm trembling. Having my humiliation out in the open made the pain more real, and I started breathing heavily, thoughts of my father pressing hard against my chest. Air became difficult to capture, and I could feel my limbs beginning to grow numb.

'It was an accident,' I assured myself in between breaths, sobs wracking my chest. There was no sense of wonder here. No reason. Just regret and despair. 'The Cold attacked me.'

'It's okay, kid,' Split said, coming over and giving me an awkward pat on the head, unsure of his movements. 'Shhh. It's okay.'

'I lost my family too,' I said, sucking in a heavy breath. 'And my friends.'

'Me too,' Shilah said gently. 'I lost my mother.'

'I lost my cousin,' Cam said, his lips twitching.

Dunes went to add something, but I quietened him with a swift shake of my head.

'I always assumed it was a Hookman that took my mother,' Shilah said. 'She was a runaway. The Coldmarch turned her down, so she was going to map a way North herself. We were going to go together, but she never came back.'

Another stone in my throat.

I tried, but could not speak.

Split's face constricted with surprise. 'Then how can you stand here while this monster—'

'Because this is not a Hookman,' Shilah said, opening her palm and moving it closer to Dunes's face so the plant's light might illuminate his features. 'This is someone trying to do something right, and if we're not allowed to change, then what's the Sun-damned point in anything. Split, everything depends on us getting to Langria, and Dunes can help.'

Split took a series of deep breaths, each one deeper than

the last. The air seemed to sprinkle sand over the flames behind his eyes. 'Dammit, fine. I'll stay.'

'Good,' Shilah said with a definitive nod. 'Micah is right. You're family too.'

The silence lasted until it turned awkward.

'And that means you'll show us the Crying Dance?' Cam asked, his cheeks red.

'I ain't going to do no dancing,' Split snarled.

Cam's mouth raised into a half smirk. 'A bet's a bet, you trash-slinging, knuckle-licking, fart-in-a-jar, sorry excuse for a swindler.'

Shilah suppressed a gasp, and I nearly toppled over into the pool. Cam's impression of Gilly was startlingly accurate, although performed at the completely wrong time.

Split wobbled a bit, blinked a few times, and then burst out laughing. The chuckles were followed by hiccups, reverberating around the cave. 'You little shit!'

Cam bit his bottom lip and then shrugged. 'Got to earn my keep somehow.'

Split sighed, slumping back next to the water, elbows again folding over his knees. The rest of us gathered beside him, taking a place along the waterline. Dunes slunk away, finding himself a nice quiet spot amongst the dark cave formations. I didn't stop him.

Shilah opened her palm, the Adaam Grass inside having already begun to lose its shiny lustre. She gave Split a questioning look, poking at the blades with her fingernail.

'The light dies when you pluck it,' Split said, rubbing the blisters on his feet. 'Something to do with the rocks.'

Shilah's face deflated.

'It's okay,' Split said with a shrug. 'You didn't know.'

She sighed, giving the dying blades a careful stroke.

I pulled another piece of boilweed from the bag and began to cover my horrible fingers, wincing each time I circled my hand.

'I've never seen a Cold wound,' Split said through his teeth. 'I didn't know that was possible.'

I continued to add layer over layer until my shame was gone from sight.

I swallowed hard. 'Neither did I.'

'Is the pain really bad?' he asked.

'All sorts,' I said.

Split's hand went to his pocket, searching with greedy fingers. 'I thought I had something to— it could help you with the . . .'

'You already gave me the vial of Dream,' I said. 'I'd rather not use it for now.'

'That's right.' Split coughed, but I could tell it was just to cover his own shame. 'We'll find you a Healer before continuing the March.' Split pointed up at the ceiling of the cave. 'I'm sure there's a few up there.'

'I don't think any Healers would know what to do with this,' I said, letting out a sigh. 'Maybe one.'

Shilah reached over and put a steadying hand on my thigh. I refused to look at her fingers, even as they gently dug in and massaged the muscle. 'Let me show you something.'

I ignored her.

'Split,' I said, thinking back to the Domestics in the cart, musing over what they'd said about the Sanctuary. Something just didn't sound right about the place, although few things in the Khatdom were actually right. 'I don't know much about things outside of Paphos. Can you tell me about the City of David's Fall?'

Split sniffed, wiping away some crust from his nostrils. 'What do you want to know?'

Shilah held out her palm. 'How about why there is still Adaam Grass—'

'Why do the Closed Eye statues all look so different?' I asked, cutting her off, telling myself it was out of genuine curiosity and not spite. 'The ones ringing the walls.'

Shilah's hand lifted off my thigh.

Split looped his finger around his head. 'Ding ding. You want to know your history then? From the beginning?'

I nodded, swallowing hard so I didn't let on how much my hand was suffering.

'Camlish' Split gave a meaningful chortle. 'Go ahead and tell them.'

Cam was sitting cross-legged, leaning towards the waters and checking his reflection. 'What makes you think I know that sort of stuff, Split?'

Split gave Cam a look as if he'd just called the Sun *polite*.

'What?' Cam said, prodding a blister on the back of his hand with a wince. 'I don't know. You tell them.'

'Rules of the Coldmarch,' Split said. 'Don't lie to your Shepherd. A High Noble spawn like you, I'd wager both my legs that you know the history of this city to the letter. You shouldn't have quoted all the old Khat nonsense to me before and given away your smarts. Not real smarts, mind you. I always said it don't take brilliance to regurgitate, only the fine ability to vomit. You probably spent most of your days in a blissfully cool library, memorizing things about the people outside. Am I wrong, Tavor?'

'It's okay, Cam,' I said. 'You can tell us.'

'Shivers and Frosts, Spout.' Cam shook his head. 'I don't want you to associate me with that kind of stuff.'

'Please,' I said, my eyelids feeling unnecessarily heavy. I'd had plenty of sleep in the slave cart, and shouldn't have been so tired, but I had a feeling my fatigue was more in the mind than the body. 'I want to know. I won't associate anything with you.'

Cam let out a long sigh. 'Fine. But if I tell them, Split, you show us the traditional Crying Dance afterwards.'

'If anyone would be in the mood to dance,' Split said under his breath.

Cam closed his eyes. His stomach gave a loud rumble. 'Can I hold the Coldmaker?'

I shrugged, looking at Shilah, who still had the machine's bag slung over her shoulder. My mangled hand left me feeling very little attachment to the invention.

'Why?' she asked.

'Can I please just hold it?' Cam asked. 'It will help.'

Shilah slid the bag over. 'You'd better not let it fall in the water.'

'I'd fall in first,' Cam said, taking the bag and letting the canvas lips fall open. He ran his fingers along the bronze Eye. 'You did a great job with the carving, Spout. And I can't believe this metal is still so cool after—'

'Quit stalling, Tavor,' Split grumbled. 'Can't you see Shilah's grass is dying.'

Shilah closed her palm.

Cam sighed, keeping his hand pressed against the machine. 'The City of David's Fall, originally called Ziah, was the site of the first Jadan rebellion after the Drought. This was their stronghold.'

Shilah gave me a playful nudge with her elbow, trying to get me to look at her, but I kept my focus on Cam. Her hand slid back onto my thigh, but I was too tired to deal with both things at the moment.

'So eight hundred years ago the Drought struck and Cold stopped falling in all the Patches of all the main cities, right?' Cam asked to no one in particular, but seemed like he expected an answer.

I nodded. 'Except Paphos.'

'Except Paphos and *Ziah*. The world began dying, and everywhere began to heat up, but not those two places.'

'And Langria,' Shilah pointed out.

Cam nodded quickly. 'Yes, but no one knows anything about Langria.'

'Split does,' Shilah said.

Split swallowed hard. 'I only know what I'm told.'

'Keep going, Cam,' I said. 'Ziah.'

Cam put both hands on the Coldmaker, his fingers shaking. 'The first Khat was already declaring himself divine, making slaves out of all the other kings and queens of the time, offering chains or death. The Khat claimed to have received his Gospels while standing out in his Cry Patch at night. Instead of taking shelter, the Khat stood in the middle of the sands, opening his arms and closing his eyes. Not a single piece of Cold struck him. Instead, when it was all over he found a Frost at his feet, the giant piece of Cold covered entirely in Ice. The Khat touched the Ice and heard the word of the Crier, telling him the decrees. So the world kept dying and the Khat spread his Gospels across the land, enlightening all the Jadan people – mind you, everyone was Jadan back then – how he had been the only one deemed worthy, and how the Crier decided to let his brother Sun cleanse the world through heat. Right?'

I nodded again. None of this information was new to me.

'But there was one problem, and this is something you won't hear in the Gospels. Ziah's Patch kept getting Cold. Every night the heavens Cried here, Cold falling vast and high on the plateaus. Nowadays it's all Noble homes and shops and monuments up there. Apparently there's a particularly decent selection of—'

'So what happened?' I asked.

'So instead of bowing to the Khat, a lot of Jadans chose to come here to Ziah. They were questioned extensively, but as long as they didn't work for the Khat they were welcomed in by King David. Given Cold and shelter and a place to pray. They built walls around the Cry Patch and dug homes into the land so there was more space' – Cam gestured around the cave – 'and fortified up their surroundings, while the

Khat amassed his armies and made slaves out of everyone else in the World Cried, claiming his divinity and making Paphos the capitol. Now, not all the books say this, and I've only found it in a few old scrolls, but apparently the more Jadans who came to Ziah, the more Cold began to fall in their Patches, almost like the Crier wanted to provide for all the newcomers.'

'Nonsense,' Split added with a huff, but his eyes did flash to the Coldmaker, his fingernails digging into his thigh.

Cam ignored the Pedlar, continuing on. 'Some stories say the Patches here became crazy fertile, like dozens-of-Frosts-a-night kind of fertile, and thousands upon thousands of Shivers and Chills. Obviously there wasn't enough space for everyone, but the Jadans spilled over the walls and made encampments outside. King David was beloved and revered.' Cam took a breath. 'And then the Khat arrived with his armies.'

My body went stiff and my vision hazy as I stared at the swirling water.

'But instead of attacking and destroying everything like he so easily could have, the Khat decided to prove to everyone that he was the divine one once and for all, and that Ziah was a false land of trickery, prospering only by the interloping of Sun. The Khat gave the resisting Jadans one last chance to come with him and declare themselves his slaves in Paphos. A lot of them buckled at the sight of so many swords, but some Jadans remained steadfast, not believing the Khat, since Ziah and King David seemed to have been chosen by the Crier as well.'

Cam paused, tapping his fingers on the bronze Eye.

'Don't hold back now,' Split said.

Cam sighed. 'So the Khat sent word to all that Ziah would burn, and anyone inside would be left to the Sun's mercy for all eternity. He kept his forces sieging the city at all sides, but didn't attack. Instead, he waited and watched, with all of his slaves and armies at his sides. And then Ziah began to heat up. It was only slight at first, but it kept getting hotter and hotter, and the ancient texts say that in a matter of days the streets were like fiery coals. All the plants and animals died and turned to ash. Cold finally stopped falling in the Patches, and their rivers and waters began to boil and the—'

'Spout.'

I sat up, the side of my head throbbing. 'Hmmm?'

'You passed out,' Cam said. 'Is it your hand?'

'You okay?' Shilah asked, more pity in her voice.

I blinked away my confusion. For a moment I saw Cam's father hiding behind his face, but the vision went away. 'Hmm?'

'Your hand,' Cam said.

'I'm fine,' I said, a little too forcefully, touching the boil-weed wrap and wincing.

'Meshua!' Dunes called from somewhere in the darkness, his massive shadow slinking between the rocks outlined by the Adaam Grass light. 'Are you in need of anything? I will get it for you!'

'It's okay, Dunes,' I said.

'Let's just get you some sleep,' Cam said. 'I can finish—'

'No,' I said, not meaning it. My hand was an endless pit of agony. 'Please. Keep going. I need to know.'

Cam looked to Split, who made a go-ahead motion.

'Ziah was burning up, the land scorching from within,' Cam said, giving me a strange look. 'And the people— you sure you're okay?'

I nodded. 'Yes. Please, I need to know.'

Cam sighed. 'The people inside the walls tried to escape, but the Khat's armies wouldn't let them, trapping everyone inside. They bricked up all the ways out. There were pleas and screaming and begging, but the Khat claimed that the Jadans had sealed their fates. He promised them that the only way they might be saved was if they destroyed their beloved temples and sculpted the perfect Closed Eye from the rubble, proving their insignificance. So, as the air inside the city grew more and more stifling, the holy houses were destroyed and melted, and every Jadan in the city frantically tried their hand at making the perfect Closed Eye. They dropped them over the walls by rope, but the Khat claimed none of them were good enough, and that every soul inside was found wanting.

'Inside, the heat became too much to bear, and all of Ziah's Cold stores were used up, Chills and Shivers, and every last Wisp, and apparently the Frosts all dissolved to dust, so one by one all the Jadans went to the cliff on the South side of Ziah and jumped to their deaths. King David himself was last to fall.'

I tried to move my fingers, but my arm wasn't responding. 'Hmm.'

Cam looked at me with deep concern. 'I thought that story might strike you as pretty rough.'

The swirling water at my feet was quite pleasant to look at, and I couldn't take my eyes away. 'For sure.'

'And those Closed Eyes on the top of the walls,' Shilah said, 'are the ones that the ancient Jadans tried to make to save their lives.'

Cam nodded. 'Yes, but remember. Don't associate any of this with me.'

Shilah licked her dry lips. 'But now it's cool here. In the city. Back to normal.'

'If you can call it that,' Cam said.

'It must have been Desert,' Shilah said, snapping her fingers. 'The Khat must have done something with Desert to kill the land here, and then done something to take the heat away afterwards.'

'You know the rumours about Desert?' Split said aghast. 'How? Did you read the book? Do you read Ancient Jadan?'

Shilah's back straightened to its characteristic rigidity. She blew the dull grass from her palm, letting it fall to the pool. I watched the warm ripples carrying away the blades, spelling something out, something important, something that I might be able to read if only I could see it from another angle. If I disrobed and slipped away from the shore. I'd let myself be carried under the waves, discovering the message on the way down.

My eyelids grew too heavy and I finally let them close.

# Chapter Seventeen

I woke up to Dunes stealing the Coldmaker.

'What are you doing?' I asked, completely disorientated by the candlelight. I tried to grab at the bag. The inside of my head was swarming with scarabs. Everything was happening too fast. I could hear my barbed tone recoiling against the cavern walls and buzzing in my ears. 'Stop!'

'Apologies,' Dunes said, stiffening, nearly dropping the bag. 'It was too close to the waters, and you were shouting and kicking in your sleep.'

'Oh,' I said, nursing my arm, glad that it hadn't actually been ripped apart. 'Sorry. I didn't mean—'

Dunes put the machine down next to me and backed away, bowing so low I wondered if he might get stuck. 'You never have to apologize to me, Meshua. I just didn't want your miracle to get lost in the waters.'

I sighed, my head throbbing. I touched my fingers to my lips and found them dry and blistered. Glancing around the ominous rocks of the cave, I found that the two of us were alone. 'Where is everyone?'

'They went to get supplies,' Dunes said, still maintaining his bow. 'Food, medicine. What your Pedlar called "decoy goods".'

'You don't have to keep bending like that,' I said.

'By your command,' Dunes said, righting himself, but then curling into his slave stance.

'On second thoughts,' I said, my mouth dry. 'Why don't you sit next to me?'

Dunes looked as if he might swoon with gratitude, a large smile drifting across his face. 'Are you sure that I deserve such an honour, Meshua?'

I sighed. 'Just come sit next to me. Don't be so dramatic.'

Dunes gracefully sat and crossed his legs all in one motion. 'After all Hamman has done to your people. For his remaining body to be treated as equal by the holy son—'

I waved him off, sourness filling my stomach. 'You've got to stop with that. I made a discovery, that's all. And my name just *happens* to be Micah. It's not some divine conspiracy to bring an end to the Drought. I'm just a normal Jadan like everyone else.' I brought my injured hand into the light. '*This* doesn't happen to saviours.'

'Of course it does,' Dunes said, giving me a blank stare. 'That and worse.'

I raised an eyebrow.

'I am reborn so I can't claim to know much about the World Cried yet,' Dunes said matter-of-factly. 'But I can guess.'

I sighed. Shilah was right, Dunes's declaration of being a blank slate was going to go stale very quickly.

'And?' I said.

'May I?' he asked, gently gesturing to my hand.

I offered my wrist, and he began to unbind my shame.

'From what I understand, you are an Inventor,' Dunes said. 'You create things that never were.'

'Haven't done much creating lately,' I said, thinking about all of the people who had either been hurt or killed since the 'miracle' machine came to light.

Now I was one of them.

'That is because of circumstance, not because of desire, Meshua. You have been run out of your home and hunted down and spun around like a wooden top with no place to land.' He gestured to the luminous Adaam Grass at the back of the cave. 'You have been plucked and have been in no position to shine, Crierson.'

I paused, too distracted by my pulsing injury to deal with Dunes's choice of name. 'Fair. But what does that have to do with my machine betraying me and taking away half of my abilities?'

'The Crier is a creator, too,' Dunes said, examining the black stain that had crawled even further along my skin. He didn't look at it with pity, however, but with a curious resolve. That made me feel a little better. 'The Crier is the greatest Creator. He made land and Cold and even life in his image.'

'And?'

Dunes cupped my wrist like a piece of art, taking it in from all angles. His touch was surprisingly delicate for someone with fingers like cudgels. 'Have you ever thought that perhaps the Crier hadn't wanted things to go back to the way they were?'

'Why would the Crier not want that?' I asked it with an edge, wondering if this was some sort of twisted Hookman logic. 'There's barely any Cold that falls any more, and everything is dead and sand and worthless. Why would he not want everything to go back to the way the world was, when it was beautiful?'

Dunes sighed. The scar on his cheek had healed up, but it was still very stark on his face, even against such dark skin. 'Because destruction is a whole lot easier.'

'Is it?' I asked, although I knew the answer. A younger, angrier me had destroyed everything I had ever invented in a matter of minutes during a crisis of faith. I took all the inventions out to the sands behind my barracks and smashed them against the bricks, caught in a spiral of rage and fear. Things that had taken me years to bring to life, countless hours bleeding from the heart, gone in a flash.

'It is. I learned that a long time ago,' Dunes said, the corners of his eyes growing damp. 'And giving in to destruction was the easiest choice Hamman ever made.'

'You have to stop this reborn stuff, too,' I said. 'I promise I'll only call you Dunes, and I'll keep you by my side, but it's not like you're a completely different Jadan all of a sudden. Life doesn't work like that.'

Dunes let go of my wrist, giving me a sad nod. 'You will feel much pain, Meshua. This is only the beginning.'

'I already feel plenty of pain, thanks,' I said, annoyed, wishing Split might hurry back soon and join me in my new-found disdain for the Hookman. Maybe the Pedlar could actually sway me to leave Dunes behind.

'What I mean is this,' Dunes said in a serene voice, once again pulling his shirt loose to reveal the rows upon rows of scars. 'I have broken one hundred and forty-five hearts. I know the sound when it happens. And I can say with absolute certainty that this world has a broken heart. I hear the eternal pain on the wind. I can hear it in the crumbling of stone and sand. I've even stood in the Cry Patches of Paphos like the First Khat and listened to the night sky. I could hear the weeping in each gracious piece of Cold falling from the heavens, the final gift of a soul with nothing left to give. The Crier has been in pain for so long. He's so broken. So lonely. Scraping from the bottom of an empty bucket. Sun has been winning in its destruction of the world. I think for the longest time the Crier had given in, contemplating the end of this great invention. Easier just to let go. It is the reason Hamman let himself become a force of destruction. It is the reason why he helped bring demise where he could, to speed up the process of mercy. To finally let the Crier find some peace.'

I looked back into the waves, and I swore I could see Dunes's words being echoed in the ripples.

'So the Crier wants us to suffer and die?' I asked.

Dunes shook his head. 'No, Meshua. Just the opposite. The world is the way it is because of circumstance, not because of desire. The Crier has been in no position to shine, either.' With a shaky finger, he pointed at the Coldmaker. 'Until now.'

'It's just a machine,' I said, fiddling with the lid so the machine might open. I couldn't use both hands, so I wasn't able to get the bow-rings to slide properly. 'It's just a damn machine!'

'It's not the machine that matters,' Dunes said, putting a hand on top of mine. 'It's the hope inside it. It's you. I believe you are the Crier's son because you represent the agony of the return. I see your scars, too, Meshua. And not just on your neck and back. To take something truly broken and make it whole is the hardest thing in the world. Nearly impossible. But the Crier is ready to fight, and has shown his resolve through you. That is what I mean when I say you will have to suffer. That is what I mean when I say you will need to feel pain. Because you will be battling side by side with the Inventor of the whole world.'

He grabbed my injured hand in a vice grip and I howled like never before.

'This is nothing,' Dunes fired back, his voice as dark and deep as the cave itself. 'This is the beginning. The bones of the world have to be set, Meshua. Destruction has been put in motion and won't sit idle. It is a great force itself, more powerful than creation in its own right, and the wounds of the past will be ripped and torn as the world tries to heal, you along with it.' Spit flew from his lips as he spoke. 'And you will bleed, Crierson. You will bleed like never before, because that is exactly what happens to saviours. That is exactly what it means to choose life over letting go. And, Meshua, that is not a guess.'

I was breathing hard as Dunes let go of my hand, and even though the pain was excruciating, I could feel my heart answering him. Maybe there was something more to all of this, something bigger than just me or Shilah or Cam. Bigger than ten years of an abandoned Coldmarch, or a single machine that creates golden beads that can freeze things to Ice and burn off skin. Because with something as simple as words, Dunes had returned something I hadn't expected.

Dunes had given me back *meaning*.

I stood up and went over to the smooth platform next to the swirling water. Up close now, I could see that the odd Crying Dance garment speared over the stone was a sort of vest, made from hundreds of Wisps knitted together with rope so it might be worn across the shoulders and dangle down past the waist. There were pieces of ribbon woven in, of every colour imaginable, and little beads hanging off, some of them even gold.

I slung the vest over my head and around my shoulders, letting the Wisps sit against my body. A handful of the garment brushed my injured hand, and I drank in the pain, letting myself be quenched. The knotted Wisps gently clacked as I moved across the stone, and I let my calloused feet feel the cool temperature of the earth beneath me.

And then I danced.

It wasn't coordinated in any way, and I didn't pretend to know any traditional steps, but rather I just let myself move to the rhythm of the silence. I let myself be free. I let myself be chained. I stepped right for every Jadan I'd hurt in the past and left for every Jadan I'd made smile. I hopped forwards for every invention I'd brought to life, all the frivolous, all the important, and moved backwards for all of the creations yet to come. Maybe I was connected to the Crier in some way like Dunes said, or maybe I wasn't, but for the moment it didn't matter. For the moment I was life. The Wisps clacked together as I jumped from heel to heel, enough to grate just slightly against each other. A profound wave of Cold washed against my body. *Inside* my body. It reminded me what Cold was, that it wasn't an enemy, like I was thinking. It reminded me that a blessing works best in the face of damnation. Cold was the path, and sky, and the tears, and the weapon yet to come.

I kept dancing, the Cold from the Wisps digging deeper into my skin. They caressed, they did not burn. Relief entwined my pain and reminded me of the connection above. Of the love my father had for me, of the time we spent together.

I finally let myself grieve.

When I was done dancing I opened the machine and refilled nearly the entire vial of tears. Dunes topped it off with his own, Jadan and pure.

And once again the Coldmaker was ready.

# Chapter Eighteen

The candles burned out, and even though we'd spotted an entire box of replacements next to one of the shrines, Dunes and I decided not to light any more. Instead we let our eyes adjust to the subtle glow of the Adaam Grass, finding peace inside the darkness of the cavern.

I couldn't see his scars, and he couldn't see the sweat beading on my forehead.

The others in the flock had been gone for hours, so we ate some of the orangefruit that Split had taken from the caravan, and I told Dunes of my past, of Abb, of my tinkering, and I explained how exactly the machine worked. From the Cold Charge to the Frost to the tears and blood offerings that had to come from a Jadan. Dunes wept for the truth and poetry in it all, and kept prying for more. He wanted to know about everyone I'd grown up with in my barracks, and I talked about it all, introducing Slab Hagan and Old Man Gum and Mother Bev. He wanted to know about Matty's game and the ceramic bird piece, and about Moussa's singing. I'd have thought revisiting such sharp memories would bring pain and sorrow, but I only found my heart swelling with reminders that my life was fluid once, not something ugly, disjointed by loss.

As I told my stories I let the Coldmaker work its magic, creating a small stockpile of Abbs I knew would be used in the quest to come. I'd have to spread the news and proof of new Cold as far and wide as I could, making sure the secret wasn't lost with me. Getting my hands on another Frost was going to be nearly impossible, but I wasn't going to get just one. I was determined to flush out every Frost outside the Khat's Pyramid. If Lord Tavor had a secret stash of the holy Cold, then other High Nobles would as well, and whether I had to barter, borrow, or steal, I would put them to use for my people. I had two High Nobles, a brilliant Jadan, and a reformed Hookman at my side.

If that wasn't a sign from above, I didn't know what was.

Dunes had asked if he might hold one of the golden beads, just for a moment, and instead I just gave him one of his own.

He wept for that too.

They were some of the finest hours I'd spent in quite some time.

I felt alive and whole.

I was just finishing up my second pile of Abbs when Split, Cam, and Picka came bursting back into the cave, the dwarf camel braying furiously. Their arms and backs were empty and their faces were flushed with terror. I knew what had happened without them having to say anything.

Shilah was gone.

'Spout,' Cam shouted, his hand tugging at his frayed hair, black with shadow. 'We were in the main market and—'

'Where is she?' I asked, slowly turning the machine off, letting the final Abb come into being. It was smaller than the rest, but it would still work. Dunes gave me a resolute nod from my side, drawing a finger across the scar on his cheek.

Picka started clomping her feet and lay down on the stone, smacking her head against the hard ground.

'Quit it, girl!' Split whined.

But the dwarf camel kept on hurting itself. Split had to grab the reins hard to keep the beast from dealing itself more damage. 'We did everything we could, I tried all my Sun-damned best peddling tricks and tones – QUIT IT – but he had so many guards with him. He insisted to the point of deafness that Shilah had to come with him, some City of David's Fall tradition – I SWEAR I WILL TIE YOU UP AND LEAVE YOU HERE, YOU DAMN BEAST – and we barely got away ourselves, even—'

'Who had guards?' I asked, trying not to let myself get overwhelmed to the point of breaking. This is exactly what Dunes was talking about. There were going to be devastating obstacles. I was going to have to struggle through them, or give up.

I was not going to give up on Shilah.

'Not the Khat,' I said.

Cam shook his head. 'He was this real charming bastard, all pomp and manners, and he annoyed the crap out of me. Called himself "Kind" or something, but he said it so quickly and with this stupid little side smirk. I wanted to hit him in his smug face—'

'Ka'in,' I said, my mind dredging up freckles. The girls must have been running away from this man for a reason, so I expected wherever Shilah was headed was not going to be pleasant. 'They took her somewhere called the Sanctuary.'

'Did you get a vision, Meshua?' Dunes asked in earnest. 'Do you see?'

'No,' I said. 'I overheard the girls in the caravan cart talking about someone named Ka'in who they were rather scared of. And to be honest the girls were all very beautiful . . .'

'Spout,' Cam said, his hands shaking. 'We need to get her back.'

I gathered the golden beads into the bag with the machine,

hurling it across my shoulder. My left hand was still throbbing and useless, and it was a good thing I had a spare.

'Then let's go get her back,' I said, marching towards the shadowy tunnel from which Cam and Split had stumbled.

'You can't bring the Coldmaker,' Split said, wrestling with Picka's reins some more. The camel was now rolling on her back, squashing the ropes out of his grip. 'What if they catch us?'

'The Coldmaker is a part of me,' I said. 'It's coming.'

'We need a plan,' Split said. 'I'm telling you, kid, he had more guards than the damned Vicaress.'

'I have a plan,' I said, not turning around or stopping. 'Dunes.'

'Yes, Crierson!' Dunes shouted, even though he was pretty much only one pace behind me, silently stepping right in my wake.

'Let's go bleed.'

For the first time in my life I stole everything.

I'd had plenty of experience plundering materials from the trash piles in the Paphos alleyways – otherwise I never would have had anything with which to tinker – but I'd done my best never to flat out become a thief. Even under the penalty of starvation, I would have let my stomach collapse before my morals. I had taken only what I thought could better my people, most of it already rubbish.

Today I took it all.

My fingers were as sticky as honey.

The markets of the City of David's Fall weren't as vibrant and varied as the one in Paphos, but still there were things there that must have been imported from every corner of the Khatdom. I treated stalls, bins, even Noble pockets as if they were my own. Dunes thought it would be safe to do only one or two passes through, but I kept at it, wreaking havoc on the Nobles' wares. While Cam and Split distracted the vendors with their outrageous bargaining, I took food, trinkets, salves, even a few Closed Eye amulets on silver chains. Even with only one good hand and the Coldmaker weighing me down, I was masterful, a true tinkerer's fingers at work, nimble and precise.

I hid everything carefully in an alleyway, brushing tons of boilweed over my plunder. Then Dunes and I hurried over to the Smith Quarters, while Cam and Split surveyed the market shops, trying to find out information about Ka'in and the Sanctuary. Logic demanded that I should have just let Cam hold the Coldmaker, but until we had Shilah back, trying to take the machine off me was like trying to remove the colour from my skin.

'You ready, Meshua?' Dunes asked, peeking in through the window of the smallest smithy, his face serious.

I took out the handful of Khatberries. Shilah had rescued me from the Vicaress while employing a similar method of disguise, back before my tinkershop days, and my stomach clenched knowing we'd parted with such unsettled tension. I was going to get her out of this Sanctuary and show her my passion without any ulterior motives. Despite whatever ancient prophecies my name implied, Meshua couldn't just be one Jadan.

No one changed the world alone.

'Yes,' I said, crushing the Khatberries in my hand and smearing the red juice all over my face.

Dunes held out his hooked blade, and I smeared some of the Khatberry juice along the metal. We had to be quick, as the street was deserted for now, but it wouldn't remain that way for long. A few Jadans skirted in the shadows of the alleyways, scattering at the sight of the bloodthirsty Hookman and his prey.

'Cunning plan to do this,' Dunes said.

'I'm not even half as cunning as Shilah. She grew an entire garden once in a cave. You should have seen it, Dunes.'

'Yes. I should have.' Dunes's face stiffened, and he cleared his throat. 'She really is quite special to you, yes, Meshua?'

'You think I'd risk Langria for anyone else?' I asked.

Dunes pondered for a moment. 'Yes. I believe you would.'

I shrugged. 'I would for Cam. He's quite special to me as well.'

Dunes's jaw tightened. 'You called me family right away, despite who Hamman was. I believe you would risk your future for any Jadan. It's the most beautiful weakness I've ever seen.'

'It's not a weakness,' I said, heat rushing to my cheeks.

Dunes gave a quick nod. 'Of course not, Meshua. Apologies.'

I peered through the window, appraising at least half a dozen Noble workers inside, and double that number of Jadans doing the dangerous work. I prayed none of them had yet seen my Wanted Scroll, as a Khatberry mask could only do so much. 'Besides, Langria wouldn't exist for me without Shilah.'

'It exists,' Dunes said, drawing the red across the entire length of the blade. 'Most of Hamman's victims were always headed North.'

I sighed, checking out my reflection in the glass and deciding that indeed the berry juice could pass as dried blood.

'You haven't been there?' I asked. 'To Langria?'

'Not past the barriers, no Hookman knows the way in, but I've seen . . . I've witnessed things.'

'What's it like?' I asked, my heart pounding.

'You know when I told you I can recognize the sound of broken hearts?' Dunes asked.

I nodded.

Dunes sighed. 'Langria is deafening.'

'How so?'

The hammering inside the smithy grew louder, startling

me and making me jump back from the door. There were shouts inside, and I hoped we could take the group by surprise. At least enough to get what I wanted.

'We need to proceed,' Dunes said, glancing at the group of fancy Noblewomen wandering down near the end of the alleyway. Most of them had impressive bellies hanging out of the sides of their dresses. Their chubby cheeks spoke of years of overindulgence, probably eating as many Khatberries and cream as they liked.

'When you got it, spend it. I always say that, ladies!' one of the Noblewomen said to the others, playing with a shiny necklace plump with painted Drafts, her parasol studded with matching Wisps. 'No point in having Cold unless it can make you pretty!'

One of the other Noblewomen aimed a kick at a passing Domestic Jadan headed for the alleyway. The Noblewoman's veiny leg barely lifted above her knee, but it was enough to throw the Domestic off balance, causing her to stumble and drop her token. The Noblewoman hocked something wet and foul on the fallen piece of metal. 'Ain't no amount of Cold in David's Fall could make you pretty, slave,' she cackled. 'Black skin is ugly as sin.'

'Poetry,' the necklaced woman chimed. 'How divine!'

'Yes, mistress,' the Domestic said, wiping off the coin on her dress – which was already stained red in many places – and stumbling away.

'Get your meanest face on,' I whispered, grinding my teeth.

'I will wear Hamman's face for now,' Dunes said with a resolute nod. 'For you, Meshua.'

'How about for Shilah?' I said. 'She's a Meshua too.'

Dunes bent over and looked me right in the eyes, his expression unreadable. But there was something soft lurking behind his blankness. It was not infuriating pity, however, but rather a swirl of understanding.

'What?' I asked, uncomfortable at my sudden nakedness of thought.

Dunes's eyes narrowed, and his entire demeanour changed. He grabbed me by the back of my uniform and hurled me through the smithy doors. From the mix of fire and Cold on my face I could tell the workshop had at least a dozen Bellows in action, all cranking the place liveable. The Noble workers stopped at once, their faces instantly as mean as Dunes's. The Jadans stopped hammering and smelting, stepping away from the hungry kilns.

'Errands or not, Hookman or not, dissa closed shop, boys!' one of the Nobles said, stepping up. He had two perfectly groomed sickles of facial hair that carved up his chin, and was dressed in a flowery blouse. He did not in the least look ready to do any smithing. 'Specially closed to your kind.'

'Crossbows!' Dunes bellowed, his voice splashing around the place like hot iron. 'I am in need of crossbows for the Khat!'

'Jadans donn get to demand nothing from meh,' he said, rubbing a bracelet of beads between his hands. 'Less you demandin death naw.'

I couldn't place the man's accent. It was close to the sound of the twin sisters in the cart, but looser around the vowels. I made a mental note to ask Dunes about it later, and then wet myself.

The more shocking the display the better.

My current trousers were soiled beyond repair, and I'd already stolen a replacement pair from a deserving vendor who'd been testing needle sharpness on whatever Jadans wandered closest to his booth.

'Ah naw!' the Noble with the crescent facial hair cried. 'Muh floor! Yuh filthy!'

Some of the Nobles fastened thick gloves around their fingers, pushing their frightened Jadans aside. They grabbed lengths of hot iron from various fires, and waved them through the air. I raised my head enough to take stock of what this shop had as far as wares, spotting racks of decorative swords, shiny breastplates, and helmets with curly horns.

Also an entire wall of the exact things we had come for.

'Crossbows!' Dunes called, lifting my feet off the ground. I went as limp as a lizard with its neck pinched, and kept my expression shamefaced. I doubled the small puddle I was leaking on the floor. Dunes thrust his blade into the air, the red juice from the berries flicking off the metal as he waved it about menacingly. This massive Jadan seemed to fill up the whole shop with his fury, and he smashed the flat of his blade on the nearest marble pillar after each petrifying sentence. 'I am Hamman the Hookman!' – *CLANG* – 'Bringer of destruction to the unholy!' – *CRASH* – 'I demand crossbows in the service of the Khat' – *SLAM* – 'or our most gracious Lord will know who delayed the capture of the New Jadan Brotherhood of Menace and Terror!'

We'd discussed a few different names – testing out alternatives, like Sun-Demons and Sun-Worshippers – but Dunes liked this one best, claiming he could make it sound the most authentic. From his perfect delivery, I was almost ready to believe that such a fearful group had been terrorizing the city as of late.

'The who?' the Nobleman asked, taking one step back, his voice discernibly meeker than before. 'Wuzzat?'

'The unworthy scum who've been hiding in the Eastern Dunes and stealing your Noblewomen for the past week!' Dunes shouted, spit flying from his lips. He ripped open his shirt and revealed all the scars. 'I've seen more than most, but this is the worst enemy to face the Khatdom in a century!'

One of the Noblemen near the front turned to another and gave an obvious sort of nod, as if this was common knowledge. I nearly broke character and smirked, but instead I let out something between a whimper and a squeak.

'I haven't heard of dem . . .' the hairy Noble said, giving a haughty sniff. 'Are you sure—'

*CRASH.*

The blade reverberated for a few moments this time. Dunes huffed and broadened like the front wall of a sandstorm, and the fire in his eyes negated all the Bellows in the place. He was the single scariest thing I'd ever laid eyes on in my life, making the Vicaress seem like a sweet lady who only carried around a knife to cut up figs.

'It may be your Noblewoman who is stolen next!' Dunes seethed, smashing the flat of the blade against his Closed Eye brand and then pointing it at the small man, who let out a similar squeaky noise to mine. 'They stalk the unbelievers first!'

The Nobleman swallowed hard, the lump stopping halfway down his throat. 'Not muh sweet Bethildah.'

'IF YOU DON'T GIVE ME CROSSBOWS THEN BETHILDAH IS AS GOOD AS GONE!' Dunes pressed the hook to my neck. He was so deft with the blade that he was able to believably dig into my flesh without drawing any real blood. 'I caught this Jadan beetle spying and tortured it all out of him. He broke so easily it was pitiful.'

'Pitiful!' one of the Nobles near the back added with a smile. 'The weakest of the weak, their kind is!'

Dunes nodded, and then snarled. 'I learned it all. Turns out there's a hundred Jadan escapees from the Glasslands all festering together in the Eastern Dunes, making a base in Hillel's Crag. They stole a whole caravan cart of Cold, and have been gnawing on the bones of your sweet Noblewomen for food. That's how they've been hiding out there so long. I know it all now, and I sent the signal, and my Hookman brothers are on their way. I need five crossbows so we can take the demons out. We need to be able to fire arrows into all those dark places where the Jadan scum are hiding and stealing your Bethildahs.'

'Not muh Bethildah,' the Nobleman gulped. 'You can get them? You can kill dem slave bastards?'

'With crossbows!' Dunes shouted, tossing a golden token at the man's feet with the Khat's seal on it. I assumed it was a Hookman thing. 'The Khat will reward you handsomely for them! But the New Jadan Brotherhood of Menace and Terror has a secret way into the city and has spies on the walls and I believe they watched me capture this Coldleech. I need to get to Hillel's Crag now! No time to waste, my masters!' – SLAM – 'No time to waste, or the Jadan enemy shall feast like the Khats of old on the chosen flesh of all those—'

The lead Nobleman held up a hand with a grimace, smacking his lips distastefully. 'Okay. No moah, puhlese.' He ripped off his gloves and snapped his fingers. 'Get dem crossbows for the Hookman. Derriss. Moussa. At the quick, yah lazy scum.'

I nearly spasmed out of Dunes's grip at the name, but I looked up and saw that it was a different Moussa he was referring to, this Jadan much lighter-skinned and with shorter hair. Still, I had to work to compose myself, having almost fainted from dread.

'Wass wrong with him?' the Nobleman asked, gesturing at me and giving another sniff. 'Pissin on mah—'

'I cut out all his teeth and slit open his stomach and then sewed them inside his body!' Dunes roared. SLAM. CRASH. 'And I promised the little stain worse if he makes another sound!'

The Nobleman almost fell backwards with a gag. The two Jadans sprang into action and grabbed some of the crossbows from the walls, rushing them over to Dunes and kneeling next to the puddle at his feet, presenting the weapons with shaking hands.

The man who'd called my people pitifully weak raised a flabby fist, nearly jumping into the air. 'Huzzah! Kill them all, Hookman!'

'I am not a Hookman!' Dunes shouted, waving his blade, his teeth wild and bared. I noticed even his gums had rows of scars.

The whole room went silent, Noble heads cocked and confused. There were a few murmurs as the fires sizzled in their kilns, waiting for clarification.

Dunes paused, his hands stiffening on my shirt. I could feel him turning from side to side, trying to figure out what to say next. I held my breath.

'No! Not a Hookman!' Dunes said with confidence, drawing his tongue across the blade, licking up a long line of the red. 'For them, I am Death itself!'

More rounds of 'huzzah' filled the air as the two Jadans stumbled away. One of them eyed the piss, and we both knew he was destined to do some putrid scrubbing in the very near future. His nose was wide and his brow prominent, and I remembered the face, promising myself I'd bring him an Abb for his troubles when all this was over.

Dunes sheathed his blade in his belt and grabbed all the crossbows at once with a meaty hand. I took a moment to look them over and I noticed the bolting mechanism looked shoddy and crooked. It took everything in me not to shake my head at the smiths' lack of skill.

'The Khat will reward you all for your valour and crafts-manship, fine Noblemen!' Dunes bowed, drawing one finger down his cheek. 'You are all heroes to the city and to the Crier above— shall I one day feel his mercy.'

'Bring back their skulls!' one of the Nobles shouted. 'We'll solder them together and turn them into something. Maybe a tub for the Jadan slaves to shit in!'

'Or we'll use them for target practice,' another one of them said, gesturing to the remaining few crossbows on the wall.

'I will bring you fine masters a trophy, but I cannot delay!' Dunes shook with power, flexing for the whole room to admire. 'For I shall bring the end to the Jadan tyranny and bring stability back to the City of David's Fall.'

'You talk a little fancy for skin that colour, Hookie,' another Noble said, this one still holding one of the smouldering pieces of iron. 'What's that about!'

*SLAM.*

'I am the Khat's blade in the darkness!' Dunes shouted, pounding a fist against his chest. 'I am the Crier's wrath!'

It didn't really answer the question, but it sounded fierce, and the guy backed away with a shrug.

Dunes bowed low and then turned, heading for the door. I grabbed the handle for him, since his hands were both occupied when—'

'Wait a damn minute naw!' the lead Nobleman shouted.

The Jadans began backing away into their corners, positioned in their slave stance.

'There's no time to delay!' Dunes said, his back still to the room.

'Yuh turn around this instant, slave!'

Dunes swung around. I was still dangling from his hand, so I careered along with him. The Coldmaker bag carried on and slammed painfully into my knee, but I still didn't regret having the machine with me.

The Nobleman's face was creased and sneering. He scratched at the puffy facial hair on both sides, an odd look coming to his face, as if he were having second thoughts.

'Aint gunna skewer those Sun-cooked bastards without arruhs,' the Nobleman said finally. Snapping his fingers, he beckoned again to the two Jadan boys, who moved so quickly I thought they might have been anticipating the command.

I could feel Dunes's relief at my back.

Dunes bowed. 'You prove why my kind is here to serve. Yes, arrows. Most grateful.'

Derriss and the other Moussa grabbed a few quills of

ammunition and came our way. I did a little quick-fingered manoeuvre into the Coldmaker bag while they scurried. When the Jadans were close enough, I reached out and really played up my pain, grabbing this new Moussa by the shirt.

'Plsss!' I screamed, making my voice indiscernible, wrapping my lips around my teeth, trying to make it sound like Dunes had actually ripped out my teeth. 'Hllpme. Hlleppmee!'

Moussa pawed helplessly at my hand. 'I— I—'

I grabbed him closer. 'Hllppmmeee!'

A quick thump rocked the back of my head, again believable, but not enough to actually hurt me. Dunes was proving to be quite an asset. I went limp, but not before dropping one of the Abbs in this Moussa's pocket.

Dunes stormed out carrying everything, myself and the Coldmaker included, and shot right into the shadows of the alleyway.

'Brilliant work, and quick thinking,' I said as he put me down, looking around to make sure we weren't followed. 'And damn, you were scary.'

All the angry creases in Dunes's face came to a rest. 'Not me. Hamman. But he's gone again.'

I examined one of the crossbows, looking down the barrel. The rivets were about the right size. With a few minor adjustments they were going to be perfect. 'Think *you* could be that scary for me? If I need you to.'

'For you, Meshua,' Dunes said, knuckles squeezing around the handles of his hooked blade. 'No.'

'I—'

He pounded a fist against his chest again, his face darkening with rage. 'For you I could be worse.'

# Chapter Nineteen

Cam thrust a floppy straw hat on top of the Khatmelon and then stepped back with a flourish. The plump fruit had been speared over the tip of the thinnest rock Pyramid in the cave, which looked a little like a slouching body. The juices from the fleshy melon had streaked the stone, imitating long trails of wet blood, making my heart beat a little faster. I never thought I had the lust for battle inside me, but I kept telling myself that, for now, it was a necessary compulsion. The guards at the Sanctuary were surely going to try to kill us at every corner, and the force I wanted to embody couldn't sit around and hope things passively worked in my favour. For the good of the Crier, Coldmaker, and for Shilah, I had to put aside compassion and become deadly.

I looked at my boilweed-wrapped fingers, understanding now that the painful blackness creeping along my skin was not a plague as I'd previously thought.

It was a sign.

All along I'd been underestimating the Coldmaker. It was as if I'd been focused only on the illuminated side of a parchment, too afraid to turn it over and look under the shadow. The machine really was a miracle. I'd been viewing the whole thing as a grouping of materials that together made something astounding; but in doing so I was discounting one of its biggest virtues. In making Cold, the machine was more than just a sum of its parts; it was in direct opposition to the Sun. It represented something much greater than the single Abbs formed at its mouth. The machine embodied the fighting spirit of the Crier. It was the piece of the divine that clung to life, regardless of the pain grinding everything towards oblivion.

The Coldmaker was a weapon.

And I was going to learn how to use it.

Cam and Split weren't able to get their hands on any proper armour to hang on the stone, but the texture of the rock would work just fine, as it was hard and unyielding. I needed to know how the Abbs would react to different surfaces in order to plan accordingly for our ambush. It was all the preparation I was allowing, however, because I had no idea what sort of horrors were happening to Shilah in that Sanctuary. I wasn't going to leave her there any longer than I had to.

'What do you think?' Cam asked with a smirk, flicking the brim of the floppy hat further down over the melon. 'Accurate enough?'

'Wrap the face of the melon in boilweed, so it's a little spongier,' I said, continuing to scrape the blade into the groove of the last crossbow, widening it so the Abbs could roll evenly. I was doing my best with only one good hand. 'And I think it needs to be more evil. Can you make it more evil?'

'I could name it "Dad",' Cam said.

I shook my head. 'That only works for you.'

Cam shrugged. 'That's true. You lucky bastard, Spout. You got a good father *and* you get to be Meshua. Not a bad haul. All I got was insanely good looks and a brain like a . . . no, that's not right.'

'Like a what?' I asked. I didn't shut down at the thought

of my father like I had before. Instead I listened intently to the babble of the sacred pool at my back, hoping to catch some secret whispers. The cave was still as dark as night, but Split had lit all the candles he could, revealing contours we hadn't seen before, deeper ripples in the stone. We'd set up targets all around the cave: wood and glass and clothing from the shrines; but I considered the stone with the melon face to be the most important.

I wanted to see what my new discovery might do to a guard.

Cam bit his bottom lip. 'I wanted to say like a library, but all the libraries I know are full of lies and deceit. So it would be a very opposite comparison.'

'How about a brain like the horizon itself,' Split said wistfully, scratching at Picka's chin.

Cam beamed. 'Beautiful and endless.'

'No,' Split said with a wicked smile. 'Because there's usually not much there.'

Picka brayed happily, showing her blackened gums.

'Atta girl,' Split said, scratching deeply. His tone was light and playful, almost healed in a certain respect, and I knew my intuition about having the Pedlar be in charge of making more Abbs had been correct. It was easy work, and didn't require more than a switch of the lever, but I figured it might make him feel more attached to all of this. As coarse as his disposition had been throughout the Coldmarch, it had changed once he'd become an active participant in the making of Cold. Now he watched that machine like he would watch a new lover getting undressed for the first time.

'Maybe that's true about the horizon for now,' I said, widening the groove down the crossbow. 'But it won't be for long. Soon, Langria is going to be over every horizon.'

Split went quiet, whatever words were at his lips dissipating quickly.

Cam steepled his hands and held them against his chest. 'Look at that, Split. The saviour of the world, and he still stands up for his friends.'

'Not a saviour yet,' I said, keeping my face even. 'But I will save Shilah. Even if the machine and I have to burn every last guard in the Sanctuary.'

'Damn,' Cam said, folding his arms across his chest.

'What?' I asked, stopping and flexing my tired fingers.

Cam swallowed hard, his face flushed with something like longing. 'I'm just so proud. You're a very different Spout from the one I found on that street corner.'

I gave a single nod. 'Just wait till I get more Frosts, so I can tinker more Coldmakers.'

'I will get them for you!' Dunes called from the back of the cave. 'Anything you want, Meshua. I will storm the Pyramid and slit the throats of anyone in my way.'

I smirked. 'Thanks, Dunes, but I'm sure there will be plenty of Frosts in Langria. Right now, I just want you to practise shooting these crossbows with me.'

'By your command,' Dunes said, wandering out of the shadows, silhouetted by the candles and grass. He was standing taller than he had previously.

I nodded to one of the crossbows on the floor. 'You take that one on the left, Dunes. It's the best as far as sturdiness goes, and I believe that you're going to be excellent at this.'

Dunes bowed, looking to Cam. 'You are right about his kindness, Camlish. It will one day echo as legendary as his deeds.'

I rolled my eyes. 'I'm right here. Anyway, forget about my *deeds* and let's focus on getting Shilah back. That's all that matters for now.'

Cam smirked, tying off the piece of boilweed around the melon's face. 'Getting Shilah back will definitely count as one of your deeds. And what we're about to attempt will certainly be worthy of a legend or two. The big man's point sticks.'

I sighed, gritting my teeth. Cam wasn't taking this as seriously as he should.

'What?' Cam asked.

'Nothing,' I said.

'Does this have something to do with all that unsettled tension between you two?' Cam asked.

'No,' I said, too quickly.

Cam smirked. 'What'd you do anyway, to cause this rift? Invent a miracle with some other girl?'

'Split,' I said, looking away. 'How about making some more Abbs? We're going to need as many as we can get.'

'Has the Coldmaker had enough rest?' Split asked eagerly, eyes aglow.

'Yes,' I said. 'We're working hard. I know she can keep up.'

'*She*, huh?' Cam asked, pretending to dance with the stone dummy, gently caressing the side of the straw hat.

I shrugged, hating myself for letting a smile slip onto my lips. 'Great Gale. Mama Jana. Shilah. I've known some brave women in my day, and in that way the machine feels like a she. And, Cam?'

'Hmm?' he asked, pretending to lead the stone in a twirl.

'Do me a favour, and take this seriously.'

Cam's smile faltered as he nodded and stepped back. Once the expression faltered I could see the intense pain he'd been covering up.

Split nudged Picka's head off his lap, and jumped to his feet, the camel grumbling with dismay. I'd never seen the Pedlar move so fast as he went over to the Coldmaker. He flipped the lever and spurred more gold. The air inside the cave always shifted as the Abbs were being created, as if the wind was rushing towards the machine to get a better look.

Dunes, still lost in shadow, opened his arms wide and let the air caress his scars. I couldn't make out his face, but I knew what sort of serenity waited there.

'What about the fact that the Crier is a *he*?' Cam asked, not meeting my eyes. 'Like those paintings in Split's cave. The ones that look like you.'

I levelled the haft of the crossbow and rolled an Abb along the groove, noticing a few more places where it would have to be scraped open. Overall though, the weapon was nearly ready. I'd been putting off the testing until all the modified crossbows were done. I was old enough to know that sometimes hope worked better than the act itself, and I wanted to savour the anticipation. This might not work out like I expected. I dreaded the possibility of being left unarmed and unplanned while despair came crashing down.

'All the more reason for his Coldmaking partner to be female,' I said, making the final adjustments to the wood.

'You don't need to be worried about Shilah,' Cam said, poking holes in the melon's face to look like eyes. 'I know Shilah well enough to know she can take care of herself. She's probably already escaped from that Ka'in guy, and is making her way back through the caves.'

'I hear nothing from any of the tunnels,' Dunes said out of the darkness.

Cam sighed. 'Thanks, Dunes. You know what I mean, though. And I'm excited because . . . because this is damn exciting! Shivers and Frosts, Spout, imagine their faces when we come swarming in there all loaded to the teeth with—'

'Let's just make sure this works,' I said, a knot in my stomach, not trying to get my hopes up too high. Cam was right, and I knew Shilah could take care of herself, but until she was by my side, and things were sorted between us, I'd feel uneasy. I was desperate to share my revelation with her, and I had a feeling she'd be proud to finally see a matching fire in my eyes.

'Meshua,' Split called, still hunched over by the machine. 'Hmm?'

'I think it's getting slower. She's getting slower.'

'Slower?' I asked, the cool wind still kissing my face as it passed through the cave.

Split put a hand on the bronze Eye, as if checking the health of a sick child. 'The Abbs are coming out slower than before.'

I nearly threw the crossbow on the ground and swept my way over to the machine. I nodded to Split as he stepped aside so I could look at the catch-point. Indeed, the gold was piling on itself slower than before. Not by much, but there was a small delay in the creation. With gentle motions – so I wouldn't send pain up my fingers – I flipped the knobs and slid the levers of the Belisk-style puzzle, lifting the lid of the machine.

'It's nothing,' I said, after a long spell. 'I think it just needs more salt in the Cold Charge.'

'Salt like what we took from the caves?' Cam asked, perking up. 'We still have those pieces—'

'I'll do it later,' I said, waving away his concern.

Dunes flung himself out of the shadows, his blade swinging high and heavy. 'I will obtain any salt you need, Meshua! I will march to the market right away and—'

I held up my hands. 'Hold on, Dunes. It's fine, it can wait. The Coldmaker is fine. Nothing wrong at all. And besides, we need to test out these crossbows.'

Dunes bowed, slinking back and lowering his blade. 'By your command.'

I wobbled back to the crossbows, having trouble finding my footing. I picked up the one I'd been working on and silently went back to tinkering.

'Micah,' Cam said, full of concern. 'What is it?'

'Fumes from the Cold Charge I think,' I said, wiping my

nose and blinking a few times. 'It's good to know. I have to watch out for that. Anyway, let's see if this plan works.'

'It definitely will,' Cam said, swinging around by my side and putting an arm over my shoulder. 'We're going to have Shilah back in no time, and we're going to blast fear into Noble hearts as we do it.'

I held out the crossbow to him, my hand shaking.

'You kidding me?' Cam asked. 'This is *your* idea. You go first this time.'

I pulled an Abb out of my pocket and loaded it onto the crossbow before I realized I hadn't cocked the actual bow back yet. Then I stared at my useless hand. 'Oh, wait.'

Cam gave my shoulder a reassuring squeeze, and took the crossbow, his face going red as he strained to get the bow taut, handing it back. 'Don't be nervous.'

I swallowed hard, putting the Abb in place and lifting the sights so they lined up with the melon guard. I had no idea how something so round and small would fly, and I hoped my aim would be true.

Dunes swung directly in my line of fire, broad and looming and in serious danger of getting hit.

'Tears above!' Cam exclaimed. 'What are you doing, man?'

Dunes kneeled down, spinning so his back was to us, keeping his chest wide and exposed as he stretched his arms as wide as they would go. 'Fire over me. In case the Cold wave comes back, I will be known as the shield that protected Meshua and his second-closest companion.'

Cam gave a conceding nod. 'Thanks, Dunes.'

I heard Split grumble something from the shoreline of the sacred pool, but I couldn't make it out clearly. Picka made a similar noise, looking longingly at her Pedlar.

'Ready for this?' I asked, desperately trying to sound positive. I was sure even Picka could tell I was faking it.

*Obstacles*, I reminded myself. *It's just another obstacle.*

'Hey, Split?' I asked.

'Yes?'

'Any pointers? I think you're the only one of us who's used one of these.'

'Sure,' Split said. 'Same as peddling. Start with your prices too high. You can always negotiate down, but you can't go up.'

'I meant about shooting a crossbow,' I said.

He gestured for me to raise the tip of the weapon.

I nodded, aiming above the melon to compensate for any arch. I should have thought to do that myself without being told to.

*Just another obstacle*, I thought, trying to regain focus.

Cam took a step back, rubbing his hands together. 'Make them shake, Meshua.'

I pressed the trigger, and the weapon bucked with power. The Abb careered off the wooden shaft too fast for me to see, far faster than an arrow. Dunes didn't spasm to the side in a cloud of brutal Cold, so I knew at least the golden bead made it past his kneeling form.

The melon was unharmed.

There was a crackling explosion along the back of the cave, however, near the Adaam Grass. Then a blast of Cold slammed through the entire cave. The shrines tipped. The sacred pool shuddered. Even the last of Split's wispy hair blew back and revealed burns and baldness. Cam and I exchanged a look as the Cold brushed our faces. At the same time, we began running to see what kind of damage the Abb had done. I grabbed a lantern on the way, and Cam doubled back to grab his own, the candle inside flickering as he ran. Dunes remained kneeling, drawing two fingers down his cheeks and muttering something under his breath.

Picka was braying wildly, rolling on her back.

Cam and I stormed deeper into the cave. A cloud of Cold

swirled and found shape in front of us, thick and fierce, and
Cam and I halted at the edge to wait for it to dissipate. We
held up our hands and tried to feel where it was bearable.
About five paces from the wall the air was now painfully
Cold, and I stuck my head further into the cloud and gasped.
The air nearly froze my lungs. I could just make out a heavy
sheet of Ice spreading across the entire section of stone wall
at the back, like our Ice bridge turned up on its side.

I kept my limp hand behind me to stave off further injury.

If an Abb held all of this power, how had I escaped with
only a few dead fingers?

At my feet, all the blades of Adaam Grass had tilted towards
the Cold, their light growing brighter with every passing
second, more vibrant and defined. The candles became unnecessary. The entire back portion of the cave was cast in soft
green, leaving the various rock shapes and patterns outlined
with unusual depth.

Cam burst into celebratory whoops, pointing through the
cloud to the spot where the Abb had struck. He gave a little
yelp, yanking his finger back and putting it in his mouth.

I tried to quell the whimpering boy in me and let the
Inventor take the lead. *Just another obstacle*, I reminded myself.
*Don't think about it*.

I needed to know everything about our capabilities for
when we stormed the Sanctuary, especially now that I knew
our weapons would be limited. I couldn't let myself miss a
single detail. The Ice on the wall was at least as thick as my
finger. It had expanded along the stone about about ten paces
wide, with various shapes at the edges, the right side looking
particularly—

'Spout!' Cam shouted, pointing again through the cloud,
but this time with his elbow. 'Look!'

'What?'

'Do you need my presence, Meshua?' Dunes called.

'No,' I said. 'I'm fine.'

'Look what you hit!' Cam exclaimed.

I squinted, trying to focus on the centre where the Ice was thickest. That would have been the impact spot. Beneath the Ice, distorted, the shape hinted at the 'unusable' sign, like the one the Jadan at Gilly's had branded on his neck. Or the ones that Jadanmasters drew on Street Jadan foreheads when they were being punished. Once I'd had the symbol etched into my tongue, which was rather unpleasant.

Normally it was a triangle with a verticle line through the middle, but this was different. This line didn't extend past the edges of the Pyramid; instead it zig-zagged through diagonally, and after a moment I realized it was bisected by multiple lines.

'It's the Khat's Pyramid!' Cam shouted.

'No, it's not,' I said carefully, the shape barely even visible through the Ice and cloud.

'It is!' Cam shouted, taking a deep, blissful breath through his nose, almost smug. 'You shot the Khat's Pyramid, and it's cracking down the centre. It's another sign. Ha!'

I had to examine it more closely, but it did look somewhat like the Khat's Pyramid. There were small lines forming on the slabs of stone, but the structure had a large crack through the centre. The refracting Ice gave it the appearance of crumbling apart at the seams.

'That's just a coincidence,' I said, pointing around to all the other drawings on the wall. There were Opened Eyes, and maps, and faces and names and prayers. 'It could have hit anything.'

Cam took the crossbow out of my hands and kissed it. 'But it didn't hit anything. And I don't see any other Pyramids anywhere.' He kissed the weapon again. 'Damn, I wish my father could see this thing.'

'You do?'

Cam held it up to the wall, lining the sights with the crumbling Pyramid. 'From the wrong end.'

'Meshua!' Split called.

'Yeah?'

'Do you want me to make more of the Abbs?' he asked, and I could hear the excitement in his voice.

'Not yet,' I said, trying not to choke on my words.

'Let's practise,' Cam said, his smile ear to ear. 'And then go get Shilah.'

I hesitated. 'Fine, but not too many times, okay?'

Cam looked up from the sights, giving me a curious look. 'I thought you wanted all of us to get good before we went to—'

'I just don't want the cave to get too Cold.' I pointed down. 'And I don't want the Adaam Grass to die. And besides, I want to get going as soon as possible.'

Cam shrugged, his face uncharacteristically serious. 'Not going to argue with you there. I'm worried about her too.'

We tried out a few more targets, learning how the Cold reacted to different surfaces, and got a rough estimate of the trajectory of the Abbs. We became proficient, and after a few attempts each we could all get close to the intended mark. If the Abbs exploded *near* a target, they still almost always sheeted the whole thing in a solid tomb of Ice. Any direct hits would not only incapacitate our enemies, but do much worse. The guards might end up looking as blackened and dead as my fingers.

Each eruption was magnificent, and proved how much of a blessing the crossbows would be in the upcoming fight. But each eruption also made me wince, my new secret growing heavier with each wasted miracle.

Because even as I was learning about the Abbs, taking in everything with my eyes and ears and nose and heart, I was elsewhere. I kept looking over at the Coldmaker after each shot of the crossbow, trying not to sink.

There was a reason the Coldmaker was slower in making the Abbs than before. Something I didn't realize until I looked inside the bronze box.

My one and only Frost was shrinking.

The Coldmaker was going to die.

# PART THREE

# Chapter Twenty

'They just had to use torches to keep them lit at night,' I said, trying to keep the tears from spilling into my eyes. 'They just always have to twist the Sun-damned blade.'

The Sanctuary was one of the biggest buildings I'd seen outside the Khat's Pyramid. The cathedral of clay and stone could have housed at least five of my barracks inside its grounds, a large dome and pillars sitting as a crown. There were no other buildings in its shadow, leaving an open moat of sand and dirt around the perimeter, which meant fewer places to hide on an approach.

And fewer ways to escape.

The Sanctuary sat at the entrance to the southern cliff face, the site of the infamous Fall. The building was walled up like the city itself, with sleepy towers strategically perched around the perimeter. Dim lights flickered inside the lookouts, but illuminated no faces. Even though I hadn't spotted any yet, I could only imagine the number of guards, taskmasters, and High Nobility between us and Shilah. Finding her in such a massive maze of rooms, gardens, chambers, and towers might take all night.

None of that factored into my thinking at the moment.

I'd become paralysed with rage and indignation after seeing what they had suspended over the front gates. My feet wouldn't move. My eyes wouldn't surrender. I couldn't focus. The Sanctuary had struck me a heavy blow, tossing me into violent currents of anger.

All this, with something as simple as windows.

'Come, Meshua,' Dunes said, looking across the expanse, most of his bulk hidden behind the empty outpost where we were all hiding. He had his crossbow slung over his back, his blade at the ready instead. 'Ignore it and let us find a way in.'

I held my ground, gnashing my teeth so hard I could feel my jaw spasm. Fire ran through the veins in my left arm. I wanted to burn the whole place to the ground. A part of me was grateful to see such a terrible display of windows before attempting such a heedless rescue, as it intensified the blood-lust tingling in my hands.

These glaring windows, captured in beautiful detail and adorned with flame, summed up just about everything that was twisted about the World Cried.

'You want a sign,' I said to Cam, my voice gritty. 'There's your sign.'

'What?' Cam asked, neck craning back with a snap so that he could stare up at the stars. Khatberry juice darkened his fair skin to red so he could blend in better with the night, but despite how much I tried, I couldn't disguise all the colour in his hair. His movements were haloed with secret streaks of gold. 'Are they shooting?'

'No,' I said. 'The torches. Lighting it up so we can see it all.'

I didn't understand why the windows irked me so deeply, considering I'd seen far worse atrocities done to the Jadan people in real life; but I didn't think it was so much the fact of the deeds themselves, but rather that everything had been glorified with such fine detail, exalted with such artistic skill.

These Nobles were not only proud of their brutal history. They were boastful.

'We must keep moving, Meshua,' Dunes urged, motioning with his massive blade. 'We should not attack from the front. I believe we'll have an easier time penetrating at one of the side entrances.'

I lifted my crossbow and aimed it at the windows.

The front section of the building was one giant tribute to the Fall, played out in a stained-glass mosaic. The city and cliff were represented by thousands of colourful shards, fitted together to form vivid pictures. Near the top were scenes of Jadans burning alive, both on their knees in prayer and rolling on the ground to try to quench the flames. Dozens of poor souls were shown spilling off the cliff. Lots of red glass had been utilized near the bottom of the windows. There were babies pictured too, mothers having put them in baskets before tossing them off the cliffs. The wicker was being eaten by fire. And looming above everything was an intricately done Closed Eye, refusing to acknowledge the pain happening to his children below.

The torches ensured the entire heart-wrenching scene could be enjoyed day and night.

'They can't just be satisfied with their control,' I said between closed teeth, itching to load my crossbow so I might destroy the terrible display. I couldn't waste Abbs. 'They have to make sure everyone else is crushed. It's wrong.'

'Are you really surprised?' Split asked.

The Pedlar's ashen skin and relatively smooth head had been much easier to smear with the dark Khatberry juice than Cam's. Split dug his little finger into his ear, rubbing away some of the disguise, and I hoped he wasn't going to be a liability. I was tempted to give him a bit of the leftover Dream, just to steady his withdrawal.

This idea came mostly from compassion, as I was having withdrawal of my own.

For the first time since starting the March, I was separated from both the Coldmaker and my World Partner. Picka was guarding the machine back in the cave, and so I felt naked and broken and exposed. Vile things had already slithered into the gaps.

'He is Meshua,' Dunes announced in serious tones.

'I wasn't arguing that,' Split chided, his eyes narrowing.

'No, I'm not surprised,' I said, my eyes refusing to move from a poor Jadan whose eyes had been done in black glass. Fire peeled back the skin on his legs revealing a delicately coloured bone. The artist had found accurate shades, careful in the selection. 'I'm furious.'

'Then let's go steal their most prized possession,' Cam said, rubbing his hands together.

I cocked my head, looking him over. Beneath the Khatberries, my friend's skin was no longer the smooth, pampered texture of his kin. He was hardened, weary. There were more lines crinkling his eyes. Something was missing.

'I mean Shilah of course,' Cam said.

I paused. 'Damn.'

'What?' he asked.

I forced a smile, even though everything inside me was nails and stingers. 'You're different from when I met you, too.'

'How could I not be?' Cam ruffled my hair. 'Isn't that what saviours do? Change things?'

'I don't know.'

Cam set his hand on the back of my neck, gently cupping it. 'You will. And just wait until we get you some more Frosts. Not that you need them.'

'I don't like how I feel,' I said softly.

Cam gave my injured hand a concerned look, still wrapped in boilweed. 'Is it getting worse?'

'Not that,' I said, hiding my hand behind my back. Indeed, the pain was getting worse, but I wasn't going to admit that at the moment. 'I'm just so angry. I want to hurt people.'

Cam gave a resolute nod. 'Good. Do it. They deserve it.'

Split's knuckles went white around his crossbow. 'Looks like me and you finally have something in common, Spout.'

Dunes let his head sag, his crossbow rattling.

I paused. The secret I was so desperately clutching kept trying to escape. 'Do you think they have more Frosts inside?'

'That Ka'in bastard seems the type,' Cam said. 'Smug enough to have one at least.'

Dunes's face shot up, eagerness returning. 'Is that what you wish, Meshua? I will deliver you more Frosts.'

I shook my head. 'Deliver me Shilah.'

Cam put a hand on my shoulder. 'We're going to get her back, Spout. I've never felt more confident about anything in my life. Except for when I felt confident that you'd be a good assistant for Leroi.' Cam tapped his lip, smirking. 'But I guess I was wrong about that.'

I finally looked at him, brow furrowed. 'Why would you say that?'

Cam drew out one of the Abbs and rolled it in his palm. 'Because I think he was more a good assistant for *you*.' He loaded the Abb behind the special ridge I'd built into the crossbow's shaft, which held the bead tight until the trigger was pressed.

'You're a good friend, Cam,' I said.

He swallowed hard. 'Let's just hope I'm as good a warrior. I've been a good friend for a while. But I've never been in a fight before.'

'What is your command, Meshua?' Dunes asked, glancing up towards the dark sky.

I understood this moment was going to come. Years of nightly plundering the boilweed piles had left me adept at sneaking around, but I'd never led a whole group of people before. I prayed I wasn't going to get any of them killed. If I had the Decoy Boxes that I'd made back in the Tavor tinkershop we could at least have caused a bit of a diversion. I thought about the Domestics from the slave cart who'd escaped, knowing there had to be some secret entrance to the Sanctuary. We needed to get in now. I preferred tact, careful thought, and tinkering to anything rash, but Shilah might not have much time.

I wiped a hand across my forehead. Beads of sweat greased my fingers. 'We sneak around the perimeter and find an entrance on the side, out of sight from the towers, and hopefully a guard there will tell us what we need to know and let us in.'

Dunes licked the last bit of Khatberry juice from his blade. 'I'm sure he will.'

And he did.

Even Split looked begrudgingly impressed.

'If you are lying to me,' Dunes said calmly to the guard, 'I will not kill you. I will find you wherever you may be – Hookmen are the best at finding runaways, which I believe you must know – and take you back to a very dark, very isolated place. And there I will practise on you. And I will tell you this, Noble guard, I am very good at the everyday sort of torture.' He thrust the tip of his hooked blade back into the man's palm and the guard broke with pain. 'As you can clearly see. What I need practice on is the darker things, the *experimental* things. So I will ask you one time. Is everything you told me true? You scream again and I remove your tongue. Another thing I am quite practised at.'

The proficiency of the torture reminded me of the Vicaress, and normally I would have buckled with sympathy. Now a part of me wanted to learn from Dunes. This guard was part of Shilah's abduction, even if he wasn't the one who took her. My blood was burning with indignation, I had a sick desire for the hooked blade to scrape bone. I *wanted* this Noble to scream.

The boilweed strip came away from the guard's mouth and he kept relatively composed, most of his whimpering happening in his eyes.

'I'm not lying, Hamman,' the guard babbled. 'I promise you that they would have taken her—'

The handle of the blade went swinging, and before I knew it, the guard was unconscious. Dunes pinned him gently against the door so the body could slowly crumple to the ground.

'He said your name. He knew who you were,' Split said, fingers furiously scratching his thigh.

Dunes shook his head, rifling through the guard's pockets. 'He most certainly did not.'

Cam and I exchanged a look. I couldn't blame my friend for his grimace. Not only was Dunes's method of torture rather severe, but what the guard had said about Shilah sounded foreboding.

I repeated his words under my breath. 'She's probably in the Beauty Room.'

'Maybe it's like it sounds?' Cam's face showed a weak twinge of hope. 'And it's not so bad, and they're just putting perfumes and nice dresses on her.'

'I don't think so,' I said, squeezing the crossbow with all the might in my fingers. 'But let's hope.'

Dunes lifted out a ring of keys from the guard's pocket and handed them to me.

Then he stepped to the side and vomited profusely, emptying his rations of figs and water. His retching was loud and violent, able to be heard in the nearest tower.

'Apologies,' Dunes said, wiping his mouth after every spurt. 'Apologies.'

'What's happening?' Cam asked, frantically looking around. 'You okay, Dunes?'

'Apologies,' Dunes said after a particularly violent spew.

Split gave me a fearful look as something sounded in the watchtower above.

'Big baby's gonna get us all killed,' Split muttered.

'Inside,' Dunes said after a dry heave, wiping the back of his mouth. 'I'll be okay once we're inside.'

'What happened?' I asked.

'I've never tortured anyone for information before,' Dunes said, his head sagging. 'I still have to get used to it, Meshua. But for you, I will.'

Split looked as if he was ready to explode, but I could see that his red face refused to look at the fallen guard. 'Are you Sun-damned kidding me? What about all those scars? You must have tortured hundreds of people before.'

'No,' Dunes said. 'Hamm—'

'Hamman is gone,' I said simply, so Dunes didn't have to. 'I understand.'

Dunes gave me a most appreciative look.

I tried the keys one by one, frowning after each one, failing and starting back at the beginning of the ring. I hurried as best I could. I didn't have a waterskin, so I couldn't do the Ice trick with the lock again. There was a cough and a soft rustle of cloth from far above: it was obvious that the guard was coming to see about the retching sound. The tower door was out of our line of sight if we pressed against the wall, but seeing nothing would only heighten the guard's curiosity. A steep staircase led down to the ground not too far from where we stood, and I loaded my crossbow and aimed it at the top of the flight. Split did the same, his hand unsteady.

Then a tense pause and the distant sound of footsteps.

'All okay down there, Gabe?' a voice shouted from above,

fingers curling over the top of the wall. 'Runaways? Why'd they go out of your gate?'

A pit should have formed in my stomach, but I was ready for whoever was up there to try to stop us. Anger bubbled at my core, and I was ready to take out my fury on the first Noble who dared get in my way.

Split's finger twitched over his trigger, and he almost let an Abb fly. I gave Dunes a silent plea, gesturing for him to load up his crossbow.

'Gabe?' the voice called down again.

Another tense pause.

All of our weapons were now pointed upwards.

'I was just thinking about the kind of women you like!' Cam burst out, in a decent approximation of the guard's voice. 'Made me hurl!'

Then silence for an uncomfortable length of time.

'Why you always gotta be so mean, Gabe?'

The curled fingers retreated from the wall, and I heard footsteps headed back towards the tower. We waited until it was all silent, and then I gave Cam a pat on the shoulder.

'Looks like you're a good warrior,' I whispered.

'That's not being a warrior,' Cam said, although his face flushed with pride.

'Then surround me with bad warriors.' I kneeled down and reached under the fallen guard's shirt. Out came a necklace with a single key at the end.

Dunes had the unconscious guard over his shoulder before I could so much as blink. Limp arms flopped down, brushing against Dunes's scarred cheek. 'By your command, Meshua.'

I opened the door with this new key and peered inside at the empty hallway. 'Bring him in here.'

We all filtered in. Dunes had to hunch and turn at an odd angle to fit himself and the guard through the threshold. I kept my crossbow raised, pointed towards the end of the long hallway in case any backup came. The passage was dimly lit with something else that made my knees weak with memory.

'Those look like the lanterns Leroi used in his tinkershop,' Cam said.

'They're called Sinai,' I said.

Split nodded. 'I've seen one from another Pedlar before. Came to my shack trying to sell me one for practically nothing. High Noble bastard reeked of desperation, so I turned him away.'

'Remember to aim at the floor if they're not wearing armour,' I said, running on fury now. I was ready for these Nobles to feel the Coldmaker's wrath.

We'd discovered that the Abbs didn't explode against soft, fleshy things like boilweed. We couldn't actually test against skin, only soggy melon, so we had to assume it would act the same. Our quest might end abruptly and painfully if any of the Abbs flew back in our direction. It had happened twice back in the cave, and one of the golden beads had nearly frozen the sacred pool.

'Shall I use my blade first?' Dunes asked, gently dumping the limp man into a pile of shadows. 'Less conspicuous.'

'Yes.' I nodded. 'We still need to find out where this Beauty Room is.'

'Just don't toss up your figs again, Hookman,' Split grumbled.

Cam tried to skirt in front of me again, as he'd done in the first stretch of the Coldmarch, but I shook my head and waved him back.

'Dunes,' I said. 'You go first. The rest of us will hide behind you so we might take them by surprise.'

Dunes flashed to the front of the group, his blade ready.

We crept onwards, my ears tense and ready. The first few hallways were silent except for the subtle buzz of the Sinai. Other than the expensive lights, however, this place was full of a rather odd set of decorations. From the stained-glass windows out front, I expected the whole place to be done up in Closed Eyes and reproductions of the 'The Cause' by Armus Josiah – the most famous depiction of our unworthiness.

But the pictures here displayed the very opposite.

'They're Jadans,' Cam said, his face going slack with shock. 'Beautiful Jadans.'

Hanging on the walls were dozens of portraits of Jadan women, all done from the neck up. Mostly the artwork depicted younger Jadans about Shilah's age, but some frames captured faces with a smattering of grey hair and wrinkles. Indeed these paintings had some of the most beautiful features: the smoothest skin, and the most startling eyes I'd ever seen in my kin. The subjects were all unique, and there was a date etched into a plaque hanging below each face.

Cam stopped to examine the nearest one, running his fingers over the etched-in numbers. 'This one is from last year.'

'It's probably when they were painted,' Split said, waving us onwards. 'Let's not lose focus, children. We have a battle to wage.'

I noticed Dunes had gone suspiciously quiet, keeping focused on the middle of the hallway.

'Do you recognize any of them?' Cam asked me, tapping my shoulder.

I shook my head, staring at Dunes's broad back. The big man was breathing faster now, every pull shallower than the last.

'Not every Jadan knows each other, Tavor,' Split said with a snort.

Cam blushed. 'I meant, like, are these well-known Jadans or something?'

Split smirked. 'Why would Jadans be well known?'

Cam's blush deepened as he stepped away from the plaque. 'I don't know, never mind.' His lips parted as if he was going to say something, and then he reeled it back in. 'Spout's going to be well known.'

'It's okay, Cam, I know what you meant,' I said. 'But no. I don't see anyone that I know.'

We followed Dunes further down the hall, more paintings and Sinai turning up at every corner. The girls in the paintings were getting even more striking the deeper inside we went. There were round-faced girls with thick, frizzled hair, toting lusty expressions. Others had faces shaped like tears, their eyes haunting. I was reminded of Leah's pouty lower lip that she had offered in the caravan cart. But her beauty would stand out even on these walls.

Then I noticed something strange tying all the paintings together.

'They're all dated the first Khatday of every month,' I said, confirming my suspicions on another plaque.

Split checked the few nearest paintings, giving an appreciative stroke of his cheek stubble. 'Well sand in my figs, you're right.'

Cam chimed in eagerly. 'I told you something was off about the date.'

'Did you?' Split asked with a smirk.

Cam frowned. 'Didn't I?'

'And that's coming up,' I said, staring at the likeness of the Jadan girl. Her eyes were as green and vibrant and lovely as the Adaam Grass. 'Only a few days from now.'

'You think that's why he abducted Shilah and took her to the Beauty Room?' Cam asked. 'To dress her up and then have her picture painted?'

'Dunes, do you know anything about this?' I asked.

The large man was still facing forwards, the pace of his breathing frantic now.

'Dunes,' I said gently.

He shook his head, not turning around.

I paused. 'Can you *guess* for me, Dunes?'

'Yeah, do that,' Split snarled. 'And while you're at it, guess why that guard back there knew your name.'

I shot Split a warning look.

Dunes turned to me, a hard lump having formed in his throat. Worry sat at the corners of his eyes, his wide nostrils flaring. 'I guess the first Khatday of the month is always a very bad day for the Jadans here.'

'Like a Procession?' I asked, remembering what the Vicaress did to us every first Khatday of the month back in Paphos.

'Worse,' Dunes said, looking at his blade. 'Probably.'

I nodded, not needing to press him any further to understand the severity of the situation. I lifted my crossbow, plucking the rubber bowstring with my unwrapped thumb, appreciating how the weapon was as ready as I was.

'We are going to find this Beauty Room,' I said. 'As fast as possible.'

'By your command.'

Dunes hurled himself down the hallway.

I was surprised at how stealthily our little group moved in his wake, everyone's feet falling lightly. Split had to stop a few times, looking woozy, but no one accidentally discharged a blast of Cold. We made our way along the deserted corridors, which ended in two different offshoots and a thick door, soft light spilling between its cracks.

As we got closer, the Sanctuary offered its first real signs of life, all of our ears pricking up as we huddled against the fine wood.

I expected to hear whips and screams of pain and cries for mercy.

But there was none of that.

There was laughter.

And music.

And beautiful floral scents trickling through as well.

None of it made any sense. The Domestics in the slave cart had seemed petrified of this place, eager to escape, and dreading their return.

Quickly I closed my eyes and prayed, trying to summon some courage from above. The Crier had trusted in me enough to destroy two of my fingers as a sign, and I hoped that he was still here with our group, waiting to show us the way.

Dunes had his blade at the ready. He nodded, stepping aside so I could pass, drooping into his submissive stance.

'Don't stand like that,' I said, giving his broad back a gentle pat as I passed. 'You're my sword, not my slave.'

He jerked up straight, prouder than I'd ever seen. He pressed a hand over the scar on his cheek.

I crept up and opened the door a crack, just enough for me to peek through. A massive courtyard waited beyond. It took me a few moments to process what I was seeing.

I nearly dropped my weapon.

'What is it?' Cam whispered at my back. 'Do you see Shilah?'

'It's, it's—'

I swallowed hard, not able to articulate.

'What's happening?' Cam asked.

'It's a banquet,' I said, steeling myself to say the next part. Admitting it made my head swoon with confusion, replacing all my readiness for battle. 'A banquet, for the *Jadans*.'

Gorgeous Domestics were everywhere amongst the lush gardens, at least fifty strong, dressed up in gowns and holding plates piled high with the most decadent foods I'd seen in quite some time. Cheeses, orangefruit, dates, and even some cured meats, all being devoured without the slightest bit of desperation, as if these Domestics ate in such abundance every night. Groups milled about, chatting with one another, smiling, and some even dancing. Many held chalices filled with dark red liquid that might have even been wine. One short-haired beauty plucked a Wisp off a pile of hundreds and dropped it in her drink, smiling as she swirled the Cold around. Almost all of them had colour smeared above their eyelids like Noblewomen, and some even had flowers woven into their hair. A small gathering of Domestics was lounging by a large pool, carelessly tossing Wisps into waters teeming with small fish.

In the middle of the courtyard was a group of Jadan women on a raised platform playing wood and string instruments, together making extraordinary, complex music. I hadn't known my people were capable of such songs. These Domestics handled harps and lutes and small drums with practised ease, swerving together through delightful melodies. They smiled and laughed as they explored melodies that were foreign to my ears, a far cry from the Khat's Anthem. A few of them looked to be gambling at a long glass table shaped like a tear, playing Conquer. They giggled as the cards turned, putting up things like jewellery, and books, and even full Chills.

Then I spotted the thorn in the garden.

Flitting amongst the crowds of beautiful Jadans was a single man.

His skin was fair – obviously Noble – and his hair was even more yellow than Cam's. He was dressed in the finest robes, cut in black velvet and accentuated with a high collar to hide a lithe neck. This Noble was unusually tall, his cheekbones pronounced, chin strong and stubbled. He would be handsome in every light through which he travelled, starlight or Sinai.

He moved from Domestic to Domestic with an impossibly broad smile stretching across his face. Bending over, he offered each girl a light kiss on the cheek, or a delicate brush on the shoulder, or a deep bow of respect. I could see him talking to all of them, and if I didn't know better I would have said he was doling out small bits of flattery, his eyes glinting with desire and appreciation.

This was the opposite of what I was anticipating.

Perhaps this place really was a Sanctuary.

To make things even more disconcerting, the Domestics all seemed receptive to the man's charm. They smiled and curtsied and gently touched a ring on his hand as he passed. For all I could tell, this was the happiest gathering since the Great Drought.

I stumbled back, even my feet seeming unsure of themselves now.

'Can I look?' Cam asked, his face sullen and concerned.

All of a sudden pain pulsed into my injured hand. I touched my dead pinky finger and winced.

At least I wasn't dreaming.

'Shivers and Frosts,' Cam hissed as he looked through into the courtyard. 'What in the Crier's name is going— that's him, Spout. That's Ka'in, in the middle, talking to all of them. Damn, he's so smug I just want to punch him in his face and rip out his yellow hair.'

'I figured as much,' I said, a sour taste in my mouth.

Cam peered through the crack silently, taking it all in. After a few moments he stepped back and let the door gently close.

'Whelp,' he said, clucking his tongue. 'I hate to admit it, but I'm rather jealous.'

Split frowned, pushing forwards. 'Let me see.'

'That is one grand banquet,' Cam said as the Pedlar wiggled past, giving me a conceding flip of his palm. 'Way better than the ones back at the Tavor Manor. Maybe Shilah would want us to rescue her tomorrow so she could fill up on good food.'

'No,' Dunes announced, his voice low and gruff. 'She won't be out there. Tomorrow will be too late.'

'I don't know,' Cam said, smiling. 'There's a whole plate of honey-crusted yams that—'

'We need to find her right away,' Dunes said, pressing his knuckles against his scarred cheek.

'Sun-damned blisters, boy,' Split said, pulling away from the door and rapping his knuckles on Cam's head. 'I think you missed a very important detail.'

'What?' Cam asked, holding a hand against where Split had struck. 'That tub of Khatapples near the fountain?'

Split rolled his eyes. 'Did you even look *up*?'

'Maybe.' Cam gave a sheepish shrug. 'Okay, no.'

Split shook his head. 'You're lucky you're good at accents.'

'I'm a good warrior,' Cam said.

Split stepped away, gripping his crossbow tightly. 'Take a see for yourself, Spout.'

This time I tilted my face sideways so I could see above the courtyard.

Five crossbows wouldn't be enough.

Just like the walls of the city itself, the Sanctuary courtyard was fully lined along the top. But instead of Closed Eyes, the whole place was ringed with Nobles. I did a quick count and lost track once I hit thirty bodies. The Nobles didn't quite look like guards, though. They weren't armoured, instead they were wearing silk robes and masks of black velvet. They surveyed the banquet with devious eyes, scratching quills against parchment. Some of them chatted quietly to their neighbours, but others seemed deeply lost in thought as they scribbled.

I shook my head as I retreated from the sight, further in a daze.

'Who do you think they are?' I asked Split.

The Pedlar turned to Dunes, suspicion all over his face. 'Any *guesses*?'

Dunes shook his head, but he did it far too quickly for me to feel confident.

'Dunes,' I said. 'Please. I need to know. They outnumber

us almost ten to one. And they're not wearing any metal to aim for.'

The big man let out a long breath, not meeting my eyes. 'Hamman knew about a ritual.'

'What sort of ritual?' I prodded.

'Something to do with the Fall itself. It's not good.' Dunes's gaze went to Cam. 'Horrible things that I would never want to be associated with, especially in the eyes of the Crierson.'

'Is Shilah in danger?' I asked.

'Yes,' Dunes said without pause.

'Any guesses as to where this Beauty Room is? This is a big place.'

Dunes shook his head. 'This is a guess I cannot make. But I swear by every star in the Crier's sight that I will—'

A squeak behind us cut him off.

All four of us swung around, crossbows aimed and at the ready.

A lovely Jadan with a floor-length gown and long hair was standing in the middle of the hallway, both her hands held over her head. She must have turned the corner and found us huddling by the door, but froze instead of running away. She was also tattooed with freckles, and I almost couldn't look at her straight on for fear of being distracted by her beauty.

'I just needed to relieve myself,' she said, her voice trembling and afraid. 'I promise I won't scream whatever you do, but you must know that he won't be happy if you touch me. I've been made beautiful, just for him. He even promised my name wasn't going to be in the scrolls this month.' She slowly lowered a hand to the strap of her dress and let the front of it fall away, revealing the scarred breast beneath. 'I'm his.'

Cam gasped, looking away and holding his hand in front of his face.

I glanced away too, but not before noticing the horrible

thing that had been done to her body. Her entire breast was covered in scars from neck to stomach, the skin marred from some sort of cutting or burning. A wave of sadness steadied my resolve.

'Don't worry,' I said, focused on my feet. 'We're not here to hurt you or touch you or anything. We just want to find our friend. She was taken here today by Ka'in.'

The Domestic nodded, dressing herself once again. There was something telling in her eyes, wily even.

'You know this place well, darling?' Split asked, lowering his weapon.

'I do,' she said, her voice meeker than her expression.

'You said "made beautiful",' Cam said. 'Does that have anything to do with a Beauty Room?'

The girl swallowed hard. 'You said your friend was taken here today?'

'Yes,' I said. 'Please. Help us find her.'

The girl gave a single nod.

And then she began to scream.

# Chapter Twenty-One

'Move!' Dunes made a vast sweeping gesture with his arms and then broke into a run towards the girl, charging at her with all the force of a battering ram. 'Get Meshua away from the wall. Get him away now!'

Cam thrust an arm protectively over my shoulder, ushering me down the hall, keeping my head tucked against his neck. I couldn't hear much over the sound of the Domestic's intense cries. They would be heard by every ear in the courtyard. They would alert the eerie masked men huddling above the banquet. She had her hands at her sides in fists, twisting the fabric of her dress, squeezing sound from every crevice in her chest. I'd never heard a Jadan make so much noise by herself, even under the touch of the Vicaress.

Split huffed beside Cam and me, trying to keep pace. His crossbow smacked against the wall, ripping off one of the paintings, and the Abb was knocked out of the shaft. My heart jerked, sending me backwards to go after the rolling bead. Cam grabbed my arm and gave me a panicked look, his fingers firm and digging in.

'Leave it, Spout!' he shouted, yanking me towards Dunes, waving with his crossbow for Split to do the same.

'No, I—'

The girl's screeching reached a new level.

'We'll make more!' Cam bellowed. 'Come on!'

'Sorry!' Split called, his pinky twisting back in his ear. The reverberations of the girl's scream were so violent I wondered if the Pedlar's fingers were going to come away bloody. 'I didn't mean to lose it!'

I swallowed hard and then stopped my foolish attempt at recovering the Abb, letting Cam lead me down the hallway. I couldn't let him know about the Frost. Better to let one Abb get away than let my secret get out.

Dunes already had his hooked blade sheathed on his hip, instead holding the boilweed strip he'd silenced the guard with earlier. He swung behind the girl and wrapped her mouth. Her cries were shrill even after being muffled by the grey strip.

'Behind me, all of you!' Dunes commanded. 'Now!'

Even in such a crisis, with an army of enemies bearing down from the other side of the door, Dunes exuded enough confidence to give me strength. His nostrils flared wide as he breathed, the rest of his face motionless. He didn't flinch even as the girl whipped her elbows backwards and landed bony knobs into his stomach and thighs and chest.

The rest of us rounded behind Dunes as he raised his crossbow towards the courtyard door. His arm was as straight and unyielding as a spear, even as the voices on the other side grew louder, clearly coming our way.

They'd be on us at any moment.

'May I shoot, Meshua?' Dunes asked, completely serious. 'By your command.'

The Domestic then tried using her feet to kick back at Dunes's groin. She directly connected with one of the blows, but his grip still didn't budge. I winced for him. His crossbow focused on the door, waiting for my signal.

'Yes!' I let out. Individual voices could now be heard in the courtyard. The door was about to swing open. 'Shoot!'

Dunes pulled the trigger and the Abb went soaring.

He was the best shot of the four of us, and as expected the golden bead connected right in the centre of the door.

The wave of Cold that resulted was so violent that it knocked us all backwards. Even Dunes stumbled. Impossibly cool wind burst across my face and arms, even thrusting into the boilweed wrapped around my fingers, making me gasp. The crack of wood was nearly as loud as the girl's screams.

A thick layer of Ice had shot across the blast point, waves of clear crystal sealing the entire wall around the door in the blink of an eye. The blockage was thick as a fist near the middle, sloping down as it met the corners of the corridor. The white tendrils steamed with mist and grasped their way towards the nearest paintings.

No one would be breaking through any time soon.

Dunes had accidentally let go of the screaming Domestic, who was now splayed on the floor, gaping in disbelief as she appraised the Ice. Her dress had ridden up, and I noticed more scarring on her thighs. She was no longer making any noise. Her lips trembled as her fingers caressed her face and the tangles of her hair, obviously in shock over the lingering Cold.

'Is this one of his tricks?' she babbled, hand smoothing her clothes back down. 'I did everything he wanted. I'm beautiful. I'm his.'

'It's not a trick,' Split said, making a calming gesture. 'Everything is okay. I felt the same way the first time I saw the Ice.'

She looked up at Dunes, full of awe and wonder. 'Are you the Crier? But your skin . . . it's like chocolate.'

Dunes gave a heavy shake of his head. 'No, child. Of course I'm not.'

'Then who are you?' she asked, her tone completely different now, every word genuine. Her hand shook as it pointed towards the mass of Ice, her eyes growing wet and red and distant. 'Have you finally come to save us?'

'I am only a protector,' Dunes said, gesturing towards me with the crossbow. 'He is the one—'

Cam stepped in front of me, opening his arms wide and bowing towards the big man. 'Don't listen to him. This is Meshua. And yes, he's come to save you.'

'That's your name?' she asked Dunes, the freckles on her cheeks glistening from spilled tears. 'Meshua. What does that mean?'

'My name is Dunes,' he said, with all the gentleness of a broken bone.

Someone pounded from the other side, the sound diminished to a gentle thump by the Ice. The door didn't budge. The blows doubled, then tripled, but the sound could barely be heard, the danger in the hallway no more than a distant memory.

Sanctuary.

'I don't understand.' The girl put her thumb in her mouth, biting down hard. 'It's so Cold. I don't understand. Who are you Jadans?'

She said 'Jadans' as if she wasn't one of us. I frowned.

Cam made a wild gesture with his arms at Dunes. 'He's Meshua. The Coldmaker. The Crier's son. The—'

Dunes looked at me with a face full of horror. 'I am most certainly not!'

I dropped my crossbow and kneeled down at the girl's side. 'It doesn't matter. But we're here to find our friend. Please, will you take us to find her? She needs help.'

Any mischief in the Domestic's face had changed to pure terror. Her eyes were locked over my shoulder, bulging at the sight of the Ice. She was even more beautiful up close, her hair thicker than the bow on my weapon. I made sure not to inhale the intoxicating smell wafting from her neck.

'I can't,' she whispered, completely afraid. 'It's a trick. I know it's a trick. I'm loyal and beautiful.'

'Please,' I said, imbuing the word with everything I had in my heart.

She paused, looked me in the face, and then shook her head. Her expression became distant and haughty. 'Never. I am his.'

I sat next to her, defeated.

'Please,' I said, one last time.

Then she started screaming again, her face full of defiance, eyes spilling over with hate.

Dunes came over, lifted her up, and then snapped her smallest finger. The screams stopped as the girl stared at her hand, her finger now sideways and angled.

Then the screams doubled.

'What are you doing?' Cam yelled, hands over his ears.

Panic settled in my chest. I was too overwhelmed to know what to do.

Dunes muffled the girl's mouth with the boilweed and then growled in her ear, wearing the mask of Hamman. 'You disrespected the merciful Meshua. I am not merciful. You will lead us to this Beauty Room. And every wrong turn you lead us down I will break another one of your fingers.'

Without so much as a pause Dunes had her next finger ready to snap.

The girl started sobbing beneath the boilweed.

Split looked as if he might cry in sympathy. 'Dunes.'

'I'm so sorry,' Cam said, tugging at his hair. 'He didn't mean that.'

'I mean it,' Dunes growled, his teeth gnashing. 'Which hallway to the Beauty Room? Left or right?'

'Dunes, stop,' Cam whimpered, staring at the tilted finger.

'We will find Shilah,' Dunes barked. 'And this girl knows where.'

The Domestic took one more look at her pinky and then shook her head. She looked much less sure of herself this time.

Dunes tilted his head, looking confused, and then he vomited. A little splashed into the girl's hair on the way down. She looked mortified, more so than when he'd broken her finger.

I stepped back, away from the foul puddle, although not much had come out of him this time.

Dunes took a deep breath, the fury returning to his face. 'Which hallway, girl? Now. Left or right?'

The girl hesitated, closing her eyes, trying to escape into her head.

Dunes turned to me, bile dripping over his bottom lip. 'By your command, Meshua.'

'She's Jadan,' Cam said, terror in his words.

I looked inside myself for the Spout from the barracks. I called out for guidance, trying to summon the Inventor. This girl was family, and it wasn't right to torture family. She was born Jadan, which meant she never stood a chance at a fair life, and whoever she was now was not her fault. There would be another way. I yelled all that and more into the abyss.

The words disappeared.

Something did rise back up, however.

Shilah's face stared back at me, rigid with pain. Her normally straight back was spasming in all directions. Her braid was whipping as her neck snapped back and forth. She wasn't screaming out, but instead, a single golden tear spilled down her face, burning a trail in its wake.

I opened my eyes. It had to be done.

The Inventor was missing.

The Warrior stood in his place.

Cam shouted something, but it didn't change my mind. This Domestic was family, but she was also the only way to find Shilah. And now, because of this girl's choice to scream, the Nobles and guards would be after us. They would find another way around our Ice, and hunt us down. The other Hookmen and the Vicaress were sure to follow suit. We no longer had the luxuries of stealth and time because this Jadan girl had chosen Nobles over family.

'Do what you have to,' I said.

Dunes snapped the next finger.

It wasn't long before we were standing outside the Beauty Room.

'You're sure this is the place?' Dunes asked the girl, who was still suspended in his arms. She was like a lifeless puppet. 'You're *sure*?'

The Domestic nodded to the heavy door at the end of the hallway, clutching her shattered hand to her chest. There were no paintings on the walls down here. No shrines. No stained-glass representations of the suppression of my people. There were only hallways painted black with a single Sinai for light in the centre. It would be the perfect place for the guards to ambush us. Dunes would be thinking something along the same lines.

Dunes grabbed hold of the girl's middle finger next, right below a jewelled ring. 'Because if you are lying!'

'She's not,' Cam said, his hands trembling at his sides.

Split gave Cam a *told-you-so* sort of look, flipping up his palms.

'I'm not,' the girl whimpered without any further squirming. 'Please.'

She used the same desperate tone as I had when asking her about Shilah. I pitied what agony she must be feeling. Filtering through the catacombs of the Sanctuary had given me time to second-guess myself. I felt a bit of remorse, which stirred the acid in my stomach, but I also knew remorse wouldn't change what needed to be done.

Dunes lowered the girl to her feet and then pressed his fingers on her collarbone and neck, pinching like a scorpion. Her eyes bulged for a moment, she swayed, and then collapsed into his arms.

Dunes let Hamman's face slide away as he set the girl gently on the stone floor.

'I will get used to it,' he said, mostly to himself.

'What'd you do to her?' Cam asked. 'Is she dead?'

'I am not without mercy,' Dunes said. 'She will sleep through pain.'

'Yeah?' Split asked, full of spite. 'And how do you know how to do something like that if you've never tortured anyone before? Did you *guess*?'

Dunes looked away.

Then a shout from the other side of the heavy door.

It wasn't a scream of pain, or one of surprise, but more of a battle cry.

It was Shilah. I was sure.

'Crossbows,' I said, making sure my Abb was still in the altered shaft. The rest of the group did the same.

I nodded to Dunes, my weapon at the ready.

We would deal the Khatdom a significant blow if we got Shilah out of here unscathed, leaving behind a burning wake of Ice.

'Break it down,' I said.

Dunes smiled, giving a sigh of relief. 'By your command.'

He rushed at the door and knocked the whole thing off its hinges with a single slam of his shoulder. The heavy wood went sliding across the polished floor, which was slick with blood and grease and piss and other fluids I couldn't place. The slab came to rest against a row of cages.

And in that instant I changed.

Perhaps changed wasn't correct, but rather I was *revealed*.

There hadn't been many times in my life where a single event knocked my view into an entirely new perspective. Where everything I thought I understood about life had been diminished, my past experiences only to be proven a thin veneer cast over truth. Even the discovery of the Coldmaker didn't jolt me as deeply and profoundly as did this moment. I'd seen many horrors over my lifetime, had experienced a lot of them first-hand. I thought I knew my limits.

How wrong I was.

I could finally understand the dark things that had always gripped my soul. The forces I chose to ignore, distracted by my curiosities.

I was rage.

I was fury.

I was vengeance.

I was destruction.

I was bloodshed.

Shilah was strapped down to a metal table, her shirt torn open and crumpled to the side, her face stretched wide with pain. She wasn't crying, however, instead her teeth were bared and she stared up at her assailant as if she was going to bite out his throat if he came close enough. Already a whole portion of her left breast was sizzling with fresh burns, and the Opened Eye tattoo on her arm had been inked Closed and then branded to a blur.

Spout walked out of the room.

Meshua took his place.

I was the Crier's weapon.

I was his justice.

Shilah's torturer wore a velvet strip on his face like the other men encircling the courtyard, but this one was over his mouth and nose, presumably so he wouldn't have to breathe in the smell of roasting skin. His eyes still lingered with a sick pleasure, although now more struck with curiosity. He didn't look particularly fearful, which only made me boil with anger.

Hanging on the walls behind him were diagrams of split limbs painted on scrolls, as well as depictions of wounds in various stages of bleeding and healing. There were body parts on the tables, arms, fingers, legs, clamped in vices, and it took me a moment to realize that they were only clay models. This was unsettling in its own right. Vials of powders and potions waited in cabinets around the room. The whole place was an apothecary gone wrong.

The cages off to the side had figures huddled together in the shadows, arms wrapped around each other in both fear and comfort. I could only make out vague, shivering forms.

The masked Noble lording over Shilah had some kind of branding tool in his hand, dangling above a solitary flame.

I knew in my heart that this Noble was going to die.

I just needed to decide how.

Shilah's face fell to the side, her eyes glazed over with pain but she spotted me instantly. She saw the crossbow and then nodded, her face flushed with an emotion I couldn't read.

'You're interrupting my work,' the Noble sneered from behind the velvet mask, dropping the branding tool in a bucket of water. It made a violent sizzle. His voice was pompous and proud, his body angled towards Cam. He wiped some blood off his plump wrists with a clean strip of boilweed, staring at the fallen door. 'She escaped twice and caused all sorts of mischief. Any problems you have with the beautification of these creatures should be taken up with Ka'in through the proper channels. This specimen was particularly nasty and in need of more extreme—'

It didn't take long to decide.

'Cut his hands off,' I said to Dunes, my voice shaking.

Dunes stormed through the room like a dark wind. 'By your command, Meshua.'

'Halt yourself, slave!' the man said, stumbling back against one of the walls, knocking a whole table of the clay models to the ground as he scrambled away. 'Wait. Aren't you Hamm—'

Dunes pinned the man's hands above his head and then swung the blade with a single chop, powering through the skin, meat, and bones of the wrists. He drove the curved metal straight into the wall. The Noble didn't even have time to take off his mask.

The man screamed horrors into the velvet strip, looking at the stumps at the ends of his arms, blood spurting out, some of it landing on Dunes. The sight of white bone left me drunk with vengeance. Dunes dropped the hands to the ground, the wrists leaking gristle and blood.

'Shivers and Frosts,' Cam exhaled, stumbling backwards.

Split's fingers flexed at his sides, hungry to get in on the action himself. He was the only one of us staring into the cages.

Dunes cupped the velvet mask harder over the Noble's mouth, wrapping his body up from behind, muffling the shouting as the severed arms continued to spurt. I wished I could turn this leaking Noble into a sick diagram of his own. Propped on the wall to witness the consequences of his treachery forever.

Or at least until I burned this Sun-damned Sanctuary to rubble.

'What shall you have me do, Meshua?' Dunes asked calmly.

I was already rushing up to Shilah, my shirt in my hands, gently placing the layer on top of her, making sure not to scrape any of her burns.

'Spout,' she said with a weak smile, walking her fingers through the air, as far as her bound wrists would allow.

'I know. Always slow.' I put down the crossbow and took her hand in mine. 'So you escaped twice, huh?'

She gave a single nod. 'I was trying to save you. But I couldn't find a way out.'

I nearly choked out a laugh. 'Save me from what?'

She squeezed my fingers, a tender look reaching her eyes. Then she studied the crossbow for the briefest of moments. 'You tinkered it so it would fire Abbs?'

'I did,' I said, going at her bindings.

'Does it work?' she asked.

I ripped off the camel-leather straps holding her down. 'I think you're going to be pleasantly surprised.'

The handless Noble continued to scream into his velvet mask.

Shilah sat up, holding my shirt over her chest. Her face was alight with pain, but she didn't cry out. Her eyes found Cam, who had his hand over his mouth and had begun to weep. I looked to the vials in the nearest cabinet, looking for groan salve, but found none. The containers were mostly filled with irritants, like sand, gravel, and glass shards, and all of a sudden a fresh wave of hate surged through my chest.

'And your hand?' Shilah asked carefully.

I held up my wrapped fingers. 'A sign.'

She raised an eyebrow.

'Later,' I said, swallowing hard. 'And your— and you?'

Shilah shrugged. 'We're going to give them worse.'

More murmurs escaped from the cages behind me, but I was still too focused on Shilah to let anything else have my attention. She must have been in extraordinary pain from the burns, but my heart swelled because she was alive. Relief overtook the force of rage, and once again life made sense.

Through the corner of my eye I saw Split and Cam move up to one of the cages, examining the strength of the bars.

'Meshua,' Dunes interrupted, still holding the Noble tightly.

The man was whimpering now, but it wasn't enough to satisfy me. 'Shall I put this monster to sleep too?'

'He gets off on the screams,' Shilah whispered, looking over at the masked Noble, her face distorting with fury. 'But I wouldn't give him any. Keep him awake. Let him hear his own.'

I used to be afraid of the fire she kept inside. I thought I might get swallowed or burned if I got too close. Now I found the intensity comforting. I understood her urges.

I touched a hand to Shilah's lower back, feeling a sheen of sweat.

'I have no doubt,' I said. 'You *are* Meshua, after all.'

'Damn right I am.' She smiled wildly as she rolled her unlocked wrists and looked at the Noble's severed hands on the floor. 'And damn right you are too.'

More murmuring from the cages. I thought I heard one of them whisper: 'He came back for us.'

'It's a trick,' another voice said from within the shadows, one I thought I might have recognized. 'Always a trick.'

'We're going to get you out,' Cam said. 'Don't worry, we're not with Ka'in.'

'You said the bastard likes screams?' I asked Shilah.

She nodded, pointing to the scrolls on the wall. 'Said they inspire him.'

'Dunes,' I called, flattening my hand against Shilah's back, feeling her wet heat.

'Yes, Meshua?' Dunes asked. The big man was starting to look ill again, but I knew he could handle a little more duty.

'Cut off his ears next,' I said.

'By your command.'

Two more small body parts slapped against the floor.

More muffled screams.

I helped Shilah off the table and looked away as she discarded the tattered rags that were once her shirt. She pulled mine over her injured chest. I took that time to search the room for any smaller Cold I might steal for the cave, but there didn't seem to be any, only the sickening diagrams and scrolls and clay body parts. Shilah's hand curled around the back of my neck, and she pulled our foreheads together.

'Thank you,' she said softly.

It was the most vulnerable I'd heard her, and I wished I could have Dunes chop the Noble's hands off all over again.

'Spout,' Cam called. 'We need to get them out.'

Shilah nodded, letting her fingers slide off my numbers. 'We do.'

I ran up to the cage. To my astonishment I recognized the Jadans inside. The caravan cart was back together again. At least most of it. On the wrong side of the bars were the two sisters, Ellia and Ellcia, each with a puffy eye. Leah was pressed between them, her luscious hair slashed and cut at odd angles and burned along many of the tips. She was nursing her right hand. All the fingernails had been removed. The layers of grime and blood did absolutely nothing to diminish her beauty.

'Yes,' Cam said, his voice almost squeaking with nerves. He couldn't take his eyes off Leah. 'We're going to get you out.'

Leah reached through the bars with her good hand and placed it on Cam's stomach, just above his belt line. 'We will be forever appreciative, master Noble.'

Cam froze up, his whole body tense.

'Get yah hand away, priss!' Ellcia hissed at Leah. 'Thum's part of a trick. Always a trick with Ka'in.'

'It's nuh trick,' Ellia said in sheepish tones. 'Yah saw whut boyfriend did in the cart. He brung Cold from the air and brought little sis to life.'

Cam looked at me and mouthed: *boyfriend?*

I shook my head.

'It's a good trick,' Ellcia said, pushing her sister. 'And number four gone died anyway. Ka'in is always in dem trick.'

'Ice no trick, sis,' Ellia said.

That answered one of my questions.

A part of me had known that the unconscious girl from the cart might not make it, but hearing of her death carved another slice from my heart.

'Are yuh blind, sis?' Ellcia shouted. 'That's dah Hookman standing right there!'

'I am not a Hookman,' Dunes said.

'Yuh the Hookman who got us in the first place!' Ellcia shouted. 'Hummun.'

'He's pledged himself to me now,' I said. 'He's changed. Hamman is gone.'

'Trick!' Ellcia said. 'That's a Hookman!'

Leah's hand slipped under Cam's shirt, her fingers caressing his stomach. She gave him a sincere look through the bars, pleading almost. 'Are you real? Is this real?'

Cam nodded slowly. 'Um. Yes.'

'Will you get us away, Noble sir,' Leah asked, digging her fingers in. 'Take me away with you.'

'Keys,' Cam choked out, looking my way.

I'd already spotted a whole ring of keys sitting on a nail just out of arm's reach of the cages.

They always had to twist the blade.

I went to grab the keys, but Ellia protested. 'Thums keys a trick!'

Ellcia reached over and tugged her sister's hair. 'Stop it. You gunn make things worse when Ka'in shows up. He always shows up.'

I grabbed the keys, a hundred different sizes and types jangling on the ring.

Leah pulled Cam closer, her voice soft. 'Those keys actually *are* a trick, sir. Those are not real. He uses them as decoys.'

'Where's the real one?' I asked.

Ellia pressed herself against the bars, gesturing wildly towards the cabinet. 'Keeps it in a different vial every night, won't let us see. Puts nasty stuff inside thum so if anyone tries tah dig they gunna get cuts and the likes.'

I would have had Dunes interrogate our masked Noble to find out, but since the man was no longer conscious – and no longer had any ears – I figured we had to do things the hard way.

'Split,' I said. 'Close the door, please. This is going to be loud.'

Split shut us in, and I gave the vial cabinet a satisfying push. The glass jars shattered against the floor, splitting out in a mess of tiny grit. I moved to start sifting through the wreckage, but Dunes was already in front of me, holding me back, the Noble's velvet mask in his hand.

'Absolutely not, Meshua,' Dunes said, strapping the mask over his mouth and nose. 'This is my task.'

And with that he was sifting through all the glass and splinters and powders, ignoring the spray and pain he had to endure. Shilah came over and took my hand in hers. I could tell she was trying to grip hard, but there wasn't much strength left in her fingers. I needed to get her back to the cave as soon as possible. I'd find her food and medicine, and we could heal together.

Split was at the cage, his forehead pressed against the bars. 'I'm so sorry this happened to you, girls. You will never be treated like this again, I swear on the memory of my wife and daughter.'

Ellcia groaned, retreating back to the shadows. 'Lies.'

'I'm so sorry this happened,' I said softly to Shilah.

She let her fingers entwine with mine and looked down. 'Just so you know. I wasn't manipulating you.'

'Hmm?'

'When I kissed you.' She looked up and stared straight ahead. She kept trying to straighten her back into the way she usually stood, but winced after each attempt, having to settle for a hunch. 'I was kissing you. I wasn't manipulating you.'

I nodded. 'I know.'

'And if I was manipulating you . . . I'm sorry,' she said. 'I won't do it again.'

I smiled. 'I won't either.'

'And . . . look, this is what I wanted to show you before.' Shilah pulled down her bottom lip, revealing a stain of black, deep under her gums. It looked much older than her other wounds. 'I tried smuggling half a Wisp when I was younger. You're not the only one who got hurt by Cold, partner.'

I took her hand in mine, squeezing tightly. Cam looked at us, his eyes tender.

Dunes eventually came back with a silver key, held triumphantly over his head. His forearms were prickled with splinters and glass, burned with caustic powders, but he didn't seem to care. 'For you, Meshua. I will get you anything you need.'

I was quick to unlock the bars. Shilah swept past me, going right into the cage. 'You can trust us.'

'Couldn't trust you in dat cart, priss,' Ellcia hissed, holding up her fists. 'You left us.'

Shilah turned to Ellia. 'Well, we're leaving now, together. Convince your sister.'

'She's right, Ellcy. And if yuh stay, how we gonna get past thum guards on selection night,' Ellia said. 'Where we gonna hide?'

Ellcia groaned. 'Thum gunn try and torture us if we leave. Issa trick.'

'No more torturing, ever,' I said, grabbing my crossbow. 'We're going to take you on the Coldmarch. We have a secret place too, where they won't be able to find you.'

Cam was staring at Leah's hand, still reaching up his shirt, his mouth agape.

'He's really not a Hookman any more,' Shilah said. 'And you can trust these Nobles.' She nodded towards Cam. 'I swe— you don't have to put your hand on him like that, Leah. We're not going to leave you behind.'

Leah's palm pressed tighter, ignoring her.

'Please, beautiful Noble,' Leah said. 'Keep me safe.'

Cam swallowed hard. 'Yes.'

Still Ellcia hesitated. I couldn't imagine what had been done to her after she'd been returned here.

Shilah wrapped the freckled sister in a hug, which I knew had to be extraordinarily painful considering the fresh burns on her chest. Shilah held tightly, even as Ellcia struggled. She whispered something into the girl's ear, and all of a sudden the resistance stopped. Ellcia gave a single nod, letting herself be led out of the cage. Ellia trailed behind, and Leah filtered out, going right for Cam's side, demure and poised.

Cam looked as if he'd just swallowed a Wisp whole.

I gave Shilah a questioning look, but she only returned a beguiling smile, shaking her head.

'Dunes,' I said.

The big man stood at attention. 'Yes, Meshua.'

'Are you okay?' I asked.

'I am in your service,' Dunes said. 'I am the best I've ever been.'

'Good,' I said, lifting up my crossbow. 'Help me lead us out of here.'

Dunes stepped over the broken Noble and wrenched his blade out of the wall. 'By your command.'

# Chapter Twenty-Two

Leah told us that the secret way out of the Sanctuary was in something called the 'Clean Room', calling out directions as we fled. Considering what the Beauty Room turned out to be, I prepared myself for the worst.

We rushed down the empty hallways. Dunes brought up the rear at a brisk charge. No guards or masked Nobles came jumping out of the shadows or hopped around corners. Everyone in the Sanctuary must have been pondering the magnificent shield of Ice blocking the courtyard door. The Cold would have seeped through the wood, and been felt even in the garden itself. I prayed everyone was still in shock, searching the sky for answers, instead of the hallways.

Shilah hunched as she moved, not able to stand up straight, and the sisters winced behind with every step. Leah showed signs of abuse too, having to walk a bit bow-legged, one leg limping.

Severed ears and hands weren't enough.

I wanted to go back and cut out that bastard's heart myself.

'Left,' Leah called, her fingers dancing through the air in front of her. 'Up the stairs!'

Dunes shot a questioning look back at me, the same way he'd done after every one of Leah's directions.

I nodded.

Dunes swung left, barrelling into possible danger. Cam, Split, and I followed right at his back, weapons at the ready.

'Cam,' I said.

He kept pace by my side, crossbow raised, but his focus kept flicking backwards to a certain Domestic. 'Yeah, Micah?'

'What do you think?' I asked quietly. My heart was a hundred hands banging on a single drum.

'About what?' Cam asked.

I paused, breath coming heavily. I seethed to the core. 'How do we fix all this?'

Cam gave me a soft look. 'We stick by you.'

'I mean it,' I said. 'This can't be how it is.'

'It won't be for—'

A rip from behind.

Dunes swivelled his crossbow, high and deadly, his whole body tense. Ellcia finished tearing a painting off the wall, the frame smashing on the ground.

'Don't care if this a trick. He dunn get tah look at them,' Ellcia said, going to the next nearest painting. 'S'not right.'

Ellia hesitated and then followed her sister's lead, ripping off a painting of her own. She looked rather proud beneath her puffy eye.

'What's not right about them?' I asked.

Shilah touched my wrist, shaking her head.

'What?' I asked. 'I want to know.'

Dunes gestured us onwards. 'We have to move, Meshua. They'll be looking for us.'

We trudged onwards, with Ellia and Ellcia ripping down paintings as we fled. It slowed the group down, and made far more noise than was necessary, but I let them have their moments. The sisters stood a little taller after each one they destroyed.

Dunes flinched at each crash of the wooden frames.

'What's your name?' Leah asked Cam, having moved to his side.

Cam gulped. 'Camlish.'

'You're beautiful,' she said, eyes on the floor. 'Will you really keep me safe?'

Cam nodded, his face stiffening with unease. He looked as if he was trying to dredge up something smart to say. The veins in his neck strained, but he remained silent.

'Go right, sir!' Leah called out to Dunes.

Dunes looked to me, and I nodded.

Leah turned her attention back to Cam, her leg dragging. 'I know this is a strange request, Camlish, but will you braid what's left of my hair? When we get to your safe place?' She tucked her injured hand tightly against her chest, nestling underneath the fabric, revealing a healthy swell of breast. 'I don't want to be *his* kind of beautiful any longer. I want to be *your* kind of beautiful.'

Shilah rolled her eyes.

Cam just blinked, his face cycling through anxious expressions. Ellcia growled from back near the end of the hallway, tearing down a painting of a Jadan with hair dyed like flame.

'Cam,' I said.

'Yeah— yes?' Cam asked.

'Can you grab that Sinai?' I asked, holding my injured hand up helplessly.

'Good idea,' Cam said. 'Get some light for any secret tunnels. Maybe keep the Sobeks away. That's why you're the leader.' He gestured respectfully to Shilah. 'Two leaders.'

Shilah gave him a gentle nod.

'Yes,' I said. 'That's the reason.'

Needing light did cross my mind. Mainly I wanted to steal some of the Sinai's Cold Charge back in the cave. I prayed that it might at least delay the Frost's disappearance. I knew the problem probably wasn't just the salt, but I didn't have

any other ideas as to how to save the holy Cold. All I knew
was that without a working Coldmaker, Meshua returned to
the little blue book.

Shilah gave me a curious look. I turned so she couldn't
read the secret on my face.

Cam grabbed the portable light as we swept past.

Leah's head cocked sideways, her bottom lip thrust out
into an intoxicating pout. 'A High Noble taking orders from
Jadans? Aren't you the one who gave your slaves the Ice?'

Cam gulped, looking away from her. 'They're not anyone's
slaves.'

'Left, sir!' Leah called out to the front, her face growing
concerned. 'Up the staircase!'

Dunes turned to me. His dark forearms shone with pieces
of broken glass, accentuated by streaks of blood from splinters.

'You don't have to check with me,' I told him gently. 'Lead
us where she says.'

Dunes's eyes narrowed with suspicion, but he swept up
the staircase.

'Seriously. What's with the paintings?' I asked Shilah.

She sighed, wincing as she climbed the stairs at my side,
teeth clenching. I reached out to steady her, and she accepted
my strength.

'You really want to know?' she asked.

I gave her an obvious sort of look.

She nodded, taking the stairs slowly. I kept a hand wrapped
around her, lifting as best as I could. My grip slipped along
her slick skin, and I kept getting lost in the scent of her burns.

'There's a ritual,' she said. 'Once a month. They set fire to
one of the Domestics and make her jump off the cliff, a tribute
to the original Fall. The paintings on the walls are of each
girl they murdered.' She put a little more weight on my arm.
'Apparently Ka'in will just stare at the paintings in the hallways for hours. He picks a different painting to take off the

wall and into his chambers every night. There's quite a few for him to choose from.'

Dozens of paintings flanked the staircase, and I couldn't look at the girls' faces.

'You happen to see a group of Nobles in masks?' she asked. 'Maybe writing names down?'

'At the banquet.'

The next steps made her whole body shudder, but she kept going. 'They study the girls. Make bets who the *Sun* is going to choose this month. They don't even bet Cold. It's all for status and power in their Sun-damned secret society.'

'And how does the Sun choose?' I asked.

She turned to look at Leah, lowering her voice. 'The girls don't ever get to go in the Clean Room, but they know about it. I think Ka'in let the information slip on purpose. There's this big glass eye that can be rotated on an axis. And it's curved, to gather up heat, like one of Leroi's magnifying glasses.' She took a deep breath. 'So all the Domestics have their names written on scrolls, which are stuck in a thick layer of sand on the floor. Once a month those masked bastards take the covering off a big hole in the roof, so the Sun hits the glass eye. Ka'in gives it a random spin, and whatever scroll gets set on fire . . .'

'We would have heard of such a thing,' I said, my stomach tight enough to turn sand to glass. 'That kind of sick torture would have made its way to Paphos. Everything comes back to Paphos.'

Shilah gave me a weak smile, and I saw that a back tooth had been ripped out, roots and all.

I was going to kill every Noble wearing a mask.

'We have the Coldmaker,' she said. 'They have their Fall. There's more secrets in this world than you think.'

'Like Desert,' I said.

She paused, and then kissed me.

I wasn't expecting it. Her lips were hard from lack of water, and she flinched at the pressure, but she made it last as long as she could. Her breath was atrocious, but I was greedy for her warmth and taste and familiarity.

She put her hands on my cheeks and stared deep into my eyes. 'Yes. Like Desert.'

'Did you mean *that* kiss?' I asked, breathless.

She nodded, putting a finger against her top lip. 'It feels like stingers and flames to kiss.'

'I'm so sorry—'

'You're worth stingers and flames,' she said, keeping our lips close, foreheads touching. 'World Partner.'

Cam swept past us, Leah hovering a little further behind him, giving Shilah and I a suspicious glance. Dunes reached the top landing, his crossbow sweeping across the perimeter. I still couldn't understand why it was so quiet in the hallways. My best guess was that everyone was kneeling before the Ice wall, praying together. If we had any luck, they'd be praying for days.

'Go right, sir!' Leah called out.

Ellia and Ellcia ripped off paintings on the staircase. They toppled down the steps, making a spectacular racket. The sisters cackled as the paintings fell; Ellia's laughter coming a little after her sister's.

No guards came to see about the noise. I guessed we couldn't have been that far from the courtyard. Part of me was starting to panic at the silence, knowing no good would come from losing my cool.

My hands felt too clean. For all these Nobles represented, for all the pain and suffering they inflicted on us, I didn't want to leave until my forearms were tattooed red.

Dunes led us down a hallway bright with Sinais.

'Keep it up,' Shilah said.

I looked behind me, confused. We were moving at a good

clip, and the sisters were no longer removing the paintings.

'Not that,' Shilah said, making a broad gesture over my face. 'Look at you. You're determined. You're fierce. You're ready for battle. You're a new Spout.'

I shrugged. 'Probably because I'm not Spout any more.'

'You'll always be Spout,' she said, her back stiffening in spite of the burns. 'I think now it's just that you're *my* Spout.'

'I—'

'So keep it up,' she said, giving a pained smile. 'And I want a special Abb crossbow too, when all of this is over.'

'Consider it done,' I said.

'That's the one,' Leah called, her voice musical and happy. She shuddered with delight, as if we already had her back in the Coldmarch cave. 'The Clean Room.'

Cam couldn't stop staring at Shilah, his face full of sorrow.

'Still no trick,' Ellia said to her sister in hushed tones. 'Who's the priss, now?'

Ellcia made an indiscernible grunt.

Dunes stopped in front of a large metal slab with a Closed Eye painted on it in red. It was almost the same colour as alder. The symbol seemed to jump out of the door, painted with depth and shadow, making it even more ominous.

'And you remember the way through the secret tunnel?' I asked Leah. 'You've done it before, right?'

She threaded her arm through Cam's, giving a demure nod.

Cam looked too stiff to move quickly.

'Okay,' I said to Dunes, getting a bad feeling. I lifted my crossbow, just in case. 'Open it.'

'I don't like this,' Split said, weapon trembling in his hand as he looked at the sisters. 'It's too quiet.'

'Maybe we're just finally catching our luck,' Cam said.

Leah gave a dainty laugh, looking up into Cam's face with glowing admiration.

Cam blushed. 'I agree. I *am* funny.'

'What was the joke?' Shilah asked, her face stern and unamused.

'Dunes,' I prodded.

Dunes rushed to try the handle, which turned without any resistance. He lifted his crossbow and pushed open the whole slab of metal with one heave, marching into complete darkness. There were no sounds from the room, everything calm and black. I thought I heard people breathing, but it was just my imagination playing tricks again. My heart was beating as rapidly as ever.

'Cam,' I said, nodding to the Sinai, feeling a huge wave of relief.

Cam puffed himself up in a self-important way, winking at Leah as he strutted into the room.

Leah tittered once again.

Shilah groaned.

We followed Cam inside as a group, the light only just penetrating the darkness. The room was vaster than I would have thought. And still. Too still.

Something slammed behind us.

All at once the room lit up in a blinding haze, dozens of Sinais blazing to life across the room. The place was vast and long, with a low ceiling that made it feel as if we were being crushed. The floor was covered in sand, and the walls were done up with hundreds of Closed Eyes, all staring towards the centre of the room. Dunes stopped still in front of me, his huge shape burned into the back of my eyes. I had to blink rapidly to adjust to the onslaught of light, the dazzling glow catching me off guard. I almost dropped my weapon.

Leah had led us right into a trap.

I looked behind us. Two guards stood with their swords drawn, helmets down over their faces. They'd slammed the door and locked us inside.

A row of a dozen guards were lined across the room in front of the lights, swords out of their scabbards, pikes at the ready. Their armour gleamed. Behind them had to be every single masked Noble in the courtyard. They huddled in imperfect rows, sneering at us from behind their black velvet, their smiles broad and hungry. They still had their scrolls and pens in hand.

A large glass eye waited on a pedestal in the middle of the room, as Shilah had predicted. The clear pupil was the size of a caravan wheel. Beneath its gaze, dozens upon dozens of scrolls stuck out of the layer of sand. Ka'in was casually leaning against the base of the pedestal. The formation of guards and masked Nobles behind him were clustered around one of the walls, which would surely mask the entrance to the secret tunnel.

'Welcome!' Ka'in chimed, as jovial as if he were greeting an old friend. His smile was easy and languid, smoother than the velvet masks the rest of the Nobles wore. 'Come in. Let's chat! Chat about the Khat. Chat about this and that. Hamman, so delightful to see you!'

'I am not Hamman,' Dunes growled, waving his crossbow in Ka'in's direction.

Leah was huddling behind Cam, the look of terror on her face strange. Perhaps she hadn't betrayed us after all.

Ellia was looking at her sister with heavy shame, her puffy eye making it all the sadder. Ellcia took her sister under her arm, holding her close.

'Trick,' Ellcia said in hushed tones.

'Well, you sure look like a Hamman,' Ka'in said, tapping his bottom lip. 'Twins, I assume? I didn't realize that scars covering an entire body could run in the family.' At this he gave a heavy chuckle, looking to his guards, who echoed the laughter.

'Hamman. Is. Gone,' Dunes said, sounding less confident than I'd have liked.

'No matter the name you wish to call yourself, Hookman,' Ka'in said, pressing himself off the pedestal with a little skip, stepping slowly towards us. 'Once again you did a spectacular job, returning all the runaway—'

'I returned nothing,' Dunes said, crossbow high and ready.

A flash of concern ran through Ka'in's face, but it quickly returned to glee as he spotted Leah and the other Domestics cowering at the back of the group.

'Do you really think I didn't know about this passageway, ladies! I had the damn thing built myself a few years back!' He clucked his tongue. 'Ahh, hunting. What's a Noble without sport? Loose the Jadan, catch the Jadan, through the secret door. Loose the Jadan, catch the Jadan, catch the Jadan whore.'

A few of the masked Nobles chuckled.

'Or is it *who's* a Noble without Noble sport?' Ka'in pondered to himself, his smile dashing.

A few men behind him began to answer, but Ka'in waved them silent, his face distorting with rage. 'Now which of you slaves stole my Frost? Which one of you figured out how to make Ice on my courtyard door?'

The silence sat heavily, but a part of me perked up. So the bastard did have at least one Frost here. I should have felt defeated and terrified, staring down so many enemies, but I had sort of been expecting this. I was left more excited than anything else.

Ka'in underestimated us.

The crossbow felt delightfully light in my hand, practically aiming itself. It wasn't every day I got to tinker with pain.

Ka'in swayed back and forth, impatient. 'I was so good to you girls. I made you beautiful and safe. Fed you bountiful food that only the Khat eats, and this is the thanks I get? Twice runaways. Runawayaways. And you!' Ka'in thrust a finger at Shilah, and then quickly returned it back to his mouth and kissed the tip. 'On your first night here you cause such a ruckus? What spirit. I see you have the potential to be most beautiful.'

Whispers from the masked Nobles filtered around the room, the echoes tight.

Shilah straightened up, defiant as always.

'Sneaked your brother in?' Ka'in asked. 'Wanted him to be beautiful, too? Sorry, no skinny little boy slaves in my Khatdom.' He tossed his head back over his shoulder, gesturing with his chin to the army of masks. 'I'm the only beautiful boy here.'

A few chuckles from behind, but Ka'in waved them silent again, not the reaction he was wanting.

'Ready for round two, Ellcia?' he asked. 'Did you want more? Your name is going on five scrolls this month.'

Ellcia folded into herself.

Ellia folded deeper, practically disappearing.

'I mean it,' Ka'in said, walking towards us. 'I need to know who wasted my Frost. What did you do to it? I didn't even think a Frost could *make* Ice, so it's one thing to—'

'It wasn't your Frost,' I said, cutting him off. 'It was the Crier's wrath.'

'Oh, is that right, ugly little brother?' Ka'in said. 'The Ice just appeared? Conjured out of the wind?'

The masked Nobles gave a collective chuckle, the room buzzing. One of them gave an overly dramatic lick of his lips underneath the mask, his eyes pinned on Leah.

Leah tucked herself further behind Cam.

I paused. 'Yes. In a way it did.'

Silence.

'Oh, don't fret, boy slave,' Ka'in said. 'There might be something in my Sanctuary for you. I have sport, yes. But I also have my hobbies. Hamman, you can quit the act now. Drop that crossbow before—'

'Dunes,' I said, my heart swelling with a dark excitement.

'Yes, Meshua?' Dunes asked.

'Drop the bucket.'

'What bucket, Meshua?' he asked.

Ka'in looked around, confused. 'What bucket?'

'Never mind,' I said, steadying my crossbow with my injured hand.

I aimed just a bit higher than my intended target, and hoped my father was watching.

The glass eye exploded outwards into a massive cloud of Cold. Shards of crystal and deadly winds sprayed backwards from the frame, right into the heart of the masked Nobles and guards. Blood sprayed the Sinai. The room tinged red. Glass sluiced through Cold-burned flesh, and the whole row closest to the blast toppled over and fell to the ground. The rest of the guards tried to swat away the Cold and the shards of Ice burning into their flesh. The wave of air rebounded off all the walls, sweeping robes and feet, causing mayhem. Cold splashed my face, my cheeks trembling with rage.

The masked Nobles screamed and tried to make sense of the carnage.

My lips curled into a twisted smile as I yanked the bow back and loaded in another Abb.

Ka'in was already plastered on the sands, forced down so hard he was practically buried. All of the scrolls around him had been flattened. His whole back was encrusted with Ice. I wanted to go over and do my Crying Dance on his fallen body. This time I would move with justice and rage, burying him deeper and deeper. I would dance him into a hole so endless that not even the Sun could reach.

'Meshua!' Dunes called over the mess of screams.

'Yes, Dunes,' I replied, giddy, the cool wind still thick in my hair.

'May I shoot as well?' he called.

'Shoot everything you have!' I laughed.

I didn't care about Frosts, or the fact that our Abbs were limited. All I cared about was destroying every last one of these Nobles. I wanted to burn Ice down their throats and into their souls.

Dunes fired an Abb square into one of the guard's chest plates. The burst of Cold and Ice was so spectacular that I almost felt at a loss. He must have been killed on the spot without having suffered. The crystal arms of Ice grabbed hold of his neighbouring guards so quickly that they didn't even have a chance to scream. They would spend eternity stuck together. I laughed deeper and louder.

Our group retreated towards the door. The guards waiting there were too stunned to do much of anything. Cam fired into the crowd next. I couldn't see exactly where his Abb landed, but it must have struck something solid, because once again the Nobles scattered and screamed under the resounding wave of Cold. The charged air trampled through their ranks.

My smile couldn't grow any larger.

Split let loose next, firing his Abbs in succession, shouting 'Anyah' and 'Lizah' between each concussive burst. He snarled with pure vengeance.

Dunes fired one Abb after another into the crowd alongside the Pedlar, loading the golden beads almost as quickly as they left the shaft of his crossbow. He struck the guards and Nobles trying to flee into the secret passage, freezing them on the spot. Their masked faces were left crisp and bitten, buried in a deadly mist that might never fade.

Leah, Ellia, and Ellcia looked too stunned to make sense of anything. The sisters had their hands pressed over their ears. Shilah's fists were balled at her sides. She was seething with jealousy.

'Dunes!' I shouted.

He dropped his crossbow, giving me a serious look. 'Yes, Meshua?'

I gestured to the guards by the door. The Cold cloud in the room was getting too thick, piling on itself and getting more violent, hungrier. If we didn't get out of there soon we were in danger of being swallowed too.

Dunes took his blade off his hip. Before I could even issue another command, both of the guards had been eviscerated. Two powerful blows to their necks and stomachs left them bleeding on the ground.

'Let's go!' I shouted, waving for our group to retreat back to the hallway.

We all rushed out and I slammed the door closed. 'Run! Hurry!'

The Domestics were still somewhat in shock, although they didn't seem as stunned as they could have been. We all ran, Split being the slowest, but his fingers remained away from his thigh. For once I saw peace in the Pedlar's eyes.

When we were a safe distance away I loaded another Abb into my weapon. I fired at the Closed Eye on the door and Iced the entire thing shut, sealing all the Nobles to their deaths.

I felt no guilt.

I doubted that I ever would.

'We'll leave the way we came in,' I said, the Warrior in my voice. My heart pounded at an unfathomable rate. 'No one is going to stop us.'

Shilah looked at me with a whole new respect.

The Domestics fell to their knees.

Dunes bowed.

Cam refrained from his jokes.

And so we left the way we came.

No one stopped us.

No one raised an alarm.

I assume we'd killed all the people who would have done so. So in quiet serenity we sneaked back out of the side entrance of the Sanctuary. Dunes stopped to check the pulse of the fallen guard in the corner, telling us that he lived. I wasn't sure if I cared.

When we passed by the stained-glass representation of David's Fall, I loaded an Abb and shot the windows too. The whole thing shattered into a thousand pieces of brightly coloured memory.

# Chapter Twenty-Three

For the next three days we took refuge in the cave, Dunes and I making trips back to the markets to steal supplies during the dark of night. We got caught twice, but Dunes pretended to be a Hookman again, and we were sent on our way. The whole City of David's Fall was swarming with taskmasters and guards, on high alert after what had happened at the Sanctuary. Word had it that the Khat was already on his way. I don't know how that would have been possible, since Paphos was many days' journey from the City of David's Fall, but in case there was a large force amassing our way, we gathered food, water, and stole as many vials of groan slave from the apothecaries as we could in preparation, stocking up on everything we would need to hide out and start healing.

Of the nine of us, only Picka rested particularly well.

Everyone had their reasons.

Ellcia was only able to sleep for short spells, sputtering awake with shouts of 'trick' and 'priss', and things I'd hesitate to repeat. Ellia couldn't stop staring at the empty cavern tunnels long enough to relax, jolting at every tiny sound, whether it be a soft cough or the groan of ancient rock. Shilah was clearly in too much pain to sleep, writhing on top of her blanket. She'd set up towards the back of the cave next to the Adaam Grass, trying not to move too much so she wouldn't keep reopening her wounds. Cam was too worried about Shilah to sleep. He kept bringing her orangefruit, which she begrudgingly ate. I continually offered to give her some of the Glassland Dream, but she only agreed to use groan salve, and even then, never enough, claiming she wanted to save it for the others. I didn't ask to see her injuries again, but I knew they were bad.

Leah's hands danced in the air in front of her all night, as if stroking long strings made of the darkness. She even did it when she managed to fall asleep.

Split and Picka both kept exceptionally quiet, mostly huddling together near the entrance, on self-proclaimed watch duty. Every once in a while Split would lead Picka over to Shilah to keep her company, and then return to his station. The Pedlar kept rifling through the Book of the March, as if searching for something important. I asked him what he was looking for, but he shook his head and said: 'It's like I'm reading it for the first time.'

He finally told us as much as he could about the Coldmarch, which turned out to be surprisingly meagre. The Jadans in charge of Langria were secretive, only telling the Shepherds as much as they needed to know. Split speculated that this tactic was in case the Shepherds were discovered by a Vicaress and tortured. Split had never actually been inside Langria, only knowing the location's general whereabouts, which was somewhere near the Great Divide. Dunes didn't know where it was either – the Hookmen were always stopped by hidden forces if they travelled too far North. The armies of Langria were trained to shoot arrows with incredible accuracy, and had weapons that lit the sands themselves on fire. They knew every scrap of land, and set massive traps for any invading forces.

Apparently in eight hundred years, the Khat's armies had never broken through the front lines.

'But how were you going to get us in?' I asked Split.

He simply pointed to the Coldmaker.

Later he told us about the rigorous process the Shepherds had to go through before they were trusted enough to have a stretch of March for themselves. About how the Marcheyes – which is what Mama Jana was – were always on the lookout for exceptional Jadans to send North. The allotted slots diminished every year before it was all shut down, and by the end, the prospective Jadans had to bear some characteristic from one of the prophecies to justify being selected. Shilah huffed when Split told us that bit. The Pedlar let us flip through the tome as much as we liked, and even though I couldn't read the text, I could feel its importance. Split was kind enough to translate any passages I pointed out.

There were predictions of Jadan armies rising from the dead and storming Paphos. Of a Jadan so strong that whips would break off his skin like glass against stone. Of secrets hidden in the land, that when spoken aloud would change sand to grass. Of a Jadan falling from the stars and being born in the Cry Patch. Of plagues. Of the Singe turning to stone. Of all the Nobles dying of firepox. Of the Crierson. Of peace. Of war.

None of the prophecies mentioned an invention.

That made me smile.

We waited for three days, trying to come up with a plan. But amongst the pain of healing and worry about our future, there was an air of hope.

There was even something like celebration at certain points. We feasted as much as our rations would allow, laughing and telling the best stories we knew. Split told us about Baba Levante, and the shows he would put on for his daughter, and I decided that someday I'd find his puppet.

We all knew this period of rest couldn't last, but it was joyous nonetheless.

The Coldmaker was a beacon, sitting proud and gleaming even in the dim candlelight. I turned it on and made a few Abbs so the new Domestics could see the machine in action, hoping to lift their spirits and earn their trust. I tried not to think too much about its impending demise. Gasps and prayers abounded as the gold formed, especially from Ellia, but I stopped the machine after only two Abbs. The sisters spent long periods of time kneeling next to the machine, drawing their fingers along their cheeks as they cried for their kin left behind. Leah stared at the bronze Opened Eye on the machine for long stretches as well, tracing the shape. Leah asked Shilah all sorts of things about the machine, learning its secrets, but never addressing me directly. I found this bewildering, but in a way preferred it.

I wasn't ready to reveal the dying Frost.

The flock was counting on me, and I was failing them.

I'd tried adding the Cold Charge from the Sinai while everyone was sleeping, but still the Abbs came out slowly, and the Frost continued to shrink. After that, my heart was left a little lonelier than before. I tried not to dwell on things too much, telling myself about the inevitable obstacles I would face, but it was no use. This wasn't just an obstacle. This was an ending. Soon we would be left with nothing but a vacuous hole where bright change once glistened.

Some saviour.

Shilah could tell something was going on with me, but I kept deflecting, assuring her I was just worried about finishing the Coldmarch. She didn't believe me, and was relentless.

But our stalemate held steady, and so attentions turned elsewhere. Shilah told the new Domestics about Little Langria, and I told them about my tinker-wall growing up. Dunes relayed the story about watching our little group cross the

Singe on a boat of Ice, and about Meshua. Unfortunately, even with my making it clear that Shilah and I were equal in the creation of the Coldmaker, everyone still began to look to me as a leader, even Split deferring to me over every issue.

I tried to rise to the challenge, the whole time doing my best impression of my father. I stood tall, spoke truth, and kept calm. I felt like a complete fraud. I may have had Abb's numbers tattooed on the back of my neck, but I couldn't pretend I had even half of his wisdom.

Shilah kept on about what was bothering me. The blackness on my left hand wasn't getting any better, or worse, so I blamed it on that.

She didn't believe me.

On the third night I finally broke.

I sat on the edge of the pool, my feet dipped in the swirling water. Shilah was sitting by my side, legs curled underneath her, her fingers submerged and being tickled by the current. Everyone else was asleep.

'You finally ready?' Shilah asked, her voice as soft as the waters.

I looked around, seeing no one stirring. 'For?'

'You know,' she said.

I felt heat rise into my face.

She peeled back her shirt enough to show the tip of the burns on her chest, still slick with a thin layer of salve. I only glimpsed a bit of the damage, but I could imagine the pain.

'Is this what you need to see?' she asked.

I turned my face away, mortified.

'Spout,' she said quietly.

I kept my face on the waters, trying to read them.

There was nothing there.

'You're not alone.' She gently grabbed my wrist and placed my injured fingers against her breast, so they lightly touched. 'You always think you're alone, but you're not.'

Pain shot through my arm. Shilah flinched too.

'Stop,' I said, pulling my hand away. 'Sorry.'

She grabbed my wrist hard this time and pressed my blackened fingers back on her burned flesh, staring me straight in the eyes, holding my gaze. Her beauty was only enhanced by the pain ringing her eyes, and she squeezed our wounds together, making them one. Neither of us called out, instead sharing a look that would leave its own scar.

'Don't tell me,' she whispered.

I nodded.

She let go, planting a kiss on my cheek.

'No manipulation,' she said with a smirk. 'Don't tell me.'

'The Coldmaker,' I said with a sigh, nursing my hand against my chest. 'The Frost inside is getting smaller. It's going to run out.'

Shilah nodded without any surprise, as if she already knew. 'Is that it?'

'What do you mean, is that it?'

She got up, walking over to the dancing platform. Kneeling down at the base of the machine, she flipped all the right levers to get the Coldmaker open on the first try, allowing the bronze box to reveal its inner workings.

'You remembered,' I said.

She gave me the kind of look that reminded me to think twice before saying such obvious things. I held up my hands in apology.

I glanced over to where the Domestics were sleeping, and saw that Ellia was awake now. She quickly closed her eyes and pretended she wasn't watching, but I knew that our terrible secret was out.

Shilah put her hand on the Frost. After a moment of contemplation, she nodded. 'Looks like all three of us are hurting.' Then she shrugged, a hopeful smile playing across her face. 'Doesn't mean we won't get better.'

'So you saw it already?' I asked.

'To see only with the eyes,' she said, stroking her fingers around her delicate mouth like she had a goatee, 'is to be truly blind.'

I raised an eyebrow.

'You think you're the only one who learned things from Leroi?' she asked.

'He told you that?'

'And more.' She gave me a mischievous look. 'There's more secrets in the world than you know.'

'So what do we do?' I asked. 'Because I'm feeling rather blind at the moment.'

'We have faith,' she said.

I paused, taken aback. 'I thought you don't believe in the Crier like that?'

She looked me straight on again, her eyes soft this time. 'I have faith in you. I have faith in us. I have faith that we'll find a solution, just like we always have.'

'Is that faith?'

'Just because you don't have faith in something divine,' she said. 'You still have to have faith in something. Otherwise, what's the point?'

I let out a long breath, the crushing weight beginning to slide off my shoulders. 'So what do we do?'

All of a sudden there was a rush of darkness at the edge of my vision; a shadow moving without any sound. My heart leaped as I spun towards the motion, the muddled silhouette forming into the shape of Dunes as it swept closer. He stopped at the edge of the platform, the hooked blade held over his heart. He'd refused any groan salve at all for his wounds, and his forearms were still rough and angry with cuts.

'Meshua,' he said, bowing to me.

Shilah sighed.

'She's Meshua too, Dunes,' I said.

Dunes hesitated and then nodded, bowing to Shilah as well. 'Of course.'

'So I assume you heard all that?' I asked, wondering if I'd just undone all the confidence the flock had in me. 'Our new *obstacle*.'

'Apologies,' he said. 'It was not intended. But I have the best ears in the World Cried.'

I swallowed hard. 'So you still choosing our side?'

Dunes ran a finger over the scar on his cheek. 'Forever. And I will get you another Frost. If you need another Frost I will get you another Frost. And then another. And another. You will never run out. I swear by the Crier's first tears you will never run out.'

Shilah and I exchanged a look.

'And where would you get a Frost?' I asked, remembering what had happened the last time someone brought me a Frost. I looked at Cam, who was fast asleep, a rope of drool hanging from his lips.

'The Sanctuary,' Dunes said.

I knew that's what he was going to suggest. I also knew that it would be madness for him to return there now, the one place where the enemy knew we'd been.

But I also thought of the Ice bridge.

And the crossbows.

And allowing a Hookman into our family.

Madness had a way of working in our favour.

Shilah shook her head. 'No. It'll be crawling with guards and Nobles and probably even the Vicaress and Hookmen, all looking for a clue as to how to find us. No, Dunes. We'll find ano—'

'Go,' I said.

'I will not be caught,' Dunes announced, dropping into a bow.

Shilah turned to me, her face aghast. 'Spout. No.'

'He won't get caught,' I said. 'You told me to have faith.'

'I will be silence,' Dunes said, bowed so low that I thought his blade might scrape the shine off the stone floor. 'I will be the blackness between stars.'

'Go,' I said. 'Don't get caught.'

Dunes's eyes were full of resolve. 'I will return with everything you need.'

And with a final bow he was gone.

That night I dreamt of the Vicaress.

She found us in the cave, my eyes opening from sleep to see her silently gliding through the dark, every step full of determined fury. She stepped around the Domestics, ignoring Cam and the Pedlar, and went right for me. Shilah and I had been sleeping next to the Coldmaker on the dancing platform, and she sauntered up on the polished stone edge. She hovered over me, flaming dagger in hand, and dripped some wax beside my sleeping body. The splatter smelled like the dead-carts baking in the Sun. Then Shilah got a dose. The heat of the fire felt real. The Vicaress had her Hookmen at her back, and there were five of them again. They waited just off the platform in deadly formation, more terrifying than I recalled.

Dunes was back under her command.

It seemed I was to be his final scar, marking the last patch of clean skin. He'd completed his grandest task yet: fooling the runaway into thinking he was a friend. Offering a kiss and then unsheathing fangs.

The Vicaress stepped back from my body, a wicked smile on her face. Her eyes shone crystal blue, catching the light of her flaming dagger, and she nodded to the Hookmen. She was wearing the tight black silk she always preferred, both her curves and the outline of her face outstandingly attractive, and my sleeping mind felt an embarrassing stirring between my legs. I didn't fault myself too deeply, however, because I knew I couldn't control what happened in my dream.

Ellia and Ellcia began screaming in my dream.

Leah hid behind one of the rocks in my dream.

Cam blubbered, pulling at his yellow hair in my dream. Split had the Glassland Dream in my dream, trying to get the cork out of the bottle. Everything was too vivid and uncomfortable, and I was ready to be done with it.

I sat up, blinking, trying to wake myself.

Shilah was already on her feet, refusing to die on her knees.

I worked my jaw and hammered a fist into my leg.

I could smell the Vicaress's fire in my dream.

I could feel the fear in the air, my flock deathly afraid.

I blinked and blinked, but the vision did not dissipate.

Everything stopped.

The truth struck.

It was all real.

This was not a dream.

Dunes had led the Vicaress and the Hookmen right to us.

I'd been betrayed.

'You bastard,' Shilah seethed, pointing at Dunes. 'You Sun-damned bastard! How could you do this?'

Split was standing in front of Picka, his eyes already glazed over from the grey powder. The Pedlar was smiling, a pinky twisting in his ear. 'Told you. Hah! Once a Hookman, always a Hookman.'

'You really did well, Hamman,' the Vicaress said. 'I can't believe I doubted your commitment. Once again, I offer a rare apology. Everything is as you said.'

For the first time, Dunes did not correct his name.

Hamman was back.

'They took us!' Leah shouted. 'We didn't have a choice! They stole us and brought us here in chains!'

'Trick,' Ellcia exhaled. 'We gunn back to Ka'in. We gunn get the Fall.'

Cam went to pick up his crossbow, his face full of rage, but the Vicaress waved her blade at him. 'Touch that weapon, Camlish Tavor, and I'll give them worse than death! It's an easy thing with girls. And I'll make you watch the whole thing.'

Cam paused. None of the Hookmen were wearing anything like armour, nothing solid for the Abb to explode against.

It was over.

They had us cornered.

'Cam,' I said. 'Don't.'

Cam shot Hamman a look of pure revulsion.

I couldn't even muster up any sort of hate or barbed last words for the Hookman in these final moments. I'd truly believed he was my friend. He'd played the part so convincingly that I could only stare in disbelief, my whole body sinking, melting into the stone. The final bit of hope holding my heart together had turned to dust. Everything good in me finally fell apart.

I was to end as a broken fool.

'Now then,' the Vicaress said, a laugh in her voice. 'The Crier is very excited to meet you all. To punish those who dare oppose his Gospels. You shall spend an eternity pondering your mistake in complete darkness, blind and deaf, as your skin is boiled away and your eyes are eaten by beetles. And did you know that it doesn't end? The Crier told me personally that everything will grow back and start again fresh and brutal. Oh, what agony shall be the eternal fate you have chosen. Who would like to go first?'

Hamman gave a nod to the other Hookmen. He reached into his pocket, showed them a single Abb, and then tossed it into the sacred pool.

The whole thing changed to Ice, the deep crackling resonating in my chest.

358 DANIEL A. COHEN

The four other Hookmen dropped to their knees, bowing their heads. But not towards the Vicaress.

Towards me.

The Vicaress's eyes went wild, her mouth at a loss.

'They do not kneel for you,' Hamman said, cutting her off.

She looked as if she might topple over in shock. 'Hamman. How—'

'Hamman. Is. Gone,' he bellowed.

Hope jolted into my chest.

'Get up, Hookmen!' the Vicaress screamed, waving her blade. 'Get off your knees and—'

'They do not bow for you!' Dunes bellowed, spit flying from his lips. 'You are unworthy!'

The Vicaress's mouth gaped, trying to understand what was happening. My jaw did the same, hanging low. It was the first time the Vicaress and I had something in common.

'Meshua,' Dunes said, dropping to his knees. 'We kneel for you.'

'I kneel for you,' one of the Hookmen said, making a strange gesture over his heart and then reaching out towards the Ice. 'Meshua.'

The others echoed his movements, their voices all gravelly, yet distinct.

'I kneel for you. Meshua.'

'I kneel for you. Meshua.'

Only the biggest and most menacing Hookman didn't speak.

I'd never been so out of sorts in my entire life.

The Vicaress stepped forwards, her body shaking with rage. 'Get off your knees, slaves! I don't know what you think you're playing at, it's just a trick! They are tricking you, and you will be severely punished! The Ice isn't real!'

The Hookmen all looked to Dunes, their faces serious.

Dunes gave another nod.

They rose as one unit.

'Meshua,' Dunes said. 'I have promised to get you what you need. I could not find the Frost in the Sanctuary. Apologies. The whole place is swarming with enemies. I will get you a Frost, but in the meantime, I bring you this.'

'Brought us what?' I asked, mouth dry. I didn't notice until that moment, but Shilah's hand had found mine and was squeezing tightly, her palm sweaty.

Dunes took his blade off his hip, holding it high.

The other Hookmen did the same.

'Family,' Dunes said.

The Hookmen advanced on the Vicaress, their blades gleaming. She was so taken aback that she didn't even get a chance to move away from the attack. Dunes drove his blade into her stomach, angling it so it would go in all the way up to the hilt. He lifted her whole body off the ground. The curved tip came through her back, pointing towards the sky. Her flaming blade skittered across the stone, landing on the Ice with a hiss. The other Hookmen circled the Vicaress, slashing their blades through the air, waiting their turn. One at a time they silently thrust their weapons into her flesh, the polished steel finding a home in the Vicaress's chest and back and throat, the whole platform stained red in a matter of moments. Trails of blood flowed past my feet, and I could only look down in shock.

Everything was over almost as fast as it had begun.

The Vicaress was dead.

Five blades had been driven through her body.

The Hookmen were kneeling again, hands empty. They ignored the corpse at their feet, unconcerned with the holy Noble who had once controlled their every move.

'They believe in you,' Dunes said, lifting his head just enough so he could look me in the eyes as he spoke. His face was splattered with red. 'They have faith in you now. I told them your truth, and convinced them to join the cause. We are yours. We will protect you until the final tear streaks the night. We will escort you on your most holy Coldmarch, and destroy any enemies in your path. Only say the word and it shall be done. By your command.'

'By your command,' the other Hookmen echoed one by one, the Closed Eyes that had been scarred into their heads stark from this angle. 'By your command.'

Again the final Hookman was silent, but he bowed nonetheless.

Shilah's hand was still in mine, and I pulled her off the platform and away from the pooling blood. She stumbled along, caught in disbelief as well, her eyes not leaving the fallen body.

The Hookmen pivoted to face us as we moved, remaining on their knees.

'What do we do?' I asked. 'What in the World Cried just happened?'

Shilah paused, her eyes never straying from the Vicaress. She didn't smile, but something was stirring behind her eyes.

'Shilah,' I said, totally at a loss for any other words, my heart hammering.

'The Hookmen are gone,' she said, surveying all the blood. She finally broke her gaze and looked instead at the kneeling figures, a dark smile finally rising to her lips. 'These men will need a new title.'

Dunes looked up at Shilah with a wide grin, nodding his head. 'Meshua.'

Shilah's cheeks flushed with pride.

Cam skirted over to us, tapping me on the shoulder. 'Um, Spout.'

'Yeah, Cam.'

'I think those Hookmen just killed the Vicaress.'

'The Hookmen are gone,' I said. 'But I believe you're right.'

'Did that really happen?' Cam said, tapping his glasses.

'Yeah, Cam,' I said.

'So . . .' Cam wobbled from foot to foot, staring at the whole pool of Ice. 'Are we just going to go on like everything's normal, or . . .?'

'We burn the body and finish the Coldmarch,' Shilah said. 'Take everyone to Langria.'

'No,' I said.

Shilah let go of my hand, looking at me sideways.

'Not yet,' I said, going over to these new Jadans. 'My family. Stand up, please.'

They rose as one unit, unfazed. They were powerful and mysterious and could strike fear into most every heart, Noble or Jadan. The silent one in the middle was somehow even bigger than Dunes, his brow prominent and eyes deadly.

'The Khat is coming,' I said, trying not to let my lack of confidence show.

'Yes,' Cam squeaked. 'All the more reason to leave.'

'We can't get to Langria without another Frost,' I said. 'And the Khat is on his way here.'

'You think that's a sign?' Cam asked.

Shilah gave me a gentle and knowing nod.

I glanced at the group of Jadans and Nobles surrounding me, counting on me, not only to make the right decision, but to change everything. I thought about all those Domestics still trapped in the Sanctuary, with the Khat on his way. And of all the Jadans around the World Cried still in chains tonight.

I thought about Abb, and what he might think if he could see all of this.

Then I smiled, looking at the Coldmaker.

What an absurd thing to ponder.

My father was right there by my side.

'I'm not sure about signs,' I said. 'But you know what I do think?'

Cam breathed deeply, his eyes following the streams of red streaking towards the Ice. 'What?'

'I think that we have the beginning of an army,' I said, rubbing the back of my neck. 'And I think it's time to begin the war.'

# Acknowledgements

A special thanks to an invaluable cast of characters living on the other side of these pages:

Danielle Zigner – The Mighty Pedlar

Vicky Leech – The Story Sage

Jardin Telling – The Enchantress

Steve Cohen – The Wise Father (w/Jokes)

Charlotte Webb – The Open Eye Scribe

Fionnuala Barrett – The Open Ear Scout

Natasha Bardon – The Queen

Jack Renninson – The Builder

Thomas Judd - The Bard

Stephen Mulcahey – The Artist